About the author

Christine Marion Fraser is one of Scotland's top-selling authors with world-wide readership and translations into many foreign languages. Second youngest of a large family, she soon learned independence during childhood years spent in the post-war Govan district of Glasgow. At the age of ten she contracted a rare illness which landed her in a wheelchair and virtually ended her formal education. From early years, Christine had been an avid storyteller; her first novel *Rhanna* was published in 1978.

Christine Marion Fraser lives with her husband in an old Scottish manse on the shores of the Kyles of Bute, Argyllshire.

Praise for Christine Marion Fraser

'Christine Marion Fraser weaves an intriguing story in which the characters are alive against a spellbinding background' *Yorkshire Herald*

'Fraser writes with a great depth of feeling and has the knack of making her characters come alive. She paints beautiful pictures of the countryside and their changing seasons' *Aberdeen Express*

'Full-blooded romance, a strong, authentic setting' *Scotsman*

'An author who has won a huge audience for her warm, absorbing tales of ordinary folk' *Annabel*

'Christine Marion Fraser writes characters so real they almost leap out of the pages . . . you would swear she must have grown up with them' *Sun*

D1351760

RETURN TO RHANNA

Christine Marion Fraser

CORONET BOOKS
Hodder & Stoughton

Acknowledgements
The author wishes to thank Commander John Douglas, OBE for
his help and advice on matters marine

Copyright © 1984 Christine Marion Fraser

First published in Great Britain in 1984 by Fontana
A division of HarperCollins *Publishers*

This edition published in 2001 by Hodder & Stoughton
A division of Hodder Headline
A Coronet Paperback

The right of Christine Marion Fraser to be identified as the
Author of the Work has been asserted by her in accordance
with the Copyright, Designs and Patents Act 1988.

10 9 8 7 6 5 4 3 2 1

A CIP catalogue record for this title is
available from the British Library

ISBN 0 340 73391 8

Typeset by Palimpsest Book Production Limited,
Polmont, Stirlingshire
Printed and bound in Great Britain by
Mackays of Chatham plc, Chatham, Kent

Hodder & Stoughton
A division of Hodder Headline
338 Euston Road
London NW1 3BH

For Gran: The Speyside Seanachaidh

Croft na Beinn

Ben Machrie

Hamish's/Mathew's Cottage

RUMHOR

Loch Sliach

Rumhor

Bob's Biggin

PORTVOYNACHAN

SOUND OF RHANNA

Part One

Winter 1960

Chapter One

Shona hummed a gay little tune as she energetically polished the big oak sideboard which sat solidly in the living-room of the sturdy stone house in Glen Fallan. Huddled into the lush green slopes of Ben Machrie, dwarfed by the great humping bulk of Sgurr na Gill, the house looked small and rather desolate, yet its weathered walls had stood so long they were part of the scenery and didn't intrude into the wild, solitary grandeur of the glen.

For more than eighty-six years it had been home to Biddy McMillan, the nurse who had devoted her life to the population of Rhanna, and though it had lain empty and rather neglected since her death some three years ago, to everyone it was still 'Biddy's house', and not one of the islanders ever passed it by on their travels without a smile touching their lips as they remembered the kenspeckle old figure with her black spindly legs and her eternal searchings for her specs and her 'teeths'.

Shona paused to gaze round, her blue eyes shining as she pictured what the house would look like when all the furniture was brought over from her house in the Mull of Kintyre and arranged in the rooms in Biddy's house. She still thought of it as such, though come the spring it would be home to her, her husband Niall McLachlan, and their twelve-year-old daughter, Ellie.

Kirsteen was making new curtains for all the windows and Shona's father was going to paint and paper the house with the help of Doctor McLachlan, Niall's father.

Always eager for an excuse to get over to Rhanna, Shona had arrived the day before to spend a week or two getting the house cleaned and ready. Tucking away a wilful strand of auburn hair she forgot about work and wandered slowly through all the rooms. Each one evoked a memory of Biddy and when Shona's steps finally stopped in the kitchen, her eyes were shiny with tears. She clasped her hands and put her thumbs to her mouth. It was very quiet. She could hear plainly the bubbling of the burn that tumbled from Ben Machrie and into the River Fallan which flowed under the bridge on the opposite side of the road. She remembered how Biddy had helped her through some traumatic times in her life, given her sound, straightforward advice, comforted her and taken her to her scrawny old bosom with genuine affection. Somehow Biddy had always been there when she was needed and her going had left a great gap in the lives of everyone who had loved the old nurse. But she had left behind a legacy of treasured memories in countless men, women, and children who had been 'her bairnies'. The house in which she had been born breathed of peace; the timeless feeling of old world serenity was so tangible it was like a living thing, the very walls and the bits of furniture that Shona had decided to keep had absorbed the character of the old woman who had lived there for so long. Nothing would have made Shona part with the solid wooden kitchen table, the dresser, and the crofter's bench which sat under the window.

Shona sighed deeply and with an effort dragged her thoughts away from the past and back into the present.

'This will be a happy house, Biddy,' she said aloud to the empty room. 'I promise you will never have cause to regret our intrusion into it.'

A bubble of sheer happiness burst into her heart, the first real happiness she had known for some time. Recently she had undergone the heart-rending experience of losing a much-longed-for baby. The pregnancy had been in its early stages but, even so, she had already formed a mental picture of how the child would look, definitely fair haired with Niall's brown eyes and perhaps her dimple in the middle of its chin. She hadn't visualized its sex, enough that it was a baby, warm, living, real, so welcome into the bosom of the family after all the years of frustrated longing. With delight she had hugged the knowledge of her condition to herself, welcoming the subtle changes each day brought, not even minding the occasional feelings of nausea; they let her know that her baby was alive and growing a little more each day. Only those closest to her had shared the lovely secret with her and only they had known her torment at the terrible loss she had suffered. She was glad now that she hadn't told anyone else about it, and she wondered now, deep down, if it was because perhaps she had been afraid something might happen to rob her of the thing she had wanted more than anything else in the world. It was as well she was coming back to Rhanna, back to stay after an absence of more than nineteen years. She had enjoyed her time on the Mull of Kintyre but this was where she belonged, where her heart had always lain.

She knew that Niall was slightly apprehensive about leaving his successful veterinary practice to try and make a go of it on the islands, but she shared none of his unease. She couldn't wait to start a new life and, despite what had happened, was optimistic and enthusiastic about the future. They had to look forward, it was no use dwelling on what might have been.

Turning down the sleeves of her dress she gazed round with satisfaction at the results of her morning's work. A ray of October sunshine spilled over the shining blood-red tiles on the floor; the newly black-leaded range gleamed like satin; the shelves with their rows of cup hooks had been scrubbed to a sandy whiteness. For a moment she wondered how she would take to cooking on a kitchen range after the ease of using a modern electric cooker but quickly she shrugged her doubts aside. She had been brought up at Laigmhor without the amenities everyone on the mainland took for granted and there was no earthly reason why she couldn't adapt back again. At least Biddy's house had running water and there was a good copper washtub in the wash-house situated off the kitchen. Her eyes grew dreamy again. It would be rather nice going back in time, rather like the old days at Laigmhor with paraffin lamps to light the way to bed and the warm glow of firelight to sit by in the evenings. She and Niall would have more time to talk, perhaps recapture some of the romance that had been neglected in the busy round of mainland life . . . A movement outside the window caught her eye and going over she looked towards the bronzed slopes of Sgurr na Gill. The hills and glens were ablaze with the rich hues of late autumn. The red berries of the rowans were like blobs of blood against the russets and golds of the dying bracken; the rusty purple of the fading heather was still bright against its sombre brown foliage. A wisp of green moved against the darker green of the lower slopes and Shona might not have noticed it but for the startling brightness of a mane of pale golden hair which she recognized as belonging to Ruth Donaldson, daughter of Dugald and Morag Ruadh, the red-haired, quick-tempered weaver and spinner of Portcull.

Ruth was walking slowly, lost in thought, the grace of her young body hampered only by the limp she had had since birth.

Shona went to the door and opening it she called out Ruth's name, but the girl appeared not to hear, her head was bowed and she kept on going as one in a trance.

Shona shook her head indulgently. It was quite usual for Ruth to be lost in daydreams. She was often to be seen wandering over the hills, lost in her own world of fantasies, thinking out plots for stories and poems. She had had her first story published when she was just fifteen years old and had been a regular contributor to magazines and journals ever since. She had confided to Shona that one of her greatest aims in life was to have a book published and Shona knew that she would never be satisfied until she had achieved her ambition.

Shona went down the path and, opening the gate of the weed-choked garden, ran swiftly over the road. At the sound of footsteps behind her Ruth looked up, startled, the violet of her eyes darkening to purple in recognition of the auburn-haired figure swishing through the heather.

'Shona.' Her soft voice spoke the name with pleasure yet there was a certain wariness in the tones. 'I'm sorry, I was daydreaming. I came out here to be alone for a whily.'

Despite the implication of the words Shona's smile remained warm. 'Ach, don't bother to apologize. At your age I was forever wandering about with my head in the clouds. I was wondering – would you come over and have a strupak with me? I could be doing with a cuppy and it would be nice to have company after a morning on my own.'

Ruth hesitated, glancing nervously over her shoulder to the white houses of Portcull in the distance. It was as if she expected to see her mother following her but the only people to be seen were Todd the Shod trundling home from the moors, his cart piled high with peats, and Dodie, the island eccentric, galloping to catch up with Todd's receding figure.

Still Ruth hesitated. 'I – don't know,' she said doubtfully, 'I left Kate in charge of the shop and Mam would be mad if she found out. You know she always finds fault with Kate, especially with her tongue worse than ever since Tam has been laid up after breaking his toe.'

Shona clicked her tongue impatiently. 'Ach, your mother talks too much herself. Don't you worry your head about her. This is Saturday and if I know Morag she'll be too busy seeing to the kirk to have much time to spare for anything else – besides, it's dinner time, you have the right to some time off, surely?'

Ruth's face cleared and a smile lifted the corners of her mouth. 'Ay, you're right enough, Shona, Grannie and Granda love Saturdays, it's the only day they get peace and Father feels free to go over the moors and write his poetry. I suppose ten minutes or so wouldn't do any harm.'

Shona linked her arm through Ruth's. 'That's settled then – and ten minutes nothing! An hour more like.' Her voice was firm. 'To be truthful I'm longing to give my first strupak to somebody. I've given hundreds in my time but never in my very own house on Rhanna. It won't be much, mind, just a cup of tea from my flask and sandwiches and buttered scones.' She paused to study Ruth's face. It was tired and drawn with dark circles under the eyes making them look bigger than ever. Shona frowned. 'You're pale, Ruth. Working in a shop isn't for you; what about that book you were going to write? You'll never get it done at this rate.'

'Someone has to mind the shop. Father comes in whenever he can but he's not as fit as he was. I worry about him. Och, I know he's no' as young as he was, he's past sixty now, but somehow he never seemed his age. To me he was always bright and cheery, but now there's a weariness about him that I don't like.'

Shona checked her tongue. She had been on the point of telling Ruth that anyone who lived with Morag would be weary. Her incessant quotations from the Bible were enough to try the patience of a saint and Shona had heard it rumoured that Morag's behaviour was stranger than ever of late. According to gossip she had once or twice wandered to kirk in her nightgown to play the organ at midnight and Dugald had had to follow her to fetch her back home. Though there was no concrete evidence of this, and because the rumour had originally sprung from the malicious tongue of Behag Beag, the gossiping postmistress of Portcull, it couldn't be certain if there was any truth in it or not; nevertheless no one, not the least Shona, would have been surprised to learn that this was perhaps the reason for Dugald's look of utter fatigue.

Shona shook her bright head. 'I know how you feel about your father, Ruth; just the same, you mustn't let it interfere with your own life. What about you and Lorn? He was telling me only last night that he hasn't seen you for a whily. He's quiet about it but I gathered from his attitude that he doesn't understand what's gone wrong between you. Yet when you came back to Rhanna a few weeks ago you couldn't see enough of him.'

Ruth turned away, shutting the gate carefully behind her, paying a lot of attention to the clasp which hadn't been used for years on the rusty hook.

'On you go, Shona.' Her normally musical voice was tinged with sharpness. 'If I don't fasten this the sheep will get in and eat everything in sight.'

Shona glanced round in bemusement at the wilderness that had been Biddy's garden. It would take months of hard work to get it into any kind of shape and the intrusion of the sheep was a welcome one as they at least kept the turf cropped to a bowling-green smoothness. But she sensed a strangeness in Ruth's mood and bit back the laughing remark that had sprung to her lips. Leaving Ruth to fiddle with the fastening she went back into the house and through to the sunny kitchen where she had left her flask of tea. Throwing herself on one of the sturdy kitchen chairs she ran her fingers through her hair and sighed as a feeling of foreboding needled persistently at her consciousness. At thirty-seven she looked like a girl in her mid-twenties. She was as slender as she had been before Ellie's birth; except for laughter lines at her mouth and eyes her skin was smooth and golden; the turbulence of early years had left eyes which still retained traces of childlike candour. More often these days they glowed with the confidence of ripe womanhood and sparkled with the love of life, though there were still the frequent occasions when temper got the better of her. These were the times that Niall teased her into tears of frustration by calling her 'Caillich Ruadh', the Gaelic for red witch, though he could just as easily bring her out of her mood by either leaving her to work it out or laugh her back into good humour. At his flattering insistence she had never succumbed to the temptation to cut her hair, though often enough she had actually reached the point of having the scissors poised ready, but at the last minute had contented herself with arranging the thick tresses over the top of her neat head.

That morning she had tied it back with a blue scarf though she had worked so vigorously it had come undone long before she was finished and now it tumbled about her shoulders, adding to the illusion of a child-woman. Over the years her face had changed; always cameo-like, its beauty was now further enhanced by a fine sculpting of the cheekbones and Ruth, coming in, was struck as always by the feeling that she wasn't in the presence of an older woman but one more akin in years to herself, though Shona's maturity had given her a wisdom from which Ruth had greatly benefited many times in the past. She had also been an excellent ally, stoutly coming to Ruth's defence when her life looked like becoming unbearable owing to the strict discipline laid down by her mother.

Ruth paused in the doorway and felt herself relaxing a little as Shona threw her a dazzling smile. She wondered at the older woman's strength of spirit. So much had happened in recent months, things that might have quelled the strongest of hearts. The shadow of bereavement still hung heavy over Laigmhor. Just as recently as late summer the McKenzie family had suffered the tragic loss of Lewis, struck down in young manhood by a tumour on the brain. It had been a traumatic time for everyone concerned and as Ruth came further into the room she couldn't stop herself from observing, 'Shona – I – don't understand how you can be so lighthearted after everything that's happened. You seem so – carefree.'

She was immediately sorry she had spoken in such a fashion. A cloud had passed over Shona's face and the smoothness of her brow was once more marred by a troubled frown. 'Ruth, Ruth, how can you think such things?' she appealed, her voice low, her shoulders drooping in a sudden posture of weariness. 'I cried for my brother till there were no tears left. After that came the emptiness, a great emptiness, Ruth, in which I couldn't even feel sadness – I was so numb – in here.' She bunched her hand and pressed it against her breast, a note of anger creeping into her voice as she went on. 'But I have a husband and daughter whom I love dearly and for their sake I had to force myself to go on and I don't feel guilty about that, Ruth. I'm still having to force myself and it gets easier, each day a little easier and while I'm here on Rhanna I'll force myself even more for my father's and Kirsteen's sake and if you thought anything at all of Lorn you would do the same. He went through hell when he lost the twin brother who was everything in the world to him and fine you know it too. But he had you, Ruth, he loves you and you're supposed to love him, yet according to Kirsteen you've hardly been near Laigmhor for weeks. It seems whenever Lorn tries to see you you always have some excuse to be off somewhere else just when he needs you more than he's ever needed you in his life!'

Ruth's face had gone deadly pale. She slumped onto a chair and put her flaxen head in her hands in a gesture of complete despair. 'I know, I know.' Her voice was barely audible. 'Och, Shona, I don't know what I'm doing these days – something – terrible has happened, I don't know where to turn or who to turn to – I – I can't tell Mam! I've never been able to tell her anything and I don't want to burden Father, he's so weary and his life has been worse than ever since Mam found out about me and Lewis – I'm being punished for that. I only did – what I did to give Lewis a bit of comfort in his last days and now – now . . .'

Her voice trailed away and she folded her arms on the table and buried her face in them. Shona gazed at the top of her golden head and a wave of compassion tightened her throat. Ruth's life had been an unhappy one almost from the moment of birth and if it hadn't been for the love of the man she thought of as her father it would have been worse still. Her narrow-minded, prudish mother, a confirmed spinster of many years' standing, had, in a mood of abandonment, succumbed to the lusts of the flesh she had so often condemned in others. Little Ruth had been the result of her impetuosity and though Dugald had married her without question, he had soon discovered that his wife had allowed herself to have been involved with several men, so that the question of Ruth's true identity had always hung in the balance.

To compensate for her sins, Morag had become a religious fanatic. She had condemned her husband and daughter to lives of misery which were only made bearable by their shared interest in writing and the deep love and respect they had for one another. When Ruth and Lorn had fallen in love it had seemed that at last she had found happiness, but recent events had complicated matters. Shona knew that Lewis had turned to Ruth for comfort and companionship in his final weeks of life. The affair had caused a rift between Lorn and Ruth which had eventually been healed but now it appeared that something else had occurred between them, something serious enough to make Ruth turn away from the only boy she had ever really loved.

In a rush of sympathy Shona stretched out across the table and put her hand firmly over Ruth's. 'Tell me what ails you,' she urged gently. 'It might not be as bad as you imagine. Only when we lock things away do they get blown up out of all proportion – and fine I know it too – I've done it often enough in my time, but a problem shared is a problem halved – as Mirabelle used to say after she had skited me round the lugs for sulking.'

Ruth had heard many of Mirabelle's sayings. Shona was

forever quoting the old housekeeper who had reared her and whom she had adored. Normally Ruth smiled at the amusing way Shona had of recounting such things, but there was no response from her now. For a long time she remained silent, then slowly she raised her head to draw the hem of her dress over eyes that were red and swollen, ignoring the square of white cotton that Shona proffered. Drawing in a deep shuddering breath she deliberately turned away to gaze unseeingly at the window, a small slight figure looking much younger than her eighteen years, the poise of her head, her fine flaxen hair, giving her a mantle of vulnerability.

'That's how my troubles began, Shona,' she said in a husky trembling voice. 'I made Lewis tell me his and he was only too anxious to share his burden with someone. I'll never forget that day. The sun was shining and the sky was wide and blue. It was the sort of day made for rejoicing but after Lewis told me that he was dying I felt that the sun had gone in forever and that I would never again feel joy in all the bonny things God made. I never thought I would be strong enough to bear the pain of Lewis's sorrow or be able to still his fears but I found a strength I didn't know I possessed and I was able to give him all the comfort he needed – at a terrible cost to myself. I hated myself for the things I had to do to help him but, och! He needed me so bad! What else could I do? I wasn't thinking of the future. Lewis had none and with me and Lorn separated I felt I had none either and – and now I might as well stop looking ahead for it seems I have nothing to look forward to anymore.'

Her words trembled off on a note of despair and Shona's grasp on her hand tightened.

'You were wonderful to my brother, Ruth. I knew him well – better perhaps than he knew himself. He was terrified of illness and pain and all his life he feared death – yet – when it came to the bit he was prepared to face it alone though thanks to you he didn't have to. Lewis was always a carefree spirit. Folk loved him whether they wanted to or no', but he could also be very demanding and he must have drained you. Maybe you're only feeling the reaction now and it might be that's the reason you don't want to get involved too deeply with Lorn at this stage. Believe me, I'm talking from experience and I understand. You need a wee whily to yourself – time to sort things out in your mind. If you explained to Lorn I'm sure he would understand.'

Ruth shook her head and whispered, 'I love Lorn, I always have. His is a good love, he gives as well as takes – he's already given me so much understanding. That's why I can't bear to face him now. I can't hurt him – not again. I think it might be better for everyone if I went away.'

Shona stared at the back of Ruth's head. 'Away! Och, c'mon, Ruth! Why on earth should you do that?'

Ruth shook her head from side to side and cried aloud as if in protest, 'So that I can have Lewis's baby! Maybe have it adopted so that it can have a decent start in life!' She stared down at the soft flatness of her belly in disbelief.

'It doesn't show yet but soon it will. Can you imagine it? Mam beside herself with shame; the cailleachs gossiping their heads off. They won't be able to call me the Virgin Bride anymore.' She gave a short bitter laugh. 'It will be something far worse than anything I've been called before and – and I'm just not strong enough to stand any of it. The only answer is to go away.'

Shona felt as if she had been dealt a sledgehammer blow. All the air seemed to squeeze out of her lungs leaving her breathless. It was the last thing she had expected to hear, yet somehow she felt she ought to have known what was troubling Ruth. She of all people ought to have known! She shook her head as if to clear it, but felt instead as if she was being sucked through a long black tunnel – back – back into a past she had thought buried. She had experienced the same thing as Ruth and she too had carried the burden alone, afraid to tell anyone she was expecting Niall's child. She must have been Ruth's age – no, younger; sixteen – sixteen years old, unmarried and terrified.

Biddy had come to her rescue, had made her pour it all out. Biddy had given her comfort and hope – hope such as she had to give Ruth – yet she was unprepared for the sudden pang of resentment that seared through her like a knife. Why should she? It seemed as if she was always acting the part of Mother Confessor. She had taken Ruth back to Kintyre after Lewis's death, had soothed and comforted, tried to be lighthearted when her own grief for her brother was an ever-present shadow in her life.

Was that really what was bothering her? If she was honest with herself she had to admit that her resentment might be born of jealousy. She closed her eyes. Yes, she was jealous, jealous of a girl who was expecting a baby she didn't want. It was so ironical after what had happened to her. She had craved a baby and she had lost it, just as she had lost the little son of long ago; now here was Ruth, weeping over a baby she had no desire to bring into the world. Oh, it was so unfair! If she had been younger things might have been different but soon it would be too late for her to contemplate having another child – and she could hardly bear the thought of that. Wild and impossible ideas surged crazily inside her head. If Ruth didn't want the baby then perhaps she could adopt it – bring her brother's child up as her own . . . She opened her eyes. Ruth was watching her, her white, strained face full of a terrible suspense.

Shona was immediately ashamed of her thoughts. Taking a deep breath she reached briskly for the flask. 'A good strong cuppy is what you need.' She paused. It might have been Biddy sitting in her homely kitchen saying these words. She felt as if the old woman was beside her, guiding her, making her sound full of a confidence she didn't feel. She remembered how Biddy had reached out to take her to her kindly old bosom before even attempting to offer words of advice. Shona knew that she was incapable of giving Ruth that kind of comfort. Biddy's unique ability to see things objectively had sprung from the simplicity of a life uncluttered by personal entanglements and Shona recognized that the complications of her own emotions put her at a disadvantage in the present situation. Nevertheless she had the advantage of knowing first hand what Ruth was going through and felt that she could offer some practical advice. Pushing a cup of hot tea into the girl's faltering grasp she said firmly, 'Now, Ruth, this is a case of first things first and you must begin by telling Lorn about – the baby—' She held up her hand to ward off the expected protests. 'You must at least give him the chance to hear the truth from your very own lips – let him know the reason why you've been avoiding him. Far better that than for him to hear it second hand from the mouths of the gossips. There will be plenty of that as fine you know and the important thing is to beat them all to it. Love begins as a very fragile thing, it can only be strengthened by mutual trust, and if you care for each other the way you say you must be able to talk things out face to face for no one else is qualified enough to do so.'

Ruth folded her hands on the table and lowered her head. 'What if he turns away from me?' she whispered. 'I couldny stand that.'

'You must stand it, Ruth – if it should happen that way, but knowing Lorn I don't think he's the sort to just turn his back and walk away. When is the baby due by the way?'

'April I think.' Ruth's voice was laden with shame. 'I – can't really be sure – I – I never thought of such a thing happening, I never thought of anything much at the time. It was all so unreal, as if it wasn't me with Lewis but somebody else I didn't know at all. All I could think about was Lorn – and mixed up with it all was Lewis – dying.'

Absently Shona nibbled at the corner of a sandwich. 'April,' she murmured, her blue gaze fixed on the bronzed bulk of Sgurr na Gill rearing upwards to the smoky drift of the autumn sky. 'Just about the time I'll be coming back to Rhanna.' She became brisk again, going to the sink to wash the flask and rinse out the cups, saying over her shoulder, 'I'm finished here for today, Ruth. I promised Kirsteen I'd be back early. I brought some curtain material over with me and we're going to measure it out this afternoon.' She had promised no such thing, but felt that she couldn't bear to while away the afternoon on her own knowing what she did. Laigmhor was a cosy cheerful place and there was always someone popping in for a crack and a cuppy and she knew she needed to have company around her if she was to keep her mind off this new crisis which had arisen. For a moment she wished that she hadn't asked Ruth over for a strupak, she had only succeeded in disrupting what, for Shona, had been a most pleasant and satisfying morning with nothing more important than the planning of home decor to absorb her thoughts. Guiltily she tossed her hair back from her face and turned to Ruth with a smile of genuine warmth. 'Well, Ruth, will I tell Lorn that you'll meet him this evening?'

'This – this evening?' stammered Ruth.

Shona's eyes were very blue as they held Ruth's troubled

gaze. 'Ay, this evening. The sooner you get it over with, the better. Where would you like to see him?'

Ruth stood up, running her fingers over her brow in a distracted fashion. 'Och, I don't know. I can't think as quick as you, I never planned it this way – I didn't plan anything as a matter of fact.'

'Now's the time to start. You could come over to Laigmhor. I'd see to it you and Lorn got the parlour to yourselves.'

But Ruth rejected the suggestion violently. 'No! Not there. Up by Brodie's Burn, it's where I always went when I needed to sort myself out. After tea – about half past six.'

She looked ready to faint, and on impulse Shona reached out to draw her close. Her hands were like ice and Shona picked up her own woollen cardigan from the back of a chair and wrapped it round the girl's slim shoulders. 'Come on, I'll walk you over the glen. Kate will be wondering what's happened to you.'

She guided Ruth outside, very conscious of her fragility and of the limp that marred her otherwise graceful movements. 'Is your leg bothering you again, Ruth?' she asked kindly. 'It seemed so much better when you were staying with me in Kintyre.'

Ruth flushed, embarrassed as always by any reference made about the thing which had always been the main source of her mother's demented guilt. 'It always gets worse when I'm bothered about something. I'm used to it.'

'You'll feel better when you've had your talk with Lorn.'

Ruth shivered. 'I don't know about that but I don't feel nearly as bad as I did. Talking to you has helped. I don't know what I would do without you, Shona, you always seem to be at hand to thole my ails with me. I wonder you're not sick of me by this time.'

Shona didn't answer and they went on in silence. The sun's rays were slanting over the green hill slopes and pouring in cascades across the purple-tipped moors; the clean amber water of the Fallan foamed over great boulders on its way to the Sound of Rhanna which sparkled blue in the distance; the chimneys of Portcull were smoking peacefully, wafting the distinctive scent of burning peat into the air. Shona paused for a moment to absorb the sounds of the moors. Far over the tracts of empty moorland the piping of golden plover came plaintively, mingling with the bubbling of the curlews and the strange lost cry of the oyster catcher. At that moment the sky became patterned with formations of great birds streaking in an excited gaggle towards the flats by Loch Sliach. The barnacle geese which came every winter to Rhanna were arriving in their hundreds and their excited cries as they swept in over the Atlantic were almost as spectacular as the grandiose manner of their flight.

A little smile of pleasure touched Shona's lips and she breathed deeply, revelling in the breezes which caressed her face and lifted her hair to toss it in disarray over her shoulders. Everything was going to be all right. She and Niall would come back to Rhanna and it would be a wonderful occasion in their lives. Niall wouldn't be here all the time, of course, but she wouldn't weary during his spells away. She would have her father and Kirsteen, Phebie and Lachlan, and so many folk to visit there wouldn't be enough hours in the day. She also planned to see a lot of her friend, Babbie Büttger, the district nurse, and when Ellie came home from school during holidays, her days would be busier than ever ... She came back to reality and again glanced rather guiltily at Ruth. She had been so wrapped up in herself she had almost forgotten Ruth's presence. She was very quiet, walking rather unsteadily, her purpled gaze faraway, not seeing any of the beauty that surrounded her.

Shona felt suddenly oppressed, as if Ruth's unhappiness had draped over her in a stifling shroud. She was almost relieved to see Dodie loping quickly towards them, his thin lips already stretching into the familiar 'He breeah!' with which he greeted everyone.

'Ay, it is a fine day, Dodie,' agreed Shona. She eyed his gaunt frame critically, glad to see that he had good colour in his somewhat wizened cheeks. 'You're looking well enough. I'm thinking that your stay in hospital has maybe done you a lot of good.' Immediately and self-consciously Dodie's blunt, calloused fingers shot up to rub the side of his nose from which, until recently, a large growth had sprouted. For years Lachlan had wanted Dodie to have it seen to, but the old eccentric had resisted the suggestion fiercely, his fear of 'furrin parts', which included mainland Scotland, making him suffer the inconvenience the growth had caused him. But some months ago it had begun to cause him real discomfort and without ado Lachlan had set about persuading him to go into hospital to have it removed. Dodie, though terrified at the idea, had finally capitulated and for the first time in his life had made the trip to the mainland. Now, the rigours he had undergone while in the hospital were only a memory though he never tired of speaking glowingly about the 'fine leddies' who had tended to his every need and who had put him in mind of Biddy. Only to a privileged few had he admitted to the embarrassment he had undergone during the trauma of 'bathing his private body in front o' wee bits o' lassies', an event which had overshadowed the very operation itself, for hardly at all had he mentioned the apprehension he had felt during the preparations for surgery.

On his return the men of Portcull had treated him kindly, though few were unable to resist teasing him. Dodie had remained primly tight-lipped about his experiences and had now reached the stage of being quite proud of his new appearance, to the degree of carting around a small milk churn which he held up every so often to view himself at different angles.

'Carry a mirror in your pocket,' Tam McKinnon had urged him. 'It would be a sight easier and no one will be the wiser.' But Dodie had turned up his new nose at this. 'I would be the wiser and I will no' turn into a cissy for you or for anyone else for that matter. Anyways, the milk churn is only in case I meet Ealasaid, it's easier to carry than a pail.'

At Shona's words he smiled gloomily through his fingers, his grey-green eyes alighting with deference on Ruth whom he had held in some awe since she had had her first story published, a fact which put her ill at ease in his company for he was inclined to eye her from head to foot as if she wasn't quite real and might disappear from view at any moment. 'Ay, thon hospital is a fine place just,' he enthused, his broken teeth showing for a moment. 'I am knowing now what it feels like to lie back and be treated like a lord. I had a fine rest though I couldny sleep much at night wi' the noise o' motor cars an' folks shoutin' in the street outside. I wouldny like the likes o' that life all the time. I missed my bonny cow, that I did, but it was lovely just to get off havin' to work for a whily.'

Shona held her counsel knowing it would be useless to bring up the subject of the Old Age Pension for which Dodie was eligible but refused to collect. 'I dinna want it,' he had protested disdainfully. 'I'm no' auld yet and they can just keep it till I'm no' young enough to work.'

So he continued to 'work to Burnbreddie' and to do his rounds of farm and croft, taking any odd job that chanced along, though he was not averse to making an easy shilling when the opportunity presented itself, as his next rather breathless words proved. 'I have just come from Ranald's,' he blurted, drawing his greasy cuff across his nose with a loud and satisfying sniff. 'He asked me to come over this dinner time to see would I collect some nice shells for the shop he is thinkin' o' openin' for the towrists.'

'A shop?' asked Shona in some distraction, sensing an unusual restlessness in Ruth, who, completely uninterested in Dodie's ramblings, was gazing over his bent back to the village beyond.

Dodie nodded excitedly. 'Ay, just that. A crafty shop or something grand like it. Him an' one o' they artist wifies are gettin' together this winter to turn his big boat shed inside out. She's goin' to be paintin' pictures to sell and Ranald wants me and Hector the Boat to collect and polish all the shells we can – bits o' driftwood forbye.' He ended, full of amazement at the idea of anyone paying good money for hunks of wood washed up by the tide.

Shona couldn't suppress a giggle. The artist woman that Dodie had referred to was none other than Barra McLean, a distant cousin of Behag and Robbie Beag, who more than thirty-five years ago had taken her leave of the island to study art in Glasgow. Though remaining a spinster, she had done well for herself and with a lifetime of teaching behind her she had retired back to Rhanna and was living in one of the harbour cottages. Her somewhat unconventional form of dress had caused a furore among the island women, led in their disapproval by Behag who was petrified at the idea that any relative of hers should bring disgrace upon the family name. In a loud voice she had denounced Barra, interspersing her words with sniffs of indignation. 'Hmph, have you ever seen the likes? Smokin' like a lum and wearin' the trowser like she was born in them! I wouldny be seen dead wi' thon cratur' and that's a fact. As for that Ranald McTavish! He should think shame of himself but then, he's the sort that would do anything for sillar and from what I hear that – that person is no' short of a shilling or two.'

'So, you wouldny be seen dead wi' Barra?' Kate had said thoughtfully. 'Well, you'd best get used to the idea for wi' her bein' a relative o' yours it's quite on the cards you will get to be nose to tail wi' her in the kirkyard one day. Oh ay, it's no' daft we are, Behag. I am after hearin' she's the selfsame cousin o' yours who went away to the mainland years ago – and a nicer, kindlier woman you couldny meet anywhere – even though she does wear the trowser – and enjoy a dram the same as yourself. I tell you, she's a mite too nice to be a relative o' yours – at least she has a civil tongue in her head, which is more than can be said for you.'

At which point the purple-faced Behag had flounced into her back shop leaving Kate skirling with such infectious laughter she soon had everyone laughing with her and looking askance at the outraged Behag's disappearing back.

Ruth smiled absently as Dodie came to the end of his monologue and, shrugging herself out of Shona's cardigan, she handed it back and murmuring something about getting along to the shop she limped hurriedly away.

Dodie gazed after her and shook his head sorrowfully. 'Poor lassie, she's no' lookin' like herself – but then she has good reason. I am after hearin' that besom Morag is doin' strange things in the middle o' the night—' He paused cryptically and gave Shona a conspiratorial flutter of his eyelid which was meant to be a wink. 'I saw her wi' my very own eyes, wanderin' over the Hillock in her goonie. I was that feart I near died for at first I thought she was a spook comin' out of the kirkyard to haunt me. I was just fleein' away when I heard the organ bein' played in kirk an' I knew it was that Morag Ruadh, for no one else plays it wi' a louder foot. It is a wonder to me she never wakened the whole of the island wi' thon thing echoin' over the hills – just like a spook it was – screamin' in agony.'

Shona paused with her hand on the gate. So the rumours about Morag were true after all. She wondered if Ruth was aware of her mother's odd behaviour. She had given no indication that things weren't as normal, if normal could be applied to the kind of life she led. But Shona knew that Ruth was fiercely loyal and would never let slip by a single word that her mother's behaviour was giving her cause for concern. Shona sighed. As if Ruth hadn't enough to worry her. It was little wonder that she looked so pale and distraught and not in any frame of mind to be bothered passing the time of day in frivolous chatter.

Shona laid her hand on Dodie's arm. 'Dodie, don't be saying a word of what you saw, for Ruth's sake.'

He stared at her in amazement. 'I wouldny do that,' he protested indignantly. 'I'd be too feart that witch Morag found out and would maybe start hauntin' me in the middle o' the night. She's daft, lassie,' he stressed gently. 'She doesn't know if her head's on back to front or if she's comin' or goin'. I just walk the other way when I see her for the last time she grabbed hold o' me her eyes were glitterin' an' she looked mad as a peat hag. She was lookin', at me – yet she was lookin' right through me – as if I wasny there and when she started rantin' at me for no' goin' to kirk on the Sabbath I just tore myself away from her an' ran all the way home.'

He glanced round his shoulder in some trepidation, as if expecting to see Morag bearing down on him, and with a breathless 'He breeah!' he was off, his long loping stride taking him to the foot of the hill track, almost before Shona had turned to shut the gate behind her.

Chapter Two

Fergus looked up as Shona came through the door, rapturously welcomed by Sheil and Ben who had been having their midday repast from bowls set out on the cobbled yard while Bob, their master, was inside as he always was at this time of day, sharing the McKenzie table.

The kitchen was warm and peaceful with the cats stretched out by the range and the old clock on the wall ticking the seconds away. It was much the same as it had been when Shona had lived at Laigmhor and that was what she loved about it. People had come and gone, time had changed many things, but the house had remained untouched by it all, its sturdy walls occasionally embellished by new paint and the ornamentations placed on them by human hands. More importantly, they had absorbed atmosphere and seemed to breathe gently of the many souls who had lived and loved and died within the homely shelter of the time-worn bricks. For a moment Shona was whisked back to childhood, seeing in her mind's eye Mirabelle at the fire, her plump face flushed as she cooked dinner or stirred the morning porridge over the flames. Shona realized that her mother must have stood at the very same fire a long time ago, just a young girl who thought she had all her life in front of her, but who had died as her daughter was born. It was difficult for Shona to get a mental picture of her but she could well imagine her smiling, the way she smiled from the photograph Shona kept among her personal possessions and which she looked at often. Her father had always sat in the same place he was sitting at now, on the same high-backed chair, the dents on its shiny leather surface bearing witness to its years of usage. She studied him for a moment. Time had been kind to him, his tall, muscular body was still lithe and lean, his face certainly bore a few lines but they only added to its ruggedness; his hair, though threaded through with white, was in the main still as black as night, the crisping curls at his nape straggling over the collar of his green serge working shirt. His eyes were dark and lively, smiling as they had smiled at her in yesteryears when she had run in from the meadows to recount some trivial incident that had been of universal importance to her at the time.

'You're back early, mo ghaoil,' he observed. 'Don't tell me you're scunnered with housework already.'

She started out of her reverie. 'Ach no, it's daft to be doing much cleaning with the house still to be painted. I just wanted to polish the furniture to keep it in good condition. Tomorrow I'll go and cover everything ready for you and Lachlan to get over there with your paintbrushes. You could start it while I'm here and I could give you a hand.'

He made a rueful face at the suggestion. A man of the outdoors, he had never been one to lavish a lot of attention on decor, though Kirsteen had seen to it that the rooms at Laigmhor were kept fresh and presentable.

Bob scraped a slice of crusty bread over his plate and sniffed scornfully. 'All thon painting and papering is just a lot o' palaver and a waste o' time and money. My own walls look just as good with a bit of distemper brushed over them. The way folks slap paper on their houses you would think the damty things were going to fall down at any minute. Good walls don't need the likes o' that to hold them together.'

'Ach, Bob, if you'd had a wife things might have been different,' giggled Shona, sitting down at the table to reach for a buttered scone. 'It would have been the making of you and your home – and just think, you would have had someone to darn your socks and wash your shirts for you.'

'A wife!' Bob snorted in outrage. 'What would I have done wi' a wife? Just buggering nuisances – the lot o' them.'

Shona's eyes twinkled. She was thoroughly enjoying the opportunity to tease the old shepherd who had always scorned marriage but who had nevertheless hankered after a family to look after him in his old age which, though he was eighty-six, was to him very much in the distant future.

'Oh, so you've had a lot of experience with women

33

then?' Shona said mischievously. 'And here was me thinking you were just an innocent bodach with only your dogs to keep you company.'

Fergus threw back his head and roared with laughter as the indignant Bob exploded into wrath which was belied by the twinkle in his faded blue eyes. 'My dogs is all I ever wanted and that's a fact! If I had taken a wife like you, I wouldny be here to tell the tale o' the kind o' life you would have led me. It's all the cleaning that I canny bide. It's just a waste o' precious time. I have dust on my mantelpiece that was there twenty years ago and if I cleaned it off tomorrow it would just come back as thick in a month.'

'If you cleaned it off tomorrow you would smother yourself to death, Bob Patterson, and you'd never live that down for the rest of your life.'

Kirsteen appeared at that moment, smiling as the sounds of merriment filled the kitchen. 'If that's not a Highland way of putting things I don't know what is,' she said, sinking down into the inglenook by the fire. 'It's good to have you home, Shona. You're the only one who can keep the men in their place. Have you had anything to eat? I didn't expect you back so soon but there's plenty left in the pot.'

'I've had something, Kirsteen,' Shona said quickly. 'I'm just being greedy helping myself to your scones – I never could resist them.'

Under the veil of her long lashes she observed the older woman, saddened anew at the changes the last few months had wrought in her. She was careful to maintain a show of cheerfulness but her defences were down just then and Shona noted the tired droop of her shoulders and the somewhat defeated angle of her head. Gone was all the youthful buoyancy of spirit, the still, golden beauty that had been peculiarly hers had disappeared, her fine face was thin and drawn and there was more white than fair in her springy, curling hair. Shona felt sadness clutching at her heart. She had lost a brother, but Kirsteen had lost a son and Shona knew only too well that maternal love was one of the deepest, fiercest loves of all.

She crumbled her scone into her plate, her appetite suddenly gone. Broodingly she wondered how Kirsteen would take the news of Ruth's pregnancy. What if the girl decided to go away and have the child adopted? Kirsteen would never be able to bear the pain of that – she wouldn't allow it to happen . . . Shona pulled herself up abruptly. She was letting her thoughts run riot. She had to wait, allow one thing to happen at a time. She wished that Niall was here, he was so steady and sensible, his rational way of thinking allowing him to work out the best way of dealing with things. She half thought of phoning to ask him for his advice but almost immediately shrugged the impulse aside. Far better to wait; after all if any decisions were to be made it was up to Lorn and Ruth to make them and they wouldn't welcome her interference at this stage.

'Where's Lorn?' she heard herself saying somewhat automatically.

Fergus glanced up quickly. 'You sound strange, mo ghaoil, the way you used to sound when you had secrets you wanted to keep from me.'

She felt a slight sense of panic at his words. He knew her so well, almost as if he could read her very thoughts. It had been like that in the old days when it had been just she and he at Laigmhor. Each had been so atuned to the other, a telepathy that existed between them had been uncanny. She had thought that the passage of time might have erased that often disturbingly close bond but knew in those moments that it was something that would always remain with them.

With a toss of her head she shook his words aside and laughed as she got to her feet. 'Havers! You're growing too imaginative in your old age – nearly as bad as myself. Is it so unusual to want to see my very own wee brother? It's ages since I've seen him and we have a lot to catch up on. Just you tell me where he is and I'll leave you to have your afternoon nap in peace.'

She found Lorn in one of the sheds that flanked the cobbled yard. He was cleaning mud off the tractor but glanced round at her approach. Again she was struck by the notion that this broad-shouldered boy wasn't Lorn, but Lewis – Lewis as he had been, a strong, healthy young rascal who had laughed at life. Lorn had always been the more frail of the two but now he was growing stronger every day and had the look of someone who had never known a day's illness in his life. His sleeves were rolled to the elbows exposing brown muscular arms; the collar of his shirt was laid back to reveal a deep, manly chest. He was as Lewis might have looked if he had lived, but there was also a strong resemblance to Fergus in him. It was there, in his dark intense eyes and in the powerful facial structures which were beginning to mature into young manhood. On an impulse Shona put her arms round him and gave him an affectionate hug and he laughed, a deep warm laugh tinged with embarrassment. 'Hey, c'mon, I'm too grown-up for that sort of thing,' he protested. Nevertheless he didn't pull himself immediately away but hugged her back, his embrace filled with the love he had felt for her all his life. Playfully he tugged at a lock of her hair and stood back to survey her.

'What brings you out here? Have you come to help me clean the tractor? If so you're welcome. As you know I was always better suited to grooming horses.'

Shona wrinkled her nose. 'Me too, you can keep your noisy tractor. Actually – I came to tell you that I have a message for you – from Ruth.'

'From Ruthie?' He sounded wary, and a little sulky. 'What is it?'

'You have to see her this evening, up by Brodie's Burn – don't ask me what it's all about – she'll tell you herself.'

He turned away but not before she saw a slow flush creeping over his smooth, tanned cheeks. Self-consciously he brushed an impatient hand over his face as if to wipe away the tell-tale crimson that so easily betrayed his inner feelings, and it was so quiet for a few moments she heard plainly the faint rasping as his fingers slid over the stubble of tiny fair hairs on his chin.

'I don't know if I'll be able to make it tonight,' he said gruffly. 'I promised Tam a game of cards.'

'I think you'd better see Ruth,' Shona said imperatively. 'It's what you wanted, surely. You haven't been moping around all these weeks with a bellyache, that I know for a fact.'

He looked at her strangely, his fine mouth curling ruefully. 'Ay, it's what I wanted right enough – but not this way – secret meetings arranged behind my back. Ruthie should have come to me if she was so anxious to see me – unless of course she's in some kind of trouble.'

'Ach, you're worse than Father,' Shona said evasively. 'I'm not going to say another word on the subject, so stop looking at me as if you could read my mind. I'm away back to the house to help Kirsteen with the dishes – you had better get a message over to Tam's to let him know you won't be able to make it tonight.'

The door creaked shut behind her and Lorn stared at it broodingly, his fingers working nervously on the oily rag he had been using to clean the tractor. For a long time he remained immobile, then with a muffled oath he went out and made his way to the stable. It was warm, filled with the sweet smell of crushed hay and leather. Myrtle, the big patient Clydesdale, was in her stall, contentedly munching hay from the manger. At his entry her ears flicked back and her velvet-brown eyes regarded his with calm enquiry. He ran his hands over her broad, soft nose. 'It's all right, lass,' he murmured, 'I haveny come to bother you, I only want to talk to you.'

She snickered with pleasure and touched his neck with her gentle mouth as he laid his brow against her mane and whispered into her ears, the way he had whispered so many of his troubles in the past.

A few lights were beginning to twinkle from the harbour cottages as Lorn made his way over the slopes of Ben Machrie. There was a crispness in the blonde grasses waving in the wind blowing up from the sea, a sign that summer had crept back into the earth, in its departure leaving behind the dry, hollow stems of bracken and wildflowers to embellish the earth with their own particular beauty before they too curled up and disappeared against the onslaught of winter.

Lorn wasn't looking forward to the long dark evenings ahead – evenings that would be full of a stark emptiness without the presence of Lewis. He had made the days of winter bright, had filled them with his noisy, cheerful, often overwhelming personality. Sometimes Lorn had felt crushed by him, forced to retreat into a shell from which there had seemed no escape, but now that Lewis was dead, now that he was an entity unto himself, he began to see that it wasn't his brother who had made him the way he was. It was in his nature to be withdrawn, he was simply his father's son, the things that were in Fergus were surely in him, and no matter how much he might long to be as Lewis had been the very structure of his being made such a thing an impossibility.

Yet there remained the many quirks of nature he and Lewis had shared, and more and more lately he had felt himself to be the keeper of his brother's spirit – that as long as he lived so also did Lewis and when he too departed the earth they would both go on to meet eternity together. He hadn't divulged his fancies to anyone because he was afraid of being laughed at, but more than anything it was because these things were sacred to him and not to be shared lightly with others, no matter how close.

He dug his hands into the pockets of his jacket and tried not to let his thoughts wander ahead to Ruth and the reasons behind the somewhat furtive meeting, but despite himself she filled his mind and when he topped a rise and saw the unmistakable gleam of her flaxen head his heart leapt into his throat. She was sitting against the Seanachaidh's Stone, the Stone of the Storyteller, her back was to him but he knew from the tense pose of her body that she awaited him with trepidation.

'Hallo, Ruthie.' He spoke her name softly but even so she jumped and scrambled hastily to her feet. He noticed that she was pale and that her hands were clenched at her sides as if to keep them steady.

'Lorn, I – I wasn't sure if you would come. I told Mam

I was going to see Grannie and Granda so I can't stay long.' Her great violet eyes regarded him searchingly. He felt his breath trembling in his throat, making it difficult for him to speak. He wanted to rush forward and take her in his arms; to stroke the strands of hair from her brow; to kiss the sweet inviting fullness of her lips, but he did none of these, instead he sat down a few feet from her and pulling at a piece of wind-bleached grass snapped it off and inserted the end between his strong white teeth.

In the silence the rushing of the burn was like thunder in his ears though he could hear plainly the scrunching of her feet as she shifted slightly. She didn't sit down. He was very aware of her standing so close beside him and though he didn't look directly at her he knew that she was gazing longingly into the blue-grey mists of the gloaming as if mapping out the quickest route of escape. It was the way she had looked in days gone by when their mutual shyness had seemed an insurmountable barrier between them. He had suspected that this was to be no ordinary meeting, and now he knew it for a fact. He wanted to go to her, to reassure her, yet he couldn't do it simply because he felt so helpless himself. Lewis would have handled the situation with ease, made some laughing remark that would immediately have lessened the tension. Lewis would have – I'm *not* Lewis! an inner voice protested passionately. I'm *me*, Lorn Lachlan McKenzie! I am separate, I am whole, I am different!

'Shona said you had something to tell me, Ruthie.' His

slow calm voice did not betray his inner conflict. 'Come and sit by me and coorie in – it's cold up here in the wind.'

'No!' Her protest was sharp and more gently she whispered, 'I'd rather not be near you, Lorn, if you don't mind. When you've heard what I have to say you might never want to look at me or touch me again.'

Lorn drew his knees up to his chest and lowered his head to gaze contemplatively into the peaty, umber water tumbling over the stones. 'I know what you're going to tell me, Ruthie.' He pronounced each word carefully, forcing them to come out in a cool semblance of order and he was glad that his voice held no tremor. At least he had the satisfaction of having sounded perfectly in control of his emotions.

'You – you know?' Ruth was staring at him wildly. He saw her hands unclenching, saw the trembling of the long sensitive fingers before they curled back up once more into small fists. 'Did Shona tell you?'

He knew then that his solitary wonderings of the afternoon had not been the product of an over-imaginative mind. 'No, Shona didn't tell me – I guessed. God Almighty, Ruthie!' He exploded at last, all the pent-up grief, hope and love of many weeks boiling outwards in a torrential outpouring. 'What the hell do you take me for? Do you think I'm stupid? Oh ay, I'll admit I must have been pretty thick not to have guessed sooner, but this afternoon I worked it all out. All this time you've been avoiding me I wondered if you had changed your mind about me. I went through hell, damn you! I tried to convince myself you weren't worth it all. Sometimes I hated you, at other times I hated myself for wanting you so much. Right now I hate myself for being so bloody stupid about the whole thing but I couldn't think straight and couldn't see what was happening under my nose. If you're having Lewis's baby it doesn't change the way I feel about you. I love you, Ruthie, I always have – oh hell,' he punched his knuckles together, 'why do I feel so angry? I want to hit somebody – I could – I could—' His voice tailed off and he shook his head from side to side, unable to go on. His deep, dark eyes were blazing in his white face, the big strong knuckles he pressed suddenly to his temples, shaking. There was silence. The wind whined through the heather, moulding the hill grasses into tawny waves, sending shivers of light over the crystal stream spilling its way over the hill slopes.

Ruth stared at his crown of earth-brown curls and a sob broke in her throat. 'Lorn,' she murmured, 'how can you love me – how can you? Knowing what you do about me?'

'Because I'm not your God Almighty mother, that's why!' he yelled in torment. 'I don't need a Bible in my hand to tell me what I should and shouldn't do. I'd be lying if I told you I didn't hate the thought of you and my brother together but what's done is done and there's nothing can take that away – it was meant to be.'

A slow haze of tears drowned her eyes and she spun blindly away from him. 'Ay, that may be so, Lorn, what's done is done, there's no turning back now – but no one in the world – not even God – can stop me doing what *I* want to do. I'm always having to please somebody and it's time I pleased myself – I don't need to have this baby.'

He glared at her, fury sparking out of his eyes. 'God might not be able to stop you but I can – by Christ I can! Oh, your mother would say He was just using me, but this is me speaking, Ruthie – not God. I want to marry you, to rear my brother's child as my own. I want to take care of you and give you some happiness – and – dammit – I want to hear you telling me that you want me too!'

His voice ended on a note of exhaustion and Ruth felt an unbearable pain searing into her heart. 'Lorn – please – I want to believe you, more than anything in this world I want to believe you – but I don't want you to say such things – because you feel you have to.'

Wordlessly he rose to his feet and strode over to stand above her, big, looming, his muscular body outlined against the sky. Her heart hammered in her breast, tearing the air from her lungs. She felt strange and weak and ready to faint – something stirred in her belly, something that might have been a heartbeat – a tiny vibration surging within – but it was too soon for her to feel such a subtle quiver of life and she realized the feeling belonged to herself, a pulsing nerve that throbbed rhythmically to the beating of her heart.

'Ruthie.' Her name was a mere breath on his lips. He was staring at her, as if he couldn't get enough of her, his eyes so dark and intense they were like the blue shadowed pools of the forest. 'Oh, Ruthie – I've waited so long.' He put out a tentative finger to touch a lock of her hair then with a little half sob he gathered her into his arms. The sheep bleated from the corries of the shadowed hill and far in the glen below a dog barked, the sound filtering peacefully through the gathering night, but the two young people heard only the surging of their own swift heartbeats and the exciting echoes of quickening breath.

'I don't have to do anything,' he said softly into her ear, 'except – this.' His lips came down to claim hers and with a helpless moan of resignation she melted against him. It had been so long, an eternity since she had felt the cool pressure of his mouth on hers, but now there was something else, something that transcended those early inexpert seekings, now there was power, a sure possessive urgency born of need and want and love. The awkward boy had grown into a man and Ruth revelled in the glory of those moments. The earth reeled and turned upside down and there was no one else but them, lost in the wonder of their love. Ruth knew that this was how it should always have been and there were tears in her eyes for time lost, for things past that she would regret forever. But it was also a time for looking forward, for rejoicing in the fact that Lorn wanted her, despite everything he still loved her and she vowed then that she would never make the same mistakes as her mother, never never would she cast the burden of her guilt on those she loved, instead she would do everything in her power to make Lorn happy and she knew that by doing so she would find happiness herself. A flame of desire seared into her, awakening her to a passion that was outside the bounds of her experience. His hands on her breasts were like thistledown yet they aroused in her a raw craving which beat and pulsed into the very core of her being. She was aware of his quickening breath and from what seemed a great distance she heard him groaning deep in his throat.

'Lorn, Lorn,' she breathed, reaching up to entwine her arms about his neck and entangle her fingers in the thick hair at his nape.

Over and over they kissed while night crept in to drape itself in velvet folds over the stark hill peaks and over the vast reaches of the wind-tossed sea. The cool of the autumn air seeped into the earth but didn't touch Ruth and Lorn and when he finally released her his brow was damp with perspiration and his body burning with heat. 'Ruthie, Ruthie.' He cupped her face in his hands and covered it with kisses. 'You're so lovely. I can't get enough of holding you and touching you, I can't trust myself to behave when I'm with you and that is why we must be married right away.'

'As – soon as that?' The words were tinged with a mild panic, yet there was a note of happiness in her tone, something that had been missing for a long time.

He nodded, running his hands over the soft contours of her belly. 'Ay, as soon as that and as far as those outside our families are concerned, the baby's mine and if that bugger Lewis is watching us right now I haveny a doubt he'll be as pleased about it as I am, though if I know him he'll be too busy chasing the lady angels to have much time to spare for the likes of us.'

'Oh, Lorn, I love you so,' she burst out, lowering her head so that he wouldn't see the tears spilling.

He crooked his thumb and placed it under her chin, forcing her to lift her head and meet his eyes. 'That's all I wanted to hear you say, Ruthie, all I ever wanted.'

She shivered and he put his arm protectively round her shoulders. 'C'mon, we'll go and break the news to our folks. If you like I'll come and give you a bit of support, knowing your mother I can't see her doing a dance of joy round the kitchen table at the idea of having me for a son-in-law. We haven't exactly been on the best of terms since I got drunk at Burnbreddie's dance.'

But she shook her head vehemently. 'No, Lorn, I'd rather tell her myself. Mam can be gey queer at times and I know best how to handle her. You go along home, there's so much to think about and I want to be by myself for a whily – I can't take it all in, there's an awful lot to arrange and we haven't even discussed where we're going to live.'

He laughed and pulled her closer. 'Stop havering. Just take one thing at a time. Even if we have to live in a shepherd's bothy in the hills we'll be all right as long as we're together.'

An unnatural quietness prevailed over the village. Hardly a soul was to be seen, only the old men making desultory conversation with the fishermen down by the harbour. There was little to disturb the peace of the October evening. Although more and more of the mainland ways were reaching the island, the Sabbath was still a pious day and Saturday nights were set aside in preparation. Within the walls of croft and cottage children queued to be bathed, old men steeped their feet in steaming basins set by cosy peat fires while the womenfolk shut themselves into their sculleries and fastidiously attended to matters of personal hygiene. Many of the houses now had the luxury of a bathroom, but, although many wouldn't admit to the fact, these were abandoned in the winter nights in favour of the comforts of washing by the fire and old-fashioned zinc tubs were furtively resurrected from the wash-houses for this purpose.

Many of the crofthouse windows were curtainless and those that took the trouble to hang drapes might as well not have bothered as the business of the household could easily be seen through various chinks and folds. Passing Murdy's house situated close to the Fallan, Lorn smothered his laughter into Ruth's hair as they caught sight of him stripped to the waist at the window, diligently shaving with one hand while the other beat time to the Scottish dance music pouring from the wireless. At the foot of the path leading to Ruth's house Lorn took her in his arms once more and nuzzled the lobe of her ear. 'Are you sure you don't want me to come in with you? I don't like the idea of you facing your mother on your own.'

'I won't be alone, Father will be there,' she said steadily

enough, though all her instincts made her want to run from the place.

'Goodnight then – mo cridhe,' he added the endearment rather shyly. 'Will I see you tomorrow?'

'Ay, you can be sure of that. I'll be at kirk in the morning but after dinner I'll be down at Mara Oran Bay.'

His cool firm mouth touched hers briefly and his hands slid intimately over her waist before he reluctantly let her go. She waited till the sound of his footsteps had died away before she went slowly up the path. For a long time she stared at the dark oblong of the door before she straightened her shoulders and turned the handle.

Lorn started as a car drew up beside him and Lachlan's head popped out. 'I see I'm going your way. Can I give you a lift?'

Lorn settled himself into the passenger seat, smiling to himself at the collection of odds and ends which littered the interior of the Austin A45. Something jabbed into his spine and raising himself up he removed the doctor's stethoscope and stuffed it under the dash. The little car wheezed and groaned on its tortured springs as they made their way into Glen Fallan and for a minute or two neither of them said anything, Lorn knowing only too well that it took a lot of concentration to steer any vehicle over the bumpy road surface.

'I was just going to pay McKenzie a visit tonight,' said

Lachlan in his deep pleasant voice. 'I met Shona this afternoon and she was on about getting her house painted so I thought I had better look in and get my orders.'

Lorn merely grunted, his dazed mind so full of half-formed plans he couldn't make sense of his jumbled thoughts.

Lachlan sensed his mood. 'It's far in the distant past but I seem to remember a preoccupation with my thoughts when I was your age. Girl trouble?'

'No – yes. Och – dammit, yes!' On impulse he told Lachlan about Ruth. He had always been able to confide in the man who was as much a friend to him as he was a doctor. Both Lachlan and his wife, Phebie, seemed more like family to him. During the years of his illness, Lachlan had always been at hand with his advice and sympathy. He had become like a second father without the complications that a father-son relationship sometimes brought and Lorn didn't feel it so odd to be confiding the things closest to his heart.

'So,' said Lachlan at length, 'Ruth is expecting a bairn which she isn't officially expecting till the pair of you are wed – is that right?'

Lorn didn't comprehend the meaning of his words and Lachlan took one hand from the wheel and gripped the boy's shoulder. 'In my experience there are such things as premature births – the island's full of them. Ay, many's the bouncing full-term babe I've slapped on the backside and the mother telling me, as innocent as you like, how surprised she was that a premature baby could be so big.'

His infectious laugh rang out. 'The cailleachs will talk but just you keep them guessing. After all, you're not the first couple to conceive on your wedding night and you won't be the last.'

'Bugger me, I hadny thought of that!' Lorn's tones were filled with awe and Lachlan smiled. How like Fergus the boy sounded, the same timbre of voice, the same terminology. They were also alike by nature, though there was one important difference in Lorn, an acceptance of the vagaries of life and a willingness to meet the twists of fate laid at his door. In his youth, Fergus had been too complicated, too proud to accept the tricks of life though maturity had mellowed him, had dampened the fire of his ready temper and for that Lachlan breathed many a sigh of relief.

He brought the car to a halt outside Laigmhor. 'Away you go in, Lorn,' he instructed. 'I can see your father another time, your news is more important.'

'Thanks, Doctor,' Lorn said briefly. He banged the car door shut and watched till the tail lights receded into the distance before turning his steps towards the house.

The peace of evening lay over Laigmhor, a soft light shone from the kitchen window, the sharp fragrance of peat smoke filled the air, strains of Scottish dance music filtered from the parlour. Lorn breathed deeply, loving the sight of the sprawling farm with its outbuildings huddled into the night shadows. The kitchen was empty but for the animals heaped contentedly at the fire. Lorn took another deep breath and squaring his shoulders crossed over the silent hall to open the door of the parlour. Fergus was dancing with Shona, whirling her round with his strong right arm. Kirsteen was at the fire, busy with a pile of woolly socks which were always needing to be mended. At Lorn's entry she glanced up, her expression unchanging but a light in her eyes at sight of her youngest son. She wondered why he had gone out of the house with a darkened brow and why he had returned full of a suppressed excitement.

'I have something to tell you,' he said and his voice was clear and strong. 'Would you mind switching off the wireless?'

Fergus complied with his wishes and silence flooded the room. In a breathless rush Lorn imparted his news then paused to look at each face in a mixture of defiance and joy. 'Well, aren't any of you going to congratulate me? It isn't every day I ask a lass to marry me.'

Without ado Fergus went to the sideboard to withdraw glasses and a bottle of whisky. 'I'm thinking this calls for a dram – in my case a big one.' The hand that poured the whisky was not quite steady but by the time he held up his glass to toast the future happiness of Lorn and Ruth he was himself again, his black eyes showing his genuine delight when he said, 'You're young to be taking a wife but I can't talk for I was not that much older myself when I got wed. Young marriages seem to run in the McKenzie household and I wish you every happiness, son. You'll make your home here till we can fix you up with something else. Matthew was talking about going to live beside Tina's mother in Portcull and it's quite likely their cottage will be free soon. The bairn will be born here—' He laughed. 'It's time these old walls heard again a baby's voice, it will bring some life to the place.'

Kirsteen had said very little. She hugged Lorn before slipping quietly out of the room, her eyes very shiny. Fergus found her in the kitchen, leaning against the mantelpiece, her head on her arm, the firelight finding every hollow in her face and gleaming on the tears staining her cheeks.

Fergus took her tenderly in his embrace and kissed her wet face. 'Mo cridhe,' he whispered huskily. 'Did I do right telling Lorn that he and Ruth could live here? I didn't give you any say in the matter.'

She leaned her head on his shoulder, loving the strength of his body. 'Fergie, Fergie, they were the nicest words I've heard spoken in this house for many a long day – oh, my darling,' she snuggled her face into the warm hollow of his neck, 'I love you for so many things but tonight I love you more than ever for being the man you are.'

He held her away from him, his dark gaze very intense. She was smiling, a smile of radiance that all at once banished her weariness. 'You look so happy,' he said wonderingly. 'Like the Kirsteen I knew long ago with the sunlight in her hair and the summer in her smile.'

She laughed, running a finger over his firm rebellious mouth. 'Just when I think we've had all our romance you speak the words of a poet but you're right – I *am* that girl of long ago – at heart anyway.' She drew a deep breath.

'Oh, I'm so happy – I feel as if – as if Lewis was about to come back to us – he'll live on in his bairn.'

'Ay, but you must think of it as Lorn's – we all must think that.'

'Och, I know, I know, it will be Lorn's but – just occasionally I'll look – and I'll remember Lewis.'

In the parlour Shona sat with Lorn, both of them lost in their own separate thoughts.

'Was it very difficult to accept – the thing that Ruth had to tell you?' Shona said eventually, tearing her gaze away from the leaping flames in the hearth.

Lorn nibbled at a thumb nail, a habit of his when he had a lot on his mind. 'She didn't tell me – I had already guessed. It made it less painful for her – oh, we had a bit of a scene, she's got a lot of pride in her and thought I wanted to marry her just to give the bairn a name.'

'And – aren't you?'

He glared at her. 'You should know better than that, Shona!' he ground out. 'What a daft thing to say. You know how I feel about Ruth.'

The blue of her eyes deepened and she smiled. 'I just wanted to hear you say it. She's lucky to have you, Lorn. She could travel the length and breadth of the globe and never find your like.'

'I just hope that witch of a mother of hers thinks so too. She doesn't trust the McKenzies.'

'Morag Ruadh doesn't trust anyone,' said Shona with a shudder. 'Not even herself. That's been the root of her troubles all these years. She'll go to her grave with an uneasy mind – you mark my words. It's a good thing Ruth's getting out in time, it's her father I feel sorry for – poor old Doug, he deserved better than Morag – yet – in his own way he's fond of the caillich – he seldom speaks ill of her. Any other man would have left her years ago.'

'He stayed for Ruth's sake.'

'Ay, but he'll stay long after Ruth's gone, he'll see it through to the bitter end – and it will be a bitter one. Morag will pay a terrible price for her years of self-loathing and I doubt it will be a price not even she bargained for.'

The carbolic smelling kitchen was faintly lit by a single paraffin lamp which cast shadows over the ceiling and softened the harsh outlines of the sparsely furnished room.

Thanks to Dugald the fire was piled amply with peats, and its warm glow was about the only source of welcome the house had to offer. He was sitting beside the range in his rocking chair, his mop of silvery white hair shining like a beacon against the drab walls whose only embellishment took the form of religious samplers hung in places where they were sure to catch the eye. Recently he had rebelled and had nailed up several of his own little watercolours of wildflowers and birds of the seashore. They had stood out like jewels and Ruth's heart had lightened every time she looked at them. The delicate hues of summer had been captured in each petal and she could almost smell the sweet fragrance of each bloom filtering through the perpetual taint of disinfectant.

But the joy had been brief. One day she found every one of the paintings gone and on questioning her father had learned that Morag had taken them all down and wouldn't tell him what had become of them. Ruth had felt a great, overpowering sadness washing over her. Her father had looked so lost, a defeated droop about his shoulders that made him look old, yet, when Ruth had cried aloud in anger he had put his fingers to her lips and said, 'Weesht, Ruthie, I can paint more. Your mother is no' too well the now and you mustny say a word to her about them.'

He had omitted to tell his daughter that Morag was becoming less and less responsible for her actions and he had never mentioned that he had had to get out of bed on more than one occasion to either prevent his wife from her nocturnal wanderings or to bring her back from them. On the last occasion she had led him to the kirkyard, a ghostly apparition in her white nightgown, moving through the darkness, following a pathway which she had trodden many times during her life. The hairs had risen on the back of his neck when her steps had finally stopped at the kirk on the hillock and she had begun to sing, a thin high sound, eerily enhanced by the silence of night and the ghostly sight of gravestones rising out of the gloom. The scraping of the kirk door had leapt out at him like thunder, startling him into action, forcing him to go forward just as Morag was about to enter the old church. She had shown no surprise at his sudden appearance and had allowed him to lead her home, her hand in his like a trusting child. She remembered nothing of such happenings and so Dugald struggled to keep his secret to himself. As a result he was so exhausted it was becoming more and more difficult for him to maintain a show of normality to the world, though for Ruth's sake he strived to remain cheerful.

Ruth's gaze swept over him as she entered the kitchen. He was sticking pictures of his beloved birds and flowers into a big scrapbook. Earlier in the evening Morag had accused him of idleness but he had ignored her and had gone on quietly with his hobby.

'You're back, Ruthie,' he smiled in greeting. 'Would you like a cuppy? The kettle's on the boil.'

Ruth went to stand by him, laying her hand on his thin shoulder. 'No, Father, I'm fine – I – there's a few things I'd like to say to you and Mam.'

Morag didn't hear. She was flouncing about more than usual, lifting pots from the range and banging them down on the shelves of the larder.

'Just where have you been all this time, my girl?' she asked through tight lips. 'I said you could go over to your Grannie's for a whily but I didn't mean this long. You know fine that Saturday is a busy day for me. Is it too much to expect a bit o' help from you?'

Fine Ruth knew what Morag meant. For as long as she could remember, Saturday nights in the 'temple' were a bustle of relentless activity. Everything that could be scrubbed was attended to with a thoroughness that left wooden objects as bleached as dry bones. Though the floors and walls were washed every morning with carbolic, they were treated to another onslaught on Saturday nights till it seemed that the very plaster cried out for mercy. Afternoons were spent preparing food and the evening spent cooking it so that there would be nothing to do on the Sabbath but serve it.

On summer evenings Dugald was able to escape to his boat or to the moors but with the onset of winter he was forced to resign himself to the house and somehow immerse himself in the harmless pastimes which Morag despised.

Ruth watched her mother for a moment before she made a reply. She had grown thinner of late but she was agile as ever, her lithe body encased in a homespun jersey and skirt, her legs swathed in long black woollen stockings which she had knitted herself. Her hair, though spiked with white, was as flamboyantly red as it had ever been and she never ventured outside without a severe black hat jammed on so tightly only the more unruly strands could find an escape.

Ruth licked her dry lips, wishing that she had been able to get her father on his own. She hated herself in those moments, knowing that she was about to heap more coals onto those which already consumed his life. She hesitated, wondering perhaps if she ought to wait for a while. But no! If she didn't speak now she might never recapture the courage she had plucked up on the way up the path.

'I wasn't at Granny's, Mam, I was with Lorn McKenzie.'

Her voice came out strong and clear, the confident ring to it as much a surprise to herself as the words were to Morag. Ruth had found that strength was the only effective weapon against her mother. She laughed at anything else, gentleness was to her a sign of weakness and because Dugald had used it over the years she was scornful of him and though she never said as much she made it plain he was to be despised for his patient endurance.

Morag paused in the larder doorway and slowly, as if afraid she might drop it, she lowered a heavy pan carefully onto the top of the sideboard.

'What was that you said, Ruth?' she asked, her voice ominously quiet.

'I said I was with Lorn, Mam.' Ruth's own voice remained steady, though inwardly she was trembling so much she felt that if she stayed on her feet for very much longer she would faint. All her life she had dreaded her mother's rages. She rarely shouted or indulged in verbal battles but gave out the impression that she would explode at any moment, like a volcano that had been simmering for years and seemed ready to erupt into uncontrolled violence. There was also about her a frightening intensity, an eerie quality of rage in continual ferment beneath a flimsy surface. Ruth had always known that her mother's strength was purely physical and lately she had come to see that the spiritual props upon which she had built her life were beginning to crumble. She was turning more and more to her Bible and finding nothing in it to sustain the warped beliefs she had harboured for so long. It was a crazed and fruitless searching for spiritual sustenance and she was poorly equipped to deal with the realities of her own and her family's existence.

Every time Ruth or Dugald brought the cold realities of the everyday world into the house she was genuinely shocked and unable to face them rationally and she experienced a sense of panic as she heard the determination in her daughter's voice.

'Wi' Lorn, eh?' She struggled to sound cold and detached. 'And what pray were you doin' wi' him when you were supposed to be wi' your grandparents?'

'We – we were just talking, Mam.' Ruth felt herself faltering and gathered up her strength for the onslaught that must surely follow her next words. 'We're going to be married, Mam – I – I hope you and Father are pleased.'

Colour suffused Morag's ruddy face. 'Married? Married to Lorn McKenzie! And how did this come about, my girl? If I'm no' mistaking I was led to believe it was his brother you were caperin' about with. Ay, he's dead now but he had his use o' you first—' Her voice rose slightly. 'He violated you, Ruth! My lassie, my very own lassie, who never heeded any o' my warnings about men but just threw herself at the first lad who came along. What sort o' a girl are you, Ruth? Giving your body to one man one minute and the next tellin' me you're goin' to be marryin' his brither? The de'il is in you, Ruth, and no mistake and may the Lord forgive you!'

All the power left Ruth and her voice broke on a sob. 'Mam, I love Lorn, I've always loved him! I only went with Lewis because he was dying and needed me more than he ever needed anyone in his life. I never loved him – but – but I'm expecting his baby and Lorn is going to marry me because he loves me more than his pride – more than anyone in the world ever loved me – except – except for my father. He's the only one who ever showed me what it was like to be loved and it's nice, Mam, to be loved. I'm truly sorry it had to happen this way but – you had to know and there's nothing you can do about it – except – tell me that you care more for me than you care about the gossips and what they'll say!'

There was a long silence in the room. Dugald prepared himself for Morag's reaction even though he himself had been poorly prepared for the blow of Ruth's news. He adored the flaxen-haired girl and fully believed she was his daughter. For years he had doubted this to be the case, but more and more, as time passed and the little quirks of nature that were in him became apparent in Ruth, his doubts had become fewer and had reached the stage where they were practically non-existent. She was his child, the startling fairness of her hair and complexion had been his as a lad, she had inherited his gift for writing and just lately had shown that she had a talent for painting. She was the only thing that made any sense of his life, she *was* his life and now she was going to be married, she would go away from the house never to return, taking everything that meant anything to him for without her nothing was worthwhile – he was condemned to living alone in the house with Morag and he couldn't take any more of her – he couldn't . . . Shame washed over him. Ruthie, his Ruthie was expecting a child. She was only a wee lassie herself yet she had never by a single word given her secret away. How she must have suffered . . . He sucked in his breath and reaching out he seized Ruth's hand and pulled her down beside him. He couldn't speak, couldn't tell her that she and Lorn had his blessing, but she didn't need to hear him say anything, it was all in his eyes, those honest grey eyes which so easily conveyed his emotions.

Morag seemed to have shrivelled in the last few minutes. All the colour had drained from her face except for two flaming spots high on her cheekbones. She sagged against the sideboard, its bleached surface supporting the weight of her gaunt frame on arms that were rigid. The silence stretched, a tangible force, filling the dark corners with insidious waiting. The very house seemed to be holding its breath in suspense. Ruth could bear it no longer. The wrath that she had dreaded was suspended, unspoken words of anger hung in the heavy air like poison-laden barbs.

'Mam!' Ruth struggled to her feet and limping over to her mother placed a hand on her arm. 'Mam,' she appealed again, 'are you all right?'

Slowly Morag raised her head and the girl saw that her strange green eyes were glittering unnaturally in the faint light. 'All right, all right,' she hissed through lips that were deathly white. 'How can you ask that, my girl? How can you speak to me – knowing the things you've done? I will be the laughing stock of this place.' Her tone became a lamenting wail. 'I will never be able to hold up my head in pride again – never, as long as I live. You've brought a curse to the good name of this house, you wanton, brazen hussy that you are . . .'

'That's enough, Morag!' Dugald could hold his tongue no longer. 'What kind of a mother are you to be thinking o' your damned pride at a time like this? Your lassie needs you more than she's needed you in her life and all you worry about is what folk will say. Are you human at all? Have you ever loved anyone in your life besides yourself? For that's all it is wi' you, Morag! All this bowin' and scrapin' to the Lord is just an excuse for self-indulgence—' His voice became harsher. 'Ay, you've revelled in it, Morag, being a martyr to first your parents and then to yourself. God Almighty, woman,' he exploded, 'there's a world outside that barrier o' guilt you've built round yourself! Ruth is in that other world and so am I – the husband you used to cover your so-called sins. I could have forgiven that, but I canny forgive the hell you made Ruthie and me go through! Ay, it's been a hellish existence livin' wi' you, woman, but thanks to my lassie I've been able to thole all the filth you ever threw at me!'

'Oh weesht, weesht, Father,' Ruth implored but it was too late. It was all coming out at last, all the things he had bottled up for years. He pushed Ruth's protests aside and with jutted jaw and flaring nostrils ground out, 'And just you leave my Ruthie be. She is going to marry Lorn and that's final. She is no' the only lass who ever had to get married – no – nor will she be the last. You of all people should see the truth of that, Morag, oh ay, you're an expert on the subject. It was the start of all our troubles when years ago you let your hair down for the first time in your life and actually started to behave like a flesh and blood woman. At least our lassie has one over you – she knows who fathered her bairn.'

He subsided back into his chair, trembling, his ragged breath coming from high up in his lungs. Morag too was shaking, her entire body seized by spasm after spasm. Her pupils were like needle points, something in them that was difficult to define, a strange silent yearning mingling with a look of naked relief. She spread her long supple hands, curling the fingertips into a gesture of beckoning. It was an oddly frightening, childlike appeal made doubly so by the fact that her lips were moving but no words would come out.

'Father,' whispered Ruth. 'She wants you – she wants you to go to her.'

Dugald arose and going over took Morag's hands and led her to the fire where he put her gently into a chair. Obediently she remained where she was. Her lips moved again but only a whimper came out, and for a long time Dugald stayed by her side, her steel-like grip on his hands making it impossible for him to break away. Slowly her head came up in a series of jerks, like a puppet controlled by somebody else.

'Dugald,' she spoke his name with a great effort, 'I'm – sorry.'

The words were barely audible but to Ruth and Dugald they were the sweetest that had been spoken in the house for many a long day. After their utterance Morag remained staring at her husband for endless moments, then her chin sank to her bosom and putting her red head in her hands she gave vent to a quiet, helpless release of tears.

Ruth had never seen her mother cry and the sight both frightened and awed her. She knew that something momentous had happened that night in the temple, something that seemed to reach out and enshroud them all in a mantle of peace. Ruth shivered and for the first time felt that the Hand of God had touched every one there with its wonderful healing powers. It was as if a miracle had happened.

'Is – Mam all right?' she asked in a hushed voice, unwilling to shatter the spell that had fallen over them.

Gently Dugald freed one of his hands and reaching out he pulled Ruth into his embrace.

'Ay,' he said softly. 'She is right enough. I only wish I had spoken out sooner – ay – I should have done it a long time ago.'

He looked at Morag's bowed head, a great sadness in

him knowing that, for her, the supplication had come too late. The delicate balance of her mind had long been in jeopardy and he knew, deep in himself, that the final thread was ready to snap.

Part Two

Spring 1961

Chapter Three

The passengers crowded to the rails of the steamer as she sailed round the headland which sheltered Mara Òran Bay from the Atlantic swell. The curving sweep of the bay with its petticoats of pure white sands brought forth murmurs of appreciation from the visitors and they stood in contented silence, eagerly pointing out the various aspects of topography which appealed to them.

Down in the saloon Shona grabbed Niall's arm and pulled him to his feet. 'C'mon, lazy, let's go up. I always love to watch the island coming nearer.'

They were the only passengers in the saloon and Niall grabbed his wife round the waist to pull her to him and kiss her intimately on the mouth.

'What was that for?' she asked, leaning against him and nuzzling his ear with the tip of her tongue.

'Just because I felt like it. After all we are starting afresh so there's no earthly reason why we can't pretend we're just newly married. Tonight when we're in bed I'll treat you like a new young bride and be very tender and patient with you.'

'Daftie,' she giggled. She gazed seriously into his eyes. 'Are – you glad we made the move?'

'It's a bit late to have doubts now and of course I'm glad. I'll miss Frank for a whily, he was a damned good partner to have and I feel just a wee bitty scary starting out on my own but we'll survive. I've paved the way well so there's no reason why it won't be a success.'

Long before he had even considered branching out on his own he had sounded out one or two of the smaller islands to see if his proposition would be a viable one and had discovered that the crofters and farmers were only too anxious to have the services of a good vet. Long before they had made the move from the Mull of Kintyre he had had several enquiries from farmers wanting to know when he was coming over to see to their beasts.

Ellie came skipping down the stairs towards them and sighed as she saw them standing close together. 'Really, this is no time to be canoodling,' she grinned impishly. 'We're almost there and everyone is really excited by something written on Ranald's big boat shed. I got a glimpse of great big letters and I think they said something about a fart studio.'

'*Ellie!*' Shona tried to sound shocked but was unable to suppress a burst of laughter. Grabbing her daughter's hand they went up on deck to be assailed by loud and varied comments reeling through the salt-laden air. They joined the throng, pushing their way to the rails to see for themselves what was causing the fuss. Shona watched the hills coming closer and happiness tugged at her heart. It was a bright fresh day with the April sun spilling over the rain clouds to make vivid patterns over the moors. The Sound of Rhanna was a flurry of sparkling blue waves racing to break themselves violently against the black hidden reefs of Port Rum Point. The huddle of white cottages round the harbour gleamed whiter than ever, the occupants having taken advantage of a recent spell of good weather to paint out the ravages of winter in time for the 'towrist season'. But for once the charms of the harbour failed to hold the attention of the crowd at the ship's rails. All eyes were turned on Ranald's boat shed, now converted into an art and craft shop with one of the smaller sheds made ready to dispense tea and home baking. The roof of the big shed faced out of the harbour and was one of the first things that people saw as they neared the island. With this in mind the ingenious Ranald had made his sign as big as possible and everyone was gaping in amazement at the bold white lettering which read 'Craft Shop and Fart Studio, Genuine Scottish Crafts, Everyone Welcome'.

Shona almost choked. Beside her Niall snorted and they doubled up in a paroxysm of mirth. 'That's what I call an unusual welcome home,' gasped Niall at last. 'Somebody's done the dirty on poor old Ranald.'

The comments of the visitors were ranging from disapproval to downright enjoyment. A child's rich Glaswegian voice shrilled through the air. 'Look, Mammy, there's another yin!'

Everyone stampeded to gape at a smaller sign propped against the side of the building. Laboriously painted in a decorative scroll it grandly proclaimed 'Fart classes by arrangement. Beginners welcome. Outdoors weather permitting.'

With few exceptions the crowd erupted into gales of laughter and the people who were waiting at the harbour for the arrival of the boat craned their necks to see what could be causing such a furore aboard the vessel.

Captain Mac, his bulbous nose a brilliant shade of red after a session at the bar with his cronies, came pushing towards Niall. A ship's master for many years he was now retired and resented travelling on any boat in the capacity of a passenger. The ocean was in his blood and when Niall had offered him the chance to skipper for him he had jumped at it and had already made it his business to familiarize himself with *The Sea Urchin*, the twenty-five-foot motor launch Niall had acquired for his trips to the islands. As Captain Mac was now a widower with relatives on just about every one of the Hebridean islands, the arrangement was a perfect one, allowing him to keep in touch with his family and yet able to remain in contact with his beloved sea.

'Bugger me, son, have you ever seen the likes o' that?' he greeted Niall, his craggy whiskered face a picture of delight. 'It'll be that crazy Tam McKinnon that's behind it – mark my words. When I was over here a couple o' weeks back he was just sayin' he would love to do something to bring Ranald down a peg or two and from the look o' it he's done it. By God he's done it! I doubt he'll have the towrists queuing at the door askin' to be shown the right way to blaw off wind.'

'It's a bit drastic,' said Niall. 'Ranald has worked hard to get his business going.'

Captain Mac pushed his fingers into his thatch of white hair. 'Ay, he has that, but this will no' do him any harm. At least his shop is going to be famous quicker than he thought and wi' Ranald's luck he'll be doin' a boomin' trade before you can say fart!'

He went off to superintend the tying up of the boat, and because to the crew he was still a figure of great authority not one of them raised a voice in objection.

Lorn was waiting at the harbour and ran forward to greet Shona and Niall as they came down the gangplank. Shona dropped the cases she was carrying and without hesitation threw her arms round her young brother's neck. 'Congratulations, you young devil,' she laughed while Lorn squirmed with embarrassment and glanced round furtively to make sure none of the village lads were watching. 'Oh, stop wriggling,' scolded Shona, 'I want to look at you to see if fatherhood has changed you at all.'

'Have a heart, Shona,' he protested though he couldn't refrain from smiling at her enthusiasm. 'It only happened four days ago. I'm hardly likely to have grown white whiskers in that time.'

Fergus had phoned through the news to Shona and Niall a few minutes after Ruth had given birth. 'It's a girl,' he had boomed joyfully. 'At last, a girl. I was beginning to think the McKenzies were fated only to have sons.'

'I should have thought that after me you wouldn't want another girl in your house again,' Shona had told him with a laugh. 'No doubt the cailleachs' tongues will be busier than ever now. Just you tell Ruth from me to ignore the old hags and they'll soon get sick of the subject.'

The rushed marriage of Lorn and Ruth had caused the usual stir of interest among the womenfolk of the island and when it became evident that Ruth was in an advanced state of pregnancy the interest turned to gossip and speculation had arisen as to when the baby would be born.

'She's had that bun in the oven longer than she's been wed, that's a surety,' had stated Merry Mary with conviction.

'Ay, folks were right when they said her mother's ways would turn the lass to sin,' nodded Elspeth Morrison, the sharp-tongued housekeeper of Slochmhor, though her tones weren't lacking a certain amount of sympathy.

'No one can call her the White Virgin anymore, and that's a fact.' Merry Mary followed Elspeth's sympathetic line. 'My, the times I felt sorry for the cratur' decked out in all thon white frocks. At least she has the look o' a normal body now – and she has a good man there in Lorn McKenzie – he was aye a laddie after my own heart and that's a fact. He wouldny be the first to take advantage o' a lass – no, nor will he be the last.'

'My God, would you just listen to the lot o' you?'

Kate had snorted with chagrin. 'You have marked that fine young couple down as sinners before they have even had a chance to get a leg over. Where do you get your ideas from I'd like to know? Maybe they are the things goin' on in your heads that you would like to have done yourselves. It's well known that Mistress Morrison here would have taken her breeks down to a pygmy if she had thought she might get a bairn out o' it! As for you, Merry Mary, it's well seeing you are a spinster woman wi' all these wild fancies you have in your head about men. Of course, it's common knowledge you get a lot o' your ideas from they wimmen's magazines you keep piled up in your house. You have had too much time on your hands since you gave up the shop. You used to have a kinder tongue in your head but now you're just as bad as all the rest o' the cailleachs.'

But despite staunch people like Kate the gossip reached a peak when Ruth had her baby after barely five months of marriage, but Lorn and his young wife had never been happier and his face was glowing when he was surrounded at the pier by the village menfolk and his hand shaken heartily. 'You have done right well, Lorn lad,' beamed Todd the Shod. 'My cailleach had our Mairi six months after the ring went on, but you have beaten us.'

Mollie, who was standing nearby, grew red in the face and hooted indignantly, 'And was not our Mairi a mite too soon in comin' into the world? A tiny wee thing she was and you only have to look at her now to see that she is still a delicate lass.'

'All ten stone of her,' smirked Todd in a quiet aside.

Niall was surrounded by a group of children clamouring to know when he would be able to come and look at their pet dogs and cats and patiently he told them that, if they brought their animals over to his house, he would take an hour or two out of his few days' holidays that he had planned, to attend to their ailments.

'Here.' Todd, not to be outdone, bustled over. 'You are just the very mannie I am needin' myself. Old Foxglove is skitterin' herself to death and I'm buggered if I can cure her. She is as dry as a bone forbye and we are havin' to buy our milk off that Tam McKinnon – and the mean bodach takin' the money too,' he ended in aggrieved tones.

Dodie loped over in time to hear what Todd had been saying and he eyed Niall with mournful appeal. 'My Ealasaid hasny been too well this whily and seein' you are back home to do your doctor I was wonderin' if you could come over and take a wee look at her.'

'Ay, Dodie, I will that,' Niall agreed with admirable calm, though his brown eyes sparkled at sight of Shona hiding her smiles in her hanky.

Tam McKinnon hove into view. There was an air of suppressed excitement about him as he came over to greet the McKenzies and Niall gave him a conspiratorial wink. 'You've done it, Tam, the boat was in an uproar coming into port. Ranald will have your lugs for purses when he finds out about it.'

Tam's homely face was the picture of innocence. 'I

haveny the least idea what you're on about, lad,' he intoned pleasantly.

But Captain Mac left him in no doubt. He gave Tam a hefty wallop on the shoulder blades and bellowed, 'By God, Tam McKinnon, you're a de'il and no mistake! What way did you manage to climb up to Ranald's roof and you as good as crippled for life!'

Tam spluttered and regaining his breath hissed in alarm, 'Weesht, man! The whole o' Portcull will hear you and I'm no' wantin' Ranald McTavish to find out what I did to his roof – no' yet anyway. I want to teach the bugger a lesson he'll no' forget in a hurry.'

'*You* did to his roof!' exploded Todd indignantly. 'Of all the damty cheek! It was your idea, I'll grant you that, but it was me and the other lads who near broke our necks gettin' over those rocks wi' the ladders while you just stood wi' your hands in your pouches and gave the orders.'

'Ay, and I was the mug who went up the ladders to paint on that big F,' supplied Angus McKinnon loudly. 'I got that much paint on my hair Ethel didny know me when I went home last night. She thought at first I was a spook.'

'Ach well, I'm no' as fit as I was, son,' Tam murmured placatingly, 'I would have been first up the ladder if I was able.'

Lorn was looking from one face to the other in some bemusement and Shona hastened to enlighten him. By the time she had finished her colourful description of Ranald's roof everyone was helpless with laughter.

'Why have you got it in for Ranald?' Lorn asked when he could catch his breath.

'Ach well, the bugger has been goin' around like a constipated peacock since Barra came home and we thought it was high time he learned a lesson.'

'Ay, and he has been up to other queer high jinks forbye,' nodded Jim Jim darkly, shock on his face as he recalled walking past Barra's house in the early hours and seeing her half naked in front of the mirror with Ranald an interested spectator in the background. In a stage whisper Jim Jim recounted the story for the umpteenth time, amply embroidered for the benefit of his audience.

'Ach, there will likely be a good explanation,' laughed Shona. 'Barra was an art teacher, remember, and it's quite on the cards she was either doing a self-portrait or teaching Ranald the intricacies of the human form.'

Todd spluttered and almost choked. 'Teaching him, ay, but I'm thinkin' it had nothing to do wi' art. Barra has had a lot o' experience wi' her bein' at art college, she is bound to have picked up a lot o' queer ways and wi' her living in the city for so long she'll be a wanton sort o' woman.'

'Ay, wantin' things that Ranald canny give her,' smirked Tam.

Barra walked past just then, a plump, pink-skinned little woman with a mop of curly grey hair and an air about her of someone who was never quite sure of herself. She smiled shyly at the throng surrounding Lorn's tractor, and Tam grinned back, his polite 'Good day to you, Barra' making

Shona shake her head and say, 'You two-faced bodach, Tam McKinnon, as well as that you're two-tongued, one coated with silver and the other like a piece of barbed wire straight off my father's fence. You should be ashamed of yourself. Barra's a nice wee soul and from what I hear she and Ranald have worked hard to make their shop a success.'

But Tam's grin was unrepentant. 'It's no' Barra, she is a nice body and I wouldny mind gettin' my hands on some o' they things that Jim Jim was able to describe so well. No – it's that Ranald who needs to come off his pedestal and when he finds out about his fart studio he might come down to earth wi' a good big bang.'

Niall threw the suitcases into the tractor. 'Don't be surprised if he takes you with him,' he warned. 'Ranald is slow to rouse but has quite a temper when he gets riled.'

Lorn climbed into the tractor and started it up. It had been the only mode of transport available but not an unusual one on an island that made use of a variety of vehicles. 'You had better get going,' he shouted above the engine. 'Mother's making a special dinner and she'll be mad if you keep her waiting. I'll take the cases on up to your house but I'll be home in a few minutes.'

He lumbered noisily away, leaving the others to follow in his wake. Ellie was in a jubilant mood and taking Niall's hand swung it back and forth like a pendulum. She was full of enthusiasm for coming to live on Rhanna and in her child's way had given him a lot of encouragement in his new venture. Already she had christened him 'the sailing vet' and she was presently employed in knitting him thick woolly socks together with a bright red woolly cap 'to keep his brains from freezing up'. Whenever she had a moment to spare out came her knitting needles and she clicked away laboriously, her tongue sticking out in concentration while seemingly endless inches of badly woven yarn sprouted from her needles. Anything she tackled of a domestic nature had to be attributed to necessity as, other than cooking and baking, her interests lay in outdoor pursuits. Now thirteen years old she was tall and leggy with expressive golden-brown eyes and a ready smile. She was at the gangling awkward stage and moved Shona to despair because nothing she wore would sit on her properly. But she had the makings of a beauty and Niall had reminded his wife that at Ellie's age she had been an impossibly skinny bundle and she had laughed at his vivid descriptions of her teenage years.

The fields were dotted with snowy white lambs. Among them strode Bob with his two sheepdogs and Matthew's son, Donald, a strapping young man who was a born shepherd and whom Bob trusted as he trusted no other when it came to handling sheep. He had taken over the training of the sheepdogs and every summer at the sheepdog trials held in one of Laigmhor's fields, he took the dogs through their paces and had earned quite a reputation for gaining top placings at almost every event.

Fergus was coming off the hill some distance away and

Shona ran to meet him, throwing her arms round his neck and smothering him with affection. 'Hey, let me breathe,' he protested laughingly. He held her at arm's length and nodded his approval. 'Just like old times, eh my bonny lass? All of us together again.'

'Ay, Father, just like old times,' she said quietly and tucked her arm through his. He smelt of grass and sweat and of the sharp clean air of the hill. It was his morning smell and she knew it would soon be replaced by the perfume of soap mingling with the warmth of damp hair crisping to dryness in the heat of the kitchen.

Ellie dashed up to throw her arm round his waist and he kissed the top of her silky head as they made their way over the grassy lane to the cobbled yard. Lorn came in at their back and bringing the tractor to a halt he jumped down and joined them as they crowded into the kitchen which at first glance seemed to be full of people.

'What on earth?' grinned Niall at sight of his father ensconced in the inglenook drinking whisky and his mother in the rocking chair by the window feeding a tiny newborn lamb from an enormous feeding bottle. She had tucked a baby's bib round its neck to catch the milky drips running from its lips and every so often she propped it up and rubbed its back to help it to break wind. She was rather flushed looking and her son looked at her suspiciously but she only raised a languid hand and apologized for not getting up to greet him properly.

'We're having a celebration dinner,' explained Fergus.

'To welcome you young McLachlans back to Rhanna and to celebrate the arrival of Lorna Morag.'

'What a bonny name,' murmured Shona, accepting the glass of whisky offered by Lachlan. 'Who chose it?'

Lorn turned from the sink where he and Fergus were vying for a place to wash. 'I chose Morag, and Ruth decided on Lorna.'

Niall looked rather surprised. 'I should have thought you wouldn't want to be reminded of that caillich.'

'I don't.' Lorn's answer was frank. 'I just happen to like the name, that's all and anyway, there's no' a sign of Morag in the bairn – she's – she's like Ruthie and she was never her mother's daughter – she aye had the look of Dugald about her.'

Lachlan, his thin face unusually pink, pressed a drink into his son's hand. 'Come on, drink up, we're celebrating two new beginnings, yours and the bairnie's. There's more where that came from.'

Niall realized that everyone was acting in a manner out of keeping with normal dinner-time behaviour. Kirsteen was giggling as she basted a sizzling turkey and Phebie, having tucked the satiated lamb into a dog basket, was now in the procedure of setting the table. She had begun by carefully setting down the cutlery only to discover that the dessertspoons were in the wrong order and from there her judgement went from bad to the ridiculous. Suddenly, in a mood of total abandonment she gave a wild whoop, cried, 'Oh, to hell with it!'

and began tossing forks across the table to land where they would.

'Mother! You're drunk!' Niall accused, then in a spurt of amusement, 'I doubt you're even steady enough for me to chase you round the table.'

Phebie raised her brows in horror. 'Don't you dare, my lad! Forbye being much too auld for your nonsense I'm far too busy.'

Niall advanced and everyone laughed at the look of dismay on Phebie's rosy face. But instead of chasing her round the table as was his habit, he put his arms round her in a bear hug and lifted her several inches off the floor.

'What an example to set your only son,' he scolded her in mock reproach. 'Here I am, about to take up house just along the road from my stable old family home and what do I find? A decidedly pie-eyed mother and a father who's obviously the worse for drink. Neither of you are fit to be seen by your granddaughter.'

A delighted Ellie shrieked with joy. She was never happier than when she was with her grandparents. Lachlan unashamedly spoiled her and Fergus indulged her to such an extent Shona had felt moved to protest and he had said slightly shame-faced, 'Ach, Shona, I know I shouldny maybe spoil her the way I do but there's no' many lassies in the family for me to spoil.' His dark eyes had held hers for a long moment and he had shaken his head. 'I missed the chance to indulge my own lassie and I've regretted it a million times, so don't deny me the opportunity to make it up to my granddaughter. Maybe I'm getting old or a wee bit wiser but I've come to see that to show love isn't a sign of weakness – the very opposite in fact.'

Phebie had flopped down once more in the rocking chair to fan her hot face with a corner of the tablecloth. 'All we need now are Grant and Fiona to complete the picture. It's a whily since they showed their faces.'

Kirsteen glanced rather dazedly at the potatoes boiling merrily on the range. 'I don't know if there would be enough to go round,' she said doubtfully and wondered why Fergus let out a shout of laughter as he grabbed her round the waist and kissed the little spots of red high on her cheekbones. 'You've had one too many, my girl,' he whispered into her ear. 'I'm going to make you a cup of strong hot coffee.'

Ellie had inveigled Lachlan into the inglenook and they were soon engrossed in a murmured conversation. Everyone else was full of good intentions but in the process of peeping into pots and into the oven where the turkey had been incarcerated for the final golden brown crisping, only succeeded in getting in the way.

When Bob appeared at the door, followed by Sheil and Ben and half a dozen beady-eyed chickens Kirsteen banged her cup onto its saucer and raised her eyes to the ceiling.

'Right, everyone,' she cried, 'out of my kitchen at once – no, I didn't mean you, Bob,' she hastened to add as the old man tossed a reproachful glance in her direction. 'You stay and have your wash and your usual smoke in the inglenook but everyone else – out! Fergus, you take the men into the parlour and Shona, you take Phebie upstairs to see Ruth and the bairn.'

Phebie curled herself further into her chair and smiled sleepily. 'Och, Kirsteen, show some consideration for an auld wifie. I doubt I'd collapse halfway up and besides, I've been to see Ruth twice since I arrived.'

Kirsteen's blue eyes twinkled indulgently. 'Ach, right enough now, we're forgetting your advanced years. I suppose we'll have to make allowances for the elderly in our midst.'

Shona picked a piece of meat from the turkey now cooling on the table and nibbled it. 'I'll go up on my own. I meant to as soon as I came in but got sidetracked by my mad kinfolk.'

Niall glanced at her, a furrow on his brow. 'I thought you would have made it your business to see the bairn the minute you got home. You've talked about it often enough over the last few days.'

'Oh, don't fuss!' she answered sharply. 'I can't do everything at once and Kirsteen needed help with the turkey.'

Kirsteen didn't say anything. She had sensed Shona's hesitancy the moment she came through the door. Over the years Kirsteen had come to know her well and very often could anticipate her moods. Her zest for life was boundless, her enthusiasms infectious and often exhausting. She rarely shied away from anything new and Kirsteen knew that she had her reasons for holding back now.

'I'll go up with you, Mother,' Ellie offered, jumping to her feet with alacrity. 'I've already been up twice. Wee Lorna is such a bonny baby I could look at her all day.' She hummed a catchy little tune as they went into the hall. She was a child who was always singing and very often Shona joined in, even though she might be in another room at the time, but today a sharp rebuke rose to her lips and Ellie stopped singing at once.

Shona stole a glance at her crestfallen daughter and saw that her proud little chin was trembling, the way it had done when she was a chubby infant and Shona had delighted in putting the tip of her pinky into the cheeky round dimple. Everything about Ellie was golden that day, her skin was the colour of rich honey, threads of gold shone in hair the shade of an autumn beech leaf, but it was her eyes which Shona loved most. They were big, expressive golden-brown orbs with a look of soft velvet to them. Occasionally they sparked fire but mostly they were meltingly gentle. Just now they were shiny with hurt and Shona was immediately sorry for her harsh words.

'Oh, Ellie, I'm a bitch of a mother to you sometimes but I don't mean to be. You're so young and uncomplicated and you have a right to sing today of all days. We've just come home and there's so much to be happy about. C'mon, I'll sing with you and if we waken the baby it's just too bad.'

They marched arm in arm up the stairs, carolling away merrily, yet they were able to surprise Ruth and Lorn who had hidden themselves in a little recess on the landing and, oblivious to everything, were locked tightly in each other's arms.

'Uncle Lorn!' said Ellie, shocked. 'You aren't supposed to do these things in public!'

Lorn, still young and inexperienced enough to be easily embarrassed, flushed and said rather snappishly, 'It wasn't public till you arrived on the scene.'

Ellie nodded in unperturbed agreement. 'You're right, I'm always doing it to people. I did it to Father and Mother on the boat earlier on when they were down in the saloon kissing and snuggling like mad.'

Lorn's spurt of ill temper disappeared like a puff of wind. 'Really?' he grinned. He put his arm protectively round Ruth's waist and lowered his dark head to kiss her on the mouth. 'If the McLachlans can do it then so can the McKenzies. We might have a public contest sometime but right now I'm clearing off. When a few women get together and start talking baby talk it's no place for a man.'

Ruth's face showed her pleasure at seeing Shona. She had lost her look of fragility and was rosy and sparkling. The few months she had been married to Lorn had been the happiest of her life and she had fitted well into the McKenzie household. It seemed that the dark, unhappy years she had spent in the temple belonged to another life. Only when she went home to visit did all the reality come back like a bad dream. Morag was living a semi-real existence, sometimes frighteningly like the Morag of old, at others like a child who had lost the way and didn't know how to get back again. During these times Ruth glimpsed something in her mother that was almost beautiful. She was trusting, gentle, and affectionate and Ruth was finding a love for the lost lonely creature that she had never had before. She mourned for what might have been, pined to have had a mother that she could always have loved instead of one who had shunned all that was tender and good.

As Morag's mental condition gradually deteriorated, so too did the layers of self-deception she had built up round herself and the raw emotions of a woman who had craved human contact became exposed at last. Dugald had grown increasingly exhausted, yet his devotion to his wife never faltered and people nodded their heads sadly and told each other, 'He is a good man is Doug, it is just a pity Morag Ruadh was always too blind to see it.'

Often she would rise in the middle of the night to spin, the steady thump of the treadle echoing eerily through the house. Once she had packed a suitcase and had wandered down to the harbour in her nightgown to board the steamer. Dugald had been so tired he hadn't been aware of anything unusual till a knocking at the door roused him and he had gone to find Morag hanging trustingly onto the hand of a young galley boy.

On several occasions Dodie had been frightened out of his wits by a ghostly apparition floating among the gravestones in the Hillock Kirkyard and he had heard a thin voice wailing out a shaky rendering of 'Nearer My God To Thee'. In terror he had blabbed out to everyone that a ghaistie was haunting the cemetery and though the villagers scoffed at him they took good care to give the Hillock a wide berth after nightfall.

Lachlan had quietly suggested to Dugald that he could arrange to have Morag looked after in a nursing home but he had rejected this and with the help of Isabel and Jim Jim continued to nurse his wife. He had been overjoyed at the birth of his grandchild but when he broke the news to Morag she looked at him oddly and had gone upstairs without a word. Later he found her sitting by the cot that had rocked Ruth and she was talking softly as if to a baby. That was when a new deception began in her life. She spoke about Ruth as if she was still the babe of nineteen years ago and spent hours sitting by the cot, crooning lullabyes. Dugald hadn't told Ruth about this latest development, unwilling to rob her of her newfound joy, but she had discovered it for herself and when Morag said to her, 'Ruth, it's long past your bedtime, you will never grow to be a big strong lassie if you don't get enough sleep,' Ruth knew that for her mother, there would be no road back to sanity.

But today she was too full of happiness to let her innermost thoughts get the better of her and as she led the way into the bedroom she couldn't suppress a dance of pure joy.

Shona eyed with approval the soft blue wool dress she was wearing. 'You're up and dressed, Ruth. Lachlan will give you a spanking if he catches you.'

'Och, I'm sick of bed,' said Ruth, going to the mirror to brush her hair. 'I heard you all laughing downstairs and decided to get up for dinner – to tell the truth – I got up yesterday too and sneaked over to see my mother. Kirsteen almost had a fit but promised not to say anything.'

'Mother, come and look at the baby,' said Ellie impatiently. 'She's lovely.'

Shona went slowly over to the family cradle that had rocked so many McKenzie children. Lorna Morag was awake, her wondering blue gaze directed at the ceiling which was pale blue and matched the wardrobe and chest of drawers which Lorn and Lewis had used during all the years they shared the room. The only differences now were the double bed and the feminine touches added by Ruth. Shona found herself feeling relieved that no one had thought to use the room that she always thought of as hers. Privately she had christened it the 'golden room' as everything it contained was in shades ranging from bronze to yellow and from childhood had reminded her of sunlight even on the dullest days.

Shona gazed at the baby, aware that she couldn't possibly see anything clearly as yet, but so frank and assessive were the big round eyes she had the strangest feeling that she was being studied. Lorna was one of the most beautiful babies that Shona had ever seen with honey-gold hair and skin unusually smooth in a newborn infant. The notion struck her that she had seen the child somewhere before and then she realized that she was the image of Ellie as an infant. Almost unwillingly she reached out to stroke the soft hair; a tiny finger came up to curl round her thumb and her heart was captured.

'Isn't she bonny, Mother?' Ellie's voice seemed to come from a long way off. Unwillingly Shona struggled out of her trance and was taken aback by the arrival of Babbie into the room, her freckled face glowing from a brisk walk up from the village. She had grown plumper of late and put it down to too little exercise so today she had left her car behind and had made her rounds on foot, determined to be as fit as Biddy had been from a lifetime walking the hills and glens.

'You were not made to be skinny, liebling,' Anton had told her that morning, his hands lingering on the softness of her breasts and she had kissed him and told him she wasn't meant to be fat either.

'Phew, I'm wabbit,' she laughed, plunking herself into a chair and fanning herself with her hat. 'And to think I struggled all this way only to find Lachlan here and you out of bed, Ruth. Who gave you permission?'

'Me,' dimpled Ruth mischievously.

'Ach, you're as well; it's the thing now for new mothers to be up on their feet as soon as possible but if you're thinking of going downstairs you can think again till I've made sure you're fit enough.' She glanced at Shona, a roguish glint in her green eyes as she observed, 'It's yourself, Shona McKenzie, slim as a yardstick. God, I'm jealous. When did you arrive by the way?'

Shona glared at her. 'Today! Just now! Babbie Büttger! Don't tell me you've forgotten I'm back to stay for good.'

Babbie ran her fingers through her red curls. 'Is that so! May the good Lord help us all. We'll never get a minute's peace now.' She jumped to her feet and hugged her friend affectionately. 'Daft thing! Of course I remember. How could I forget with your father and Lachlan dinning it into my lugs at every opportunity? By the way, have any of you any idea about what's going on in the village? I know Ranald and Barra have just opened their craft shop but I honestly didn't think it would attract such a crowd so soon. There's a queue more suited to Sauchiehall Street waiting to get in.'

Ellie covered her mouth with her hands to smother a shriek of mirth. 'It's the fart studio,' she spluttered in delight. 'All the towrists will be wanting to see what it's like.'

'The *what*?' Babbie's face was a study.

Shona plunged into another account of Tam's handiwork and long before she was finished both Ruth and Babbie were helpless.

'Come to Rhanna and get your education right enough,' gasped Babbie at last. 'I doubt Ranald hasn't found out about it yet. He was standing at the door of his shop rubbing his hands when I passed and Barra was inside ringing the till fit to burst.'

Shona shook her head. 'Tam has done them a good turn after all. He might think twice in future about trying to get one over Ranald.'

Fergus's voice floated upstairs, announcing that dinner would be ready in five minutes. Shona looked at Babbie. 'You'll stay and have a celebration drink, I hope?'

Babbie's eyes widened. 'You don't think I came all this way just to see you, do you? A droppy is just what I need to get my feets going in the right direction.' She giggled. 'Remember Biddy always said things like that as an excuse for a dram?'

'I remember,' Shona said, her smile faltering a little as Babbie lifted Lorna out of her cradle and kissed the top of her downy head.

Chapter Four

Ellie skipped away ahead of her parents and she was singing again as they made their way through Glen Fallan to the sturdy house set close to Downie's Pass, a narrow cleft carved out between the hills. To everyone the house was still known as Biddy's house and though the young McLachlans still thought of it as such they had christened it Mo Dhachaidh which was the Gaelic for My Home, hopeful that the passage of time would mark it down as the happiest of houses to all who entered it to ceilidh or strupak. Niall was whistling, the way he always did when he was particularly happy. Shona looked at him, remembering the young Niall who had gone away a lot from the island but whose return home was always heralded by that jaunty whistle. How eagerly she had strained to listen for it all these years ago and it had become so familiar to her it was imprinted in her heart.

Despite her happiness that fresh windy April day, Shona was aware that a strange sadness lurked under the surface and she was angry at herself because she felt that way. Yet she knew that poignancy was justified on such an emotional day and she smiled even as her eyes misted at sight of the tiny white hairs at the side of Niall's head. His hair was so fair and shone in the rays of watery sun slanting through the clouds but the little white hairs shone brighter. Strange to think that he was forty now, she mused tenderly. She never gave much thought to his passing years. He was tall and strong with glowing tanned skin and a boyish way of laughing that reminded her of Lachlan, and when he made love to her it was with all the undiminished passion she associated with youth and vigour. He had never made a fuss about passing birthdays and seemed careless about the subtle changes each one made to his appearance yet he had surprised her on his fortieth birthday by commenting in dismayed tones, 'Hell, I'm forty, I never thought it was that close. Where have the years gone? They've flown in and suddenly I'm no' as young as I was.'

The mark of the scar he had received at Dunkirk stretched in livid pallor across the mahogany skin of his neck and she caught her lip on a sob. Niall stopped whistling and turned quickly to look at her, the hearing of his good right ear razor sharp. His brown eyes regarded her quizzically and he cocked his head in a typically enquiring gesture. 'You are bubbling over with joy, I hope,' he said with mock severity.

'Of course I am, what else?' she said quickly.

He took her hand and squeezed it. 'I just wondered if you were feeling the same as me, that's all. To tell the truth I'm feeling different to what I thought I would. We've come back to the island a hundred times since leaving but today we're walking up Glen Fallan to our house, and I keep remembering things I thought I'd forgotten – things about us as bairnies. I was just thinking about the cave at Dunuaigh. In a way it was our first home really. Mind how we carried chairs over the moors on a June morning? And how we fell asleep after we had gorged ourselves on chocolate and liquorice?' He chuckled at the reminiscence. 'I was never away from the wee hoosie that day and Mother kept asking me if I'd been at the syrup of figs. In the end Father had to give me something to dry me up.'

'Really?' Shona giggled in delight. 'I never knew that. I wish you'd told me for the exact same thing happened to me and Mirabelle was so worried she was all for taking me to see your father before I skittered myself away to a shadow. It's a good job I was back to normal the next morning. If Mirabelle had carried out her threat your father might have put two and two together and made us eat more liquorice as a punishment.' They both shrieked with laughter and Ellie came dancing back, splashing in the puddles, her long legs carrying her swiftly. Positioning herself between her parents she coaxed them to make a half-hearted attempt at skipping.

'Ach, you're both getting old,' she taunted mischievously. 'I've seen hens that could hop better.'

'Old! Of all the cheek!' spluttered Shona, tossing her mane of hair back from her sparkling face. 'We'll show you what *real* skipping is, you impudent wee wittrock.' And suiting her actions to her words she took to her heels so swiftly the others had a job to keep up.

They arrived at the gate of Mo Dhachaidh in high spirits. Niall glanced up at the windows of the house and said softly, 'We're here, Biddy. The McLachlans have come home.'

'Ay, we're home, Biddy,' echoed Shona. 'And the first thing I'm going to do is tidy up the garden, it's like a jungle.'

Niall winked at Ellie. 'The first thing I'm going to do is take your mother over the threshold so that she can make us a cuppy.' Without more ado he swept Shona into his arms and she shrieked with fright, clutching frantically at his head and covering his eyes in the process so that he charged blindly up the path, a giggling Ellie running to open doors, guiding him through with yelled instructions. Charging into the kitchen he dumped Shona unceremoniously into a chair before collapsing into another one to gasp for breath.

'I'll make the tea.' Ellie swung the kettle over the fire which Fergus had lit that morning, anxious to make the house as welcoming as possible. 'You two had better take a rest. I told you you were too old to be capering around and I was right!'

Later Shona went upstairs, following the sound of singing to the room which was to be Ellie's. She had chosen the wallpaper herself, white decorated with sprigs of green leaves and sprays of harebells, and she had helped to paint the doors and surrounds in a cool shade of forest green. Shona stood at the threshold, watching her oblivious daughter unpacking the cases that Lorn had brought up on the tractor.

'You're so happy, Ellie,' Shona observed softly.

Ellie looked up in some surprise. 'Of course I'm happy, I'm always happy when you and Father are feeling right with the world. Happiness is like the measles – it's infectious.'

Shona sat on top of the bed and gazed out of the window. A perfect rainbow was arched against the hills, embracing the peaks in a shimmering mist. 'Look, Ellie, a rainbow; make a wish before it disappears and one day you might find a pot of gold.'

Ellie left her unpacking and going over to the window gazed out in wonder. 'Good luck,' she murmured with conviction. 'That will be our pot of gold. We're going to have good luck in this house.'

'I hope so, Ellie, I hope so.'

Ellie studied her mother's lovely face and said thoughtfully, 'Why were you so sad today when you looked at Ruth's baby?'

'Was I?' said Shona rather sharply. 'I don't know what makes you think that.'

'Ay, but you do know,' Ellie persisted. 'It's because you'd like another baby yourself, isn't it?'

An angry retort sprang to Shona's lips but a glimpse at her daughter's earnest face quelled it. Until recently she might have thought the child was being merely impertinent but lately she had noticed a change in her attitude to life.

Her observations were more mature, she was growing up and anxious to show that she could take part in sensible discussions.

She took Ellie's cool little hand and held it tightly. 'Ay, you're right, you wee wittrock,' she admitted huskily. 'I must be daft but I'd like another the same as you. Your father and I wanted a few bairnies.' She smiled absently. 'In the mad rosy idealism of youth we thought we had the world at our command and could make all our dreams come true – but real life isn't like that, Ellie, things happen that none of us can foresee.' On impulse she told her daughter about the baby who had died, as she talked her thoughts carrying her back to the dreadful day when she thought Niall had been killed at Dunkirk and like one demented she had run over the moors to the cave at Dunuaigh where her tiny son had been born.

Tears glinted in Ellie's eyes. 'What was his name?' she asked in a faraway voice.

'Niall Fergus.'

'And what was he like?'

'Fair, like your father, a teeny fair-haired wee boy. He would have been a young man now, at least twenty.'

'I wish I'd known him.' Ellie sounded wistful and Shona looked at her surprised. Never by word or by deed had she ever indicated loneliness but in that moment she gave herself away.

'You would have liked a wee brother or sister, then?'

'Ay, but it wasny to be.' The child sounded wiser than

her years, her golden-brown eyes filled with understanding as she returned her mother's gaze. 'Anyway, whenever I get lonely now I'll think of Niall Fergus and imagine a big brother who sticks up for me all the time and always lets me get my own way.' She laughed. 'In real life he would likely have bullied me and called me a nuisance or he might never have bothered his head about me so in a way dreams are better than the real thing – you can make them go the way you want them to go.'

She glanced rather shyly at her mother, colouring a little as she asked, 'Do you believe in dreams coming true – even though a lot of yours didn't?'

Shona paused in the act of folding Ellie's new school blazer over a hanger. 'Of course I do, though some of mine didn't, a lot of my nicest dreams became reality – your father was one and you were another.'

The child laughed. 'I never thought of myself as a dream – I'm too noisy – no – I mean things that you want to do with your life but you're not sure if you're clever enough to make them happen.'

Ellie's modesty about her abilities had always been one of her most endearing traits and the words were typical of her.

'What is it you want to happen so badly?' asked Shona persuasively. 'Tell me and I'll tell you if I think you can do it.'

Ellie's eyes sparkled. 'I want to be a doctor like Grandpa Lachlan. I spoke to him about it when you were all being drunk earlier and he says he thinks I might make it if I work very, very hard. It's what I've always wanted to do but never said anything till I was old enough to be taken seriously.'

Shona smiled. How like Niall the child was. His ambition to be a vet had never faltered and despite difficulties with his hearing he had become a successful animal doctor though he was often doubtful of his abilities. It seemed the trait had passed on to Ellie and Shona was confident that she would become as brilliant as he was in her chosen career. 'I would have taken you seriously if you had talked to me about it years ago because your father was determined to be a vet from the minute he knew which end of a horse was which and I'm delighted that you want to be a doctor like your Grandpa Lachlan – meantime, what exactly is that hideous thing you're arranging on your dressing table?'

'A sheep's skull.' Ellie patted the object fondly. 'I found it on the verge. I'm going to be studying skulls and things from now on and while I'm home these holidays I want to visit Lighthouse Jack. He's got a marvellous collection of skulls, mostly marine things like whales and sharks . . .' She looked rueful. 'The only thing I don't like about us living on Rhanna is having to go away to school in Oban. I hope I'll like it.'

'Of course you will,' assured Shona. 'Just you tell them that your uncles, Lorn and Lewis McKenzie, went there.'

Ellie made a face. 'Maybe I'd better not, Uncle Lewis was a bit wild, wasn't he?'

'Ay, he was that,' agreed Shona. 'A real young devil at times but everybody liked him just the same.'

'What a shame he died so young.' Ellie's face had grown solemn.

Shona nodded and said softly, 'Ay, it was a terrible tragedy.'

'Sometimes I look at Uncle Lorn and imagine he's Lewis and in that way I keep them both alive – sort of like looking in a mirror and seeing a reflection. Maybe Uncle Lorn does that too, he looks in the mirror quite a lot.'

Shona laughed. 'That's because he's vain and because he doesn't think a nosy wee madam like you is watching. It's natural to look in mirrors, we all do it.'

'I don't, I'm not bonny enough.'

'You will be, you'll grow up to be quite a beauty, Helen McLachlan, all the boys will be after you and I'll be a grannie before I know it.'

Ellie gazed at her mother's face. 'You'll never be a grannie – even if you live to be a hundred, you're too young ever to be old—' She threw down a dress she had been folding. 'I'm going down to tell Father about me wanting to be a doctor, if I talk nice to him he'll maybe let me go on a trip with him these holidays – after all, a constipated cow is much the same as a constipated cailleach though I'm not sure if you would stick a suppository up a cow's backside!' She shrieked with laughter and left the room with alacrity, dodging the cushion Shona threw at her.

Some minutes later Niall's shout of approval came from one of the downstairs rooms and Shona smiled.

She went to the top of the stairs and looking down saw her husband and daughter dancing in and out of all the rooms . . . She experienced a pang of pure joy. What a loving and happy relationship existed between the two people who were her life. From personal experience she knew that there was a special love between a father and a daughter and she was glad that Ellie had been brought up in such a happy atmosphere. Everything had gone quiet downstairs and she guessed that the two had collapsed with sheer exhaustion.

'Father, can I come with you on one of your trips?' Ellie's voice floated upstairs clearly.

'Ay, you can that,' Niall acceded readily. 'Only give me some time to get the hang of things. Wait till the summer, the sea is kinder then. Meanwhile you can come with me after tea to look at Todd's cow and maybe diagnose what ails it.'

Ellie giggled. 'It isn't constipated, is it?'

'The opposite – what on earth made you ask that?' Niall sounded surprised.

Ellie's giggles changed to a snort of uncontrollable laughter. 'Och, I just wondered if you would give a cow a suppository, that's all. I'll just have to go on the rounds with Grandpa Lachlan and watch him doing the real thing.'

'Father will have none of it!' laughed Niall. 'Can you imagine him letting a wee lassie like you see a thing like that?'

'I have to learn sometime.' Ellie sounded as if she was holding her breath. 'Anyway, I've already seen it being done. I went with Babbie once and sneaked up to the window of old Jock the Fiddler's cottage. It wasn't a suppository but an enema which was even better because the noises he made into the bedpan frightened his dog so much it ran outside and had the skitters!'

'You wee besom!' Niall's explosion of laughter was an even match for Ellie's shrieks as she flew from him pleading for mercy, her breath wobbling in her throat all the way up the hall and into the garden.

They were having tea in the kitchen when Ellie wriggled round in her seat to look thoughtfully at the window set into the thick wall above the crofter's bench. It was a deeply recessed window, with a view looking towards the rugged shoulder of Sgurr na Gill and the winding road through the glen. Its broad ledge shone with fresh white paint and was already adorned by a posy of wildflowers which Ellie had picked from the shaded banks of the River Fallan. 'I've been thinking,' she said dreamily, 'I'd like to have a corner of this window all to myself.'

'Whatever for?' asked Shona as she dished steaming portions of shepherd's pie.

'For Biddy's picture, that nice one you keep in your bag, the one where she's wearing her teeths. I mind the day you took it. She was moaning because it was such a hot day and you told her she was too grumpy looking to have her picture taken and made her go into the house to put in her teeth. She came out smiling because Woody had sneaked them into his bed and had chewed away a wee corner. Biddy said it proved even the cat didn't think much of artificial teeth.'

Shona paused with the serving spoon in mid-air. 'Ay, I mind that day fine, how strange that you should have taken in every little detail like that.'

'I couldn't help it,' choked Ellie. 'She looked so funny trying to smile and keep the chewed denture in at the same time – and – in the end they fell out and we all had to get down on our knees and look for them in the grass.'

She finished her account on a shriek of mirth which was echoed by her parents who could so easily conjure Biddy's whimsical ways to mind.

'I think it's a lovely idea,' Shona said at last, wiping her eyes with a corner of her apron. 'And I also think Biddy deserves to have something nice to make up for our intrusion into her peaceful home. We've been here only one day and already it's like bedlam.'

'Biddy wouldn't mind.' Niall pulled in his plate and scooped a generous helping of pie onto his fork. 'She liked to have life about her and the house has been empty for so long it needs a lot of laughter to waken it up.'

'You'll waken it up all right if you choke on that mouthful you have on your fork. Honestly, it's a miracle Ellie has any manners with a father like you as an example.'

'She wouldn't have a father at all if I starved myself to death,' Niall said, unperturbed, winking at Ellie who with great self-restraint was taking dainty mouthfuls and trying hard not to laugh.

It was fun that first evening at Mo Dhachaidh, washing dishes in the bright, airy, newly painted kitchen. Afterwards they walked arm in arm down to the harbour, taking up the width of the road, Niall whistling, Ellie and Shona humming a gay little tune.

'I ought to get a wee car for you,' Niall said. 'My own will be over in a few days but you'll only have the use of it when I'm away. You could be doing with something to get you around.'

But Shona shook her head decisively. 'Not yet, I want to walk over the hills and moors the way I used to. I didn't need a car then and I don't now – and don't you dare look at me like that, Niall McLachlan! I know what you're thinking, that I was younger then and more up to it. Well, I'm good for a few years yet and I'll get myself in trim again, living on the mainland made us all soft – besides – who needs a car when Biddy's old bike is lying in the wee shed at the back of the house just crying to be used.'

Niall grinned. 'But it's ancient, almost as old as Biddy was herself. It'll fall to bits at the first pothole.'

'Ach, stop havering, these old bikes were built to last and I'm going to make use of it so that's the end of the matter.'

There was quite a bustle at the harbour. The fishing boats had just arrived, watched with interest by the old men who spent their days exchanging sage gossip and occasionally giving the young fishermen the benefit of the knowledge they had reaped during their own years at sea. The children were playing on bicycles or pottering about with old tyres and home-made rafts in the shallows, watched placidly by the cattle who were often to be seen standing in the water in an effort to ward off the perpetual flies which had come out early that year because of the mild weather. Many of the fisherwives were in their gardens, arms folded on dividing walls as they enjoyed a blether with their neighbours, but by far the greatest number of people were hovering round Ranald's craft shop, curiously watching a queue of village men at the door.

'Daft, daft they are,' was the opinion of Canty Tam who was pursuing his favourite occupation, that of staring vacantly out to sea as if in the hope of catching a glimpse of the Green Uisge Hags who were reputed to lie in wait beneath the waves for the unwary boatman who ventured out too far.

The McLachlans went over to join the queue and were greeted with enthusiasm by the village worthies.

'You have come to learn it too,' grinned Fingal McLeod, nodding vaguely into the dim interior of the shop.

'Learn what?' asked Niall innocently.

Fingal removed his pipe from his mouth, stooping to tap it out on the scratched surface of his wooden leg. 'The art of farting, of course. Have you no' seen the advert?' He winked meaningfully and showed broken teeth in a wide grin. 'Mind you, I am hoping myself we will be practising out of doors for I wouldny like to be inside when that lot get going, the cailleachs have been feedin' them up wi' pans o' broth and we all know what that does to the insides.'

There was a commotion from within and Ranald appeared, pulling Tam by the scruff of his neck. 'Just you show me what you have done to my bonny sign,' cried Ranald angrily, 'I knew there was something funny goin' on this mornin' but I was so busy I had no time to spare to see what it was all about!'

'Ach, c'mon now, man,' protested Tam jovially. 'Are you no' after admitting that you have had a fine busy day – busier than you ever hoped to be in a lifetime. Your fingers must be red raw from bangin' away at that till all day.'

'What have you done to my sign?' persisted Ranald grimly.

Tam looked greatly discomfited. 'Ach well now, me an' the lads were just after thinkin' that you had a very fine sign there, Ranald, very fine indeed but too severe – ay, much too severe and ordinary like so we thought it would do no harm at all if we added one o' they wee gimmicks they big businessmen use all the time in advertisin'.'

'No harm at all,' echoed Todd the Shod, his round, craggy face the picture of benevolence.

'Get on wi' it, you bunch o' mealy-mouthed dumplings!' ordered the seething Ranald, giving Tam a shake to show he meant business.

'Well now, if we could just take one o' your wee boats to the mouth o' the harbour I'll be showing you,' suggested Tam, striving to remain calm in the face of Ranald's ire.

Without a word Ranald led the way down to the rocks where his boats were lying and in minutes a small dinghy was in the water. Giving Tam a none too gentle shove he made him scramble to the thwart and directed him to man the oars. The crowd on the shore watched with interest as the boat bucked out of the bay to the mouth of the harbour. For a short time it remained there before a great screech of indignation floated over the waves, sending the gulls soaring up from a sandbank in a flurry of beating wings.

'That was Ranald,' nodded Jim Jim. 'I wonder will he maybe drown Tam while he has him out there.'

Canty Tam grimaced at the sky. 'The Uisge Hags will be waitin' for him,' he prophesied with fiendish certainty. 'If they get their claws on the like o' Tam McKinnon there will be no mercy for him. My old mother calls him the De'il's Disciple and warned me a long time ago no' to have anything to do wi' him for it's like as no' he'll come to a sticky end.'

'Weesht, you glaikit bugger,' warned Jim Jim, prodding him in the ribs. 'It's you and that old witch you call a mother will come to a sticky end – right in the middle o' your very own dung midden too. It's near as high as that old Sgurr back there and if you didny waste so much o' your time on silly fancies, you and the cailleach would be out spreadin' it on your land.'

Ranald and Tam had arrived back on shore, the former scrambling with agility over the rocks and running to his shop to put his head inside and bawl, 'Barra! Barra! Would you believe what they have done to our sign! It is no wonder we were gettin' some gey queer looks from the towrists and all that other smirkin' and laughin' behind our backs.'

Barra appeared, her plump face flushed after a hectic day, her grey curls mussed attractively over her brow. Rapidly Ranald explained what had happened but before he was halfway through she dumped herself on a nearby rock, threw up her hands and gave vent to gales of laughter.

'This is serious, woman.' Ranald looked at her in dismay but she was beyond hearing him, the tears were pouring down her face and she could do nothing but wave her hands and occasionally manage to splutter, 'Outdoors, weather permitting,' before she was off again, clutching her wobbling stomach and mopping her face with her hanky. So infectious was her laughter that very soon everyone joined in. The harbour rang with the sounds of merriment and the children giggled at the sight of all the adults in various poses of prostration.

'Ranald! Ranald!' gasped Barra at last, her shoulders still twitching. 'Stop wetting your breeks for a minute –

and listen to me. Tam has done you a favour today. I have never seen a new shop having such instant success. Ach, ach! Stop gaping like a dead fish and thank Tam McKinnon this very minute.'

'*Thank him?*' yelled the astounded Ranald.

'Ay, thank him. Because o' him you have made pounds instead o' pennies and have sold nearly all the trinkets in the shop. You will have to get a hold of Dodie and old Hector to see if they can gather more shells – after you have paid them for the last lot of course.'

Tam rubbed his hands together and cocked a beady eye. 'I'm thinkin' I maybe deserve a cuppy and some o' that fine home bakin' o' yours, Barra – and I wouldny say no to a wee droppy o' the good stuff either.'

'You can all have a strupak,' beamed Barra, bustling to her feet, aided willingly by several pairs of hands whose owners grinned delightedly at the feel of amply rounded flesh rolling over their fingers.

Ranald was left speechless at the door as everyone made a bee-line inside and Todd shook his head as he walked up to the Smiddy with the McLachlans. 'That's a turn up for the books right enough. She's a good soul is Barra and if it wasny for this damt cow o' mine I would have had first go at that whisky Ranald has been hoarding like a miser since Ne'erday – after all, it was me who risked my neck gettin' up to his roof to paint on that big F for him,' Todd finished in aggrieved tones.

It took Niall only five minutes to diagnose and treat

Foxglove's malady and much to Ellie's disappointment the cow had no need of a suppository or anything else so dramatic. After a strupak with Mollie, Todd accompanied the visitors outside with the pretence of seeing them off.

'I will just walk wi' you a wee way along the road,' he said loudly and obviously for Mollie's benefit for he was no sooner two seconds outside than he sprachled away with agility in the direction of Ranald's craft shop.

Niall took Shona's arm. She felt cool yet warm, the shy smile she threw at him filled with the secret intimate promises of things yet to come, things which he knew were for him alone when the time finally came for them to shut the world away.

His fingers probed the warm hollow of her palm and she shivered in anticipation of their first night alone in Mo Dhachaidh, but she said nothing, instinctively knowing that no words were needed to convey that his message had been received and understood. He had changed into his Rhanna clothes, a lovat jersey and a McLachlan kilt and he felt hard and masculine, the narrow lean edge of his hips brushing hers with every step he took.

'Will you always love me?' The question was as sudden as it was unexpected.

Through the gathering darkness she studied his face, looking for a sign that would tell her he was only half in earnest but she saw only seriousness in the intent lines of his expression. The wind was ruffling his fair hair, blowing it over his brow and she felt an overwhelming urge to take him there and then into her arms.

Ellie was out of sight, the shore was deserted, the sigh of solitude breathed over the Hebridean landscape.

Without hesitation she wound her arms round his waist and pulled him in close to her. Despite the rugged maleness of his body she was aware of an unexpected vulnerability in him that night, a strange uncertainty that reached out to her and pierced her heart. In the darkness she gave an odd little smile. Men were like that, her Niall was like that, he gave the impression of always being in control, of containing within his virile body a supreme strength that could never falter – but it could – sometimes it could, and then he was like a small boy seeking reassurance.

Leaning forward she kissed him on the lips. 'Of course I will always love you, darling, darling Niall. But what makes you ask a thing like that? These are the sort of questions I usually ask.'

'Sometimes men have to ask them as well,' he said and his voice was low. 'Maybe it's because everything today is new and different and I want you and me to always stay the same.' His fingers explored the warm satin skin at her nape before he bent his head towards her and took possession of her lips, his tongue making a little circle of fire against hers. 'We'll make tonight a night to remember,' he murmured huskily into her ear. 'So that we can always look back and smile our secret smiles whenever we think about it.'

She felt warm and confused and very aware of the

passionate flame that had kindled between them and she was reluctant to relinquish the sweet intimacy of the moment even though she spotted Behag's face spying on them from her window. Mischievously she thought of prolonging the interlude for Behag's benefit, but Ellie appeared on the shore by the Fallan bridge and Captain Mac was down by the water's edge preparing to take the dinghy out to *The Sea Urchin* which he had earmarked as sleeping quarters, and she stepped out of Niall's embrace, contenting herself by taking his hand and holding it tightly.

As if by magic half a dozen children materialized beside Captain Mac, clamouring to help the popular old sea dog, and under his bellowed orders the dinghy was afloat in no time. The whole proceeding was watched with interest by old Joe who at the grand old age of a hundred and one was still able to participate in marine activities. When he wasn't on the water he was usually to be found pottering about on the shore and at sight of Niall he scrambled to his feet and walked over the shingle with the easy rolling gait of a veteran sailor.

'That's a fine boat you have there, lad,' he observed, prodding his pipe towards the harbour, his sea-green eyes bright with admiration. They were strange eyes; children looked into them and saw a kaleidoscope of memories. It was as if patterns of light were refracted into swiftly changing scenes and with a little imagination it was possible to look into his eyes and see sunken treasures, mermaids and other fabulous creatures who inhabited the magical lands under the waves. Old Joe had a fund of sea adventures to relate and whether they were real or imaginary generations of children had never tired of hearing them. 'I was too busy lookin' at her to notice you two kissin' up there,' the old man went on innocently and Niall's fingers tightened on Shona's as a smother of mirth escaped her.

Niall gazed with pride at the trim white hull of *The Sea Urchin* rocking elegantly on the waves. 'Ay, she's a good-looking boat right enough, Joe, but more importantly she handles well in the water. Mac has had her over to Barra in a swell and he was singing her praises.'

'I would like to be havin' the feel o' her planks under my own feets,' hinted old Joe gently and Niall glanced at Shona.

'What do you say, mo ghaoil? Will we all take a wee trip over to *The Sea Urchin*?'

'Why not? We can do anything we like tonight and the water is fine and calm.'

To show his delight old Joe made a faultless spit into a rock pool some distance away before plodding off to catch Captain Mac who was getting ready to set off.

It was cool and peaceful aboard the boat. The men went down below to sample some of Captain Mac's Jamaican Rum Cocktail, a potent concoction which he claimed could 'ca' the feet from an elephant'. Shona stayed on deck with Ellie, gazing at the dark drift of the Rhanna hills etched against the smoky blue velvet of the eastern sky. The cries of the newborn lambs echoed from the fields; the barking of a roe buck bounced from the hill corries to drift plaintively over the mysterious silent plains of the Muir of Rhanna; an oyster catcher piped a melancholy tune from the calm secret inlets which nestled below the great brooding cliffs of Burg; the lights from the cottage windows shivered down into the black water of the harbour, piercing tentatively into the splashes of spray beating against the treacherous rocks of Port Rum Point. It was a fresh cold night with a bite in the breezes singing in from the open sea, and to Shona the tang of peat smoke had never seemed sharper, the haunting peace of the amber-flecked sea had never before invoked such contentment; the elusive quality of the misted night hills had never been more filled with the solitude of lonely high places.

'Oh, Ellie, I love it so,' she breathed passionately. Reaching out she put her hand on her daughter's slight shoulder. 'You're young, my wee lamb, and although I knew at your age that I liked solitude I can't exactly remember the emotions it brought so you tell me what you feel.'

Ellie rubbed her cold arms. 'I feel strange – in here—' She placed her hand over her heart. 'I feel very small and yet I also feel big – as if I could touch the hilltops and push my pinkie through the middle of that big golden moon sailing above Sgurr nan Ruadh . . .' She shivered suddenly. 'I also feel a bit cold and all sort of itchy and scratchy.'

Shona burst out laughing. 'You daft wee thing! I can understand the cold but not the itch.'

Ellie wriggled and reaching inside her jersey pulled out a tiny black sleepy kitten. Niall appeared in time to see the latest arrival. 'You wee wittrock – where did you get *that*?'

Ellie giggled and kissed the kitten's moist nose. 'Todd gave her to me in return for what you did for Foxglove.'

'Oh, did he now?' Niall's eyes gleamed. 'We'll see about that – we'll never earn a living if we get paid in kittens.'

Ellie's smile trembled between disappointment and hope and he relented. 'All right, you conniving wee devil, you can keep the kitten but I'll get over to Todd's in the morning and collect what's due me – and I don't mean a barrowload of dung or another kitten either.'

Ellie lifted the kitten to the warmth of her neck and whispered in its ear, 'I'll call you Woody. That was the name of Biddy's cat and every time I call on you she'll feel really at home.'

Niall looked at Shona. 'She's like her mother, utterly devious and entirely without principle—' She pushed her fingers into his palm and a warm reassurance flooded his being. 'Ay, she's like her mother all right,' he murmured softly. 'Able to get round any man by just cocking a wee finger and smiling.'

Part Three

Summer 1961

Chapter Five

A gust of rain-spiced wind propelled Kate into the village corner shop and the door banged shut behind her of its own volition as the gale sucked in its breath before skirling away to see what mischief it could wreak elsewhere.

The violent opening of the door had set the bells above it jingling discordantly and Merry Mary came out of her back shop in time to receive a shower of cold droplets from the outsized oilskins which had ballooned round Kate's ears and which were being treated to a thorough shaking at the mercy of Kate's big capable hands.

'Mercy, what weather for June!' Kate greeted Merry Mary breathlessly. 'The damt wind is so strong it just wheeched up my raincoat and treated the world to a rare view o' my breeks.' She banged her shopping bag on the counter and wiped the glistening raindrops from her fresh, ruddy cheeks. 'Ach well, never mind, at least they're clean and there's no holes in them so Behag will have nothing to say on that score. I saw her auld face peeping out the window o' the Post Office and knowing her she'll soon have it about that I as much as stripped to the skuddy in the middle o' the village street.'

She paused for breath and grinned broadly at Merry Mary who had taken up her favourite stance behind the counter, her arms folded comfortably on the piles of newspapers which had arrived on last night's steamer and which no one had yet braved the elements to collect. Her bright cheery face was full of anticipation, for Kate could always be relied upon to relate a piece of juicy gossip and was adept at finding things out before anyone else. Some said she made it her business to know other people's, but as these observations were confined to the 'nosy cailleachs' of the district no one bothered to take their opinions seriously.

'I must say, it's nice to see your face behind the counter again, Merry Mary,' said Kate. 'Is it no' just like old times?'

Merry Mary positively beamed. 'Ay, I feel like I've never left the place and though it's only for a wee while it will give poor Dugald a chance to decide what he's going to do about it. I have a feeling he doesny want to let it go till he sees will Morag Ruadh be sent away to a home that deals wi' ailments like hers.'

Kate clicked her tongue. 'Ach, he'll no' let her go. The Lord knows why he's hangin' onto a woman who made his life a hell but there you are, it's the way o' things. Strange things can happen to folks who have been conditioned to years o' misery. They have a name for it but I canny just mind what it is.'

'It is a fetish.' Merry Mary's tones were triumphant

though she didn't tell Kate she had only that morning gleaned the word from an article about sexual deviations in one of the magazines which she always read from cover to cover before putting them out for sale.

Kate nodded. 'Ay, it will be that,' she said with assurance, unwilling to let Merry Mary have the satisfaction of knowing she had no earthly idea what it meant.

Merry Mary clucked sympathetically. 'Poor mannie, I am after hearing that she is as demented as a clockin' hen and goes around singin' lullabyes to an empty cradle. She is just like a simple bairnie, poor sowel. Isabel tells me that she sits in the bath and allows herself to be washed without so much as a murmur though last week she stood up wi' the soap bubbles flyin' off her bosoms and began rantin' about the comin' o' the Lord and what He would do to all the sinners of the world. I wonder Dugald doesny pack his bags and run away. It's no' safe to have a body like that in the home and folks are terrified when she takes it into her head to go wanderin' all over the place. Some o' the young lads are sayin' they can see right through her nightgown.'

'Havers!' Kate rejected the suggestion energetically. 'No mortal body could see through thon goonies o' hers. I swear they're made o' double layers o' flannelette. Doug must wonder what a woman's body looks like for I doubt he never clapped eyes on one inch o' Morag's bum. Mind you ...' she leaned over the counter and though there were was no one else in the shop, lowered her voice to a conspiratorial whisper, '... there's aye Totie wi' her fine big breasts and other parts that men like to play with. She's been Doug's fancy woman all these years – I'm certain o' that.'

'Ach, get away wi' you now.' Merry Mary was enthralled. Impatiently she tucked away a wilful strand of ginger hair in order to see Kate better. 'If it was the case surely Behag or Elspeth would have got wind of it by now?'

'They have been discreet, very discreet.' Kate sounded slightly peeved because discretion of any sort made her all the more determined to get at the reasons behind it and in the case of Dugald and Totie she felt badly let down because she felt that they were too clever even for her. She wasn't sure if a chance sighting of them walking together over the cliffs was any reason to suppose that they were no more than good friends and hastily she changed the subject, broaching the one she had come into the shop to discuss in the first place. Taking the cup of tea that Merry Mary pushed over the counter, she stirred it thoughtfully. 'I was after seein' the new minister this very mornin',' she imparted between sips of tea, 'walkin' in the garden o' the Manse like a body lost in a lot o' thought and though it was pourin' from the heavens he had no coat on and not so much as a halo to cover his head.'

'And what is he like?' asked Merry Mary eagerly, the arrival of the new minister the day before having caused much interest and speculation, for he came alone to the island, a point not in his favour. Rhanna liked its ministers to be family men. There was 'something no' natural' about a man who walked alone. A good deal of secrecy surrounded the new man which not even the church elders had managed to penetrate. The Reverend John Grey, now retired, had been reticent on the subject of the minister's background. The only fact which had been made known to the community was that he had come from Glasgow to the island because health reasons wouldn't permit him to continue with a large parish.

'Well, I didny get a close look at him wi' all that rain in my eyes.' Again Kate sounded aggrieved. 'But from what I could see he is a fine big chiel wi' hair as black as night and broad shoulders to him that would sit better on a farmer – he certainly didny have the appearance o' a frail mannie.'

'Ach my.' Merry Mary clicked her tongue in dismay. 'He will no' be liked. A good-lookin' single minister is just askin' for trouble. All the young lassies will be so busy gigglin' at him and runnin' after him they will no' take in a word he has to say about the Lord. The mothers will no' like it either for young folks are silly enough these days and the kirk is about the last place they want to go anyway.'

'It will be popular now, mark my words,' predicted Kate, helping herself to the biscuits on the counter. 'The Reverend Mark James will be havin' a full kirk next Sabbath and no mistake.'

The door flew open once more to admit Barra McLean. She came in a flurry of raindrops and a gust of bullying wind which catapulted her plump figure to the middle of the floor. The door swung back and forward, brushing the bells with such vigour the chain snapped and they went crashing to the floor in a tinkling heap. Kate put her back to the door and with Barra's help banged it shut. Barra took a step or two forward and bent her head to look in some confusion at the severed bells. 'I'm right sorry about that, Merry Mary, I'll get Ranald to come over and fix them back up.'

Kate gave her a knowing wink. 'Ranald eh? My, Barra, is it no' time you were gettin' the bugger to pay you back for all the effort and money you have put into that shop o' his?'

Barra's pink face grew pinker. 'Well, Kate,' she began doubtfully, 'I don't want paying back. It's a joint venture. Ranald has put a lot into it as well and neither of us will see the benefits for a whily yet.'

Kate nodded her head indulgently. 'Now, Barra, you know fine what I mean. You and him are a mite more than just business partners, we all know a thing or two about that. After a man gets below the top layers he has more than one kind of business in mind. The trick is no' to let him get too far, for then he'll think you're a wanton woman and free into the bargain.'

Barra pulled herself up to her full five foot one inch and treated Kate to an unusually baleful glare. In all her years in the city she had never come across the likes of Kate McKinnon and didn't quite know how to deal with such an outspoken and utterly frank woman. Despite having been away from the island for so long Barra had still retained many of her whimsical ways; the inherent politeness that had been instilled in her from the cradle was still very much to the fore and she had fully believed that as a native of Rhanna she would have few problems on her return. She had, however, soon found she was far wrong and was finding herself at a great disadvantage. In her years of living in a city she had readily fitted in and had been openly accepted wherever she went, but on Rhanna, she was finding it hard to integrate and to adapt herself back to the island ways. She had forgotten that certain things which were perfectly acceptable on the mainland were looked on askance by a community that was rather conventional in its outlook. She had found it easier to get on with the menfolk and in a seeking after company had turned to them for a certain amount of solace though nothing on the scale as suggested by Kate, who, though more sympathetic about her habits and her mode of dress, was nevertheless one of the key figures in the village and a person not to be trifled with. She was therefore slightly on the defensive with the formidable McKinnon and dreaded situations which took her among groups of gossiping women with the able Kate at the forefront.

Also she had her cousin Behag to contend with. From the beginning she had made it plain that Barra was to be treated with contempt and she had managed very successfully to make her feel something of a black sheep, someone not fit to bear the good family name. She had just come from an errand to the Post Office and after five minutes of Behag's tight-lipped silence was in no mood for Kate's insinuations.

'I think you are talking a wee bit out of turn, Mrs McKinnon,' she imparted stiffly. 'I don't like what you are implying about me and Ranald.'

Kate stared at her in genuine surprise. 'Ach, Barra, I'm no' criticizing *you* – indeed I'm thinkin' you've livened the place up since you came. You are a spirited woman and I'm glad that you are no' allowing that old prune o' a cousin o' yours to get you down. Whatever you and Ranald get up to is your own business but I am just sayin' you mustny let him think he owns you just because you allowed him into your house after a respectable hour. He might get queer ideas and if he's anything at all like my Tam he will have got it into his head that he's in there wi' a shout. Once a man has got a leg over the door he will no' be long in lettin' you see the hairs on it and anything else he might have in mind. Men are all alike when it comes to the bare facts and I am just warning you for your own good.'

Merry Mary folded her arms and nodded her wispy ginger head in agreement, but Barra's thundery look suggested that she was feeling anything but appeased.

'Just what do you mean by that, Mrs McKinnon?' she asked through tightly folded lips. 'My home is just as respectable as any other body's in this village – no' that that's anything to be proud of,' she added spicily. 'In all my years in Glasgow I never saw the likes o' the things I am seeing here. Oh ay, you are all the Lord's angels in the broad light of day but come nightfall the angels turn into devils and that's a fact. As for letting Ranald into my house when all you poor innocent cratur's are supposed to be tucked up in bed (praying no doubt to the Lord to save your lilywhite souls), the only time he came to see me was one night after I had gone to my bed. His chappin' on my door and hissin' through my letter box would have made a ghost rise in a panic and I got him off my doorstep in a hurry, knowing what would be said of me if one curtain had tweaked. The silly man had spilled beer all over a painting I had just finished. A watercolour it was, of the sea crashing over the rocks at Bodach Beag, and by the time I had finished trying to get the stains out, the sea had turned brown and the Bodach Beag tilting so much you would have thought he was as drunk as Ranald—' A twinkle in her eyes wiped away her sternness and Kate threw up her hands, giving her lungs full throttle in the process.

'Ach, Barra, it's a brave woman you are right enough. Just wait till I get my hands on that Jim Jim – I'll choke all the fables out o' him, that I will!'

'Will you be havin' a cuppy, Barra?' Merry Mary pushed a steaming mug over the counter while Kate produced an innocent-looking cough bottle from her shopping bag. Uncorking it she poured a generous amount into the tea and winked. 'Seeing you are no' everybody. Tam wouldny mind I know; he has never stopped singing your praises since thon trouble you had wi' your lovely sign.'

Barra had swallowed her tea in a few gulps. At Kate's words she gave a shriek of glee and all three went into raptures as she enlarged on her reactions to the sign.

Taking out a large square of red cotton from her sleeve she blew her nose and shook her head. 'Never have I laughed so much,' she spluttered mirthfully. 'The idea of all the towrists sailing into the harbour and seeing that sign, my God, it was priceless!'

She went into fresh peals of laughter and when she finally subsided, exhausted, Kate wagged a finger at her. 'Now, Barra, you mistook my meaning about Ranald paying you back for everything you've done.' Her eyes gleamed. 'As you know he is a bachelor mannie and you are a spinster woman and I'm thinkin' the pair o' you are just made for each other wi' all these crafty interests you share.'

Barra looked at her blankly. 'But Kate, it is not like that wi' me and Ranald. Oh, he's a good man and quite a considerate gentleman in his own way but never once has he hinted that there is anything more than a business arrangement between us.'

Merry Mary shook her head knowingly and chided gently, 'Barra, you have not yet found out all there is to know about Ranald McTavish – oh no. He had a very strict upbringing you see. His mother was aye warning him about the temptations o' the flesh and she told him never never to get mixed up wi' the wild women from the cities. She said they would be no good to him and would just be waitin' till he took his breeks off before they robbed him of his wallet . . . you will have seen that he is a mite fond o' sillar?'

Barra couldn't deny this and Kate rushed into the

breach. 'Ay, it's been a weakness o' his all his life. Whether it was his mother's influence or just that he was born a miserly bugger he has always watched his pennies with the excuse that he was savin' up to provide a good home for a wife when he became old enough to be wed.'

Barra blinked in astonishment. 'But surely – the cratur' must be sixty if he's a day. Maybe he feels he's past the age to be taking a wife.'

'Ach no, no, Barra,' sighed Kate patiently. 'The bodach has it in his head that he's too young yet to be settling down.'

Barra giggled girlishly. 'I could say that now I've heard everything, but no doubt I'll be learning a bit more before I'm through.'

'Indeed you will that,' nodded Merry Mary. 'The islands are full o' middle-aged men who believe they are too tender an age to be trauchled wi' a wife. Wi' some it's calculated, mind. They wait till pension age then take a wife o' childbearing years so that they can sit back and let the wife and bairns look to them in their old age. It works too, I'm tellin' you. Old Padruig of Croy lives in the lap o' luxury wi' his pension, his wife and four strapping sons doing all the work about the croft. The only time he has to lift a finger is when he needs to pee.'

'So Ranald is not the exception then?' Barra sounded unconvinced.

'Indeed he is no',' Kate assured her. 'But he is just ripe now to be takin' a wife and you could do worse for yourself, Barra. He has money and he is still a handsome enough chiel if you forget the wee twist he has on his face and the bunches o' hairs growin' out his lugs. He's a fine clean mannie too and some are no' so fussy about hygiene when they get older – but of course most o' them have got their woman at Ranald's age and wouldny care if their feets never had a single sniff o' soap and water.'

Barra was thoroughly enjoying herself. For the first time since her arrival she felt herself to be one of the community and as such allowed into its secrets. 'You are forgetting I am one of the wild city women Ranald's mother warned him about. He'll have no eye for the likes o' me.'

'You are an island woman who went to the city to find work – there lies the difference,' said Kate knowingly. 'Ranald had his eye on you from the start and I wouldny be surprised if he ruined that bonny painting on purpose just to make an excuse to get inside your house.'

'Get away!' Barra's laughing tones suggested that she was greatly amused by the whole thing and Kate regarded her seriously.

'You can joke all you like, Barra, but you would be wise to take heed. I have a wee suspicion you have been washing and mending his socks for him – am I right?'

'Ay, indeed, I saw no harm in helping a poor lonely man.'

Merry Mary and Kate exchanged meaningful glances and the latter shook her head and said cryptically, 'There you are now, I was right, Ranald has got it bad and no mistake.' She lowered her voice to a compelling stage whisper. 'No one single woman on this whole island has ever been allowed to touch McTavish's personal items of clothing. Some have tried, mind, but all have been refused in no uncertain manner. You are honoured, lassie, ay indeed, and if you're wise you'll waste no time gettin' his ring on your finger.'

'His ring!'

'Ay – and make sure the bugger has the weddin' soon after. Some men think an engagement ring is as good as a passport to the bedroom and once that happens you can just forget about the weddin'.'

'That's true, that's true,' supplemented Merry Mary sadly, her own personal experiences on the subject having led to her own state of spinsterhood, of that she was certain. 'Just you keep your finger on your halfpenny till your weddin' night and you will never regret it.'

Barra, still taking it all as the joke she was sure was intended, grinned affably, 'And I suppose wi' me being a virgin woman it will not be unseemly to go up the aisle in white carrying my lilies and the white Bible my mother gave me when I was twelve.'

'You have every right of all that,' Merry Mary and Kate assured her in unison. 'And just think,' added Kate, 'thon nice new minister who came yesterday will be the one who will get the pleasure o' marryin' you. Yours might be the very first weddin' he will get to perform on the island so we'll have to make it a special day for the pair o' you –

and seeing you are no' as young as the usual kind of bride we will maybe only ceilidh for two nights instead of four, though of course you'll be too busy enjoyin' yourself on your honeymoon to care how long we ceilidh.'

Barra glanced from one earnest face to the other and was seized with an irresistible desire to laugh but having made such notable headway with two of the island's worthier characters, she daren't risk giving offence and managed to compose her plump face into serious lines.

'You know, ladies,' she said soberly, 'I'm beginning to look forward very much to the pleasure the new minister will get when he marries me. A friend of mine always suspected that men of the cloth only wear a dog collar for one very good reason.'

'And what would that be?' asked Kate eagerly.

A grin split Barra's rosy face. 'To hide the ravishes of passion that wanton women like myself have laid upon them. The marks o' love are no' easy things to disguise so what better than a dog collar to cover them up.'

Both Merry Mary and Kate erupted into skirls of laughter but then the talk turned to more sober things with Kate for once looking unusually worried as she talked about her daughter Nancy who had recently undergone major surgery.

'Ach, my, the poor cratur',' said Barra sympathetically. 'But she has you to look to her, Kate, and Lachlan forbye, and no doubt the new minister will be payin' her a few visits – what is his name by the way?'

Kate supplied the information and Barra said almost to herself, 'Mark James. I know the man – so he has come to Rhanna to forget – poor, poor soul.'

'What is that you say, Barra?' asked Merry Mary curiously. 'You say you know the mannie?'

Barra straightened, and said hastily, 'Not at all, I was just thinking the name was familiar, that is all. I hope the folks here will be kind to him; it is never easy coming to a new place as fine I know myself.'

The two women looked shamefaced. 'We will treat him as we would our own kin,' vowed Kate, 'never you fear, Barra. It will be hard for him when he takes his first sermon this coming Sabbath but the christening of wee Lorna McKenzie will maybe ease matters. There is nothing melts the heart more than to see an innocent babe being received into the kirk for the first time. We are all lookin' forward to it.'

Barra cocked her head to one side and said rather breathlessly, 'Robbie is coming, I would know those steps o' his anywhere.'

Robbie padded shyly in, the stealth of his walk attributed to the years he had been ghillie to Burnbreddie and also to the years Behag had made him walk in stockinged feet through the house, claiming that his slippers gave her a headache. Mostly it was reasoned he had acquired the catlike tread during his endeavours to sneak out of the house in order to be away from his sister's watchful eye.

He twisted his cap in his hands and glanced awkwardly

at Barra, his blue eyes unblinking in his pleasant round face. 'It is yourself, Barra,' he acknowledged in a breathy whisper.

'Ay, it is that, Robbie,' she nodded, keeping her eyes averted from his penetrating stare. 'And I'm away now before Ranald thinks I have got lost.'

The door swung shut behind her. Kate shook her head. 'She is a fine wee body and she has a sense o' humour into the bargain.'

'Indeed, she'll be all right now that she is finding her way around better.' Merry Mary looked at Robbie. 'Is that not so, my bonny mannie?'

Robbie pulled a thread from his cap and seemed unaware that the peak was now just hanging from a frayed edge. 'Ay, that is so,' he agreed, gazing rather forlornly at the door from which Barra had just departed.

Babbie settled herself comfortably into the big old armchair that had been Biddy's and gratefully accepted the cup of coffee which Shona handed her. They had both gone over to Rumhor that morning in Babbie's car and Shona had thoroughly enjoyed the opportunity to stop for a crack in the crofts and cottages she had known so well as a child. Yet she had felt saddened at the changes the years had brought to the people who had been young to middle-aged the last time she had seen them. In a strangely childish way she had expected that they would have remained the same and was seized with the notion that her return to the island wasn't going to be at all as she had pictured in her mind.

A visit to the Taylors of Croft na Beinn had helped cheer her up considerably. Nancy Taylor was Kate's eldest daughter. She had worked at Laigmhor when Shona had been an infant and some of Shona's earliest recollections were of buxom Nancy shocking Mirabelle into gales of helpless laughter with her colourful descriptions of her courtship with Archie Taylor. Many of Shona's first words had been gleaned from Nancy's unique vocabulary much to the dismay of Mirabelle. When anyone came to the house she hastened to whisk the infant away lest she exercise her new words in front of her more prim friends. Mirabelle too had been prim in her own way, but she certainly hadn't been prudish and had laughed at Nancy's sayings till the tears rolled down her smooth, plump cheeks.

Nancy was now a grandmother but she had retained the zest and mischief of her girlhood and so ably had she entertained Babbie and Shona they had spent the time in her company laughing. Yet Nancy had recently had an operation for breast cancer and anyone else in her position couldn't have been blamed for feeling self-pity. But not Nancy.

'Ach, it has taken a weight off my chest,' she grinned irrepressibly. 'I was always well endowed with big breasts. Mither swore blind I was born wi' them and she might be right for I can never mind a time when I was without the buggers. When me and Archie were courtin' he said he could always tell me from the other lassies by the way they bounced up and down wi' an extra shoogle to the side for good measure – ach, poor Archie,' she said fondly. 'He was aye a one for breasts – the things he did wi' mine is nobody's business—' Unconsciously her hand moved over the flatness of the left side of her chest. 'He will only have the one to play wi' now but och – it's maybe as well – at his age it should be more than enough. Besides, the next best thing for him is legs and I've got plenty and enough meat on them to keep his passions going for a whily yet.'

Giggling she had slapped her ample thighs before sinking into a chair to accept the strupak Shona had made for her. 'Ach, it's good you are.' She studied Shona's face. 'My, my, you're as bonny as the day you were born. I mind it fine though I was just a slip of a girl, your poor mither upstairs in labour, your father near demented wi' worry, Mirabelle clumpin' upstairs wi' hot water for the doctor and bakin' sody for auld Biddy.' Her cheery face grew sad. 'It was a dark dark time for everybody, that it was, but then you popped your wee face into the world and suddenly it was morning and the storm was over and though your bonny mither had drawn her last breath you were bawlin' out wi' all the buggering strength in your wee lungs. My, you were a bugger betimes. Poor auld Mirabelle was near demented but och, she thought the world o' you, that she did and her heart was brimful o' pride for McKenzie o' the Glen – poor Alick too for all he was a wild, wild laddie.'

Shona had been enthralled by Nancy's revelations.

Often in the past she had experienced an impatience with the eternal prattlings but now she realized that, with the exception of her father and Lachlan, Nancy was the only person left who could give her a first-hand account of those early days at Laigmhor.

Babbie had smiled indulgently at the look of interest on her friend's face and she had listened patiently as both Nancy and Shona plunged into long reminiscences about things dear to their hearts. From her experience with people Babbie knew that the chatter was beneficial to both women, especially Nancy whom she suspected was hiding a lot of apprehensions behind a cheery facade.

At the door she glimpsed a little of the real Nancy. Shona had braved the elements to go outside and pick some cuttings for the garden she was presently cultivating and Nancy was bending over to move wellingtons and shepherd's crooks out of the way. A spasm of pain twisted her face and she clutched at the pathetic flatness of her chest. 'The bugger is sore betimes,' she gasped and her black eyes fastened on Babbie's face, the fear in them stark and naked. 'I don't want to know what is ahead o' me,' she stated bluntly. 'Whatever it is I will fight it wi' every last breath that is in me.'

Babbie laid a comforting hand on her arm. 'Ay, you will that, Nancy, you have spirit,' she uttered with conviction, her admiration strengthened for this brave, gentle McKinnon, who, despite all her boisterous ways, was one of the kindest people that she had ever met.

'I didny want to let Shona see how I was feeling.' Nancy was herself again, a beaming smile spreading over her smooth attractive face. 'I have always thought o' her as a wee lass. It's easy to feel that way about her for there is something in her that has never really grown up. No' that she isn't brave and proud like all the McKenzies – oh no – 'tis just that she shies away from reality and is more inclined to think of life as a fairy tale—' She paused. 'It will take her a whily to find her feets on the island, she has come back as the young lassie she was when she left. She will expect too much too soon and will be disappointed many times before she learns that she will have to let go of the past if she wants things to work out for her and Niall and the bairnie.'

It was a profound observance. Babbie was taken aback but had no time to orientate her thoughts. Shona was coming back, fighting her way through the squalls of rain which blotted out the hills and the sea, and they had to make a mad dash to the car to avoid a drenching.

Babbie sipped her coffee thoughtfully, one green eye fixed on Shona who was arranging a dewy bunch of late primroses in the vase in Memory Corner.

'What a lovely idea that was of Ellie's,' Babbie said and Shona turned a sparkling face.

'I know, she's a deep thinker for such a young lassie. I've looked out a lot of tiny picture frames and when she comes home she can arrange them to suit herself.'

'She's coming back on Friday, isn't she?'

'Ay, and don't I know it. She's written me every other day this week reminding me. As if I could forget. It will be so good to have her here for company and she'll be in time for Lorna's christening on Sunday. She was afraid she would miss it even though we all kept telling her we had arranged the date to suit her.'

Babbie watched her friend for a few thoughtful minutes. 'You're missing Niall, aren't you?' she said eventually.

Shona flicked her hair carelessly over her shoulder. 'Ay, it's natural. Wouldn't you miss Anton if he had to go away every other week?'

'Like my right arm,' said Babbie fervently, 'I'm used to having him around.'

Shona rounded on her, eyes flashing blue sparks. 'Then why ask such silly questions if you know how I'm feeling?'

'It is called making polite conversation.' Babbie's tones were dry.

Shona was immediately sorry for her outburst. 'Och, Babbie, I'm a bitch, I don't know what's wrong with me. I'm not sleeping. I miss Niall at every turn and it's so strange not having him in bed beside me. I lie awake hearing every rafter creaking and the mice squabbling in the heather. It's making me a bitty irritable. Oh please don't think I'm unhappy, I love being back on Rhanna, I adore this dear old house – it's just – when Niall's away I find myself counting the days till he gets back.'

'You've got too much time on your hands,' said Babbie

bluntly. 'You ought to think seriously about taking on a job. You enjoy coming with me, I know, but let's face it, Shona, you're doing it more for the company really. It seems a shame to let all that good nursing experience go to waste, so why don't you consider becoming my assistant? The Lord knows I could be doing with some help.' She ended with a weary sigh.

Shona studied her friend's face and for the first time noticed the tiny lines etched on her clear pale skin. For a few moments she argued with herself. Babbie must be in her early forties now, a few lines were to be expected – on the other hand they could have been prematurely brought about by the demands her job made on her – she shrugged. 'You're havering, Babbie Cameron – sorry – I mean Büttger. There is no such thing as a post available for an assistant. If I'm minding right you made it plain to the Medical Authorities you didn't need one.'

Babbie grinned ruefully. 'I was young and full of enthusiasm then. I'm sure a post could be created for an assistant if I made an issue of it.'

Shona examined her nails. 'It's good of you to think of me but I don't want to be tied down to anything – not yet – I've got so much I want to do – so much to catch up on. I'll always be on hand if you need me of course, but right now I'm perfectly happy the way things are.'

Babbie knew it was useless to pursue the subject. She was well used to Shona's stubbornness. When her mind was made up only Shona herself could change it and with a resigned nod Babbie changed the subject.

'Elspeth tells me the new minister has arrived and from all accounts he doesn't fit into the usual concept of how a minister ought to look. Elspeth has already condemned him as being too modern looking though she grudgingly had to admit that he has, what she calls, a good honest bearing. The poor soul will have his work cut out with the Elspeths of the community.'

'He certainly sounds different from our own John Grey,' mused Shona. 'It will be interesting to see what his sermons are like. When I was a wee lassie I mind how terrified I was by all the hellfire and brimstone that flowed over the kirk every Sabbath. It was years before I finally realized that the Reverend Grey was a human being and not the awful ogre he made out.'

Babbie laughed. 'No doubt the Rhanna folk had a hand in converting him. To see him pottering about in his garden you would never think that such a pink-faced, silvery-haired gentleman kept the old folks in terror of losing everlasting salvation.' She put down her cup and made to rise. 'Not that any of it ever bothered me. I'm too fond of my Sunday long lie-in to care if all the demons in hell came skirling about my lugs. You're different, you always went to kirk.'

'Old habits die hard. I've rarely missed a Sunday from the day Mirabelle hauled me along for the first time complete with black woolly stockings and a clean hanky tucked into my pouch. I was always scared to use it in case I would ruin the beautifully ironed creases.'

Above the hissing of the rain on the panes Shona heard a movement outside and she glimpsed a tall fair-haired man at the door. For a joyful moment she thought it was Niall coming home sooner than expected but it was Anton who came into the kitchen, the rain streaming down his handsome bronzed face. 'Ah, liebling, I thought it was your car at the gate.' He embraced his wife, grinning as she protested at the wetness of his garments. 'I was over seeing Johnston of Croynachan and stayed to have a wee strupak with them.'

Over the years he had adopted much of the island ways and his charming broken English, liberally sprinkled with Scottish words, was a delight to the ears. He was an excellent farmer, the well-tilled fields of Croft na Ard bearing testimony to the long hours of labour he lavished on the land. Though he was a man who guarded his privacy he wasn't jealous of it and the door of the croft was always open. In the months of summer he organized horse-riding events on the wide flat fields above the cliffs and he had made it his business to learn the language of the Gaels. As a result he could converse with the old people in the tongue they knew best and was able to listen to the wonderful tales that had been handed down from generation to generation. During the course of his learning he had taught some of his own language and the Rhanna folk took a positive delight in slipping the odd German word into a Gaelic conversation, especially when being asked directions by a wandering tourist. It all added to the fund of tales to be related at the ceilidhs with everyone vying to recount the best 'towrist tale'.

Anton greeted Shona, his keen blue eyes appraising her slender figure appreciatively, a look which wasn't lost on Babbie.

'I knew I should have stuck to my resolution not to use the car,' she wailed. 'I'm getting fatter and losing my husband's attention to my best friend. I think I'll have to go on a diet.'

He slapped her playfully on the bottom. 'Do that and I'll lock you up in the house and force feed you. I love you as you are, *liebling*. If you were to lose your nice plump bottom where would I warm my hands on a cold morning?' He winked at Shona. 'It is the nicest time, just before rising, snuggled into my soft little dumpling, all warm and steamy – as if she had just come out the oven.'

'Anton Büttger! What did Tom Johnston put in your tea?' demanded Babbie.

'Well, it certainly wasn't bromide – I can't wait to get you home.'

Despite herself, Shona had to laugh at Babbie's outraged look. Seeing the two of them together made her long for Niall all the more and when Babbie issued an invitation to come over for dinner that evening she hesitated. It would be strange going anywhere without Niall, she might feel left out, Anton and Babbie wouldn't do it deliberately but their very closeness made it unavoidable. She declined the invitation with the excuse of getting Ellie's room ready, avoiding the reproach in Babbie's eyes.

Babbie turned away and opened the door. A concoction of scents wafted in, tossed by the warm wind and rain into a deliciously heady blend. The mist was still drifting over the hills but there was a heat in the air and a hint of blue sky over the sea to the west.

'There's the new minister,' she said suddenly. 'I recognize him from Elspeth's description.'

Shona looked over Babbie's shoulder and saw through the drizzle a tall lone figure walking along the grey ribbon of road, shoulders hunched, head bent against the weather. *How lonely he looks.* The notion came unbidden to her mind.

'I wonder if he's coming here,' she said aloud. 'The kettle is just off the boil.'

But just then the figure turned, heading back towards the tiny white houses of the village lying against a slate-blue sea. Shona experienced a sharp pang of disappointment. It would have been nice to have entertained the new minister in the bright, cosy living-room of Mo Dhachaidh. She was in the mood for company and she might have succeeded in making him feel welcome to the island.

'If you hurry you can perhaps offer the fellow a lift,' Anton suggested to Babbie. 'I came over on Corrie and I want to get him back to his stable.' He smiled. 'I have never known a horse to dislike the rain as much as he does.'

They dashed along the path, hand in hand, Babbie giggling as a gust of wind blew up her coat, revealing her shapely legs. At the gate they parted company, Anton to mount his disgruntled horse, Babbie to jump into her car and thankfully pull the door shut. She waved cheerily as the engine coughed into life. Shona watched her progress along the road, held her breath as the little car stopped beside the mysterious stranger, released it again as Babbie moved away. The road stretched, grey and deserted, Anton having galloped away ahead of his wife.

The silence enclosed the slender, auburn-haired woman at the door. She gazed at the wind-wracked trees which hugged the windings of the Fallan, then her eyes travelled slowly upwards to the grey-green slopes of the bens, aloof behind their transparent veil of mist. A golden eagle planed majestically over the crags then swooped down to be lost in the corries.

The ewes with their well-grown lambs were cropping the juicy unfenced turf at the side of the house, amongst them strutted the hens, pouncing on the insects stirred up by the animals' hooves. The contented sound of clucking, mingling with the purling of the nearby burn, was music to Shona's ears. She had acquired the chickens soon after her arrival and now the brown, black, and white mosaic they made against the green of the grass was a part of Mo Dhachaidh.

As she watched, a slinking black form appeared round the side of the henhouse and she gave a soft little chuckle of anticipation, her former feelings of loneliness dispersing in the joy she felt in her surroundings. Woody was up to her tricks again. From kittenhood she had taken a delight in stalking the hens, the satisfaction on her pussy face as she scattered them, a joy to behold, and though they were fly for her now, their beady eyes trained on her creeping progress, they seemed to enjoy the game and tormented her by waiting till the last minute before fluttering out of the way.

Another movement caught Shona's eye and she raised her head to see a black-clad figure coming towards her through the rain. For a moment she thought it was the minister again till it came closer and proved to be Dodie scampering swiftly along. He was the last person she wanted to strupak with just then. Having gone from a longing for company to an appreciation of the utter peace of her environment she was in a mood to be alone and half thought of closing the door and pretending she hadn't seen him. Shame, hot and remorseful, flooded her being. How could she? Who was she to deny such a harmless creature a few minutes of her time? He was an old man who spent far too much time on his own. True, he would have died without his freedom but everyone needed company at some time. He was an undemanding soul whose needs were few, but she knew he enjoyed an occasional strupak though only if he was specifically invited to partake of one. Of all the folk on the island he was one of the few who didn't make a habit of ceilidhing or popping in for a crack and a cuppy.

She hated herself for ever thinking of shutting him out and almost before the familiar 'He breeah!' burst upon her ears she was at the gate to throw it wide and usher him through.

His enormous wellingtons squelched muddy footprints all along the hall to the kitchen where he stood, his layers of oilskins making a horseshoe pattern of drips on the red tiles of the floor. His manner was half-shy and nervously he scratched the gnome-like ear that escaped his sodden cap, his lips stretched wide in an apologetic attempt at a smile.

'I didny know if you would be in, I wasny lookin' for you,' he lied, having made the journey specially to see her. 'I was just comin' along this way to see would I maybe find some nice flat stones in the river.'

He gazed at her soulfully for several seconds during which a fat bubble of water gathered under the peak of his cap, matching the one which was suspended precariously on the end of his nose. With a sudden decisive movement he delved into his roomy pocket to withdraw a tissue-wrapped bundle which he placed on the table, drawing his hand away quickly, as if afraid the object might bite.

'I was hoping I'd maybe catch you in to give you this wee thing I made,' he explained rapidly. 'I was after speakin' to your wee Ellie when she was home at Easter and she was tellin' me about her corner o' memories so I thought it would be nice if I could give something for it too. Biddy aye liked flowers and if her photy is maybe turned to look at this it will be mindin' her o' the moors,' he finished in some confusion.

Shona unwrapped the mysteriously heavy package. It was a large oval stone, flecked with the browns and the greens of the river from whence it had come, one side of it displaying a handpainted spray of bog myrtle intertwined with the delicate purple flowers of the shy little butterwort. It had been carefully varnished to protect it, including the shaky letter D unobtrusively and painstakingly scratched in one corner. Shona turned it over in her long fingers, unable to believe that such a detailed piece of artistic creation could have sprung from the old eccentric's thick, calloused fingers.

'Did you do this?' she asked in some wonder.

'Ay, it was my first and took me a long time.' Dodie fingered the buttons of his oilskins nervously. 'I was aye tellin' Barra that her paintings were beautiful just, and she brought all her things over to my house, once a week last winter, and showed me what to do.'

'Barra did that?' said Shona softly.

'Ay, she is the only woman I have ever been alone wi' in my very own house.' Dodie gulped at the memory. 'But she never once gave a glance to the wee bitties o' dust on my shelves. She was too busy wi' the paints and tryin' to show me how to use them,' he finished anxiously, eyeing Shona to see if her face registered approval of his gift. She continued to gaze at the stone and he reddened, taking her silence as a polite way of letting him know she didn't like it.

'I meant to bring it over sooner, as a wee present for your house,' he wailed dismally, 'but that Ranald has kept me so busy huntin' for shells I hadny the time for any of the things I like doin' wi' myself. Now he is on at me to paint stones for him too and I'm feart I'll no' have any more time to enjoy findin' things.'

Shona went over and propped the stone on the window ledge, opposite Biddy's photo. 'This is a small masterpiece, Dodie,' she told him gently. 'I feel very honoured that you thought to give me such a beautiful treasure and I know Biddy will appreciate it as much as I do – and just wait till Ellie sees it – she'll be wanting you to show her how it's done.'

Dodie blushed to the roots of his hair while his grey-green eyes regarded her in a slow dawning of dazed joy. 'I like it fine myself,' he enthused. 'But I wasny sure if it was grand enough to stand in your window. It is kind you are just for likin' it so much.'

Something that might have been a tear gleamed in his eyes and he gave his head a violent shake. Both drips descended simultaneously, one to roll in a tiny rivulet over his brow, the other to plummet over his chin to be lost in the dirty nut-brown crevices of his neck.

Shona made him remove his oilskins and motioned him to sit by the glowing embers of the peat fire then she went to prepare a special strupak, in the process surreptitiously cutting an onion which she placed innocently on the draining board by the sink.

Dodie beamed with rare contentment into the fire and allowed his big-boned frame to relax. 'My, this is a nice house,' he commented approvingly, his gaze roving over the homely arrangement of furniture. 'It minds me o' Laigmhor and I aye felt like bein' myself there, especially when Mirabelle was alive.' He stretched his lips, showing his broken, tobacco-stained teeth. 'I am thinkin' you have taken up a lot o' her wee habits for she was aye rushin' to cut an onion whenever I called for a strupak. Quite a few folks hereabouts have copied her for they all seem to be slashin' onions when I am in their houses and I'm aye wishin' they wouldny for I canny bide the way they make my eyes cry when I myself am no' feelin' at all sad.'

Shona had to hide a smile. Dodie was as oblivious to his own peculiar smell as he was to the various repellents that people dreamed up to combat it. It had been Mirabelle's belief that the pungent juices of a cut onion killed smells as well as all living germs and quite a few people had followed her example, with the result that her method had come to be known as 'Mirabelle's cure'.

Woody had returned from her adventures and was now perched on Dodie's shoulder, purring with pleasure as his big gentle hands caressed her ears. Shona went to the sink and scooping the onion into a pan closed the lid firmly on it. 'I was just going to make some onion soup but you enjoy your strupak first,' she told him, handing him a plate piled high with a variety of home baking.

Dodie smacked his lips as his fingers closed over a huge bun filled with fresh cream. 'If it's no' one thing it's another,' he told her. 'Now my eyes are dry but my mouth is waterin'.'

He settled back in his chair, unconcerned by the fact that Woody was licking the cream oozing onto his chin. 'I was just thinkin' – maybe the new minister would like a painted stone to welcome him to the Manse. I was hearing he came yesterday and no doubt he will be feelin' new for a whily. Folks that don't know the ways o' the island must feel gey lonely till they get the hang o' things.'

Shona squeezed his bent shoulders affectionately, struck as always by his regard for other people's feelings. 'Ay, that's a lovely idea, Dodie, and don't you be worrying your head about that greedy Ranald. Just you do your stones as you feel like it and to hell with the rest of it. When you've had your strupak I'll put on my jacket and we'll go down and have a word with Mr McTavish. Tell him straight that you'll gather shells for him but that's all. By the way, does he pay you enough for all your efforts?'

Dodie sniffed, thinking of the last time he had hinted to Ranald for payment only to be put off by a rather feeble excuse. 'Right enough, as long as Barra is there to make sure I get it. Old Hector was just sayin' he's no' goin' to gather anything else till he gets some money and I'm thinkin' o' tellin' him the same.'

'Right, you can tell him today,' Shona's tones were resolute. 'And don't you worry, I'll be there to keep you right – you know you can rely on me.'

He threw her a look of trusting adoration. Ever since she was a small girl he had trusted and loved this bonny female McKenzie and furthermore she had always had a knack of making him feel at ease. Happily he tucked into his cream bun, ably aided by Woody who had bunched one agile paw into a scoop and was using it to scrape the cream from Dodie's chin and onto the pink curled flap of her mobile tongue.

Chapter Six

Shona walked along the scented ridge of the fields towards the woods where in days gone by she had waited for Niall to come off the boat. And now she was back to waiting again. He wouldn't be home till Sunday night and would miss Lorna's christening, though he had promised to try and come home on Saturday if it was at all possible.

She glanced up at the vast reaches of the sky. The squalls of rain and wind had gradually blown themselves out and that morning had dawned clean and clear with a great golden sun bursting up over the seas to pour its warming rays over the island. It was a truly golden Hebridean summer's day and Shona paused to gaze over the warm green fields to the Sound of Rhanna sparkling like a sapphire-studded ribbon in the distance. The hills were blue and appeared very far away with the haze of heat blurring the corries and softening the ragged peaks. The hayfields were knee high with a soft blonde tinge to the heads of the ripe grasses swaying lazily in the breezes. Scents of rowan and hawthorn blossoms mingled with the warm fragrances of purple clover and bird's-foot trefoil whose plump yellow petals were alive with bumblebees prodding in a search for nectar.

Shona stood for a long time, the tips of her fingers clasped to her lips, a slender figure dressed in blue, her neatly tied auburn hair burnished to flame in the sunshine. On impulse she stooped to gather a posy of harebells and clover which she placed carefully into her shopping bag, her fingers lingering on the delicate petals of the harebells.

By the time she got to the harbour the boat was already tied up and the passengers were streaming off. She caught a glimpse of several well-known faces and giggled as the good-natured arguments of Tam and his cronies reached her ears. They were at the pier with their carts and were supervising the unloading of the coal from the ancient barge which called several times a year with its precious cargo.

'Mother!' Ellie's joyful greeting rang above the general noise and she came flying towards Shona, a bundle of arms and legs and unruly hair. Shona gasped as she was enveloped in a bear hug and she had to struggle a bit before she could break the hold of her daughter's thin, strong young arms.

'Oh, Ellie, it's grand to see you again. You've grown taller but you haven't filled out yet. Did you have company on the journey?'

'Ay, Rachel and Jon and Tina and Eve. They were the best because Eve was showing her mother how to put on make-up and we went into their cabin and had a great time. Tina got her eye shadow all smudged and

Eve and me were so busy laughing we couldn't do a thing to help her.'

Shona spied Ruth's bright head among the crowd. Beside her, talking quietly, was the tall bespectacled figure of Jon Jodl and hanging onto his arm was the unmistakable form of Rachel McKinnon, her arresting good looks making her stand out from the rest. Almost a year had passed since her last visit to the island and during that time she had married Jon, the young German who had worshipped her from her childhood. He had exchanged his post as music teacher in Oban for one in Glasgow so that he could be near her while she pursued her studies at the Atheneum.

Ruth had Lorna Morag in her arms but Rachel wasn't showing a great deal of interest in the baby. Ruth had chosen her to be the child's godmother and Shona had thought it wasn't a very suitable choice. Rachel wasn't very keen on children, partly because she had had her own brothers and sisters thrust upon her since she was old enough to change a nappy and handle a feeding bottle, and partly because the mothering instinct wasn't strong within her.

Shona had hoped Ruth might ask her to be godmother, and had experienced a pang of resentment on learning that it was to be Rachel – yet her common sense told her it was only natural. The two of them had been friends from an early age and who was she to think she had any right to Ruth's baby? After all, she hadn't done all that much to help Ruth – except – except in the beginning when Ruth had needed help so desperately – she had helped – she had ... Yet, she also had to admit that she had given Laigmhor a bit of a wide berth since her return to Rhanna but she had never stopped to ask herself the reasons behind her avoidance. Now, as Ruth spied her and came towards her, Shona faced some of the truth. She envied Ruth her beautiful infant and it had taken her time to adjust to the idea of a baby who wasn't hers wakening all the rooms at Laigmhor with its cries.

Her cheeks reddened as Ruth's sweet face broke into a rather hesitant smile. 'Shona, your father was saying he wondered why you hadn't been over for a whily. I didn't see you on the road.'

'I came over the fields,' Shona said, more curtly than she had intended. 'It's a day for walking amongst the grass and the flowers.'

She turned her attention to Rachel. She was dazzling, a windswept beauty with a vibrant, expressive face and smouldering dark eyes which were filled with a turbulent restlessness that marriage to Jon had barely tamed. Yet she obviously adored her husband and kept her long fingers tightly clasped over his while her eyes moved rapidly along the length of the harbour, as if she was seeking someone desperately, yet an uncertainty in her glance showed that she knew her search was in vain. Shona felt shut out from Rachel's private world and the greeting she had been about to voice died in her throat. Ellie was crooning over the baby, thrilled when the grasping little hand closed over her finger.

The dimpled wrists were enclosed in fringes of pure white lace, the tiny face, already showing traces of healthy golden suntan, was shaded by a white cotton sunhat from which escaped silken threads of fair hair.

'Oh, Ruth, she's beautiful.' The words came unbidden to Shona's lips.

Ruth nodded slowly. 'I know,' she said simply and somewhat distantly and Shona realized that she wasn't the only one who could be moody when she felt like it.

She sighed and turned away to see Lorn striding past the Post Office, his hands in his pockets, a determination in the way he moved. Shona's heart lurched. For a split second in time she thought that Lewis had come back and wondered if it would always be like that. They had been so alike, the twins, except that Lorn had been the smaller of the two, now he was as strong, perhaps even taller than Lewis had been, but for that there was little that set them apart.

Rachel obviously thought so too. An odd expression had crept into her dark eyes. The full, beautiful mouth that had never uttered a single word, trembled and half-formed a name. Her hand curved upwards, as if she was about to raise it in greeting, then slowly it fell back to her side. She had loved Lewis. Oh, how she had loved the handsome, roguish young McKenzie. Part of her had died when she had made the final break from him, never dreaming that death was soon to carry him over the Great Divide which no mortal could reach, no love could span. The break was forever but Rachel knew that she would never love another as she had loved Lewis McKenzie.

Lorn's straight youthful figure wavered till he was like a mirage, never coming nearer, never going away. A tremor passed through her and she felt as if she was the only person left in the world – alone – so alone . . . Jon's fingers tightened on hers and she straightened – she had Jon, dear, kind, gentle Jon who was always there when she needed him. She could never be alone as long as she had Jon.

She made her smile ready for Lorn so that by the time he reached them she was able to face him and look steadily into his blue unwavering stare.

'You look well, Rachel, you too, Jon.' His greeting to her was brusque and she knew why. She had hurt Lewis, had hurt him very badly when she turned away from him and it would be a long time before Lorn could forgive her for that. 'What do you think of my daughter? She's beautiful, isn't she? Maybe one day you'll have one like her – if you're lucky.' The questions were harsh, voiced in such a way they weren't meant to be acknowledged. Ruth flushed and threw him a look of appeal, but he wasn't seeing her, he was too intent on getting it through to Rachel that he wasn't glad to see her, didn't approve of the fact that his wife had asked her to be the baby's godmother. But Rachel sensed something else in his words, overtones of accusation that had nothing to do with Lewis – or rather nothing to do with her having left him – or was she wrong – perhaps it had everything to do with her desertion of Lewis . . . a shiver went through her . . . she had heard about Lewis and Ruth – he had turned to her for comfort and . . . She studied the baby's face for the first time and something clutched at her heart. The child's eyes were blue a very dark, intense blue and she remembered eyes that had gazed at her with passion, lips that had carried her into rapture . . . Lewis looked out of the baby's eyes – but so too did Lorn, each of them vying for a place in those beautiful orbs – then Lorna broke through and pierced the bubble containing Lorn and Lewis – but Rachel knew – she knew who had fathered Ruth's baby – she looked directly into Lorn's eyes and saw resentment smouldering in their depths – and she wondered if he was happy having married so young with a ready-made family . . .

Lorn hated Rachel in those moments of meeting her after so much lapsing of time, of so many happenings. He blamed her for the thing that had happened to Ruth, for the trauma of events succeeding the death of Lewis. It all came flooding back, the grief, the uncertainty, the doubts, the fears that sometimes beset him when he sat back and saw in retrospect the magnitude of the responsibilities he had shouldered – yet he had wanted it that way, it had been the only way to keep Ruthie. Perhaps it was natural to have doubts, they were young, still inexperienced about life, still getting to know one another, he couldn't imagine an existence without her . . . if only . . . the muscles of his jaw tensed . . . if only she was more assertive, if only she didn't try to please him all the time. After a while it could be very trying – yet – he loved her.

He glanced at his sister and saw that she was watching him. Telepathy passed between them. She knew, Shona always knew what was going on in his mind. She had done it with Lewis and now she was doing it with him. He smiled, a brilliant smile that lit his eyes and took away the darkness from his brow.

'Shona, 'tis nice to see you, are you coming up to Laigmhor for a bite? I have strict instructions from Mother to invite you and Ellie over, so you'd better not refuse.' With an oddly deliberate gesture he took the baby from Ruth and dumped her into Shona's arms. 'You have a shot at holding her, she's getting spoilt and girns when anyone but Ruthie lifts her.'

Ruth's cheeks grew brighter still. 'I don't like her disturbing you, that's why I pick her up so much, especially at night knowing you have to get up so early.'

'I told you I would take turns with her and if she disturbs me it's too bad. Babies are like that, Ruthie, it's in their nature to disturb people when they least want to be disturbed.'

Ruth's face showed her hurt and she turned away so that he wouldn't see the tears glimmering in her eyes. She was feeling depressed a lot these days. It had come on after Lorna's birth and her mother's illness wasn't helping matters. She and Lorn seemed to be snapping at each other a lot of late – an old doubt wormed its way into her consciousness – should she have married Lorn to give the baby a name? She loved him, more than ever she loved him – but had she done right by him?

The warmth of Lorna's chubby little body seeped into Shona till it seemed her very skin glowed with it. She stared down at the small, contented face. The baby was watching her, a frown creasing the smoothness of its brow, then it chuckled and regarded her with wide-eyed expectancy. Shona smiled and pressed her lips to the softness of the rounded cheeks. A few strands of silken hair tickled her nose and the faces she made were received with delight. Shona felt a sense of personal triumph. Despite what Lorn had said the baby hadn't cried, rather she had received the attentions of her aunt with gurgles and smiles that bordered on the rapturous.

Rachel and Jon stood a little way apart, feeling shut out. Rachel's eyes scanned the harbour once more. The gulls were settling back to favourite perching places, ruffling their feathers and muttering indignantly about the disturbance that the arrival of the steamer brought to their lives. The visitors were drifting towards the hotel, a few breaking away to gaze into the window of the Craft Shop; Tam and his cronies had temporarily abandoned the loading of the carts and were sitting along the harbour wall, companionably sharing tobacco and cigarettes with the skipper of the cargo boat. A tall Nordic figure with a sheaf of blond hair was striding past the cottages, skirting the War Memorial by Murdy's house. Rachel's fingers tightened compulsively on Jon's and she stood on tiptoe, as if trying to see beyond the unmistakable figure of her stepfather, Torquil Andrew. But he came alone, walking down to pick up the cases and the musical instruments which Jon had left standing against the wall of a nearby cottage.

Torquil's blue eyes didn't give much away as they alighted on Rachel. 'Your mother is sorry she couldny come down to meet you. She is busy wi' the babby but knew you wouldny mind if I came along. Dinner is nearly ready so you are to come along at once – you and Mr Yodel.'

A black mask fell over the bright expectancy in Rachel's eyes, dulling them into lethargy. It was almost a year since she had last seen her mother, yet she was too busy to come to the harbour to meet her and welcome her home . . . Why did she remember her father so clearly at times like these? Big, grizzled Dokie Joe, with his rough tongue and his heart of gold – lifting her up, his black eyes snapping with pride, always slightly puzzled because his beautiful clever child could never communicate with him when there was so much they needed to talk about . . . Rachel's head went up and the tempestuous look was back again in her eyes. Torquil felt uneasy in her presence. She had never accepted him, and always he was aware of her resentment. She and Jon would be here for a month and Torquil wasn't looking forward to it a bit though he liked Jon and got on well with him even though he was always on guard, always ready to defend Rachel if the need arose.

Ruth went over to Rachel and took her hands; all the misunderstandings that had been present between them at Lewis's funeral, forgotten.

'I'll come over to see you tomorrow, Rachel,' she said eagerly. Beside her friend she looked small and vulnerable yet for all her delicate appearance hers was not a lesser strength than Rachel's. They had different levels of physical endurance, different ways of looking at the world and it might have been because they were such opposites that theirs had been a rare and enduring friendship. 'We could go for one of our wanders over the moors and you can tell me all your news.'

Rachel's eyes glowed and she nodded. Ruth was talking about the Rhanna she loved, the moors, the glens, the wide clean shores where on barefoot days she had embossed her footprints in the sand and swum in the bays with Squint, her little spaniel, paddling at her side. The tension oozed from her limbs and she glanced up at Jon who smiled. 'Of course you can go with Ruth, I won't intrude, never fear. I have a lot I want to do myself and a visit to Anton and Babbie is the first thing on my agenda.'

Keeping her eyes averted from Lorn, Rachel nodded her goodbyes to the others and moved away along the pier, her tall, arresting figure causing several male heads to turn in undisguised appreciation.

Lorn threw his arm round Ellie's shoulder and they began to move towards Glen Fallen, Ruth deliberately lagging behind, a glint of anger replacing the joy in her eyes. Lorn had been positively rude to her friend and she had no intention of behaving as if nothing had happened.

'I must get some things at the Post Office.' Shona stopped outside that establishment and checked her bag to make sure she had her purse ready. 'Ruth, can I keep Lorna with me a wee while longer? She seems quite happy with me.'

'Ay, of course you can.' Ruth's voice was unusually gruff.

'Tell the others to go on. I'll catch them up.' She withdrew the crushed posy of wildflowers and handed them to Ruth. 'Tell Ellie to put these in water, I forgot about them but they'll live with a bit of care.'

The interior of the Post Office was as dim and musty as it had always been. The strong odour of ink and apples vied with the fusty smell from the bags of broken biscuits which Behag sold to the village youngsters, eager to spend their pennies on something substantial enough to keep them going between meals.

Behag was sitting on a hard-backed chair behind the high counter, her needles clicking rhythmically, unintelligible murmurings coming from her throat as she counted the stitches. Only the top of her checked woollen headscarf showed, bobbing back and forth, back and forth of its own volition, a palsy which had begun some time ago and which had worsened with encroaching years. The needles came to rest and as she stretched the furrows of her neck to see who had entered her premises, her facial features became evident, the little beady eyes darting suspicious looks in Shona's direction, her down-turned mouth twisting into something that was meant to be a smile.

'It's yourself, Shona McKenzie, complete wi' a bairnie.' She never conferred on Shona her married title and Shona had put it down to mere forgetfulness though she suspected Behag as merely acting true to form and being insulting.

'Ay, it's me, Behag,' Shona nodded. 'And I'm in a hurry.'

Immediately she knew she had said the wrong thing. If she had indicated that she was in the shop with plenty of time to spare Behag would have scuttled about with energy, and would have made sure she was seen off the premises in a hurry. As it was she rose to her feet stiffly, muttering something about being riddled wi' the rheumatism and no' able to hurry for anybody. She fumbled with the ties of her scarf, tightening them round wizened jowls which plunged into the scrawny layers of her neck. With a disdainful sniff she scrunched her bony fingers through a wad of forms lying on top of an ink-splodged blotter. 'Damty forms, sometimes I'm thinkin' I should take down my Post Office sign and put The Bureaucracy in its place – but, ach –' a smile startled the grim contours of her countenance, '– we have to move wi' the times – that we have. I was never a body to shirk work – and there's been a lot o' it ower the years – a damty lot but no one can ever accuse me o' laziness.'

Behag was retiring soon and Shona knew she had her

reasons for her quick change of face. Since Biddy had acquired her MBE it had been a burning ambition of Behag's to have a similar honour thrust upon her and knowing that she would have to be recommended for it she had become unnaturally agreeable of late and it was even rumoured that she was making life bearable for her brother Robbie who had hitherto lived a miserable existence.

'There is no dog I know would put up wi' the kind o' life Robbie has led,' Tam asserted to Kate on several occasions. 'I have come upon him on the moors wi' his face in his hands and the tears croakin' out o' him something sore.'

'It's the Uisge Beatha does that to Robbie,' Kate said bluntly. 'But you're right, Tam, the poor sowel would be better livin' in a kennel than wi' thon dried-up old crone. But she'll get her come-uppance, you wait. One o' these days Robbie will do something that will scare the shat out o' Behag.'

Shona made her purchases and searched through her bag for her purse, her movements restricted by the baby in her arms.

'A fine healthy bairnie you have there,' nodded Behag. 'She sits well in your arms and wi' her havin' the stamp o' the McKenzies on her she might well be yours – of course –' she sniffed again, '– she could be anybody's from what I've been hearin'. Ruth is her mither all over again and history has a habit o' repeatin' itself. That good brither o' yours took on a handful there – oh ay. The bairnie has the look o' Lorn to her right enough – and of course –

she is like Lewis too. A wild wild laddie was that brither o' yours – a typical McKenzie if ever there was one – he and Ruth were more than a mite friendly. I saw them wi' my very own eyes, caperin' about behind Lorn's back. Poor wee babe, she wasny long comin' into the world after the wedding, my, have you ever known such a rush – and all within a month or two of Lewis havin' his accident. No' that I'm one to pass judgement – oh no – it's just things a body hears and wi' me in my position I canny help hearin' what other folks are sayin' . . .'

Shona's brow had darkened dangerously and her eyes were blue glittering ice pools. Before Behag came to the end of her monologue she leaned over, grabbed the rubber date stamp, and in a flash had imprinted several tattoos all over the crêped skin of Behag's bare arms. The postmistress was rendered speechless, her mouth falling loosely into the sagging layers of her jowls. Shona banged her money on the counter and made for the door. 'There you are, Behag,' she imparted triumphantly. 'All stamped and ready for the post. I'll tell Erchy to bring over an extra big sack and to be sure and put you on the next cargo boat – preferably one that's heading for the Antarctic – you'll soon melt the ice with that peppery tongue of yours.'

A screech of outrage followed her as she rushed outside and banged the door. Shona was helpless with laughter. Oh God! If only Niall was here, how he would have enjoyed her descriptions of Behag's astounded face. She dashed away from the door to almost collide with a tall dark man rounding the corner of the Post Office. Shona recoiled and in doing so glimpsed Behag's scowling countenance peering from behind her twitching blind and on a surge of mischievous impulse Shona lifted her fingers to her nose in a positively rude gesture. Behag's eyes bulged, her lips pursed and the blind fell back immediately. Lorna was gurgling, as if she too had enjoyed the joke, but Shona's high spirits were receding, making way for the dull steadying influence of sobriety and her cheeks were pink as she said breathlessly, 'You must think me mad, I just couldn't stop myself doing that – to be honest . . .' Her dimples came irrepressibly, 'I enjoyed every second, I felt like a child again, not caring what anybody thought, but I'm not a child and you must think I'm – I'm crazy . . .' Her voice tailed off. The stranger was grinning, an engaging grin that lifted the corners of his wide, beautiful mouth, and he was introducing himself though there was no need. Her view of him on the glen road had been brief, yet she would have recognized his broad-shouldered masculine figure anywhere. There was something about the way he held himself, a pride of bearing, that singled him out as an extremely individual man. She was horrified at herself, what a way to meet the new minister, he must not only think her mad, but bad into the bargain. Yet he was still smiling, as if he too had enjoyed the interlude, and he was speaking again, in that cool deep voice that impinged so acceptably on her senses.

'You mustn't look so embarrassed,' he told her with

a laugh. 'Ministers can see the funny side of life too, you know, and I don't doubt for a minute that your urge to express yourself in such a manner came about from sheer frustration.'

'Och, I can't excuse myself that easily – it was just – well, to be frank, our postmistress has a knack of goading people into doing things they – they wouldn't normally dream of.'

He nodded sympathetically. 'I know, I had heard about Miss Beag, so don't worry yourself any longer.'

She studied him through her long eyelashes. He was dressed in fawn slacks and a tweed jacket and his white shirt was open at the neck. The thick black cap of his hair was laced with white at the temples but nowhere else; his face was too lean, bordering on thinness yet there was an unexpected attractiveness in the angular cheekbones. It was a face of character, enhanced by a deep cleft in the strong chin and the far-seeing expression in eyes of a smoky blue-grey circled by a ring of dark navy. Her proffered hand was seized in a firm clasp and as she introduced herself and explained where she lived his face lit up.

'*That* house? I almost reached it the other day but instead accepted a lift from the district nurse. She assured me that I would have been invited in for a cup of tea if I'd been brave enough to carry on.'

She had allowed her hand to stay in his longer than she intended and somewhat awkwardly she pulled it away, fighting down the bubble of awareness that had arisen in her breast. 'How do you like the island so far?' she asked politely.

'The island I love – the people – well to be truthful I have this awful sinking feeling that I'm being sized up with some suspicion. Mr Grey told me it's natural for newcomers to be subjected to a certain amount of scrutiny but I think I'm getting more than my fair share.'

Shona played for time before answering and threw back her head in order to escape the full effect of his all-seeing gaze. Her hair escaped its bonds, cascading over her shoulders in waves of exquisite sheen.

'Damt hair! I swear I'll get it cut whatever Niall says . . .' Her hand flew to her mouth. 'There I go again – forgetting who you are – och, to hell! What does it matter? You're human after all and it's easy to forget you're a minister. That's why the islanders are sizing you up – you don't quite fit the usual mould. We've been used to the straightforward sort who made sure you never forgot who they were.' She giggled. 'Your predecessor wore his cloth even to go fishing though if the weather was bad he smothered himself in oilskins and the men visibly relaxed – Graeme Donald forgot so well he once spent ten minutes cursing before he remembered the minister was on board.'

The minister showed white teeth in a wide grin. 'If they like informality so much then surely they ought to feel at home with me?'

'Och, they will, give them time. They're holding themselves back so that they can get it into their heads that you
are a man of the cloth because later, when they're feeling
at ease with you, they'll remember not to let themselves go
too much.'

His smoky gaze stayed on her sparkling face. 'That all
sounds rather complicated but I think I can see what you
mean. I'm glad I bumped into you, Mrs McLachlan, you've
helped to make me feel a bit more hopeful.'

'Ach, call me Shona, everyone does, the old folks are
a bit more formal about such matters, but when I get my
official title I find myself looking over my shoulder to see
who's behind me.'

'All right then – Shona – if you promise to call me
Mark during informal interludes like these.'

She didn't answer but stepped back in some confusion
and he looked at his watch.

'I'd better go, Tina will have my meal ready.'

Shona remembered that Tina, Matthew's wife, had
mentioned something about seeing to the new minister but Shona hadn't taken her seriously. Tina was an
extremely easy-going woman with a devil-may-care attitude
towards housework. Time meant nothing to her though
somehow she had always managed to be prompt with the
family's meals.

'Tina is looking to you then?' The verification was for
her own benefit and she was unable to suppress a smile
at the remembrance of seeing Tina dusting shelves, her

method being to trail a feather duster along a set course while she had her nose buried in one of the romantic novels she avidly devoured.

Mark James reciprocated her smile. 'Yes, she's my housekeeper and suits me down to the ground. I can't stand fastidious women and when I instructed Tina never to disturb my desk she looked at me blankly and I realized that the idea of looking in my study, let alone tidy it, had never even entered her head.'

'That's Tina all right. She's such a peaceful soul you'll often wonder if she's in the house at all.' She glanced along the road. 'My daughter will think I'm lost, I'll have to go.'

He glanced at the baby who was studying him with wide-eyed absorption. 'You have an older child then?'

'Oh, this isn't mine, she's my brother's baby, Lorna McKenzie. My daughter's thirteen now.'

'I'd never have believed it.' The grey-blue eyes were on her again, assessing her face. 'You seem – so young.' She reddened and was at a loss for words and he pulled his gaze away. 'Please – I wasn't being personal – just surprised.' He nodded towards the glen. 'You're a McKenzie then which means your father must be McKenzie of the Glen. I'm going up to his house later to arrange some details about the christening.' His attention fastened on the baby. She was blowing bubbles, her rosy lips pursed, her hearty chuckles designed to bring a smile to the dourest face. 'So this is the wee one I'll be christening on Sunday. She's a bonny baby – a bit like you round the eyes.'

'She's Lorn's double – and of course she has her mother's colouring – I wish I could lay claim to her but . . .' She stopped, feeling she'd said enough, and rather more abruptly than she intended, made her goodbyes to the minister.

At the War Memorial she paused and looked back. He was walking along the harbour to the Manse, a tall straight figure with that distinctive air surrounding him like an aura. There were quite a few people busying themselves along the shore but Mark James might have been alone. For all his upright carriage, for all the strength and self-sufficiency she had sensed in him, he looked vulnerable and strangely heart-rendingly lonely.

Ellie had run ahead to Laigmhor, leaving Lorn and Ruth to follow slowly in her wake. Lorn was very quiet and Ruth stole a glance at him, knowing that he was angry because she had made a fuss over Rachel. The sunlight was in his hair, lighting the earth-brown curls to rich copper. His young face was set and stern looking and she saw more of Fergus in him than she'd ever seen before.

They were walking in the shade of the birchwood, the branches were throwing out delicate fronds of cool greenery; sunshine dappled through the leaves, making a golden pattern on the dusty surface of the road; from high above a song thrush was pouring forth a fountain of song which echoed far back into the mysterious shadows. It was all so beautiful and peaceful but it failed to bring comfort to Ruth. She wanted to reach out and touch her husband. Her husband – it didn't seem quite real yet, everything had happened so swiftly since that fateful meeting by Brodie's Burn. The hastily arranged marriage followed by a few days on Coll for their honeymoon; Christmas, gone before she had really prepared for it; Lorna's birth, on her before she realized it was actually going to happen; getting to know her baby before she'd had time to really get to know Lorn, to find out the sort of things which angered him or made him happy. He wasn't in the least like Lewis, he was much more complicated and stood firm in the things he believed in – to the point of stubbornness. It was a trait she was fast discovering in all the McKenzies and often found difficult to handle. Even so she enjoyed living at Laigmhor, Kirsteen and Fergus had been wonderful, understanding and discreet – yet – she often found herself longing for a home of her own, how much easier it would be to talk to her husband about private matters, to make up differences when they felt like it instead of having to wait till they could be alone in their bedroom. Matthew and Tina were intending to move to a cottage in the village beside Tina's mother who was getting old, but the house needed a lot of work done on it and it would be a while before it was ready.

She longed to say something to Lorn to break the silence that had fallen between them, knowing he wouldn't speak first. She had learned that early on in the marriage and as a result it always fell to her to make the peace. But she was damned if she was going to do it today! Although he had objected when she told him she was asking Rachel to be the baby's godmother he had eventually relented though not without a certain amount of bad grace. He had known that she was going to the boat to meet her friend and there had been simply no call for him to stomp down at her back. She knew he had only done it to embarrass both herself and Rachel. He was behaving like a spoilt and unreasonable child and unconsciously she lifted her head in a gesture of defiance and kept her lips firmly closed.

The feminine scent of her wafted enticingly to Lorn's nostrils and from the corner of his eye he appraised this new little wife of his with her child's face framed in its cloud of silky hair. Child she might look, but the soft flowing dress she wore gave lie to the milky skinned curvaceous body underneath. Her small rounded breasts with their pink, flower-like nipples, would have stirred desire in any man as would her hips, creamy and smooth, a sensuous movement to them when desire robbed her of shyness and suffused her limbs with careless freedom. During the first nights of their marriage she had held herself back, the inhibitions instilled in her from the cradle battling with her awakening desires. But he had been patient with her, allowing her time to adjust, time to blossom out and come to him when she would. Her full awakening had caught him unawares, he hadn't been prepared for the wildness in her, for the throwing off of conventions which had cloaked her inner self for so long. It was as if she was reaching out, discovering, taking all the pleasures of the universe at once, carrying him with her into the realms of a new and exciting world. She had been wild, passionate, fierce, gentle, demanding, drowning him in wave after wave of ecstasy. An echo of that night came to him now, making him feel hot as he observed the freckles on her small straight nose, the proud tilt of her firmly rounded chin.

'Ruthie.' His hand strayed over the gap that separated them, bridged it by laying his fingers on her arm. 'I'm sorry about this morning. I still don't think you should have asked Rachel to be Lorna's godmother but she's your friend and you have a right to ask who you like.'

She kept her head high. 'Indeed I have, Lorn McKenzie! And I'll go on having my friends even though they may be people you don't care for. I don't have many friends I can feel at ease with and those I have I intend to keep – despite what you stubborn McKenzies think or say.' She gave a sarcastic laugh. 'Oh ay, you're no' the only one, Shona doesn't approve of Rachel either. She's jealous I didn't ask her to be godmother. It's a side to Shona I've never really seen before and I don't like it – just as I don't like you telling me what I ought or ought not to do at every turn. I'm sick of it! All my life I had Mam ranting on at me – don't do this – don't say that – well—' Her chin went up further. 'I've had enough. I've tried to please you ever since we got married – tried to show you how grateful I was that you had forgiven me for what happened between me and Lewis. I admired and loved you for it but I'm human, Lorn, and I canny go on being grateful all my life. I'm me – Ruth Naomi McKenzie – and I won't be beholden to anybody anymore.'

His shout of delight startled her. His blue eyes were sparkling and with a quick flick of his wrists he pulled her into his arms to kiss her lips and nuzzle her ears. 'At last, Ruthie! At last you've answered back! I can see life with you is never going to be dull – there will always be something new to discover – you've got a lot of coming out ahead of you and my God! I'm the lucky bugger who's going to be there to see all the changes.'

She was staring at him in bemusement, her face flushed and warm. 'You mean – you're not – angry?'

'Angry! The opposite. A man likes a wife to please him but he also likes a bit of spirit. You've been so anxious to give in to me at every turn I was beginning to think you had no will of your own.'

Her brow cleared, she said wonderingly, 'You spoke first – I've just realized it – always before I gave in and made the first move.'

'Ay, you did that, you'll have to be firm with me, Ruthie, I'm just as pigheaded as my father but Mother doesn't allow him to be top dog all the time, she's got a mind of her own and isn't afraid to let him see it. I was in the wrong today and I'm not too bloody childish to admit it.' He plucked a wild rose from the wayside and fixed it into her hair. 'That's what you are, Ruthie, a wild rose, soft and shy and dewy yet capable of hurting when you feel like it, that's the way you were before we got married and the girl I fell in love with – so – if you want us to be happy – show your claws now and then.' He grinned. 'I used to think that was the reason girls grew their nails long, so they had something to help them win in a fight. Mind the uproar you caused when you nearly scratched the eyes out of John Baxter? He was calling you names . . .'

'Saint Ruth,' she interposed, her expression faraway.

'Ay, whatever it was you sent him off bloody and beaten with his tail between his legs and that's how I've always thought of you, a gentle lassie slow to rouse but able to let the sparks fly when the need arises – mind you, I hope you never have to go that far with me – I don't think I could handle you,' he ended with a laugh and she giggled.

He held her hands and studied her face. 'You look like a girl ready to go out to a dance – there's a ceilidh on at the hall tonight – we haven't been anywhere since Lorna was born – so, how about it, Mrs McKenzie?'

She sighed. 'Lord, I'd love to but Kirsteen and Fergus are going to Slochmhor for the evening and there will be no one to look to Lorna.'

Shona was coming slowly along the road, her slender figure just topping the rise by the birchwood. Lorn laughed. 'Oh yes there is, my big sister for one, she'll be delighted, I'm sure.'

Ruth looked doubtful. 'I don't know about that, I get

the feeling she canny really be bothered with babies – she shied away from Lorna from the minute she set eyes on her.'

'That's what you think,' Lorn's tones were soft. 'Ruthie, you have a lot to learn about people. Shona would give her right arm to have a baby like Lorna – she wanted a lot of bairns but only had Ellie.'

Ruth looked away. '– And the wee boy she lost.'

'Who told you that?'

'In a way she did – when she spoke to me at the time I knew I was pregnant. I wasn't sure but when I mentioned it to Kirsteen she – told me about the terrible time Shona went through – but – I thought perhaps it had put her off having children – heartache can do funny things to people – I imagined that Ellie – had been – a mistake.'

'A mistake! Ellie's the most precious thing in their lives! It wasn't heartache that denied Shona more children – it was just bad luck – you ask her about tonight, she'll jump at the chance.'

His assumption couldn't have been more apt. Shona's eyes were like stars as she heard Ruth's proposal. Gazing down at the baby she giggled. 'It looks as though you're stuck with your Auntie Shona, my babby. You and me and your cousin are going to have a bonny time.' She became brisk. 'It will be easier if she stays the night in my house. You two won't have to rush home and I won't be wandering up the glen in the small hours with bags under my eyes. I'll collect some of her things and take them back with me after dinner.'

Lorn threw his wife a grin of triumph as Shona walked beside them, completely wrapped up in the baby who gurgled in the protective circle of her arms.

Chapter Seven

Ruth gazed down at her cherubic daughter. She was peacefully asleep after a night of fretful crying during which she had roused the entire household and caused havoc with the carefully laid plans for the christening breakfast which Kirsteen had taken much of the previous evening to prepare. In the bright hours of the summer dawn everyone had at last managed to get some rest, only to waken in a panic with the realization that they had overslept.

Bleary-eyed and disgruntled they sat around the table in silence, munching burnt toast and gulping down mouthfuls of tea which, though stewed, was hot and sweet and very welcome.

'She must be teething,' Lorn decided, thinking of the time spent pacing the floor with his baby daughter bawling lustily in his ears.

'She's too young, surely,' protested Ruth. 'She's only two and a half months.'

Fergus rubbed the black stubble on his chin and grinned ruefully. 'The McKenzies do everything in a hurry and that wee besom's going to be no exception.'

Kirsteen was at the ironing board, going once more over the ruffles on the christening robe. Lovingly she stroked the cream satin of the garment which had been made by Fergus's grandmother more than a hundred years before. Each stitch had been exquisitely executed, the fine old French lace which overlaid the bodice and edged the sleeves was as delicate as a cobweb and still as good as the day it had been fashioned. Kirsteen held the smooth material to her face. 'What a lot of McKenzie bairns have worn this bonny thing,' she mused. 'Strange to think the McKenzie men were once able to fit this tiny gown – there must have been – let me see – four of your grandmother's sons and daughters – then you, Fergus, Alick, Shona, Alick's son – then – no, not Grant ...' She looked wistful at the idea of her eldest son missing the chance to wear the McKenzie robe and her voice faltered as she went on, 'At least Lewis had his turn of it though Lorn had to make do with another,' she laughed. 'Your grandmother never catered for twins, more's the pity. Alick and Mary were like us, only one of their boys got to wear it. After that came Ellie and now wee Lorna – I wonder how many more babies will feel the caress of it against their skin.'

Fergus kissed the top of her head. 'More than we'll ever see, that's for sure – and if I don't go and shave I'll be late for kirk and so will you unless you plan to arrive in your dressing gown.'

Light steps sounded on the cobbled yard and Shona

came in, delightfully cool looking in a pale green linen suit and a white blouse with ruffles at the neck.

'You look bonny, mo cridhe,' Fergus greeted his daughter, then gazing beyond her to the open door, 'Isn't Ellie coming? I need her help.'

'She was at my back when I left.' A stab of pride pierced Shona's heart. How her father adored his eldest granddaughter – adored and trusted her. From her infancy he had allowed her to do things for him which he would never dream of allowing any other. She had grown up with his disability and accepted it as easily as she accepted the cold rains of winter and the warm sun of summer. As a baby she had laboriously fastened the buttons of his jackets; as she grew older she tied his shoelaces and attempted to make knots in his tie. Now, at thirteen, she often struck the matches which lit his pipe and had become such an expert at doing his tie he often bemoaned her absences from the island.

Shona smiled at her big handsome father. 'Baby,' she teased. 'Don't fash yourself, Ellie will be here in time to do your tie.'

As if on cue Ellie arrived, her arms full of wildflowers which she stuck hastily into a vase before dashing upstairs to help her grandfather.

Ruth, still in her dressing gown, her hair unbrushed, threw Shona a look of desperation. 'I'll never be ready in time,' she wailed. 'Lorna needs changing and it will take ages to get her into that robe. She might start

185

crying again and be sick all over it and I've still to get myself ready.'

'And do you think I came over early just to sit and twiddle my thumbs?' Shona scolded. 'Upstairs with you this minute, I'll get her ready.'

With everyone dispersed the kitchen was quiet and peaceful and Shona quickly set about clearing the table before she turned her attention on the baby. When Shona went to lift her she was warm and drowsy and smelt of rosewater which Ruth had sprinkled into her morning bath. Shona carried her to the inglenook and sat to cuddle her for a few precious minutes. A pair of bright eyes fastened on her face and scrutinized her in some puzzlement.

'No, I'm not your mother,' Shona said and drew in her breath. 'Oh God, I wish I were, if you were mine I might not feel so lonely every time your Uncle Niall has to be away.'

She lifted the baby up and tucked the downy head under her chin. The feel of the trusting infant against her breast was rapture; the rapture of petal soft skin, of tiny grunts and gurgles; of soft hair that tickled and little fists that innocently touched whatever they would. Shona wanted only to sit all day in the inglenook at Laigmhor holding Ruth's baby and with a sigh she rose to fetch the robe from the wooden clothes horse where it had been warming by the fire. Some minutes later she laid the baby down to straighten out the yards of exquisite material and as she admired she felt that this must surely be Ellie lying there waiting to be carried to kirk, small hands carelessly grasping the lacy sleeves; big blue eyes adoring the patterns of light dazzling off the brass ornaments by the fire. Ellie had been the last McKenzie to wear the robe and it seemed to Shona as if the clock had been turned back to those happy hours she had spent with her baby daughter . . .

Ruth came into the room, lovely in her youth, her sun-bleached hair framing her sweet face, her pale skin showing to advantage the pink dress she was wearing.

'You look a treat,' Shona said warmly, 'I have never seen you looking more bonny and no wonder, you have the world at your feet this beautiful morning.' She paused. 'Is your father coming?'

'Ay, he is that, he's so proud of his granddaughter he wouldn't miss her christening for anything. Grannie and Granda will be there too, so Father asked old Sorcha to sit with Mam. She's a tough old lady and as deaf as a post so anything Mam says will just go over her head.'

'Does your mother know her grandchild is being christened this morning?'

'Ay, we told her but she didn't seem to take it in – she just went upstairs to sit beside the cradle and rock it – poor Mam,' she added gently, her violet eyes full of sympathy. 'She is living in her own wee world now.'

After that everyone came crowding into the kitchen at the one time and it was a happy procession that walked through the sunny glen to the kirk on the Hillock. Bob joined them on the way, a grand old Highland gentleman in his kilt and tweed jacket, his white hair brushed, his beard combed smooth, a Sgian Dubh tucked into the thick cream woollen hose which covered his sturdy calves, his brown knotted hand resting lightly on the carved bone handle of his shepherd's crook.

'God, man, you're a bonny sight,' Fergus greeted him. 'You've excelled yourself this Sabbath.'

'Ach well, it's no' every day we get a new minister,' Bob grunted dourly, reserve not allowing him to admit that he had made the effort to dress up for the christening, though his old eyes softened at sight of the baby with her clean new little face peeping out from her lace bonnet. 'Forbye, it's time my kilt had an airing. It's lain in the kist so long the hairs on the sporran have grown an inch!'

The kirk bell was tolling out, reverberating through the moors and glens, and folk were emerging from croft and cottage, a stiffness in their bearing suggesting collars hard with starch and corsets laced too tightly, combining with the instinct of never to be seen slouching or hurrying on the Sabbath. Phebie and Lachlan came along in time to hear the subdued laughter which greeted Bob's whimsical words and everyone was in a good humour when they arrived at the kirk gate.

Here Dugald, Jim Jim and Isabel were waiting, Jim Jim pulling disgustedly at cuffs so saturated in starch they were like celluloid; Isabel scolding him from the side of her mouth; Dugald, thin face rather serious under his mop of white hair, smiling nervously at Ruth who went quickly to his side to show him the baby decked in all her finery.

Rachel and Jon joined them, the latter smart in a dark suit, his young wife sophisticated in a well-cut, olive-green two piece with a scrap of green and black velvet perched on her raven curls.

Raising her head she found herself looking into Lorn's eyes. He was strikingly handsome in his dark suit, his white shirt a startling contrast to his bronzed skin. His hair had been carefully brushed but had fallen back into its natural curl; the sunlight shone through it, laving it with copper. The sky was wide and blue that day and found its mirror in his eyes. Rachel was about to lower hers when he smiled at her, a strange, sympathetic smile that was like a balm to her spirit.

Since rising that morning, Shona's thoughts had been filled with the disappointment of Niall's failure to return the night before and she was glad that she had Ellie by her side, the cool comfort of the small hand in hers bringing her immeasurable comfort. As Kate had predicted, the kirk was filled to capacity that glorious morning in June. Sunbeams slanted through the windows, the scent of roses mingled with the aroma of mint which the old folks liked to suck during the sermon though there was always the odd one rustling surreptitiously from a roomy pocket.

Totie Little was at the organ, puffing slightly as her feet worked the pedals, trying to keep the squeaking of them to a minimum so that they wouldn't be heard above the music, her flushed face made redder still by the ruby light filtering through the only stained glass window the kirk boasted, gifted by a member of the Balfour family.

The laird, his wife and sons, were sitting in their pew near the front, the eldest boy, dark haired and good looking, still a bachelor at twenty-six, ogled slyly by several young women with whom he amused himself during his spells at home, gaining himself a reputation as a womanizer as his grandfather had been before him; the younger son, quiet and thoughtful, his rangy form hunched awkwardly on the uncomfortable pew, studying with deep interest the beautiful peacock feather which sprouted proudly from old Isabel's hat, sighing a little as his thoughts began to wander, taking him far over the grouse moors with his dogs and his beaters beside him – more than six weeks to go till August twelfth – still – they would pass . . .

Babbie's bright head stood out against Anton's fair one and Shona threw her a smile as she passed which Babbie answered with a mock yawn, hastily stifled, conveying the message that she had sacrificed her Sunday lie-in to be there that day.

With birdsong pouring in through the open door, scents of sea and moor strong in the air, a bumblebee in the flowers on the chancel table, it was a time to rejoice in the glories of summer. Robbie Beag thought so too as he came respectfully inside, straightening the crease of his best trousers into which he had hastily changed after a morning spent poaching the Burnbreddie Estate. There he had roamed most of his working life, acting as ghillie, half-heartedly chasing the rabbit catchers and the trout baggers who, unrepentant, shared their spoils with him at the end of the day. Now he was retired and delighting in participating in the pursuits he had so often envied. At his back came Tam McKinnon and Fingal McLeod, boldly slipping into their places, ignoring the meaningful looks thrown at them from their womenfolk. But Robbie was possessed of a gentler nature and his expression was hangdog as he took his place by his sister's side, her glare of outrage though only glimpsed, enough to make him redden and stare down soulfully at his boots which he had forgotten to polish. He gulped, hoping that Behag wouldn't notice the scuff marks. On the other side of him, Barra suppressed a smile into her hanky, nudged him and passed him a mint imperial which he took in his sweaty palm, lifted his thumb to see what it was, turned to nod his smiling thanks, and slipped it into his mouth in the pretence of stifling a cough.

Lachlan got up to shut the door, resuming his seat as the coughings and rustlings died away, coinciding with the opening of the side door to admit the Reverend Mark James, facing his congregation for the first time. Dressed in his robes, his face clean cut above his snow white collar, he looked the epitome of strength and confidence. For a long time his eyes raked the sea of faces before him, one thumb hooked into the folds of his gown, the palm of his other hand resting lightly on the open Bible on its stand above the chancel steps. The silence stretched, during which Lorna Morag chuckled and old Joe choked so violently on a mint he had to have his back discreetly thumped by Todd the Shod. The tension mounted inside the little kirk and quite a few folk began to fidget.

Fergus fumbled with his shirt collar, pulling the tautness of it away from his skin; Ellie watched him anxiously, wondering if she had made his tie too tight; Kirsteen examined her hands lying on her lap and noted that one of the nails was broken; the Rev. John Grey blew his nose so loudly one or two children tittered.

Phebie sat with her eyes closed, thinking about Fiona, wishing that she was there that day; Lachlan nudged her and her eyes flew open to see his amused sidelong grin; Dugald stared at his shiny black shoes and wondered how old Sorcha was coping with Morag; Rachel kept her hand tightly in Jon's and wished the ceremony was over; Jim Jim was making faces at his entranced great-grandchild and glowered at Isabel in pained surprise when she poked him in the ribs and made a warning face.

Shona felt herself growing hot. In a mild panic she wondered if the minister was at a loss to know how to begin. He looked so erect, so composed, yet his hands were not quite as still as they seemed, his fingers were working against his cloth, the hand that lay on the Bible trembled slightly. He looked so alone, divorced from the throng by a matter of a few feet, the chaste light lying mellow across his face, smoothing out its angular lines.

His eyes were roaming from face to face, studying them, taking them in, remembering them, then they came to rest directly on Shona, as if he had at last found someone who was familiar to him and she felt herself to be bathed in a tranquil glow. A tiny half-smile crooked the corners of his mouth and her heart quivered, knowing it was for her alone. She was embarrassed by the intimacy of the moment and a flush of burning shame stained her neck, making her glad that she had arranged her hair in a way that hid it. It was wrong – wrong to read anything but innocence into the look but she couldn't deny that the small new awakening he had aroused in her at their first meeting came more alive that morning.

He held out his hands then, in a gesture that seemed to gather the entire congregation to his bosom, and his smile deepened, setting lines of laughter about his eyes.

'This morning I feel that I am a very privileged and lucky man, he began, the mellow fruitfulness of his deep tones reaching every corner without detracting from the peace that lay over the ancient stones. 'On this beautiful day I come to you as a stranger but I hope, when this service is over, I will say goodbye to you as a friend, I need your friendship, just as surely as I need my God to sustain me when I am alone – and we are all alone at some time in our lives . . .' He paused and gazed around, the smoky enchantment of his eyes beguiling the young girls, fascinating the children, comforting the old. He had charm all right, Mark James, but it was a clean, clear forthright charm.

When he finished speaking, everyone rose to sing the first hymn and the rafters fairly reverberated with the heartfelt strains.

The christening party were called to the font, Rachel carrying the precious infant, a picture in her satin robe, ruby light staining the peach of her cheeks, eyes, big, blue, gazing with wonder at the stiff peacock feather adorning old Isabel's hat, small fists punching the air, gurgling and smiling all the way to the font.

Rachel was taut, the roses in her face deepening to crimson as she felt all eyes to be upon her, draining her, robbing her of all the little affectations she had acquired in the city. Her legs trembled, her dark eyes were wide and apprehensive. To speak – oh to speak – just once, to hear the Baptismal Vows issuing from her lips and not from the voice inside her brain. Lorn and Ruth were repeating their vows, Ruth too young looking to be a mother, her fluffy flaxen hair, her small-boned body, giving her the appearance of a little girl pretending to be grown up; Lorn, tall, erect, his frown of concentration not marring the clean moulding of his face or the intense clearness of his shadowed eyes. The congregation then stood to repeat its vows on behalf of the child, and as Rachel handed the baby to the minister she glanced up to see his eyes upon her, lazy yet penetrating, piercing her soul with serenity. Looking up she caught Jon's encouraging smile and the day that had started so uncertainly for her became charged with sunlight.

The minister was blessing the child and the kirk was hushed; fingers of sunlight silvered the heads of the old folk and burnished the heads of the young; from the edge of the moors a lapwing piped; nearer at hand a curlew bubbled in glorious adoration of the sun-laved seas lapping the shores ...

The rattling of the stout wooden door fell like a blasphemy on everyone's ears, making them start in fright. The rattling was followed by a hideous screeching which curdled the blood and tingled the spine of everyone there. Mark James paused in his ministrations and looked through the dust-filled sunrays to the door. The kirk seemed to hold its breath and there was a dreadful tension-filled silence. Again the warped and ill-fitting door was pulled and rattled viciously then slowly it began to scrape back, squealing agonizingly where it rubbed over the top step.

Lachlan half rose, poised ready to intercept the intruder. Rachel's face turned pale, but not as pale as Ruth who was staring petrified at the door, as if she knew what was about to happen. Dugald stepped quickly to her side, his thin hand kneading her shoulder, conveying a reassurance he didn't feel.

'Mercy on us,' muttered Isabel to Jim Jim. 'It canny be, oh, God, it canny be – no' this day – oh, dear God – no' this day o' all days.'

A final tug brought the door fully open and Morag Ruadh stood framed in the arched aperture, a wild-eyed dishevelled figure, her hair standing in red spikes around her head, her sunken chest rising and falling with each painful breath, her pinched nostrils dilated. She had dressed hurriedly, creeping away to her room the minute she knew old Sorcha to be sound asleep in her chair. Her black skirt was twisted, longer at the back than the front, her tight corset showed broken bones where it stretched across her belly, a black cardigan was folded across her bosom, held together by a safety pin, her thin legs, bare and pallid, were stuck into brown brogues with the laces undone. It was a far cry from the neat and decorous Morag of old, but at least she had dressed.

Yet nothing so subtle penetrated the shocked horror in Dugald's consciousness and the hand that clutched Ruth's shoulder tightened convulsively. She was incapable of movement, unable to make any gesture of comfort towards him. The fair pallor of her skin had flamed to a fiery red, her pupils were the colour of black grapes. The June sun poured over Morag, glinting into her hair, finding the red flecks in her strange green eyes. Behind her stretched the sun-cosseted fields, the tranquil heat-hazed moors.

Not one person in kirk that morning had eyes for the view beyond the door. Everyone was staring at Morag, wondering what had brought her here, what she intended to do. She was behaving in a frightening manner, her nails scrabbling viciously at the door jamb, as if she was trying to make some lasting impression on it, her lips were working but no sound was coming, just a high wailing moan that plunged the bravest heart into abject fear. Yet she was a figure of pathos, a poor demented soul adrift in a hellish half world where there was no hope, only despair, deep and dark.

The Rev. Mark James, standing with Lorna in his arms, recognized Morag's dreadful state of mind. He had already heard about her, how she had once worshipped God in this very kirk, had played the organ every Sabbath without fail. Compassion overruled the slight feeling of repugnance that the sight of her had invoked in him. This was her grandchild he held in his arms. Dugald had told him about his wife, had explained why she couldn't attend the ceremony but he hadn't immediately collated this demented creature with local description and the sketchy gentle one of Dugald's.

Mark James strove to collect his thoughts. The congregation were looking agitated, some of the children were beginning to cry quietly. The only sounds to break the silence were the rustling of clothing and the horrible continuing notes issuing from Morag's throat. He handed the baby back to Rachel and murmured a few words in Dugald's ear. Dugald's white head nodded automatically and slowly he began to make for the door. Morag came shambling towards him, her lips stretched wide in a leering grimace, her whole being intent on reaching the font where the christening party stood. Dugald's hands reached out to her but she pushed him away, her bearing tense and pouncing, reminding the more imaginative of the Seanachaidh's tales woven round the dark mysterious legends of witches.

But it was no legend who sprung forward like a cat, one

long finger raking the air, pointing at Rachel with the baby in her arms.

'You've taken my babby!' Vindictively she hurled the words at Rachel. 'I want her, she's mine, she's mine, Rachel McKinnon, and you will no' take her from me! You were aye a queer one! Satan himself sits on your shoulders and though you may be dumb you speak wi' your eyes – things that no mortal body wants to hear! Ay, the de'il was in you from the start but you will no' sacrifice my babby to that evil house – oh no! She's mine! She's my Ruth, and I want her back. She will never grow to be like you, oh no, I will teach her no' to let any man tarnish her purity!'

The sacrilegious accusations continued to pour from her twisted mouth and Ruth swayed against Lorn who put a steadying arm around her shoulders, whispering comforting words in her ear. Isabel and Jim Jim looked away, unable to bear the shame of knowing that this was their very own flesh and blood blaspheming in the house of God, bringing the devil into a holy establishment.

The baby began to cry, a petted sobbing that made Morag look wilder still and stretch out her arms, as if to snatch the little creature away from an ungodly guardian. But Rachel, despite a swiftly beating heart, had never once flinched from Morag's terrifying figure, and now she snuggled the child closer to her breast, evading the clutching fingers which wavered towards her. Her dark, contemptuous stare fell upon her tormentor, hypnotizing, mesmeric.

Morag backed away, her hand going up to shield her eyes, her lips quivering in dread. 'The de'il is in her,' she whimpered. 'She's no' right, never was, even as a bairn.'

Mark James took Morag by the arm and she allowed herself to be led up the chancel steps and over to the altar. There the minister spoke to her quietly, his arms round her shaking shoulders, the low murmur of his voice filtering to the ears of the congregation.

'We will no' forget this day,' Kate murmured to Elspeth, who back straight, eyes fixed on the stained glass window, was moving her lips as if in prayer.

Elspeth nodded grimly. 'Indeed we will no' – and if the doctor is wise he will no' allow that cratur' to stay on the island a minute longer after this.'

The minister was coming forward, leading Morag by the hand, and she followed him like a trusting child who has at last found a friend. Bending he spoke a few words in Totie's ear. After a few tight-lipped seconds she arose and stepped down to take a place in one of the pews, leaving the organ clear for Morag, who, having sat down, was lovingly fingering the keys, her smile radiant, the glow of ruby light on her face making it soft, childlike, innocent.

Isabel fingered her peacock feather nervously. 'Ach, our poor, poor lassie,' she whispered to Jim Jim. 'She'll no' be able to play. She's too far gone to know an organ from a peat spade.'

But Morag had not forgotten how to play the ancient harmonium that had once given her so much satisfaction.

Mark James finished blessing the baby and the kirk rose to sing the baptismal hymn, all eyes on Morag who seemed to be playing a tune of her own as her agile fingers fluttered over the keyboard. Then, quite suddenly, above the squeaking of the pedals, the organ burst into life and the opening strains of the hymn reverberated round the kirk. The minister's gaze was on Morag, encouraging her, and she responded, summoning every vestige of strength to please this bonny man who had spoken to her with such understanding. The wonder of the event was strengthened as the words of the hymn rose to the rafters, *The Lord bless thee and keep thee*, sung in a mixture of Gaelic and English with a few words of German thrown in by the old Gaels for Anton's benefit. Swelling, pulsating, the voices burst triumphantly forth while Lorna Morag blew bubbles and chuckled at the feather in her great-grandmother's hat, the tip of it pointing proudly to the cobwebby roof.

Tears were pouring down Morag's face. Towards the end of the hymn she faltered but the finale spurted from under her fingers, dying away gently to leave a throbbing silence. A breeze danced through the open door, fanning the pages of Bibles and hymn books, cleansing the air, bringing freshness and life upon its breath.

Morag was spent, her shoulders sagged, her long white fingers lay still upon the organ keys, her ruddy cheeks were mottled with purple, her head had fallen forward onto her bosom.

'Ach, she is just a poor, poor lost soul,' nodded Elspeth

in a rush of compassion and those who sat beside her nodded their heads in sad agreement.

Lachlan was up beside Morag now, a look in his face that was oddly disquieting as he held her thin wrist between his fingers. Mark James went to speak to him and it was a grave face he turned to his parishioners. He apologized for the fact that his first service had been such an unusual one but, as far as the islanders were concerned, he had no need to be sorry for anything he did. Already they had responded to his charm, forgetting the earlier doubts they had harboured about 'the mannie who walked alone'. Those who had come to kirk prepared to criticize and find fault, instead found themselves looking askance at others who had dared to doubt the minister's integrity.

As the service was brought to a premature end there was quite a scuffle to get to the door to see who would be first to shake the new minister's hand. His eye fell on Barra and a strange flush spread over his high cheekbones. Taking her hand he shook it warmly. 'We meet again, Barra, it's nice to see a well-kent face.' He threw her a meaning glance and putting her fingers to her lips she shook her head, understanding the message in his eyes. Flushed but determined she ignored the curious looks thrown at her and even quite enjoyed the feeling of power within her breast. Kate and the others could question her till they were blue in the face but they would get nothing out of her. For once she had the upper hand and she walked away down the hill, her back straight.

A stream of people filed past the minister, shaking his hand, congratulating him on the success of his first service but he seemed restless, his gaze straying frequently to the interior of the kirk. Shona came out just as Babbie and Anton were making to go away.

'We won't be having the christening celebrations after all,' she told her friend. 'Morag isn't well. I – I think she's played the organ for the last time. Lachlan asked if you would go back in.'

Babbie immediately disappeared inside, going straight to Lachlan's side. Morag was very still, her face strangely immobile.

'I think she's had a stroke,' Lachlan spoke quietly to Babbie. 'We'll have to get her home so that I can examine her properly.'

Fergus ran his fingers inside his collar but his discomfort was more than physical. The strange, fixed stare on Morag's face made him feel uneasy. Part of him was aggrieved at her for disrupting the ceremony in such an unholy manner yet he knew a deep pity for the woman who had brought her life to such an unhappy climax.

'Help her,' whispered Kirsteen and he went immediately to assist the other men to carry Morag down the steps. Mark James walked beside her, his strong big hand over her frail one. 'Bless you, Morag Ruadh,' he said softly. 'And don't be afraid, God is with you.' But she seemed not to hear and he laid her hand gently back to her side and went forward to open the door wider. Ruth stood beside him as her mother was carried out of the kirk. 'Thank you, Mr James,' Ruth said softly. 'Despite everything you made the ceremony so – so meaningful. Our daughter has been truly blessed.'

Lorn nodded his agreement and Mark James's smile washed over them, making them feel it was all right to smile back, even at a time like this.

Shona's heart missed a beat and she turned away with the feeling of having drowned in a hazy blue-grey pool.

'Thank you and bless you, I feel welcome to this place now.'

The words, cool and deep, meant for Lorn and Ruth, dropped like pebbles into the depths of Shona's heightened awareness and she wished it was her right to follow Mark James into his private world and listen, just listen to his voice.

'Mother, come on, everyone is going away.'

Shona started out of her reverie to stare at her daughter's face without comprehension. She gave a little laugh. 'Sorry, I was daydreaming.'

'About Father?'

'Well, no, I was – just thinking,' faltered Shona, reddening under her daughter's frank gaze.

'Well, I was thinking about him, during the service – till Morag Ruadh came screeching in. I can't wait to see him tonight. I've finished his socks and his hat but he's not getting them till we're away on this trip. I wish he'd been here this morning, don't you? It was a bonny christening except for Morag Ruadh.'

'Ay, it would have been fine if your father had been here.' Shona spoke the words automatically, hating herself because she had barely given Niall a thought from the moment she stepped over the kirk door.

Niall was weary that evening, quite content to sit back in his chair in the parlour and listen to Ellie prattling. Each member of the family had a chair which they had claimed as their own years back. Shona's was a monstrous, well-stuffed green armchair with a sagging but deliciously comfortable seat. Niall's was identical but for a patch on one arm, Ellie's was made of pink cane with a tapestry seat and a little footstool to match. Very soon it would be too small for her and Niall studied her lazily, smiling at the sight of her scuffed brown knees jutting out from the seat.

She caught his look and her golden eyes glinted. 'I know what you're thinking but I'm not parting with it. It isn't really too wee, it's just—' She shifted her position, making her limbs fit the contours. 'I'm not sitting right. Anyway—' She jumped up. 'It's a beautiful evening and I'm going out to play with Woody for a whily.'

At the door she turned, twisting her long hair between her fingers. 'Father – you haven't forgotten, have you?'

His brown eyes twinkled. 'Forgotten what?'

'That you're taking me with you on your next trip.'

'Am I?' He sounded surprised. 'To tell the truth it slipped my mind.'

She glanced at him sideways, a smile starting to dawn across her cheeks. 'Just for that I'm not going to bother playing with Woody. Instead I'll clean your car – and if one or two of the tyres go down while I'm there . . .'

He thew a cushion at her. 'You dare, madam, and I might forget about some wee surprises Mac and me cooked up between us – such as dropping anchor at Breac Beag and spending a couple of nights there. There's an old shepherd's cottage there with the roof and everything still intact, just the right base to have adventures from. The caves are near as high as Fingal's Cave on Staffa and the rock pools so warm it's like swimming in a hot bath – oh, ay, and of course there's the fishing. Mac says he spent a night there and caught so many saithe and mackerel he was throwing them to the seabirds – but of course, maybe none of that interests you which is just as well since I'm supposed to have forgotten it all . . .'

She hurled herself at him, tickling and pummelling till he begged for mercy. 'You win,' he panted, his face red with laughter. 'I'll take you, I promise – now, get out of here and leave your old man in peace. I'm no' able for your capers now – as your Grannie Lachlan would say.'

In moments the house was quiet, the hens crooned peacefully outside the window, Ellie's voice drifted from the river where she had taken Woody to teach her how to fish with her paws.

For a while he enjoyed the peace, wiggling his toes into the pink woolwork rug Shona had made while they were living in Kintyre. It was good to be home. He missed it when he was away; only the thought of returning to his wife and daughter kept him going. He cocked his good ear, listening for signs of life, pinpointing it to the kitchen. Getting up he padded through. Shona was at the window, gazing pensively towards the hills, her chin propped in her hands, the threads of her hair caught to fire in the bright evening light. Soundlessly he went up behind her and slid his arms around her slender waist.

'You're very quiet.' His lips brushed her lobe. She tasted of warmth, the smell of new baked bread, which she had made that afternoon in defiance of the Sabbath, lingered on her clothes.

'Am I?' She didn't turn but kept on gazing outside.

'Ay, you are that.' He nuzzled his mouth into the warm hollow of her nape. 'Have you missed me at all?'

'Maybe just a wee bit.' Her voice was lazy, the smile that hovered at the corners of her mouth was secretive, inviting.

He pressed himself harder against her, his former contentment laced now with desire.

'I'll crush the life out of you, Shona, mo ghaoil – though, on second thoughts that might not be wise – your body feels very good to me the way it is.'

She twisted round to look deep into his eyes. 'I think, Niall McLachlan, I would like if you crushed me.' Her lips parted provocatively and his hold on her tightened, his thumbs caressing her nipples till they became taut.

'Ay, you would like that, Mrs McLachlan,' he whispered against her cheek. 'I think we'll have an early night.' He grinned, his boyish features illuminated. 'After all I have a very good excuse. I'm bone weary and need you to massage me to sleep.'

She laid her head on his shoulder and he let the silken strands of her hair run through his fingers. 'I'm sorry I didn't make it for the christening this morning – yet in a way I'm glad I wasny there.'

She didn't move, finding the comfort of his shoulder so relaxing she could have closed her eyes and slept in his arms. 'Why?'

He looked contemplatively from the window to the hills. 'Freedom,' he spoke as if to himself. 'The hills have their freedom – Morag Ruadh used to walk them long ago when she was a young woman, always she was a lonely strange creature but she had her freedom. Now she has none, not even her spirit is free to wander. I wouldny have liked to witness her humiliation in kirk this morning – nor that of Doug and Ruth, Isabel and Jim Jim.'

She held him tightly, a shaft of pain piercing her breast. It wasn't often that Niall was serious – yet lately he had been bemused and saddened by the changes brought by the passing years.

'Thank God the new minister was able to handle the

situation, he continued fervently. 'He sounds a good lad. Do you like him?'

Idly she traced the scar on his neck, an imperceptible shiver running through her. 'I like him – and so it seems does everyone else, even those who were all set to criticize everything he did just because he has no family.'

'How do they know that? He might have grown-up sons and daughters living away from home.'

'He might – though he doesn't seem old enough – perhaps in his middle thirties – besides, he doesn't have a wife.'

'A bit of a mystery man, eh?'

'A bit – oh, Niall.' She pressed herself closer against him, a sense of foreboding rising up inside her. 'Hold me very very tightly. I love you, my Niall, I really do love you so much, and I've missed you more than you'll ever know.'

'Hey—' He laughed and wound his arms fiercely round her. 'You've convinced me – you don't have to sound as if you're convincing yourself.'

Her eyes blurred and she was glad that her face was hidden from him. 'I know,' she spoke shakily. 'It's just – sometimes when you're away and I'm feeling lonely I have time to think a lot and there have been times when I can't seem to get your face into focus. When you're near me like this everything about you is so real and familiar and that's how I should see you when we're apart – yet, there are times when I can't – and it worries me.'

Tenderly he kissed the tip of her nose. 'That happens to me too, sometimes when I try to picture you I see a red witch instead.' She giggled then and, smiling, he went on, 'I suppose it happens to people who are very close. We eat, read, sleep together and yet we don't take the time to look at one another properly – not in the way we did when we were first going together and spent our time goggling into each other's eyes. I knew every part of you then, that the whirly bits on your right ear were slightly different from your left. Even in the dark I could find the little mole on your thigh—' His eyes widened. 'Hey! Now I can't remember which thigh it's on – maybe you'd better let me look.' He took her arm and led her out to the hall. 'Call on Ellie and tell her it's time for bed. We will then repair to our own bedchamber to catch up on our studies. There's only one way for us to refresh our memories and I have the very remedy.'

'Oh, and what may that be?' she asked coyly.

He gave her a sidelong glance. 'If you really want me to spell it out then the plan is simple. We will remove all our clothes and spend the night studying anatomy – imprint each pimple, each hair into our minds so that we shall never forget them again.'

'You dirty bugger,' she giggled. This was the Niall she loved, able to lift her out of a mood with his nonsense, able to make her laugh with his absurdities. She grabbed him and swung him round. 'Don't ever change,' she entreated him lightly.

'*I* won't,' he answered seriously.

She looked at him quickly but he broke away from her and went outside to look for Ellie.

Chapter Eight

A week later Shona took a chair to the green at the side of the house with the intention of catching up on some of the paperwork that had been piling up. Since Niall had branched out on his own the task of book-keeping had fallen to her, but she didn't mind and actually quite enjoyed it. June had slipped into July with the weather showing no sign of breaking. Each day dawned clear and cloudless, and the farmers were up before daybreak to get on with haymaking. Ellie had risen early each morning, going off as her parents were just stirring. When the weather was right like this the farmers took turns in helping each other to get the hay cut and Ellie had had a wonderful time traversing the length and breadth of the island, coming home in the gloaming atop a cart piled high with newly gathered hay, the warm fragrance of it filling the balmy air of evening.

It had been a busy week for Niall too and the phone, which normally sat quietly on its cradle, had never seemed to stop ringing.

'What did they do before you came?' Shona wondered. 'After all, there's always been animals on the island, but never a vet.'

Niall chuckled. 'Ach, the farm lads have their own remedies for ailing beasts and as a last resort they could always call out a doctor. Father has had some gey queer patients in his day and they haven't all been the two-legged variety. If I'm minding right your father was aye looked upon as a sort of unofficial vet. With that in mind I'm looked upon rather suspiciously and I never get off lightly. Old Padruig was nearly standing on top of me when I gave his cow an injection for lung worm and after I had treated one of his horses for a severe swelling he showed me a jar of crushed stonecrop mixed with groundsel which he claimed had always done the trick before vets were ever invented. When I asked him why he had called me out, he screwed up his face and told me he thought he would give me a try but threatened to sue me if anything went wrong with his horse. There's a bit of the animal doctor in them all and some of the old remedies were effective.'

Shona settled herself into her chair with her ledger but was promptly interrupted by Woody who jumped up and prepared to make herself comfortable. 'Ach, get away, you lazy creature,' scolded Shona, but feeling too lazy herself to lift the cat down she settled back instead and stretched her bare legs to the sun. It was very warm and utterly peaceful with the burn tumbling over the stones and the soft breezes rustling the leaves of the rowan trees which grew among the pines at the foot of the hill; the summer sky was blue; for as far as the eye could see, the moors stretched, green and languorous. She closed her eyes, letting her thoughts take her back once more to what had been a very pleasant week. Niall had snatched some hours off and they had gone to picnic at Aosdana Bay, paddling in the freezing water, shrieking with agony as the waves splashed them. Ellie had swum beside them, giggling at their antics.

They had all participated in the haymaking at Laigmhor and it had been lovely, working together in the scented fields, enjoying the banter, enormously hungry for the home-baked scones and thick crusty bread served with lashings of raspberry jam. They had quenched their thirst with creamy milk or the home-brewed beer supplied by Tam and poured straight from the cask.

Fergus, delighted at the sight of the furrows of cut hay spread out to dry, had started an impromptu ceilidh, there in the fields, his bronzed face alight, his dark head thrown back. Shona had marvelled at him, her father, shy, aloof, so carried away by the joy of the moment, singing as if in thanksgiving, the deep, clear notes of the Gaelic song bursting spontaneously out of him. Then embarrassment had stilled the song, and he had reddened, but it was too late, the tune was taken up till it rang round the fields. The evening that had followed was a memorable one, with everyone dancing to the tunes from hastily acquired melodions and accordions. The ineffable joy of watching Kate, skirts held high to display long pink drawers, oblivious to all but the gaiety of the moment, skirling and hooching while the sun crept lower in the western sky, was something not to be forgotten in a hurry. She was joined by her daughter, Nancy, much recovered from her recent operation, as her laughable antics ably proved.

From the high shorn fields the sea was visible in the distance and everyone paused to watch the great fiery ball of the sun wavering above water of molten gold before it gradually sank over the horizon, leaving in its wake a sky lit to flame shot through with streaks of lilac and turquoise.

Dodie, his calloused hands stained green from working in almost every hayfield on the island, got slowly and surely inebriated on Tam's beer, and when everyone began to dance again he made no objection to Mairi taking his hands and coaxing him into a shambling attempt at a jig. So carried away did he become he forgot himself completely, gave vent to an abandoned screech which was meant to mimic that of Kate's, and without any warning whatsoever he threw his legs high in the air, kicking off his big wellingtons in the process.

With exaggerated shrieks everyone had scattered but it was all lost on Dodie who, eyes closed, lips stretched in bliss, was left alone in a little clearing, dancing in stockings well ventilated by holes. His bare, mottled toes curled into the shaggy stubble of the field, making everyone shudder and wonder if he had any sensation in his soles or if the beer had rendered his sensibilities numb.

At midnight Todd had played a solo on the pipes, his sturdy figure silhouetted against the silvered sky to the north, his feet rustling through the drying hay. The haunting airs had drifted down the glen, mystical, magical, drawing the islanders from their homes so that they came to Laigmhor in an eager throng, anxious to join in the revelry.

When Todd retired perspiring, Lorn had taken up his fiddle, soon joined by Jon and Rachel who had come with their own violins. And all enmity was forgotten that endless summer night as the fiddles played and everyone danced, their moods dictated by the music, joyous and wild one minute, soft as a breeze the next.

Shona had drifted in Niall's arms, held close, contentment satiating her being. At 3 a.m. as a pale milky dawn was breathing over the eastern hills and the birds were starting to chatter, she had walked home beside Niall, Ellie asleep in his arms, her young face beatific in its repose, her long legs dangling in comical awkwardness. Shona smiled to herself at the memory of the ceilidh, thought about the enthusiasm of the villagers afterwards and their keenness to do it all again someday.

The heat of the sun was making her drowsy and she felt lulled into sleep by Woody's purrs. The pen slipped from her fingers and rolled onto the grass . . . a touch as of thistledown brushed her mouth and she smiled lazily. Only a child could kiss like that, warm, innocent, undemanding. She put up a finger to the moist little circle on her lips and murmured, 'And the child stole a kiss from her mother's lips, only to give back a millionfold the little that she had taken.'

With a start she realized she was quoting aloud a poem Ruth had written and which had been published in one of the Scottish magazines. She had cut it out and pasted it into a scrapbook where she kept all of Ruth's poems and short stories.

She opened her eyes. Ellie was standing against the sun, dressed in white shorts and a pink cotton blouse. Her legs were a deep brown lightly sprinkled with tiny fair hairs which glinted in the sun; her knees were scuffed and scratched from numerous falls and entanglements with Woody's sharp claws; her hair was in plaits, shining threads of it flying loose. The ripeness of the summer sun lay on her smooth cheeks, her mouth was curved into a smile which held traces of pensiveness. 'These are lovely words. Did you make them up?'

'No, Ruth did. I keep all her poems. You must read them sometime. Folks nowadays have forgotten the beauty of poetry.'

The little girl stood back, arranging her limbs for inspection. 'I'm ready. Do I look all right to be going on *The Sea Urchin*?'

'You're bonny, a bonny wee sailor. Have you got everything you need?'

'Ay, don't forget you've been dinning it into my lugs all week. I've got enough woollies to last a month and so many pairs of knickers I'm thinking of setting up a shop on Hanaay. My sea boots are on the boat and I've packed a bra just in case my bosoms suddenly start sprouting while I'm away.' Her dimples deepened as she glanced down at her flat chest, and made a face. 'Mind you, it would have to take a miracle but Mac's sister is said to be a bit of a speywife so maybe she'll put a spell on me, make my bosoms grow so big they'll sink the boat and all in her.'

She choked with laughter and Shona got to her feet giggling. She cuddled her daughter to her. 'I'll miss my daft wee Ellie. What am I going to do without your singing? I'll be deafened by the silence in the house. When you come back you might find that I've changed into a sad old crone, all warty and whiskery.' She bent her back and made a hideous face which brought skirls of glee from her daughter.

'Ach, Mother, you're the one who's daft. We'll only be away for a week and you could have come with us if you'd wanted.'

Niall came out of the house, laden down with cases which he set thankfully on the grass. 'Phew! What have I let myself in for? She's only thirteen and already she carts her entire wardrobe with her. Mac goes out with what he stands up in and except for some jerseys which I keep on the boat I'm wearing everything I'll need.'

'As long as you've got plenty of clean socks and pants – oh and toothbrushes – Ellie . . .'

'Ay, Mother, I've got mine,' Ellie said with calculated patience.

Niall grinned and saluted. 'And so have I.' He came forward and put his arms round Shona while Ellie folded her arms in mock resignation and lifted her eyes to the sky.

'Are you sure you won't come with us?' he whispered

into Shona's ear. 'I thought you would have jumped at the chance.'

His hair tickled her nose, his newly washed skin felt cool against her face. All week she had swithered about whether to go on the trip while Ellie coaxed and persuaded and Niall actually went as far as getting her cases down from the top of the wardrobe.

'Somebody has to look after things here,' she said evasively. 'There's Woody and the hens and the phone to answer – and I thought I might bring Lorna over here for a day or two. I'd love to have her to myself for a whily.'

'You know Kirsteen said she would look to all that.' He sounded peeved and once more she hesitated, thinking how lovely it would be in weather like this to sail in *The Sea Urchin* to the small island of Hanaay where she knew she would be assured of a welcome. The people there had taken Niall to their hearts and eagerly awaited his visits. Both Niall and Captain Mac were glowing in their accounts of the hospitality they had received and Mac's sister, Nellie, had gone as far as to get her spare room ready in case Shona should arrive. But she couldn't turn her back so easily on her obligations on Rhanna. Though Kirsteen had offered to look after things she was already fully committed at Laigmhor with several grown men to see to; over and above she had Ruth's baby to look after now that Morag Ruadh had returned from hospital where she had been kept under observation. She had lost the use of her left arm and leg and her speech had been slightly affected as well. Her return meant even more work for Dugald, and Ruth had taken to going over every day to help out, leaving Lorna with Kirsteen who, though more than willing to take the baby, was noticeably tired looking.

Shona stroked the back of Niall's neck soothingly and whispered, 'Please understand, I can't let Kirsteen take on another thing at the moment. I promised I would go over to help out, take Lorna off her hands now and then—' She paused, wondering if that was the real reason for staying behind. Not to help Kirsteen but to spend some time with a delightful infant whose tiny intelligent face creased with smiles at sight of her? No – no – She pushed the thought away. Kirsteen needed her, quite a few folk needed her. Niall and Ellie wouldn't enjoy the trip the less because she wasn't with them.

'We'll have to go.' Niall stepped back. 'Mac took supplies onto the boat last night and he'll be wanting to get off.'

He lifted the heaviest of the cases. Ellie having grabbed the lightest. His free hand went out to her and she clung to him, her face full of anticipation for the adventure ahead. They had said their goodbyes to Slochmhor and Laigmhor last night, Ellie insisting that she had to see her grandparents then, as the likelihood of finding them all at home during the day was remote.

Niall was starting to walk away, something in his demeanour suggesting that he had dismissed Shona from his mind. It was ridiculous. Niall was seldom ruffled – yet she had sensed his keen disappointment when she had finally refused to go with him.

She wanted to run after him, to tell him she loved him, to hear like reassurances coming from him. She started forward, but they were too far away now, her action would seem like too much of an afterthought. 'Take care, dearest Niall,' she murmured and raised her hand, waiting for the moment when they would turn and wave back, but they were walking on, chattering, laughing, all at once divorced from her, shutting her out.

On impulse she raced to the hill behind the house and looked down on the grey winding ribbon of the road. The two people she loved most were mere dots, enclosed by the moors, embraced by the mountains which made them seem smaller still. A great sense of loneliness overwhelmed her and she found herself whispering, 'Look back, oh please, look back.'

As if in answer to her prayer Ellie turned at that moment, waving back towards the house, making Shona upbraid herself. She should have waited, Ellie always waited till she was a certain distance away before raising her hand, she hadn't forgotten – nor had Niall. His hand came up too and they were both walking backwards, waving, shouting towards the house, last farewells she couldn't hear, their voices were being carried away in the wind.

She cupped her hands to her mouth and cried, 'I'm up here!' and waved both hands above her head, feeling somehow that it was very important that they should see her, that for them to go thinking she had turned her back on them would be something she would feel sad about for the rest of her life. Desperately she tried to attract their attention but they neither saw nor heard her and with a sigh she wandered back down to the house to resume her neglected paperwork. But a restlessness had seized her and she couldn't settle. After a few minutes of nibbling furiously at the end of her pen she jumped up and started off briskly down the road, vaguely hoping that she might catch up with them, see them to the boat after all.

But the road stretched, deserted but for the sheep and the Highland cows which roved at will, munching the succulent roadside grasses by day, plodding down to the beaches in the evening to stand with their hooves in the cool water. As she neared Laigmhor she could just see two bright heads bobbing in the distance then the road dropped and they disappeared from view.

Kirsteen hailed her from the garden and glad of the diversion, she went through the gate and up the path to the front door which was seldom used, the family always having favoured the side entrance leading straight into the kitchen. Lorna was in her pram which was parked on the little lawn to the side of the door. She lay under a cool frilly canopy, kicking her bare legs in the air, examining the intricacies of her own hand, turning it back and forth, her brow furrowed in wonder. She was dressed in a yellow cotton dress and nothing else except a nappy and a white cotton sunhat with the wide brim shading a face wreathed in smiles at sight of Shona's head peeping under the canopy.

'I'm praying she stays clean,' Kirsteen said fervently. 'Ruth's aunt is taking her back to Coll for a week. She came to see Dugald and Morag but when she realized just how difficult the whole situation is she offered to take the baby off Ruth's hands to allow her to be more with Morag.'

'What!' The question was torn sharply from Shona. Spinning round she stared at Kirsteen questioningly. 'When did you say the baby was going?'

'In a wee whily – as soon as Aunt Grace has had a bite to eat. She's a good soul and Lorna will be fine with her. As well as allowing Ruth more freedom it will give me a rest – I'm not as fit as I thought I was,' she ended with a rueful smile.

'But I could have looked after Lorna!' The words were torn from Shona in a flurry of rage. 'I said I would come over to help out. You or Ruth only had to mention it to me and I would have had the baby over at Mo Dhachaidh to stay for as long as it was needed. Oh God, Kirsteen! Surely you're not so blind as to see that I love having her – I – I've been looking forward to coming over here to help with her, take her out in her pram!' Her eyes were bright, her cheeks red with temper, but Kirsteen, weary with broken nights and busy days, was in no mood to deal with anyone's tantrums, let alone Shona's.

'It's up to Ruth to decide what's best for her own baby,' she said rather coldly. 'Besides, we were all under the impression that you were going off with your own family.'

'Who told you that?' rapped Shona curtly, fighting down an almost irresistible urge to shout. Her fists were clenched at her sides, so tightly the knuckles showed white.

Kirsteen ran her fingers through her crisp curls in a weary gesture. 'Niall did – and Ellie too – they seemed convinced that you wanted to go and were only pretending otherwise. When they came over last night Niall laughed and said you would change your mind at the last minute because all week you had been dithering about whether to go or not. As a matter of fact your father was surprised to learn you didn't jump at the chance right away. You're always saying how much you miss Niall and you do tend to moon around till he comes back, so it was natural for us all to assume you wouldn't want to be left on your own when you had the opportunity to enjoy yourself with your husband and daughter.'

'Moon around!' Shona picked out the phrase that most annoyed her. 'Just where did you get that idea, I'd like to know? I have plenty and enough to keep me busy.'

'Have you?' Kirsteen sounded unusually sarcastic but Shona was too incensed to realize that it sprung from weariness and a desire only for a little peace.

She almost stamped her foot and had to exert all her control not to do so. Cheeks crimson, nostrils white, she grated, 'Ay, I have that, Kirsteen. I'm not Ruth; you can't keep your eye on me at every turn, so can't possibly know what I do with my time. As for all these assumptions about me! It's high time everyone realized I have a mind of my own!' Kirsteen stared in disbelief at this but Shona, fury making her oblivious to the ludicrousness of her own words, went racing on. 'If I had wanted to go with Niall I would have said so from the start and that's an end of the matter.'

Kirsteen's blue eyes were sparking now. 'Good!' she clipped. 'Now we all know where we stand and for once I might get a bit of peace and quiet around here!' She turned away, throwing over her shoulder, 'It's hot, I'm going to have some lemonade. Are you coming – or can't you make up your mind?'

Shona's nostrils dilated, she hesitated, then decisively stamped after Kirsteen. The kitchen was cool after the heat of the sun, with all the windows thrown wide to catch the breezes. Aunt Grace was at the table, very erect, one finger crooked daintily on the handle of a rose-sprigged, bone china cup, part of Kirsteen's best tea service. A widow, sixty behind her, with a fat, genial pink and white face in which bright beady eyes peered inquisitively, quaintly old-fashioned in her attire, slow and calm and capable in her manner, she looked like a small battleship, guns drawn in, ready to fire them if the need arose. Her saucer placed strategically under her chin, a drip at her nose from the steaming tea, the cherries in her frayed hat dangling cheerfully over ears which looked in danger of amputation from the half dozen or so fierce-looking hatpins which held the creation in place, she cocked a beady eye at the flies sticking to the fly paper above the window, seemingly enjoying the buzzing of their trapped wings.

'Nothing like a good hot cuppy to stoke the boilers,' she greeted Shona affably, wiping away her drip with the corner of her flowery frock. 'I canny bide the coloured water they serve on the boat and I am drinking enough now to keep me going for a whily.'

Kirsteen managed a smile. Indeed it was impossible to be straight faced when in the company of Aunt Grace; one of the reasons Dugald had so enjoyed his visits to her croft on Coll. 'I'll give you a flask away with you, Aunt Grace,' offered Kirsteen. 'Though at the rate you drink tea a milk churn might be more suitable.'

Shona wanted not to like the equable little woman who was going to take Lorna away, spoiling all the anticipated joys that should rightfully have been hers, leaving in their place a week that stretched interminably ahead, a week in which there would be no Niall, no Ellie. But instead she found herself smiling as Aunt Grace giggled at Kirsteen's words and without haste helped herself to another cup of tea, her hanky fluttering over her nose as if in readiness for the coming drips.

Shona caught Kirsteen's eye, saw her ready smile. She smiled back, feeling petty and ashamed. She had vowed to help the older woman and instead she had come here today and behaved abominably, as if it was all Kirsteen's fault, as if she was the injured party in a family crisis which called for patience and understanding, not angry words and an introspective obsession with her own needs and desires. It came home to her that Morag must be really ill for Ruth to dream of parting with her baby for even a short while.

Aunt Grace put down her cup, wiped her mouth thoroughly with her hanky, straightened her hat, and with a beaming smile announced that she was ready to leave.

'I'll come with you,' offered Shona. 'You'll have your hands full.'

Kirsteen threw her a grateful look and they set off, Shona holding the baby, Aunt Grace carrying the suitcases.

'I am stopping by to see Dugald before I go,' she informed Shona. 'The poor mannie is having a hard time these days – and poor Morag too. What a way to end up, and her such an active body in her day. I mind o' her when she was just a lass and though she was aye a quiet one, there was a contentment about her and she was kindly too in her own way. She has brought all this on herself, of course, the mind can do strange things to the body and lookin' at her it is no' hard to tell she has no will to live. Any other cratur' might go on for years wi' a failin' mind, but Morag will no' last very long. If she sees the month out no one will be more surprised than myself.'

Dugald greeted his sister with quiet affection and they disappeared inside so that Aunt Grace could say goodbye to Morag. 'Though it will just be a waste o' time,' Aunt

Grace said sadly, 'the poor soul doesny know one face from another, yet there are times when she looks as if she knows more than she lets on.'

Ruth came out to cuddle her daughter and kiss her goodbye. She was thin and strained looking and Shona said sympathetically, 'How is your mother today, Ruth?'

'She ought to be better than she is.' Ruth sounded puzzled. 'Lachlan says she could recover completely from the stroke but she won't make any effort to do the things that he and Babbie tell her; also she's getting thinner by the hour. None of us can get her to eat a proper meal.'

Aunt Grace appeared, her genial face quite sad, though she made her goodbyes cheerily enough. Once out of earshot of the house however she clicked her tongue and sighed heavily. 'Ach me, thon's a poor sickly cratur' right enough. She has the look o' daith on her and that's a fact though I never said a word o' that to Dugald. Mind you, I canny be sad about it for it's what she seems to want and it would be a blessing for my brother too. I was never happy about him marryin' the lassie, she wasny the one for him – but there you are – what's for us will no' go by us but he's had to bear the brunt of a cratur' like Morag for too long now. But of course the same rule applies to us all and that which is comin' to Morag will surely no' take any short cuts round about – no indeed.'

She was puffing a little as they reached the harbour and Shona took her arm to help her over the various pieces of equipment strewn about the pier. They stopped at the gangplank and Shona reluctantly handed the baby over and on impulse stooped to give Aunt Grace a hug and a kiss on her warm cheek. The little woman beamed and patted Shona's head as if she was a little girl, then turned to go up the gangplank. Her hat was rakishly awry, the cherries glinted in the sun, dangling and swaying in keeping with the bobbing of Aunt Grace's head. Once on deck a good-natured galley-boy relieved her of her cases and led her to a seat near the lifeboat so that she would be in the lee of the wind when the boat turned.

Shona waved and turned away, her steps taking her away from the harbour and up to the high cliffs of Burg where the wind soughed and the sheep cropped the sweet turf. Here it was lonely, wide and wild with the seabirds wheeling and swooping. Far below was the great curve of the bay with its golden sands and pink rocks, further out the black ragged reefs glistening with sea spray which toppled over the fat shiny bodies of the grey Atlantic seals sunning themselves on smooth niches. Further in, under the lee of the cliff, was the Well O' Weeping, spouting up out of an underground cavern. The well, it was said, had been made by the tears of the widows who came there to mourn their menfolk when a ship was lost at sea and some of the womenfolk too had disappeared after a visit to the Well O' Weeping and had never returned. The old folks maintained that the widows, demented with grief, had simply walked into the sea and drowned, though the younger ones scoffed at this and thought it more likely that they had been unable to bear living on the island with their sons and husbands gone and had left by the usual conventional means. But even the young ones listened when the Seanachaidhs wove their own special brand of mystery into the legend of the Well O' Weeping. Gathered round a peat fire on a winter's night with the wind howling and wailing outside it was easy to believe anything told by the Seanachaidhs.

Shona's gaze travelled again to the Well O' Weeping, in her mind's eye picturing the black-garbed womenfolk at the place of pilgrimage, never finding solace in that wild, forsaken spot with the wind shrieking into the caverns and the ever-present roar of the sea reminding them continually of its might.

'How lonely,' thought Shona, a mood washing over her that she couldn't define. 'How alone they must have felt knowing that they would never see their menfolk again – how very, very lonely.'

Almost unwillingly she tore her gaze away from the oddly hypnotic spot and even more reluctantly allowed her eyes to sweep slowly over the coastline, her gaze travelling across the calm coastal waters to the broad deep blue ribbon of the Sound, sparkling spectacularly, embracing the pale horizon. The trawlers many miles away were mere specks, the steamer, well into the Sound, puffed out thin wisps of smoke from its funnels. Strange to think that Aunt Grace, to whom she had recently talked, was now some miles away – and so too was darling little Lorna.

The Sea Urchin was captured unexpectedly in her vision.

It was hugging the coastline, a tiny dot, only distinguishable by the route it was taking, set on a course for Hanaay which was a mere hazy blue blob far far away.

'I should have gone with them.' She spoke the words aloud, a continuation of the thoughts which had plagued her since their departure. 'Kirsteen was right, I should have gone.'

She put out her tongue, surprised to taste the salt of her tears. She hadn't been aware that she was crying and it frightened her because she didn't know why she was crying – except . . . The niggle of unease that had been with her all morning intensified, crawled deep in her belly so that she shuddered and turned her back on the sea, as if by doing so she could forget all the loved ones it contained on its wilful bosom.

She arrived at Mo Dhachaidh in a pensive mood, trying to shut her mind to the silence of the house, feeding Woody and the hens, filling the time with a hundred and one small tasks with which she normally never bothered. At teatime she took her tray out to the garden and whilst eating her solitary repast occupied herself by mentally marking down all that still needed doing in the wall-enclosed suntrap. Things were slowly beginning to take shape. The rambling roses decked the wall in a bower of deep blushing pink; the lupins, recently flattened by the strong winds, had been resurrected and tied on cane supports, the fuchsia bushes were a riot of purples and reds; the yellow and orange trumpets of tom thumbs splashed their vivid colours along the foot of the wall, invaded by furry brown bumblebees whose legs were made comically clumsy by little sacks of pollen.

Woody purred, the chickens clucked and she felt lazy and good – except for that odd little niggle of foreboding that was constantly at the back of her mind. After tea she resumed her belated paperwork and when it was finally complete she went upstairs to tidy Ellie's room, sighing a little at the chaos which met her, smiling as she straightened the various skulls which decorated the dressing-table top. Not until she was about to leave the room did she see the note stuck into the grinning jaws of a conger eel skull hanging on a coat hook behind the door. The writing was untidy and it had obviously been written in a hurry as scant attention had been paid to the spelling.

Mother,

I'm glad I'll not be here to hear you moaning about the mess. I couldn't find my other shorts and pulled out every drawer before I remembered you had put them in my case yesterday. If you come with us you won't find this note. I hope you don't (find the note) because Father is planning some lovely things for us to do and see. His eyes were shiny when he told me about them – that lovely big shine that comes to them when he's partic very happy (I can spell the other word but can't be bothered looking in the dictionray). If you don't come I love you anyway, if you do you'll

know I love you because I'll bring you a cuppy every morning with the milk in first the way you lick it (I mean like!).
Ellie

She threw the note down and went quickly from the room, her throat tight. When she went into her own room and saw that Niall had half-packed a case for her, remorse tore her in two, mingling with a vague restlessness that wouldn't be stilled.

Chapter Nine

The feeling was still with her next morning, and after breakfast she packed a picnic lunch and went round to the shed where Biddy's ancient bicycle was housed. Niall had stripped, cleaned and oiled it and it squeaked only slightly as she made her way up Glen Fallan towards the moors. The morning had started cool with a mist shrouding the hilltops but now it was rolling away to reveal patches of cornflower blue sky. The grass verges were bright with clover and yarrow, huge clumps of dandelions the colour of ripe butter starred the banks interspersed with buttercups and purple thistles; the scent of wild thyme was heavy in the air merging with the delicate scent of pale blue harebells. The fields of Croynachan hadn't yet been cut and the hay was a ripe yellow. Highland cattle browsed contentedly among the sweet clover-strewn grass; on the high ground a field of barley, silvered by the wind, swung its pearly fronds to and fro. The numerous reedy lochans that studded the moors were like deep blue sparkling sapphires set amongst the fresh spikes of heather growing on mossy knolls. The lochans were the nurseries for grey lag geese and Shona stopped for a while to watch the parent birds fussing around their fully fledged goslings.

Shona laughed at the antics of the chicks, peeping at her inquisitively from the cover of the reeds, one or two of the more daring paddling out for a quick swim before darting once more for cover.

Larks were trilling high overhead while peewits tumbled and frolicked across the endless acres, wild with the delight of the great empty spaces that were theirs to command. Pheasants strutted unhurriedly across the track, the bronze and purple of their plumage flashing jewel-like against the more sombre moor grasses. Shona breathed deeply, glad that she had come to a place where a sense of freedom, like no other on earth, breathed from panoramas of sea, sky, machair and moor.

The peat hags were only just starting to be opened at this end of the island and several groups of people were busy, their spades raised in greeting as Shona cycled by, the wind lifting her hair, spurring the roses to her cheeks.

She had no conscious idea of where she was going but it was enough for her to be out in the gloriously perfumed air, to feel the blood surging through her veins, awakening her senses to all the delights of burgeoning summer. When she finally arrived at the abbey ruins near Dunuaigh she propped her bike against a crumbling wall and flopped down on a heathery knoll to just sit and let the unearthly peace of the forsaken hollow soak into her. To some it was an eerie place, desolate, forgotten, but from childhood she had loved it, finding its stillness a balm to any mood she happened to be in. The old abbey itself was a place of wonder and mystery, there was an odd, poignant beauty in its mellow mossy stones which were held together by shrubby roots and by the twisted saplings that grew out of the walls. The secrets, the sadnesses of the past lay here, nothing that was of the present intruded, except for the odd pieces of earthenware left by the tinkers and which might have belonged to a bygone way of life.

As children she and Niall had played among the stones, never tiring of it, always discovering something to fire their imaginations. Once it had been a pile of old bones in a burial chamber behind the altar stone, another time they had found a piece of roughly woven cloth hidden deep in the earth and well enough preserved to make them think it might once have been worn by the monks who had worshipped here.

She had lost count of the times they had stood in the arched window apertures, shading their eyes as they stared into the distance, pretending alarm as imaginary bands of Viking raiders came ever nearer, murder in their fiery eyes, terror in their fearsome weapons. Sometimes she had been genuinely frightened by Niall's vivid descriptions of his imaginary sightings and she had wanted to jump down and hide somewhere safe. But she had seldom given in to her fears. In those days she was continually having to prove to him that she was as good as or better than any boy, showing him a toughness she didn't always feel.

She cupped her chin in her hands and let her thoughts wander, smiling as she remembered the fun they'd had, sighing a little for those magical, far-off childhood days. Echoes of things she had thought forgotten came back to her and in her mind's eye she saw herself as she had been, a skinny, leggy nymph with a mass of auburn hair and a brown, sunburned face more often than not streaked with dirt. By comparison Niall had been sturdily built, fair curls blowing in the wind, calm brown eyes regarding her thoughtfully, occasionally smouldering into anger when she threw one of her temper tantrums.

How odd, how very odd it all was, she mused, she and Niall sharing childhood days, growing up to become man and wife, having a child of their own. Yet nothing in this place had changed, a bit more overgrown perhaps, but basically the same as it had been for hundreds of years. If she was to come back a hundred years from now it might look much as it did at present, slightly more weathered, a little less of the old stone left, but that would be all. It was so far removed from the modern world, conventions didn't matter, there was no one to criticize, no one to watch, if she was to revert back in time for a little while it wouldn't matter to anyone. In a mood of abandon she removed her shoes and stockings, carrying them as she wandered through the cool tracts of mossy ground between banks of wildflowers. A surge of excitement such as she had often experienced in childhood passed through her and she began to skip the way Ellie did during walks, revelling in a carefree method of locomotion that had been forgotten with passing years. Two streams came off the hill on this stretch of moor and without hesitation she paddled in, holding her breath as the freezing water tumbled over her feet. The peaty brown water was full of small trout which nibbled her toes whenever she stood still. With arms outstretched she played the game of the stones that she had so often played with Niall in the past, following the course of the burn by jumping from stone to stone, the first to get wet feet a cissy. She forgot time, forgot everything but the pure joy of behaving like a small girl again with no one about to make derogatory comments. So wrapped up was she in her game, she didn't notice where the stream was taking her till the mewing of a buzzard made her glance up. In front of her was Dunuaigh, the Hill of the Tomb, and more immediately a tall, twisted but sturdy birch tree, its branches bearing delicate fronds of tiny green leaves which threw cool shadows on the tangle of bracken and brambles beneath.

She stared in wonder, her blue eyes mirroring her reflective mood. 'Niall's tree!' she said, remembering how he had planted it to mark the entrance to 'their' cave, never dreaming it would survive one winter, let alone – using her fingers she ticked off the years.

'Twenty-five.' Her voice came out in an awed whisper. 'Twenty-five years.' She had thought that the tree would have died long ago, beaten down by the savage winter winds and rains hurtling over the exposed land from the wild Atlantic. She hadn't been near the spot since she had left the island to make her home on the mainland, had almost forgotten Dunuaigh, the tree – the cave . . .

Her breath caught in her throat and splashing out of the burn she ran to the tree, reaching up to touch its leaves. They were smooth and cold between her fingers and for a long moment she savoured the feel of them then suddenly and imperatively she began to pull back the undergrowth, but still she was unable to find the entrance to the cave that had once meant so much to her and Niall. Snagging her clothes, pricking her fingers, stinging herself on nettles, she eventually cleared a space through which she could crawl, then she was inside, standing up, dusting herself down, pulling bits of grass and fern from her hair. The tunnel she had made through the undergrowth allowed the daylight to filter in, letting her see that it was all as she and Niall had left it last time they were here. Her brow furrowed as she tried to remember exactly when that was – 1941 – July 1941 – twenty years ago. It was too long ago to recall the exact day but as soon as she got home she would look up her old diaries. Strange that she should come back, almost as if something had pulled her to the spot. She stared around; nothing had changed; the wickerwork chairs still stood, one on either side of the stone 'fireplace'; the dolls that Mirabelle had made were lying on the shelves among cups and various oddments of kitchen utensils, all covered in dust and cobwebs.

Beside the cruisie there were even the remains of the

matches she had struck so frantically whilst in the throes of lonely childbirth – she shuddered and forced her mind away from that time, thinking instead of that day all those years ago when she and Niall had come here – there had been a reason – he had wanted to still the fears she had about marriage, to take away the guilt she had harboured since the birth of their stillborn son, she had been haunted by it and hadn't wanted to face the reality that marriage to Niall would bring. But he had stilled her fears – had loved her, tenderly, passionately, completely and he had succeeded in taking away the shadows of the past. She shivered again, wondering why her steps had led her here today, almost as if she had been meant to come back, a pilgrimage to make her realize how lucky she was in her marriage. 'Niall,' she murmured, 'we've been so happy, we've had so much love in our lives – and Ellie has made it complete.'

But she wasn't complete, that was the root of her present unrest and she faced it that morning in the cave at Dunuaigh. It had all started with Ruth and her baby – yet it went back further than that, back a long way. The advent of little Lorna had brought it all to the surface, that was all. It was as simple as that. She gritted her teeth. 'I'm not going to think about it anymore,' she vowed there and then. 'I'm a lucky bitch, I've got Ellie, she's all I want . . .'

In a burst of determined energy she set about cleaning the cave, as if by doing so she could dust the cobwebs from her mind, rid herself of useless longings. Using a hand brush and shovel she found by the fireplace she brushed furiously till the layers of cobwebs were dissipated, with her dampened hanky she lifted as much dust as was possible. Eventually she stood back, hot but satisfied, taking a last look round. 'I'll never come back here,' she vowed aloud. 'There's no reason now, it all belongs in the past.'

Rather pensively she went back outside to the sun. With a last affectionate pat on the silver trunk of the birch tree she made her way back to the abbey where she took her lunch from her saddlebag and sat with her back against a wall to eat chicken sandwiches and fruit cake washed down with a flask of cold creamy milk.

She had no desire now to stay in the hollow and getting back on her bike she cycled round to Glenriach and was nearing Loch Tenee when she saw a black bicycle much like her own propped against a rock. Beside it, gazing over the loch was the unmistakable figure of Mark James.

The brakes of Biddy's bike squealed in protest as she jammed them on and any dignified meeting she might have harboured in her mind was immediately squashed as, with one foot drawing sparks from the road, the bicycle careered on, coming to an abrupt halt at the verge, throwing her off amid thumps, squeaks and muffled curses.

Mark James was at her side, helping her up, brushing her down, anxiety fighting the twinkle she glimpsed in his eyes.

'Ach, I'm fine, go ahead and laugh if you want,' she told him sharply. 'I don't think I've broken anything so you don't have to fuss like a mother hen.'

'Fine you may feel, but you look as if you've been in the wars,' he hazarded, eyeing the red blotches on her legs and the scratches on her arms, his mouth twitching at sight of the dust marring her dress and lying in streaks across her suntanned limbs.

She glanced down at herself and laughed. 'You mustny bother about me, I've been out all morning enjoying myself.'

The engaging grin that had captivated her from the start, beamed out. 'You have some quaint ideas about having fun – you ought to bathe those scratches before they fester.'

'I'm a good healer,' she told him but nevertheless ran down to the edge of the loch to plunge her arms in. 'I'm sorry I interrupted you,' she threw over her shoulder. 'I canny bide it if anybody does the same to me.'

He came to stand by her, tall enough to make her crick her neck to look up at him. He loomed against the blue sky, clean looking in a white shirt tucked into fawn slacks, his feet encased in open sandals.

'I was only having a bite of lunch at the lochside. Tina packed it for me and then bundled me out of the Manse, complete with John Grey's bicycle, a legacy for the next in line, I suppose. Tina thinks I don't get enough fresh air. She has gone all motherly on me lately so I thought I'd better do as I was told.'

Shona straightened, keeping her eyes averted, not wanting to meet his quizzical gaze. 'I'd better be getting on, time

passes so quickly on a day like this I just forgot about it.'
She went over to examine her bike, relieved when she
saw that the jolt had made little impression on the tough
framework.

'I'm finished here,' he called, 'I'll get you along the
road.' He began to pack up, every movement slow and
leisurely, reminding her of Woody in a lazy mood. 'Which
way are you going?' he asked as he came up pushing his
bike and when she told him she intended to go back via
the high road he said easily, 'Suits me, I'm making some
house calls this afternoon and there's one or two folk live
in that direction.'

She hesitated, wondering if it was too late to change
her mind, tell him that she was going the harbour route
after all. But he was already away, wobbling a little as he
waited for her to catch up.

'Och to hell, what's the harm?' she argued with herself
and mounted quickly. He was easy to talk to, asking
her things about herself, her family, genuinely interested,
amused at some of the anecdotes she related, yet he
made scant reference to his own life and she couldn't
stop herself from wondering why. But it was so pleasant
cycling alongside him, feeling the sun on her face, the
wind in her hair, his deep pleasant voice in her ears,
that she forgot about everything and gave herself up
to the pleasures of the moment. At the hill track they
were about to go their separate ways when Dodie loomed
over the brae, his nut-brown face showing his pleasure at

sight of them. The minister had obviously encountered the old eccentric before and was ready to return the familiar greeting in kind, batting not one eyelid at sight of Dodie's garb which was the same, winter and summer alike, nary a nostril wrinkling at the smells emanating from the big, wellington-encased feet.

'I was wondering,' Dodie began, 'if you would like to be coming to my house for a wee strupak. I dinna get to come to kirk as much as I would like and haveny had a right chance to speak wi' you – I haveny the right dress for wearin' on the Sabbath and folks do nothing but sit in the pews and talk about the things you're wearing.' In his prim way he was lying. Shona knew fine that he could look smart enough when the notion took him but most of his life he had avoided going to church, only turning up in the kirkyard for funerals and occasionally weddings.

'I was aye thinkin' that God is no' just to be found in a kirk,' Dodie was explaining gloomily. 'I find Him all the time when I am wanderin' the moors. I sometimes let Him into my own hoosie forbye, but it is no' God I'm wantin' to see the day, it is yourself, Mr James. I'd like fine if you would be honourin' me wi' a visit.'

Shona eyed the old man, thinking that he was indeed growing sophisticated and she was further astounded when he fluttered an eyelid in her direction in an attempted wink and invited her along as well.

The tiny cottage in its picturesque setting of heathery hillock, flanked by a burn that tumbled over white stones, sparkled white in the sun. It had obviously just been painted and Shona suspected this was the reason Dodie had asked them back. Her suspicion was confirmed when the minister commented on the charm of the house and how well it was maintained. In an excess of pride Dodie puffed out his bony chest and nodded in eager agreement.

'Ay, ay, it's a fine wee house and does me and Ealasaid a treat. Now, will you be comin' this way, mind the sharn doesny get on your shoes, the sheeps drop it all over the place but I am no' mindin' for it makes a good manure for my vegetables, mashed in a bucket wi' a wee droppy water.'

Shona held her breath. History was about to be made. Dodie was actually leading them to his door and it would be the first time ever that a minister had been invited over the doorstep. But at the last minute he held up his stubby hand. They both stopped dead and she was afraid to look at her companion to see his reaction.

'Sit you down here.' Dodie indicated two flat rocks abutting into the cropped turf at the side of the cottage. 'I'll no' be a minute now,' he told them after they were settled. 'Just you enjoy the sun and be restin' your feets till I come back.'

He disappeared into the dim interior and there was silence. Shona looked down at her thumbs, twiddling them for a few moments before she dared to sneak a glance at the minister. He was sitting with his legs drawn up, his hands clasped round his kees – and – she smothered a giggle as she noticed that his face was red with suppressed mirth and that his lips were firmly compressed. Her strangled snort reached his ears and he simply couldn't keep back the laughter any longer. Throwing back his head he gave vent to gales of such infectious mirth she joined in, smothering hers into her hanky.

'Weesht!' she warned imperatively. 'Dodie's coming back.'

It was with little surprise that she saw what the old man was carrying and it was with a sense almost of gratitude that she accepted the big stick of juicy red rhubarb and the polky of sugar he pressed into her hands.

The minister showed admirable appreciation of the most unusual strupak ever offered him since his arrival to the island, dipping his rhubarb into the sugar with all the enthusiasm of a small boy.

Dodie, his big blunt hands folded over his chest, beamed at his visitors with paternal fondness. 'Ay, you're enjoying that and so you should right enough.' He fluttered his eyelid once again at Shona. 'This lassie will tell you it is the best rhubarb in all the island but I can trust her no' to be giving my bonny secret away.' He shuffled backwards a step. 'I will leave you in peace to enjoy it for I must go and see to my Ealasaid – dinna forget to put your polkies in your pouches – I was scunnered wi' all thon litter left by the towrists and dinna want to see the likes on my land again.'

Mark James got up and laid his hand on Dodie's bent

shoulder. 'God bless you, Dodie,' he said warmly. 'And thank you for the strupak – it's the nicest I ever had.'

Dodie blushed with pleasure and as he stumbled away he vowed to himself that he would go to kirk someday soon and this time it wouldn't be to a funeral – it would be to listen to the nice kind voice of the new minister talking about God in that straightforward way he had, no' wi' the yells o' thunder that the other ministers had unsuccessfully used to try and get their message over.

Shona was lost in thought, thinking about a day just like this when she and Niall had learned the secret of Dodie's rhubarb.

'A penny for them.' Mark James was beside her, looking down at her enquiringly.

'Och, I was just thinking. With Niall and Ellie both gone I find myself with a lot of time to think.'

'Why don't you come with me today?' The question was very direct. 'The old folks here are the most marvellous characters I've ever come across. I'm supposed to buck them up but when I leave it's with the feeling I've taken away more than I've given.'

'All right.' The answer was out before she quite realized it but it was too late to take it back. He was reaching out, courteously helping her up, his hands firm and warm in hers.

He was good company, she couldn't deny it, nor the fact that an easy rapport had sprung up between them. She also discovered that he had a sense of humour which became more apparent as time went on. At one point he halted his bike and reaching inside his saddlebag withdrew a crumpled tweed jacket which he shook briskly to remove the creases. From the pocket he extracted his dog collar and proceeded to fix it round his neck. Shrugging himself into the jacket he grinned at her rather sheepishly. 'The old folk like a minister to look the part so I always carry these things with me when I go visiting.'

'I know what you mean,' she laughed. 'Everything must fit into a category.'

'Especially ministers. I learned that lesson very harshly when I called one day at the doctor's house. Elspeth Morrison answered the door and her look of horror at seeing me minus my collar was something I won't forget in a hurry. I felt I had committed the worst cardinal sin of all and literally withered before her eyes. She was so angry at me she made no attempt to offer me a cuppy till Phebie came on the scene and sent her scuttling about her business. Behag is another who scares the pants off me. She only has to look at me and I wilt under her intimidating scrutiny. I often wish I had the courage to do as you did that day you came rushing out of the Post Office – or better—' He choked on a spurt of laughter and his eyes danced. 'I'd like to do it in front of the entire Sabbath congregation – just once, to see the horrified reaction on all those prim Sunday faces.' Shona shrieked with glee and they went on their way, indulging in all sorts of ridiculous nonsense so that, by the time they reached the first port of call, they were red faced and breathless. The house they approached was perched on the edge of the cliffs, surrounded by an oasis of emerald green turf on which a drift of fat brown hens clucked and poked. Old Meggie, a widow of ninety, came to meet them, leaning heavily on a gnarled walking stick, a tartan shawl thrown over her thin shoulders, a white peeny covering a black dress which reached to her ankles, her eyes shrewd and quick behind her glasses.

She entertained them with volatile ease, firing inquisitive questions about her fellow islanders with a speed that left them dazed, and all the while the sun streamed through the open door together with the hens and a collie dog who had one brown eye and one blue. The views across the cliffs to the Sound were entrancing and the old lady was able to tell them which fishing trawler was which, though they were just small dots on the glazed sea. 'I spend most o' my time watchin' the boats on the water,' she told them proudly. 'I like thon big fancy yachts though the wee fishing boats are the best o' the lot. I keek at them through my spyglasses and can watch them peeing over the side – ay – and a fine splash they make too if the water is fine and calm. It's no use at all on a rough sea.'

At this point the minister took a fit of coughing while Shona found it necessary to get out her hanky and blow her nose hard, both of them gratefully accepting the cup of tea proffered by Meggie whose eyes were twinkling mischievously at their discomfiture.

Before they left she hobbled to the mantelpiece where

sat a crinoline doll. With a devilishly merry chuckle she reached up a mottled hand and whipped away the doll to reveal a bottle of whisky which had been hiding under the full skirt. 'You'll hae a droppy, Minister?' she quavered and without waiting for an answer poured three good measures, downing hers in one gulp after making a short toast to Mark James regarding his new post. Shona went with her to rinse the glasses, a faint astonishment in her at the way Mark James had so speedily consumed his whisky, leaving hardly a drop at the bottom of the glass.

Old Meggie obviously approved of him, in the privacy of the tiny scullery confiding, 'He's a bonny mannie, that he is. I like it fine when he comes to visit. He can take a dram as good as the next man but you will never see him the worse for it – oh no. He's a man after my own heart for he doesny have to make you feart o' God in order to get his message over. I like the Lord better since the new minister came and that's a fact.'

She came outside to see them off, her white hanky fluttering in the wind till they were lost to view in a bend in the road.

A winding sheep track led to the home of Jack the Light, the taciturn ancient that Ellie loved to visit. Having spent much of his life alone he was shy and reserved with all but a privileged few, sharing his life with three dogs, several tamed wild rabbits, a goat, a cow and a three-legged cat who came bouncing to meet the visitors and usher them along, her tail high in the air.

Jack the Light was at his window, watching their approach, but when they went in he was fiddling with a brass ship's telescope, apparently engrossed with its workings, barely lifting his grey head to acknowledge their arrival.

Shona gazed round the room which so fascinated her daughter and found herself entranced in turn. Skulls and bones of all descriptions littered the mantelpiece and dresser, together with every type of seashell imaginable. Outside, propped against the front wall of the house, reposed the enormous jaw-bone of a whale which must have measured at least sixteen feet long.

The old man gruffly invited them to take a seat but Mark James declined, going instead to inspect the display of marine skulls on the dresser, touching each one, asking questions about them. Jack's rather grim countenance gradually relaxed, the frown lines departed as he blossomed visibly, after a while plunging eagerly into detailed accounts of how he had come by his treasures.

'Mostly they came in on the tide,' he nodded, his eyes faraway, as if he was watching the rollers tossing their spoils onto the beach. 'Every day something new, life was never dull for me in those days, oh no, aye something in the waves to occupy me – but here I am, no' even polite enough to offer you a dram – you will be havin' one wi' me?' His enquiry was anxious. 'I know fine some meenisters see it as the de'il's brew but it was the only thing that kept my bones warm in my days as keeper and I have it to thank for keepin' me alive now – my limbs get sore betimes but a droppy o' the good stuff soon puts me on my feets again.'

It was then Shona noticed that his hands were twisted with rheumatism and his walk, when he rose to get the whisky, was stiff and awkward, making him shuffle his feet like a toddler taking its first steps. She declined the whisky politely, feeling her face uncomfortably hot and she wondered at Mark James, who with a large whisky warming in his hands, gave no sign of having taken anything stronger than tea. The old man spoke about Ellie, his rheumy eyes glowing as he described her visits to his house and the interest she showed, not only in his collections, but in the stories attached to each one, though Shona suspected the same tales were repeated time and again.

'She'll make a fine wee doctor,' the old man said with gentle conviction. 'She has all the patience it takes for a job like that, forbye being as bright as a winter moon.' He got up stiffly, holding onto the arm of the chair while he flexed his knees though it was a surprisingly agile finger that he wagged at Shona while instructing her to 'Wait you there now, I have something I want you to give to Ellie when she comes home.'

He disappeared into another room and Shona, unable to contain herself a moment longer, leaned over and hissed, 'What on earth are you doing with all that whisky? Four calls we've made this afternoon, and you've had a dram at each one. You've had enough to floor a horse yet you seem as sober as a judge.'

Mark James kept her in suspense by smiling at her in a secretive fashion then he pulled back one side of his jacket to reveal a wide-necked flask reposing in the depths of an inside pocket. To demonstrate, he unearthed it, poured in his untouched whisky, stoppered it and placed it back in the pocket.

'If I was to drink all I'm given I'd be in a perpetual stupor,' he grinned. 'So I devised this little method for disposing of it. Later I'll put it into those little miniature bottles you get and give it back to the old folks at New Year.'

'Well, you cunning bu . . .' She caught the blasphemy in time as she remembered she was, after all, in the company of a minister, yet so relaxed did he make her feel it was an easy enough matter to say the kind of things she might say to Niall.

'I know,' he agreed. 'But you have to admit it's the only way to remain sober and yet not offend.'

'But – how did you manage it?' she asked in amazement. 'I was watching you all the time.'

'Not all the time. I'm a great one for stepping to the door to admire the view every so often and every one of the houses we visited today had a particularly fine outlook.'

Her appreciation of this was tinged with a certain amount of outrage. 'You might have invited me to join you in a breath of air! I feel as drunk as Tam McKinnon must feel after a night at the malt.'

He merely laughed. 'Och, c'mon now, don't get up on

your high horse. It has done you good to let your hair down and you don't have to answer to anybody. In my position I have to be careful, which doesn't mean to say I'm a stick in the mud. I enjoy a dram but there's a time and place for everything.'

Jack the Light shuffled back into the room, bearing a beautifully polished piece of wood in the shape of a seal complete with flippers. 'I found it on the shore and thought Ellie might like it. Old Dodie got his eye on it and I had a mind to let him have it but ach – he finds enough treasures of his own and had no need o' this one—' He broke off to look at the minister with respect. 'I see your glass is empty – I knew fine you would enjoy a dram and I'm thinkin' a big chiel like yourself could stand another.' But Mark James held up his hand and got to his feet with an alacrity that made Shona smile. 'Thank you, Jack, but no, I must be getting along but may say it's been a pleasure to make your acquaintance. I didn't get along as far as your house the last time but hope you don't mind if I come back.'

The old man was overcome, a gleam of tears showing in his eyes. 'Indeed no, I will look forward to it – I – well I'm no' a body who can be doing wi' a lot o' folk round my feets but sometimes it gets a wee bitty lonely and I'd welcome a crack wi' a mannie like yourself—' He lowered his voice bashfully. 'The way I like you is because you have never once mentioned the Lord to me, yet I feel, when you've gone, you will have left a wee bit o' Him behind – ay indeed.'

At the door he pressed something into Mark James's hands and red with embarrassment all but pushed him out of the door.

They were nearing the Manse when he stopped to unwrap the parcel. Nestling in the folds of paper was a magnificently curled ram's horn, its neck embedded with silver to strengthen it. A fine chain was attached to a tightly stoppered cork which came out with a pop. He sniffed. 'Whisky,' he laughed. 'I doubt if I'm not careful I'll be getting myself a reputation.' Inside the wrappings he found a hastily scrawled note which read: 'This is for your mantelpiece. It will sit there as innocent as you like as long as you never let the cailleachs catch you drinking from it. If truth be known it is them who gave us a taste for the good stuff in the first place by putting it in our feeding bottles when we were just bairnies. So if you ever want to blame somebody – blame them. Jack the Light.'

Shona gave vent to peals of laughter. 'The cratur' is right there but just the same I'd advise you never to let the likes of Elspeth Morrison catch you with that ram's horn to your lips!' She looked at him, his hair was tousled, a streak of dirt lay over the rugged contours of his face, a flush of sunburn freckled his sinewy arms.

'You have a way with the old folks,' she told him softly. 'They've taken you to their hearts.'

'I just let them talk, open out about their lives. Memories are the only things some of them have. Watch their faces when they drift back in time – they light up – glow.

Half the time I don't know who or what they're talking about, but the important thing is to let them see you're listening.' He looked at her keenly and she felt the smoky blue of his eyes penetrating deeply into her senses. 'Earlier you spoke about memories, we all have them, happy or sad they're always there at the edge of recall. The thing is not to dwell on them too much, leave that to the old, it's all they have – you have so much more and you're young enough to care what goes on in the present.'

'What about the future?' she asked quietly.

'It's important but an unknown quantity. It's natural to look forward as long as we don't expect too much, for very often you will be let down.'

'Such words of wisdom.' She wanted to make the words light but instead sounded serious.

He looked at his hands. 'I'm a rambling fool, that's all. I just – get the impression that you're going through a phase at the moment, torn between things that happened in the past and those that you would like to happen now.'

She flushed. 'You sound as if you know a lot about my life.'

'My dear Shona, I wish I did, I can only read what's written on your face – and I see a restlessness – a dissatisfaction with the things you already have which are so much more than many.'

Briefly he touched her hand then started to walk away towards the Manse, pushing his bike, saying over his shoulder, 'I have strict orders from Tina to be back by five and it's almost that now.'

In a few minutes he would be gone from her and already she felt bereft without his presence. At the last minute he turned, the smile on his lips warm. 'We must do this again sometime – it was nice to have your company.'

'Ay, we must.' She tried not to sound too eager.

His quizzical gaze bridged the distance that had sprung between them. 'Will I see you in kirk this Sabbath?'

The question caught her off-guard and colour flooded her face. He had noticed her absence from church when she herself had almost forgotten about it. She couldn't explain, even to herself, why she hadn't gone. Niall had been home and she had suggested they go for a long walk instead of the usual Sunday routine involving kirk and dinner at Laigmhor. He had looked at her rather strangely but had acceded readily enough. Yet she hadn't enjoyed the brisk walk over the cliffs; one half of her had been in kirk listening to the mellow voice of Mark James, the other half had been preoccupied in wondering what had made her break the habit of a lifetime when all the time she knew the answer and wouldn't face it.

But that day she did, looking at the tall handsome figure of Mark James standing against the sun, eyes crinkled, black hair wind tossed, she knew he had been the reason behind it all. He was in her thoughts too constantly for it to be safe and she had reasoned that the only way to forget about him would be to stay away from his magnetic presence. But it hadn't worked. The more she tried to forget him, the more she thought about him, and now she decided it might be better to behave as normal, force herself to see him not as a dangerously attractive man but as the rather mysterious minister who had come to the island with the sole purpose of carrying out his godly duties.

'I'll be there,' she said abruptly and pedalled quickly away without looking back once.

When she got home she went immediately upstairs to rummage in the box which contained all her personal possessions. There were so many diaries but it took her only a minute to pick out the one dated 1941. The entry was there all right, a brief chronicle of her visit to the cave with Niall, written under the seventh of July, exactly twenty years ago to the day.

How odd that she should go back to the spot exactly twenty years later but perhaps not so odd when she stopped to really think about it. Her subconscious had guided her to a place filled with precious beginnings. It had been the start of her life with Niall – a prelude to years of happy marriage. Today had been a kind of anniversary pilgrimage – nothing more – yet – that persistent niggle of foreboding was still in her making her feel afraid, though of what she didn't know.

Niall had been very much in her thoughts this morning, worming into her mind at every turn, making her too aware of how much she missed him. She felt suddenly cold and with a shudder closed the diary with a decisive snap. Her father had always said that she was possessed of too much imagination and he was right – the words of Mark James came to her, beating insistently inside her head, telling her not to dwell too much on things past, it was the present which mattered. She clasped her fingers to her mouth. He was right. She had so much that was good and wonderful in her life and when Niall and Ellie came home she would show them just how grateful and lucky she was to have them.

That night she went happy to bed but woke in the small hours, overwhelmed by a feeling of such loneliness she cried out and turned quickly to snuggle into the safety of Niall's arms – but he wasn't there – and she wondered if he was lying awake in a lonely bed, thinking about her, missing the feel of her arms about him as much as she missed his.

Chapter Ten

Ruth picked up her mother's dinner tray and carried it through to the parlour. Morag's bed had been brought down here to make it easier to tend her. It had been placed close by the window which afforded a view of the harbour, the kirk on the Hillock, the Manse, and the magnificent wide sweep of the Sound of Rhanna.

The weather had grown oppressively hot with thunder growling among the hills on and off for days and everyone was wondering 'if the damt thing was comin' or goin' or just hangin' about making noises like a cow wi' the wind'.

All the windows in the temple had been thrown wide but not a breeze stirred the curtains, even the cobwebs in the eaves hung grey and still.

Morag was propped against a pile of pillows, her once ruddy face pale and hollow so that her green eyes looked abnormally big. She had allowed Barra McLean to cut her hair and it sprang up in natural curls round her head, the redness of it a startling contrast to the wan face it framed. Her arms lay listlessly on the counterpane, the long bony fingers of her good right hand never at rest, continually plucking threads from the coverlet so that a ball of fluff had formed in the palm of her hand. Her other hand was limp and useless looking and lay passively on top of the Bible which never left her side, day or night.

She was muttering when Ruth came into the room, a weak unintelligible string of sounds which no one could understand. Ruth put the tray on a chair and helped her mother to sit up, talking to her calmly, chattering about everyday affairs. It was the only way she could dissipate the oddly eerie atmosphere in the room and though the sound of her own voice was hollow in her ears it had the effect of bringing some normality to bear. Patting the pillows into shape she gripped her mother's thin arm and attempted to pull her up. But she might not have bothered, Morag immediately sank back down again in hollow-eyed, hopeless apathy, her gaze fixed on the chimneys of the Manse, unblinking, uninterested.

'Mam, I've brought your dinner,' Ruth said, a note of despair in her voice as she visualized another long discourse of persuasion with little hope of any response. Since the scene in the kirk, Morag had refused nearly all nourishment, allowing herself an occasional sip of water, the only liquid she would allow to pass her lips.

'It's a nice salad, Mam.' Ruth tried to sound enthusiastic. 'And there's a dish of fresh strawberries sent over from the Manse gardens. Mr James picked them himself,' she ended persuasively.

The minister had paid several calls to the house and it was only during his visits that Morag showed a flicker of interest. He had talked to her, often for an hour and more, and the last time, while he was reading a passage from the Bible, her hand had come up to touch the book briefly before it fell back to her side. Tears had been in her eyes, spilling slowly over her face in soundless despair, wordlessly letting him know that she understood the things he was talking about.

At Ruth's words she pulled her head slowly round and one finger quivered outwards, as if pointing to the dish of fruit on the tray.

Ruth picked it up and took it over to the bed. 'That's right, Mam, you'll enjoy these.'

She held her breath as she pushed a juicy red berry between her mother's white lips. Morag lay against the pillows, the strawberry held in her mouth, but for her hair the only splash of colour against a background of white, then suddenly and violently she spat it out, wiping the juice from her chin, grimacing as if she had tasted poison.

'Och, Mam, you've got to eat sometime,' Ruth beseeched wearily. Her eyes strayed to the view from the window. Oh how she longed to run out there, away from the atmosphere of gloom which prevailed in the house. She had hardly seen anything of Rachel since the christening; how lovely it would be to go with her into the sweet green countryside where there was life, hope, freedom; to feel the exuberance of Rachel's spirit expanding her, bringing her out, making her wonderfully aware of the glories of the world – and how she longed too to see her little baby again. It had only been five days but seemed more like five months. She was only a wee thing but already she had such personality, she was so full of life, so comical with her toothless smiles and chuckles – she was joy, pure and simple. It seemed impossible to her now that she had ever entertained the idea of giving her child away to someone else and she shuddered at the very thought – She jumped out of her reverie. Her mother was talking, in a clear strong voice like the Morag of old and her words brought an icy dread to Ruth's soul.

'I've laid your white frock over the bed, Ruth, you must put it on right away – and see to it that you bathe first – clean – you must be clean, my girl, in your mind as well as all else. When you've had your bath you can read me a chapter of the Bible before your father comes home.'

Ruth felt panic rising in her breast. She was whisked back to the days of her early girlhood when her mother had spoken these selfsame words almost every waking day. Morag's green, unwavering stare was on her and, despite her shivers, Ruth opened her mouth to make some pacifying remark. Then she realized that her mother was not looking at her, but straight through her, as if she didn't exist, as if she was watching the phantoms of the past flitting through her distorted mind – but there was something else in Morag's eyes. Despite their glitter they lacked true life – there was a look of death in them – and Ruth knew in those moments that her mother didn't have long to live. She was approaching death without fuss or struggle, with her virtual refusal to take nourishment, willing the final curtain to fall over the miserable existence she had created for herself.

Ruth could stand no more. With a little whimper she limped hurriedly from the room, hardly seeing where she was going, her heart pounding in her breast so that she felt lightheaded. The walls of the kitchen closed in on her, crushing her, suffocating her . . . She wasn't prepared for another human being to be part of her terrified impressions, her father was next door, taking a break from the sick room, having his dinner in the comfortable atmosphere of her grandparents' house, but someone *was* there in her vision, a tall, dark spectre which wavered and blurred. She swayed and put out a hand to steady herself only to find it in a comforting grip. She was being led to a chair, made to sit down, a few minutes later finding a strong hot cup of tea in her hands. It burned her throat and she knew it had been laced with brandy but she didn't care and gulped it down thankfully. In a short while she felt better, her stomach had fallen back into place, her head had stopped swimming. Rachel was sitting in a chair beside her, drinking tea, her whole demeanour calm, relaxed – except for her eyes – they were dark with unease and Ruth knew she didn't feel happy in the house. The temple did that to people, unsettled them, made them look round anxiously as if seeking a way of escape. Rachel was watching her, eyebrows raised enquiringly, and in a rush it all came out, the crushing fear, the anxieties.

'Mam's dying, Rachel,' she said flatly. 'I saw it in her face just now. Sometimes she knows what's going on around her, at other times she lapses into a world of her own – she – says things. It's getting worse every day and I feel I don't want to go into her room ever again.'

Rachel stood up, a determined look in her turbulent eyes. Before Ruth could move or say anything she went to the door of Morag's room and, opening it, went boldly inside. Ruth watched, horrified. Her mother had never liked Rachel. Always she had feared the untamed, gypsy-like creature with her powerful personality and her ability to strike terror into her with just one glance of her dark, luminous eyes.

Ruth got up, almost knocking over her cup, limping over the floor to stand by the parlour door. Morag's pupils were dilated in abject fear. She had curled into a rigid ball, her good hand clenched into a fist and pressed to her chin while she cowered back against the pillows, as if trying to escape the contempt she always sensed in Rachel's attitude. An eerie whining sang at the back of her throat, her green eyes were wide and staring.

Rachel stood for a long moment looking at the pitiful creature whose weaknesses she had always loathed, especially as they had been the cause of Ruth's childhood humiliations, depths to which no human being deserved to sink – especially a sensitive girl like Ruth whose personality would have been squashed into obscurity if it hadn't been for her father. But there was no contempt in Rachel's eyes now, only pity for a fellow human who had needlessly led a life of misery and self-loathing. She took a few paces towards the bed. Morag's whimper rose to a high-pitched wail, her eyes rolled in terror, saliva oozed from her mouth to foam in bubbles over her chin.

'Leave her, Rachel,' implored Ruth but Rachel seemed not to hear. She had taken Morag's hands, holding them and stroking them in an oddly gentle gesture. Morag lay rigid, unmoving, but gradually her tremors died away, her eyes lost their wild look as they focused on Rachel's face, finding there a calm serenity that seemed to reach out and touch her. The girl's great dark eyes pierced her, driving demons of unrest beyond recall, flooding her soul with an unearthly peace.

Rachel's hands were now on her brow, stroking the temples with a soothing touch.

Gradually Morag's limbs uncurled and relaxed. She lay quite still while Rachel's hands, soft as the wings of butterflies, caressed her temples and the eyes of tranquillity gently bathed her spirit.

The Bible fell unnoticed from the bed and her eyes closed. Ruth looked on in wonder. All along everyone had said that Rachel 'had the power', was possessed of something which was beyond the comprehension of most people. On one or two occasions Ruth had witnessed the calming effect her friend had on people who were sick or afraid, but never before had she seen the extent of that gift and it awed but in no way frightened her. It was almost as if Rachel had hypnotized her mother, willed her into a near normal state of peace. Morag Ruadh was asleep, her thin face like a young girl's in its repose, all the lines of fear and anxiety erased from her brow, her mouth.

'Rachel, I love you,' Ruth said simply. 'Thank you for helping my Mam to find peace.'

Rachel smiled, a dimpled mischievous smile, and she was once again the girl Ruth knew, yet always in the future, she knew that when she thought of Rachel she would see her as two people, the lovely, self-assured, arrogant creature people either loved or hated, and the Rachel with a God-given gift which changed her into a tender, caring soul with healing at her fingertips.

Rachel indicated that she would come back later but just as she was leaving Lorn appeared. Quickly Ruth told him what had happened, afraid that he might turn his back on the girl who had so wronged his brother. But Lorn instead went over to Rachel and taking her hands looked deep into her eyes for a long long moment. Rachel felt her heart beating fast as she prepared herself for what was coming. He had hated her that day on the pier, had disliked the idea of her becoming his daughter's godmother, she had sensed his anger, his rejection of her as once she had rejected his brother – but these emotions had left him now, forgiveness was there, in the blue orbs that held her own with such intensity – and there was something else, something she didn't want to see and she turned away quickly before he could speak, pulling her hands out of his grasp, not looking again at the boy who reminded her too much of Lewis, awakened in her things she had to forget if she was to follow the course she had chosen for her life.

She was glad that Dugald appeared just then and she was able to make her escape from the house, not looking back, wondering if she had done the right thing following an impulse that had taken her to visit a woman who had always rejected her as being of evil blood. But there was no turning back now, she had promised to go back and see Morag – and after that she and Jon would go away, back to the world of music which they both loved – and she might never come back to Rhanna again. It held too many memories of things she had to forget as well as those other dangerous emotions that lurked under the surface.

Ruth was telling her father about everything that had happened while he had been absent and he sat beside her and took her hands. 'God knows we can be doing wi' all the help we can get just now, Ruthie – and so too does your mother. If she can find peace before she dies then Rachel deserves all the blessings we can give her.'

When Babbie arrived to change Morag and make the bed she was immediately struck by the change in her. Instead of objecting and complaining she lay passively and peacefully, allowing Babbie to carry out her ministrations in half the time it normally took. She noticed however that Morag was rapidly becoming emaciated and went through to ask Dugald if she still wasn't eating.

'Nary as much as a sup,' he sighed wearily. 'She has lost the will to live, lassie, that's a pure fact.'

'Let me try,' offered Babbie, but when she went through to try and persuade Morag to take a spoonful of broth she turned her head away and gazed towards the Manse. Babbie saw that the pulse in her neck was quivering weakly and she realized that Morag was nearing the end of her strength.

'I want the man o' God,' she spoke suddenly, her voice strong and determined. 'And I want Rachel.'

Mark James came immediately to the summons, taking his place by Morag's bed, but half an hour passed before Rachel came and when she did she came swiftly, running along the road, her long legs carrying her effortlessly. Morag watched as she came nearer and a wry smile twisted her mouth.

'See how the lass moves? I was once like that, able to run – free – free as a deer before I became – imprisoned.'

The normality of her words made everyone look at each other in amazement and wonder if some miracle had happened to throw Morag's decline into reverse but it soon became apparent that it had only been a temporary respite. With Mark James on one side and Rachel on the other she seemed contented and lay peacefully, her blue-lidded eyes closed.

'I'm very tired,' she murmured as if to herself, 'and ready now to go to the Lord.'

Ruth stared at her mother. Death was close, she knew, but surely – not that close. Morag's eyes opened and they were clear and strangely bright. 'Ruth, my lassie, take my hand.'

Ruth did as she was bid and Morag gazed up into the sweet young face that had so much of Dugald in it. 'Forgive me, Ruth, forgive me, my babby, for all the pain I've caused you – forgive me my sins, Ruth, I want to hear the words from your own bonny mouth.'

Ruth bit her lip. 'Of course I forgive you, Mam, it's human to sin and we are all human whether we like it or no'. Mam – oh, Mam!' she cried. 'Why have you tortured yourself so much? You areny a bad woman – you shouldn't have punished yourself so harshly . . .' She faltered and couldn't go on. Tearing her hand away she got up and stumbled away from the bed.

The clarity was going out of Morag's eyes, leaving them dull and heavy but when Dugald came to her side her long fingers curled over his with feverish strength.

'Doug, you've been a good man to me, the Lord knows you have. I'm sorry for all the heartache I've caused you. I went the wrong way, Doug, I see that now – now that it's too late. But you must go on without me and make your life. You have your lassie, you and she were aye close and will be closer still without me – weesht – I know where I'm going, I'm ready to go – you have your granddaughter too . . .' She turned her gaze upon Ruth. 'You called her after a mother who was neither here nor there to you, Ruth, it was a kindly thing to do.'

'Lorn gave her the name, Mam,' whispered Ruth.

Morag's eyes were glazing, turning inwards. 'Lorn did that?' she breathed, her sunken chest rising as she struggled to take in air. 'And I thought he hated me.'

'None of us hates you, Mam!' The protest was torn from Ruth. 'You hated yourself and that's the worst hate of all!'

Morag nodded weakly. 'Ay, lass, you're right—' She made a feeble little gesture with her hand. 'I saw nothing that I liked very much in myself. It wasny hard to feel as I did . . .' Her voice tailed off and she lay exhausted, the gauntness of her face very pronounced.

Mark James placed his arms about her and cradled her as if she was a baby while he spoke to her in a calm, soothing voice, reassuring her with his words of comfort.

Dugald took Ruth aside and told her, 'I think the time has come to call Lachlan. I'll go for him, Ruthie, and you will maybe go next door and fetch your grandparents.'

Lachlan sat down with a weary sigh, glad that afternoon visiting was over and he could relax for a while. Sometimes he felt the years weighing heavily upon him, times like now when his shoulders ached with tension and all he wanted to do was lie back and close his eyes with no sound of human voice in his ear, reciting tales of woe. A faint smile hovered at the corners of his sensitive mouth. How good it would be occasionally to stay in bed when he felt like it, to never have to look at a septic throat or make up another prescription again. Still he only had a few years to go before he retired – retired! God, how time flew. He could still remember plainly his student days, his clumsy inept attempts with needles – a scalpel – his sleepless nights of wondering if he would ever make it – ever become a qualified doctor. Now he could see it all in retrospect, his failures, his successes, recognize his limitations. The trouble was his patients didn't, they looked up to him, expected him to perform miracles, when often the answer to their problems lay within themselves, depended on their own frame of mind . . .

'Lazybones.' Phebie's soft voice broke across his thoughts – that was one voice he didn't mind, it seldom grated on his nerves. He was lucky he had a good marriage – a fine family to keep him going. Phebie was beside him, he could sense her presence, smell the freshness of her clothes.

'I'll massage your neck.' Her smooth hands were a treat on his skin and he stretched in contentment.

'Mmm, that's grand, all I need now is Ellie to fetch my slippers and put them on for me. I wonder how the wee wittrock is getting on.'

'Och, Ellie will be enjoying herself, never fear.' Phebie frowned suddenly. 'It's her mother who puzzles me a bitty just now. She was so keen to get back here yet all she seems to do is moon around – more so this whily back – since Lorna was born.'

Lachlan nodded. 'She's got baby fever, it can happen to women of her age – it happened to you and you were a lot younger than Shona. She's approaching a time when the chances of having more children might be less and she's beginning to panic a bit.'

'Ay, you'll be right,' Phebie said thoughtfully, thinking about a time when she had been desperate for another baby, her joy when Fiona eventually arrived on the scene. 'Another bairnie would have been the making of Shona, yet Niall is quite happy with Ellie.'

'Men are more contented with what they've got. It's in a woman's nature to hanker after more.' He opened one eye to look at her mischievously. 'Unlike the likes of me, they have never learned the secret of true contentment.'

Phebie smacked him playfully. 'Havers! You're too skinny to be an advert for contentment – it's plump folk like me who know the secret o' that.' From the window she saw a vehicle coming swiftly along the glen. Glancing at the clock she saw that it was five-thirty, time for the tea and scones she and Lachlan had every evening before surgery. But when Dugald's van pulled up at the gate she knew there would be no pleasant little tea break for her husband. She sighed, longing for the day when they could call time their own. But when she went to the door to meet Dugald, her face was full of the caring sympathy which Lachlan's patients had come to know and love. A swift glance at Dugald's anxious face told Lachlan that his mission was urgent and without a word he went at once to fetch his bag and followed Dugald out to his van. Morag had been one of his difficult cases, her illness being more

of the mind than the body. He had been unable to do a lot
for her, except try and make her as comfortable as possible.
There was no fight in her, none of the fierce instinctive
battle to hold onto life; rather the reverse, and his heart
was heavy as he followed Dugald into the house.

But it was too late for him to do anything more for
Morag. She had died soon after her husband left the house,
peacefully and without a murmur in the arms of the man
of God, holding the hands of her daughter, Rachel's hands
upon her brow, soothing her, sending her serenely into that
other world in which she hoped to meet her salvation. She
was peaceful and relaxed looking, free of the demons of
darkness that had haunted her for so long.

Old Jim Jim took out his hanky and gave his nose a
good hard blow, his eyes awash with the tears of a father's
sorrow. Morag Ruadh had often harassed him to the point
of breaking, she had bullied and complained till he 'was
near driven daft wi' her endless rantings'. Often he and
Isabel had wished her far away but never as far as she was
now. He looked at her lying so still and somehow small and
innocent – like the wee lassie he had nursed on his knee
many many moons ago. She was his daughter after all and
there was always something about death that wiped out the
bad in a body's life. He put his hand on Isabel's shoulder.
'She is better away, I see peace on her such as she never
had in life. The Lord has blessed her wi' His light.'

Isabel gave a watery sniff. 'Ay, you're right there, but
ach – it's sad – sad just the same – though mind,' her red

eyes lit on Rachel and the minister, 'if it hadny been for these good folk she might never have found the kind o' peace that lies on her face now. It was the one thing I was aye feart o' most – that my lassie would go to her grave an unhappy, restless soul that would never settle – a body neither o' the living nor the dead – wandering forever.'

The hairs on Jim Jim's neck rose. 'Weesht you, woman!' he rebuked sharply, the idea of a perpetually roaming Morag too much for him to bear. 'We could all be doin' wi' a dram to ease our nerves, I'm thinkin'. I know Morag didny approve but she's no' here now to be sayin' what she thinks.'

Isabel stared at him shocked and whispered, as if she was afraid of being overheard, 'Look to what you're sayin', you silly man. She *is* here unless my auld eyes are up to their tricks again. You canny say these things in front o' her.'

'Ach – balls!' Jim Jim's tones were defiant and though his steps were firm as he went from the room to fetch the whisky, it was noticeable that he took frequent looks over his shoulder as if to check that he was quite alone.

Half an hour later Lachlan took his leave, at the door taking Ruth's hand in a firm grip. 'You'll be able to have your wee girlie back home again, Ruth.'

'Ay, Doctor, I will that – it's just a pity – Mam never had the joy of her own wee granddaughter.' She took a deep breath.

It was over, finished, yet somehow she knew that it would never be over, that sometime in the future she would stop and remember a woman with fiery hair and strange green eyes, and she would feel a sadness in her for the mother she had never really known or understood.

The thunder was growling over the lowering hill peaks as Lachlan went down the path, leaving the temple behind. It was hot and clammy, making him more tired than normal, certainly too exhausted to face the prospect of evening surgery with a spring in his step – and certainly in no mood to be bothered with Behag Beag who was making her determined way towards him, her scuttling gait bringing her uncomfortably nearer, reminding him of an ancient hen in a quest for scraps.

'Doctor, Doctor, wait you there!' she ordered querulously as she crested a knoll, her head bobbing in agitation. 'I saw you from the Post Office and said to myself "there's the very mannie". I have an urgent message from the coastguard at Oban.' She sniffed. 'It's a good thing I am a diligent woman for it was past closing time when the call came through but I was never a body to turn my back on my duties. The clock might tell me it is time for me to go home and have a well-earned meal but wi' all the paperwork I have to do . . .'

'What is it, Behag?' He stemmed the flow of self-praise sharply, knowing that she had her eye on him as the vehicle through which she might be recommended for a long service award. He had no intention of giving in easily to her wiles nor was he going to tell her that her brother Robbie, for reasons of his own, had been to persuade him to set the wheels in motion. For Robbie's sake he had already spoken to the laird about it and he had promised to see what could be done when the time for Behag's retirement came nearer. Meanwhile Lachlan was quite enjoying the spectacle the postmistress was making of herself over the affair. She was altogether too nosy a creature for his liking. He wasn't the only one who resented the fact that she listened in to the conversations that came via her switchboard and could tell folks their business almost before they knew it themselves.

At his tone she sucked in her thin lips as if in preparation for one of the tight-lipped silences for which she was renowned, but this time she thought better of it and managed a sour smile instead as she imparted dourly, 'The line was cracklin' wi' all this damt thunder about but I managed to make out something about a fire on a boat. I never caught the name o' it but it is making for Rhanna wi' a badly injured body on board. The coastguard mannie asked for a doctor to be standin' by.'

'When will it be here?'

'Ach, the mannie's voice was cracklin' that bad I couldny make him out but I think he estimated two hours.'

Lachlan ran his fingers through his unruly hair. 'Well, I'd better get along to evening surgery then, and come down to the harbour later. Good evening to you, Behag.'

'Ay, to you as well.' Behag's jowls were sagging. Something in the doctor's attitude suggested an indifference towards her and she couldn't have that – not now. 'I'll get along back to the Post Office after I've had my dinner.' She managed not to sound ingratiating. 'Just in case the coastguard tries to get through again – if so I'll be lettin' you know.'

Lachlan relented. 'That's good of you, Behag, you certainly do take your job seriously. We must try to think of some way of showing our appreciation for when you retire.'

Behag's beady eyes lit up and she sprachled away with a spring in her step, only at the bottom of the hill slope experiencing a slight pang of guilt because she had forgotten to ask the doctor 'how was Morag Ruadh keeping?'

Chapter Eleven

Ellie was singing a sea shanty as she peeled potatoes at the neat sink in *The Sea Urchin*'s saloon. It had been a wonderful trip, first to Hanaay where they had stayed with Mac's sister, Nellie, in her neat croft beside the sea. There had been ceilidhs almost every other night and during the day her father had taken her on his calls. It had been great fun being a pillion passenger on his old motor bike, her arms round his waist, the wind whistling through her hair as they traversed the length and breadth of the island, visiting farm and croft. She had been enthralled watching his skilful ministrations to the working beasts, but best of all she liked the small animals, the litters of kittens snuggling in haylofts, the gangling sheepdog puppies, even a big black Mynah bird with an orange beak who, with a range of human voices at its command and a vast vocabulary of oaths, had made her shriek with merriment.

But nothing could beat the baby sea otter she had heard crying one night on the beach outside Nellie's Croft. On going to investigate she had found it to be injured and helpless. She had taken it back to the croft and her father had worked with it patiently, putting salve on its wounds, showing her how to feed and care for it. After that it had gone with her everywhere in a wickerwork cat basket, its endearing, babylike presence making up for not having her beloved Woody beside her. It had even gone to the ceilidhs at all the different houses and now it was aboard *The Sea Urchin*, her father having given her permission to keep it though he had raised his eyes and called upon God to help him. She giggled at the remembrance and went to peep at Tubby reclining in his basket, his small prehensile feet clasped round a baby's feeding bottle, his long luxuriant whiskers dripping with milk. He was perfectly at ease lying on his back, displaying the round furry stomach that had earned him his name, his eyes screwed tight shut in beatific concentration on his bottle. When he had finished the contents he gave a small chirrup of satisfaction before falling asleep with the teat still in his mouth, a most contented expression on his furry baby face.

Ellie could have stayed watching the fascinating and lovable little creature for hours but after a while she went back to slicing potatoes into chips, her eyes straying every so often to the window above the sink which afforded a view of the tiny uninhabited island of Breac Beag with its grassy plateau, white beaches and awesome overhanging cliffs. Here the gannets and fulmars made a fearsome din as they plummeted to the sea or perched on their nesting sites among the cliffs. But out here on *The Sea Urchin*, anchored in the bay some distance from the shore, the noise was softened and drifted quite pleasantly over the glassy waves. It was a hot calm day with the sea's surface visible for miles and not even the mutterings of thunder in the atmosphere could detract from the tranquillity.

This was the part of the trip she had most looked forward to and it had been everything she could have wished for. The weather had been perfect, blue skies and hot sun. She, her father and Captain Mac had swum in the sheltered bay and fished for hours in the dinghy catching dozens of saithe and mackerel. They had tramped the length and breadth of the island, seeing the bulk of Breac Mor slumbering in a blue haze a mile over the sea, finding the nests of lapwings, peewits and golden plover, discovering and exploring the numerous caves which pitted the cliffs along the coastline, spending a night in the old shepherd's cottage where they'd ceilidhed till the small hours.

Yet, delighted as she was with everything, she couldn't stop her thoughts straying to her mother, wishing she was here to enjoy it all with them. She knew her father wished so too. Often she caught him with a distant look in his eyes and when she challenged him once he had laughed in a discomfited way and said it felt strange not to have her mother's voice dinning away in his lugs.

'But – you're always away,' she had said, puzzled. 'So why are you missing her this week more than any other?'

'I'm not,' he had said seriously. 'I'm always like this when I'm away from her, you've just never been here to see it, that's all.'

'That's the only thing I don't like about coming to Rhanna,' she had said wistfully. 'You have to be away a lot and I can only come home for holidays. If we had stayed on Kintyre I could have gone to high school in Campbeltown and then I would have been home every night.'

'Ay, but there you used to moan because you didny see enough of your grandparents. Now you can have them every holiday and not just the odd one.'

She had brightened. 'Ay, that's true, I love living on Rhanna for that and for so many other things I can't count—' She had paused to study him quizzically. 'Why are you such a wise old father? I think I'll stop calling you father and call you Methuselah instead.'

He had taken her across his knee then and pretended to spank her, making her shout so heartily for mercy that Captain Mac had come running to see who was being killed.

She took the chip pan from the table and placed it on the neat little calor gas cooker. Until today her father wouldn't let her do any of the cooking, he and Mac producing the meals between them, which, though wholesome enough, lacked imagination, and after a few days all their palates had become jaded.

'Och, c'mon, Father,' she had wheedled earlier that day. 'I'm sick of tinned beans and corned beef – you and Captain Mac can trust me. I'm a big girl now and more capable than you think – and I'll be sick if I taste one more burnt baked bean!'

With a laugh he had acceded, his brown eyes resigned as always when he had capitulated to her. He and Captain Mac had gone off in the dinghy to the island leaving her to raid the cupboard, finally deciding to make fish and chips.

Tubby was making contented little chirping sounds from his basket and she twisted round to watch him, giggling as he opened wide his whiskery jaws in an enormous yawn. The table in the saloon was set, the crisply battered fried fish keeping hot in the oven. All she had to do now was wait for the chips to crisp to a nice golden brown, the way her mother made them and which never failed to draw a favourable comment from her father. She had never made chips before, and hoped anxiously that she would make a good job of them.

She glanced at the clock. The hands were at five-thirty and she wondered what her mother was doing at that exact moment. Having her tea most likely. At Slochmhor her grandparents would be having their usual tea and scones before the start of evening surgery. Grandpa McKenzie would be coming in from the fields about now, stripping to the waist to wash himself at the sink, his big brown body glistening with soap bubbles. Leaving the cooker for a minute she went to kiss the top of Tubby's silken head, wondering how Woody would react to a baby otter about the place – never mind Woody – how would her mother react? She rushed back to the cooker, saw that the chips were nearly ready and Mac and her father had still to wash before she could serve up tea. A peal of thunder directly

overhead made her jump in fright and she glanced out of
the window to see that the water was no longer calm but
rolling into the bay in big, glassy troughs. The sky was dark
and ominous looking, with a cap of thick grey cloud circling
the top of Dun Ree on Breac Beag. Big drops of rain were
starting to fall, in a few short moments growing into a
torrential downpour which pocked the shallow water near
the shore. The boat was rocking from side to side, swinging
round on its mooring so that her view was now of the open
sea. She left the cooker and went quickly to look from the
opposite window, a small sigh of relief escaping her as she
saw the dinghy casting into the water. In a short time her
father and Mac would be aboard and the chips wouldn't
be wasted after all – the chips . . . Even before she swung
round an ominous swooshing sound reached her ears. She
turned sharply and what she saw made her eyes widen in
terror, and she knew, she knew she should never have left
the cooker unattended. It was the one thing her father had
instilled into her before leaving her on her own.

Tubby had left his basket and in a playful mood had
sought out the chewed rubber ball which was his favourite
toy. Always he took it in his mouth and jumped with it to an
elevated position so that he could drop it down and watch
it bouncing. But this time he must have gone too near the
cooker and his rump had caught the chip pan, knocking it
over. It was on fire, boiling fat splashing onto the walls, the
flames spreading rapidly, igniting the paintwork, blistering
the wood. The breeze from the open hatch cover was

fanning the flames, making them whoosh outwards so that a tongue of fire licked the door frame.

Ellie stared petrified at the scene, her limbs locked with fear, her eyes huge in her drained face. In a dream she was aware that her knees were so weak they would hardly hold her up but she forced herself to move – to get Tubby. Snuggling the baby otter to her breast she bounded to the door, but it was too late. A ring of fire blocked her way, clouds of red hot smoke seared her lungs, making her cough violently. She heard whimpers of terror beating inside her head, like a puppy dog crying. For a moment she thought it was Tubby but he was cringing against her, making no attempt to break away, and she knew the sounds were coming from her own scorched throat.

The otter's eyes were rolling to white and he was chittering and whimpering in the same heartbroken voice she had heard him use on the shore before she had rescued him. Terror, livid and raw, enveloped her and she stood, not knowing which way to turn.

'Father, Father,' she whispered, 'please help me.' She opened her mouth wider to scream his name but the only sounds that came out were weak and husky, the heat in the saloon so intense it was biting into her lungs.

Her eyes were smarting so much she could barely see the inferno that was closing in on her but through a red hot misty blur she spotted the assortment of towels lying near the sink. With a terrified sob she grabbed two, throwing them into the sink to pump water over them. Into one she bundled Tubby, wrapping it round his dear plump little body till hardly a whisker showed, the other she wound round her head like a turban, covering her hair, her face, leaving only a chink to see through. Hoisting Tubby up she carried him up the steps to the top where she held him at arm's length so that she could thrust him through the wall of flame, and then she tossed him with all her strength, onto the deck, away from immediate danger. Flames engulfed her, red hot pain seared her flesh. She felt herself spinning through a vortex of living flame, her father's name was a mere breath on her lips. She fell back to the floor of the saloon, hearing a dull thud deep inside her head before she slipped swiftly into merciful unconsciousness.

Niall looked at his watch and saw that it was five-thirty. Ellie had ordered him to be back for six and he smiled as he thought of how she had instilled authority into her voice, of the way her chin had jutted – like Shona when she was putting over a point. Ellie was growing more and more like her mother every day and just before he had left *The Sea Urchin* that afternoon he had reminded her of this, telling her his life was going to be a hell with two shrewish women in the house.

'Ach, men are like babies,' she had answered ably, 'they need to be told what to do. How Mother managed you all these years I'll never know. It's a good job I'm getting old enough to give her a bit of support.'

'Come on, Mac,' he called to the old sea dog who was putting the finishing touches to the bonfire they had built on the shore round the point. It was to be a surprise for Ellie and they planned to come back later in the evening to cook sausages on it. Captain Mac drew a sleeve over his big nose and scrambled over the rocks to catch up with Niall, looking back with satisfaction at their afternoon's work.

'She'll make a bonny blaze,' he said enthusiastically. 'We'll have a fine ceilidh to ourselves and the smoke will keep the damt midgies away. I can have a dram or two behind the smokescreen, safe from prying eyes. That wee madam o' yours has been keeping an eye on me this trip and here was me thinkin' I was done wi' all that nagging wi' my cailleach out the road.'

'Ach, you love being told what to do,' laughed Niall. 'I watched you with Ellie and saw that tough old face of yours going as soft as butter.'

'She has a way wi' her I must admit,' grinned Mac. 'I told her if I could find some way o' shuttin' her up I might consider keepin' her on as the ship's mascot.'

Clambering over great outcrops of rock festooned with masses of sea pinks they came to the turf edging the bay, the green almost hidden by blue speedwell and the bright yellow of bird's-foot trefoil. The larks were singing, a swelling volume of sound that exploded melodiously into the reaches of the sky, on and on, never stopping.

Along the shore the oyster catchers were probing orange beaks into the rock pools. The colouring of the sea round Breac Beag was a delight to the eye, the tangle and sand in deep water giving alternating rainbows of mauve and green merging to blues and purples. They got into the dinghy, Captain Mac at the stern, Niall taking the oars, his strong arms taking them easily but surely out into Valsaal Bay, his eyes on the lowering clouds over Dun Ree, his bad ear crackling as an enormous clap of thunder sounded directly overhead followed by a torrential downpour that soaked them in seconds. The dinghy was like a cork in water that had suddenly turned rough and Niall bent his head into the rain as he struggled to make some headway. Mac's eyebrows were dripping rain all over his face and down his neck and he drew them close together so that they formed a hairy canopy over his eyes. He glanced up, screwing his face against the downpour, his mind on the meal that Ellie had said would be ready and waiting for their return. His eyes widened and he stared disbelievingly through the curtains of rain. His face blanched, his voice came out in a hoarse croak, 'Christ Almighty, man, the bloody boat's on fire!'

Niall's head jerked up and he twisted round. Smoke was billowing from *The Sea Urchin*, drifting across the green swelling troughs of the bay.

'The fuel tanks!' Captain Mac yelled. 'We'll have to get to her before she's blown out the bloody sea!'

'Oh, God, no!' Niall whispered, barely believing the

evidence of his own eyes, his shocked mind only able to register a few details at a time.

'*Ellie!*' He screamed the name, in his horror hardly able to make his limbs work, though seconds later he was rowing like one demented, his breath harsh in his throat as he hauled viciously at the oars, rowing as he had never rowed before, heart pounding, mouth agape. Once aboard they took in the situation rapidly. The cabin was so full of smoke they could see nothing through the dense clouds except tongues of flame licking through the perspex windows, curling over the rim of the door.

'*Ellie!*' Niall screamed the name again as he wrenched the fire extinguisher from its stay and charged with it towards the door. Captain Mac, hanging over the side soaking a rug with water, raised a sweating face. 'Niall!' he yelled imperatively. 'Put something over your head!'

But Niall was beyond hearing. With tears blinding him he played the foam along the rim of the door and in the temporary respite plunged through to stumble down the steps to drench the flames inside the saloon. The skin on his hands shrivelled, his hair and eyelashes were singed but in his anguish he felt nothing.

Ellie! Ellie! Ellie! The name swirled round inside his head. He was vaguely aware of Captain Mac coming in with a blanket in his hands. He dropped it over the stove before rushing outside for an extinguisher. Acrid smoke filled his throat, his arm brushed the red hot metal of the sink and he gave a cry of pain. With his arm over his face he fell to his knees and began crawling forward, his head cocked, listening for a sign of life, hearing only Mac's laboured breathing as he battled round the saloon, beating the flames out.

The smoke was receding slightly, allowing him to see the huddled form of his daughter on the floor.

'Ellie, Ellie,' he babbled the name then swung her into his arms to stagger up the steps to the deck. Captain Mac had picked up the foam extinguisher and was putting out the remainder of the flames, his red streaming eyes gaping wide. He saw the charred remnants of the chip pan on the cooker and went over to examine it, noting that it had tilted on the ring, splashing hot fat everywhere. That was what had happened, Ellie must have left the cooker for a few moments but that was all the time that was needed to start a fire like this . . . His shoulders sagged, he felt suddenly old.

He went on deck with a pile of soft sheets and blankets which he had retrieved from the cabins. Niall grabbed the sheets and gently wrapped Ellie in them then he knelt beside her to stroke the strands of hair from her brow. Because of the towel, her face had escaped the ravages of the fire, beyond that he hardly dared look, his mind already shocked by what he had glimpsed before he had enclosed her in the sheets.

'I'll get through to the coastguard at Oban.' Mac turned away, nausea seizing him. Hard and tough as he was his face screwed up and tears spilled onto his blackened cheeks. The radio equipment was at the far end of the saloon. Though covered in a sooty deposit it appeared undamaged and Mac sent up a prayer of thanks as he worked the switches. A bolt of thunder crashed almost directly above followed by a flash of lightning. The voice on the radio was faint, distorted by so much crackling it was difficult for Mac to assess how much of his message had been understood. He had decided to head for Rhanna, the island nearest Breac Beag with a resident doctor and he emphasized this fact together with everything else that was relevant to the situation. The voice on the other end was asking him to speak up then it grew fainter till there was nothing but crackling. Mac suddenly felt lost and helpless. Damn the buggering storm! It had to happen at a time like this! The only good thing about it was that the torrential rain had kept the deck of the boat cool and so had reduced the risk of the fuel tanks igniting.

Time was the most important factor in a case like this; the only thing to do was to lift anchor and get to Rhanna as speedily as possible. He went to the door. Niall was still on his knees beside his unconscious daughter, his shoulders hunched like an old man, shock lying stark across his face. He seemed incapable of action, so unlike the practical Niall that Mac knew so well. Mac made him take a swallow of brandy which was kept for emergencies. Mechanically his throat worked, he swallowed and coughed but kept on staring down at his daughter with unbelieving eyes.

The old sailor realized that the job of getting them back to dry land lay with him. Once more he tried the radio, but it was worse than ever and he abandoned it in favour of more practical action, glad of the chance to be doing something that he knew about. In a short time they were ready to go, soon Breac Beag was just a blur on a misty horizon. The storm had receded, the rain had been short-lived, but now a low haze lay over the water which made Mac curse.

Tubby had rolled from the towel into which he had been so carefully wrapped and stood on his hind legs chittering quietly. He dropped down on all fours and went shuffling over to touch Ellie's face with his cold, inquisitive nose; getting no response he dumped himself down beside her to curl himself into a ball, a pitiful lost cry at the back of his throat, like a baby waiting for its mother to come back from a long deep sleep.

Chapter Twelve

The boat came round the headland of Mara Òran Bay and Mac, at the wheel, gave heartfelt thanks as the harbour hove into view. Despite the haze on the water he had made good time and felt more hopeful at the prospect of delivering Ellie into Lachlan's capable hands.

Lachlan waited fretfully at the harbour with Babbie and a few of the village men who were standing by to offer their help. Everyone had wondered whether to take the lifeboat out to meet the expected vessel but had decided against it as being of little help since it wasn't clear which direction to look. The thunderstorm which had hit the island earlier had departed, leaving behind a misted blue evening with a calm sea reflecting the fishing boats tied up at the jetty. The Highland cattle had come down to cool their feet in the shallows and stood in a row, silently enjoying the cool comfort of the water; sheep bleated from the headland of Burg; seabirds called peacefully; the echoes of children's laughter drifted across the bay. It was an idyllic scene but Lachlan was growing impatient, his gaze focused seawards till the glare from the water forced him to look away.

'Come *on*,' he voiced his thoughts. 'Whoever they are

they will have a dead body on their hands if they don't get a move on.'

'It depends on the extent of the burns,' soothed Babbie. 'It might not be as bad as we've been imagining.'

Over the years she had come to know Lachlan well and she knew fine that his nerves would stretch tighter and tighter till he could put his skills and energies to good use. Not that he had so much energy of late. She couldn't help noticing the changes age was bringing to him, the signs of strain on his face, making it look gaunt at times. But at the sight of the boat his face cleared. The coastguard at Oban had been through to Behag again, telling her that they thought the name of the stricken boat was *The Sturgeon*, though they couldn't be certain of this. Lachlan's fingers tightened on the handle of his bag, as if he couldn't wait to get going.

The boat came nearer and Ranald, his binoculars at his eyes, threw back, 'It's no' her at all, Doctor, it's *The Sea Urchin* comin' home. Niall must have decided to come back early.'

Lachlan's eyes lit. God, it would be good to have them back! Shona might stop moping with Niall at home – perhaps they could all go for a picnic together, the McLachlans and the McKenzies – like that grand affair they had had one Easter over by Traigh Mor Bay. It was time they had a day like that again and Phebie could be doing with a change. So buoyed up did he feel that for an instant he even forgot why he was here at the harbour instead of at home with his feet up enjoying precious hours of relaxation.

Ranald's eyes blurred and the boat went out of focus, but not before he had noticed the blackened paintwork. His hand shook, it couldn't be . . . He called on Tam who squatted down beside him and held up the glasses. Tam's good-natured face puckered into a grimace of disbelief.

'It's her all right,' he murmured, horrified. 'She's the boat who got the coastguard to wire through a message to Behag.'

They both scrambled to their feet, their affection and concern for the doctor and his family showing in the dumb, agonized glances they threw at one another. The boat was coming closer, soon she would be tying up at the jetty where a space had been kept clear. Tam's throat worked. What to do, what to say, how to say it . . .

'Doctor, she's the boat we've been waitin' for!' It was out, unvarnished and raw, the words reeling harshly through the air. Tam's chin trembled and turning, he hurried away, the other men following on his heels, running to the jetty to await the boat.

For a few moments Lachlan didn't move. He looked as though he had just been punched, his eyes, dazed and blank, registered nothing. Babbie was aware that her legs were shaking. She stared at *The Sea Urchin* nearing the jetty. It couldn't be – her senses swam. Which one of the people on board had been injured? Captain Mac? That lovable old sea dog who in his time had weathered storm, flood, in his early days, a shipwreck . . . or . . . She couldn't think further, instead she prayed silently, God, God, whoever it is don't let them suffer. Don't let this man Lachlan know the pain of tending someone he loves . . . She was running beside Lachlan, forcing herself to keep up with his long, desperate stride. They reached the jetty as the boat was tying up. The men were at the foot of the steps ready to help . . . Lachlan cleared his throat and watched as one hypnotized as the men came up carrying a white wrapped bundle, their faces haggard, shocked—

'Ellie!' Lachlan's cry of recognition was a protest. His mouth twisted, almost as if it was painful to say the name. She was a crumpled small bundle, this beloved grandchild of his, held in Tam's arms, her golden hair spilling in a silken cascade against the rough tweed of his jacket. Gently Lachlan lifted the sheet aside – he didn't look again, instead he focused his attention on Ellie's face. She was awake, her brown eyes watching him, so big in the pale canvas of her face they were pools, sucking him in, drowning him in their pathos.

'I'm sorry, Grandpa,' she whispered. 'It was an accident, I was careful, I really was.' She shivered violently; a spasm passed over her features.

'It's all right, babby,' Lachlan assured her hoarsely. 'You lie still like a good wee lassie and we'll have you in Slochmhor in no time.'

He took Babbie's arm and pulled her aside. 'She's bad, Babbie, hardly any pain which means severe third degree burns. We'll have to get her to hospital – could you go and phone the laird? Tell him to get round here fast. We'll have to get her over to Barra and his is the fastest boat hereabouts. Alert the airport at Barra, tell them to have a plane standing by. Meanwhile I'm going to get her to my house as quickly as I can . . .'

Babbie squeezed his arm and went swiftly away. Niall was coming up the steps, trying to hide his injured hands from his father's eyes. But he needn't have worried. His father greeted him distractedly, his whole being taken up with Ellie to whom he was administering emergency treatment. Todd was coming down from the Smiddy, driving the big silver limousine he had won in a competition some years back.

'Get the bairn into this, Doctor,' he shouted as soon as he was within hearing distance. 'It has more room than yours and she will be at your house in no time.' Niall, heedless of his hands, gathered up his daughter and ran with her to the car, his father at his side.

'Grandpa,' Ellie's light voice came faintly. 'I want to go home to my own bonny room.'

Lachlan hesitated. Mo Dhachaidh was further away than Slochmhor and he had to be ready to get Ellie to the pier as soon as the laird arrived with his boat. He saw the silent plea in his granddaughter's eyes and relented just as Babbie returned, her nod telling him that help was arriving.

Old Isabel had brought down a pile of pillowcases from

her house and Babbie wound two round Niall's hands. But he had no thought for himself and sat with Ellie in the front seat, talking to her quietly, nuzzling her hair with his lips. Her eyes were growing lethargic and Lachlan glanced at her frequently, apprehension in his troubled eyes.

Shona put down the phone as if she had been scalded. She had received the call from the Post Office, warning her that Ellie had been involved in an accident and was being taken to the doctor's house. For once Behag was gentle and sympathetic, a gruffness in her voice at the thought of the little girl who came to her shop to buy sweets, a smile never far from her bonny face. She was the only one of the McLachlan/McKenzie clan that Behag really liked or understood, and there were tears of genuine sorrow in her eyes as she returned the receiver to its hook.

Something happened to Shona after hearing the news. She went numb from head to foot, her skin feeling as her mouth did after a visit to the dentist's. She remembered nothing of running to Slochmhor, of breaking the news to Phebie, of the deep shock that showed in her round, pleasant face. Vaguely Shona knew that Elspeth had come into the room, the structure of her normally expressionless face collapsing with emotional pain. More and more these days she stayed beyond her working hours, finding comfort in the friendly atmosphere of Slochmhor, which totally lacked the sterile emptiness of her own home where she was wont to talk aloud for the sake of hearing a human voice.

'No' Ellie?' she whimpered, her love for Niall's child going back to her birth. 'It canny be wee Ellie.'

Todd's car flashed past the window and Phebie recognized its occupants. All three women ran outside and over the glen road, arriving in time to see Niall disappearing upstairs with Ellie.

Shona whirled round on Lachlan but before she could speak his arms were round her shoulders and he was saying quietly, 'We're hoping to get her over to Barra, Babbie has phoned to tell them to have a plane standing by to take her to hospital. She'll need a lot of specialized care that I canny give her here.'

Shona shook her head as if to clear it. 'How – how bad is she, Lachlan?'

He took a deep breath. 'Very bad, I'm afraid. I'm going up now to see what I can do for her. Todd's away down to wait at the harbour and will come back to let us know when the laird's boat arrives.'

He went quickly upstairs and Phebie lifted her white apron to bury her face in it, her sobs coming quietly and helplessly.

'I knew something was going to happen,' Shona spoke as if to herself. 'I haven't felt easy for weeks now – I knew – but I didn't think – it would be Ellie.'

'It was an accident, lass.' Captain Mac stood in the kitchen door, his nut-brown face suspiciously wet. 'We left her to make dinner and the chip pan got knocked over.' From his jacket he extracted the baby otter. 'She saved this wee cratur'. Take it to her, she'll be wantin' to see how is he keepin'.'

Automatically Shona took the otter and went with it upstairs, her movements oddly mechanical, her steps never faltering as they approached Ellie's room. Lachlan was gently bathing her in cool water, his nerves stretched as he waited for Todd to come back with news of the laird's boat. He didn't dwell on the possibility that it might not come, instead he kept his mind busy with a hundred and one things that would have to be done when it arrived. They would have to get Ellie to the harbour quickly, after that it would be a matter of time before she was safely in hospital. He had carried out an examination of her that confirmed his worst fears. Most of her body had been affected by third degree burns, involving the dermis and epidermis. He guessed that the nerve endings below the skin had been destroyed, the reason she wasn't showing signs of feeling much pain. In fact, though pale, she was extremely calm, her eyes lighting at sight of Tubby in her mother's arms.

'Put him beside me,' she requested. 'And could I have Woody as well? She can snuggle on my pillow and keep my ears warm – Mother—' Her eyes were suddenly troubled. 'Don't be angry with me – the fire was an accident. I'll never let anything like it happen again, I promise.'

'I'm not angry with you.' Shona laid her hand on her

daughter's brow and smiled, hardly sparing a glance for Niall who, crouched by the bed, his grimy face hollow and exhausted, was obviously in a state of deep distress. Woodenly he allowed Babbie to tend his hands then quickly returned to the bedside.

'We had a good time, didn't we, Ellie?' His tones were desperate, clutching at straws of normality.

'Ay, Father, the best ever . . .' Her voice was suddenly weak, her skin had taken on a transparent pallor. Lachlan jumped up to feel her brow and take the pulse in her neck. It was weak and rapid, the skin on her face was cold and moist. He turned white. It was what he had dreaded most, the signs of delayed shock. She was speaking, asking for a drink and he went immediately to take a cup from the tray of tea Phebie had just brought in, pouring away most of it, topping it up with hot water. He held the cup to Ellie's lips and she drank feebly, whimpering a little, complaining of feeling sick.

'Isn't the laird here yet?' he demanded harshly of no one in particular. Niall seemed unable to function properly and made no move from the bedside and it was Babbie who ran down to ask Captain Mac to go out and look for signs of Todd. Just then the door burst open to admit Fergus and Kirsteen. Fergus's eyes were black coals in his face, a muscle was working in his jaw.

'Todd just told us,' he grated. He swung round on Babbie, a million questions on his lips and rapidly she explained the situation.

'As bad as that?' Kirsteen had difficulty getting the words out.

'Christ Almighty!' Fergus balled his fist. 'Not our Ellie! She's only a wee lass—' He swung round again. 'Is she in pain?' he ground out urgently. Babbie shook her head, and relief flooded his eyes, making it impossible for her to tell him that it would have been better if Ellie had emerged from the accident crying aloud in agony, the difference perhaps between life and death.

Todd came in, his round face perspiring, imparting the news that the laird had just come into harbour and was standing by ready.

Babbie ran upstairs, ready to blurt out the news, knowing it would stir everybody into much longed for action. But she stopped dead in the doorway, arrested by the sound of Phebie sobbing; the strange, unreal sight of Shona calmly straightening the collection of skulls on the dresser, straightening the bed, her movements wooden, puppet-like.

Lachlan was bending over the bed, his face a ghastly grey colour, the lock of his hair falling over his brow, his long, sensitive fingers lingering on his granddaughter's soft hair before they came down to gently close the lids over her eyes.

'It's as well.' His voice was a mere whisper. 'If she'd lived she would have gone through hell – her arms – her legs – so bad – she might never have walked again.' When he stood up his face was livid with grief and he seemed to have aged ten years in the last few minutes.

Shona was looking down at her daughter, her hand raised as if to touch the smooth young face, but she seemed to think better of it and allowed her hand to drop back to her side, as if it was too heavy to uphold. 'She got her wish anyway,' Shona spoke for the first time since her last words to her daughter. 'Like Peter Pan – she never did – grow up.'

A strangled sob escaped Niall who had been kneeling motionless by the bed. Reaching forward he pulled his child onto his knee so that her head was resting in the crook of his arm. Burying his face into her hair he began to rock back and forth, back and forth, his shoulders convulsed with harsh, helpless sobs.

'Ellie, Ellie!' he cried aloud in his agony. 'My wee Ellie! I love you, my wee lamb. Don't leave your daddy, you're mine, my babby, my own bonny little babby! Don't go, Ellie, don't go, I won't be able to live without you!'

Shona glanced at his bowed head. The fair threads of his hair mingled with Ellie's gold; the white, ragged scar showed up vividly on the taut skin of his neck; his tears were spilling over Ellie, soaking her hair, her face . . .

As Lachlan and Phebie went to comfort their son, Shona walked away, past Babbie at the door, downstairs to the parlour where Fergus and Kirsteen were impatiently waiting and Todd and Mac paced the floor, wondering what was holding things up.

'You won't be needing the laird's boat.' Shona imparted the news unemotionally. 'Ellie died a few minutes ago.'

The stunned faces were white blobs in her vision. Fergus came to her quickly, put his arm around her to draw her close. He was as hard and strong as he had always been but she could feel his grief, like a crawling nerve, tightening his muscles, trembling through his limbs. He pulled back to look at his daughter, his black eyes pain-wracked, puzzled. He studied her, trying to see what was in the pale lovely face, the wonderful eyes which gave away so much of what she was feeling, thinking. But he saw nothing, only a blankness that didn't make sense.

Her throat worked, her voice came out, normal and steady. Reaching out she lightly touched his shoulder. 'I'm fine, Father, really, I just want to be alone for a whily – none of this is quite real yet—' She drifted away towards the kitchen and Kirsteen went to Fergus to hold him tightly. 'Oh, Fergus,' she whispered brokenly. 'What will it be like for her when she comes out of that waking dream?'

'A nightmare,' he said and sounded afraid.

She shook her head. 'It brings it all back, everything we try to forget. It's less than a year since Lewis died and now – now Ellie. Will the luck of the McKenzies ever turn – will it?'

'It's life, Kirsteen,' he murmured and his voice broke. How he had loved his eldest grandchild. She had brought joy and light into his life – into all their lives . . .

'And death,' she said bitterly. 'Too much of one and not enough of the other if you ask me.'

Shona walked into the kitchen. It was still very warm though the window was wide open . . . the window. She went over to it, feeling as if she was floating on a cloud, moving without effort. She paused, staring outside. The evening air was laden with fragrances of the country – she breathed deeply – summer, how lovely . . . her gaze strayed to the pictures in Memory Corner. Biddy smiled at her—

'Ellie said this would be a lucky house, Biddy.' She spoke flatly, without emotion. 'But it's not, it's brought us bad luck—' She paused and wrinkled her brow – What bad luck? What was she talking about? Then she remembered. One of the hens had died that morning. She had found it in the henhouse, its funny big chicken legs up in the air, all pale and stiff. 'Ay, bad luck, Biddy,' she continued and her voice was pebble hard. With a sudden swift movement she slammed Biddy's picture face down on the windowsill. How could Biddy smile like that when a poor little chicken lay dead in the grave she had dug for it behind the henhouse? And the old nurse had been so found of animals too – she paused again, the frown lines deepening, trying to remember if Biddy had liked hens – or had it just been cats? She sighed. Sometimes it was difficult to remember the things that people had liked when they had been alive.

*　　*　　*

A week later Shona walked down the road towards Laigmhor, her smile dreamy as she approached the sprawling white farm buildings in their lush green setting. Puffs of peat smoke were drifting lazily from the chimneys and she knew that the kitchen would be filled with the afternoon fragrance of baking and cooking. This was her home, her only home really, the place in which she had grown up, been so happy, she belonged here and knew that she would never really feel at home anywhere else. But had she always been happy at Laigmhor? She stopped in her tracks and began stripping the heads from the long grasses by the roadside, her face set into lines of concentration.

No, it hadn't always been happy, she decided, for a start it had taken her a long time to get to know her father and there had been other things – sad things – things she didn't want to think about. It was better to remember the happy things, people smiling, never looking lost and lonely – she glanced back the way she had come and her face darkened. Niall was back there and he was lost and lonely looking and seldom smiled – especially in the last week – there had been a funeral, the funeral of a little girl, a child with sun-bright hair and a look about her sweet young face that had struck her deeply – a strange look, as of one suspended for all time on the brink of womanhood but forever remaining a child – like Peter Pan – that's who she was – Peter Pan, and somehow her death had all been Niall's fault only no one had accused him aloud. But he knew all right, no wonder he looked so ill and pale with tragedy mirrored in his nice brown eyes. The only thing she could do was to behave as normally as possible – as if nothing had happened – better to forget – it hurt too much to remember . . . She shuttered her mind and abruptly started walking again, better to keep active, busy – it was the only way to keep sane.

Kate was coming along the road. She liked Kate, liked her strong face and buxom body. There was a sturdiness about her and she laughed a lot, said funny things. No, Kate was seldom upset about anything. When she had been a little girl Kate had come to Laigmhor to see to the things her father hadn't the time to do on his own. She smiled as she thought of how Kate had swished the washing around in the tub, soap bubbles to her elbows, talking away cheerily, saying things that had made her laugh. Kate drew closer, a hesitancy about her manner that wasn't in keeping with the bold, forthright woman she knew. She stopped beside her and seemed to be studying her face and she wondered why because she was smiling and greeting her in the normal way.

'How are you, lass?' Kate's voice was full of concern, the lines round her mouth turned down in an odd kind of sympathy.

'I'm fine, Kate,' she assured. 'Isn't it a bonny day? I wonder how long the good weather will last.'

Kate shook her head in an abstracted way, that uncertainty of manner more pronounced. She eyed Shona doubtfully, noticing that her blue eyes were distant, as if she wasn't aware of anything going on around her. She had been the same at the funeral, remote and calm, not a single tear in her eyes. Kate stifled a sigh. It had been a dreadful week for the McLachlans and the McKenzies – and for the Donaldsons too, laying poor Morag Ruadh to her rest. Poor cratur', she was better away, and from all accounts she had slipped off peacefully, all her demons laid to rest, thanks to the minister and Rachel. Ay, a fine lass, Rachel, and of course with her having that strange power she had been able to do some wonderful things to ease Morag's last hours. Ay, a granddaughter to be proud of right enough. With her talents she would go far . . . Unconsciously Kate puffed out her chest proudly, her thoughts straying back to Morag.

The minister had had two funeral services to conduct that week and he had carried out his duties in a manner which had further endeared him to the island. He had been kindness itself to Dugald and Ruth, Isabel and Jim Jim, and they had been flabbergasted when he had donated a bottle of whisky to the funeral repast. But he had excelled himself for wee Ellie, had conducted the service simply, beautifully, movingly and his words of sympathy had been spoken from the heart, really meant, not just kind words to be spoken because it was his job to say them – in fact he had *cried* when the small coffin was being lowered. She had only glimpsed his face but she was sure she had seen tears on it and one or two other people had verified it – Barra had looked at him oddly, as if she was afraid for him and after the service she had hurried after him and they had gone up to the Manse together. Kate had sensed a mystery about those two since the day the minister had acknowledged her so warmly in kirk. Barra knew something she didn't, yet she hadn't been able to find out what it was which had incensed her and made her all the more determined to keep her ear to the ground. She looked at Shona again, remembering her talk with Merry Mary yesterday when Shona had departed from the shop.

'She is taking it remarkably well,' had said Merry Mary, nodding at Shona's disappearing back. 'Fancy comin' out to do her shopping and going about as if nothing had happened.'

'Too well,' Kate had frowned. 'It's as if only part o' her is here and the other part somewhere else altogether – no' just quite all there – if you see what I mean.'

'Ay, right enough,' agreed Elspeth, her gaunt face showing her own sorrow, her eyes red from continual weeping. It had been a nightmare week at Slochmhor with Phebie going about silently, stopping in rooms where she thought she would be private enough to give vent to her grief; the doctor, moving through his day mechanically, looking nearer to exhaustion than she had ever seen. 'Ach, poor Shona,' she went on. 'The Lord knows she was punished well enough all these years ago but surely she has suffered enough without paying this terrible price as well.'

'Are you feeling all right, Kate?' Shona's voice cut through Kate's thoughts and she shook her head sadly.

'I am right enough myself but I am just goin' up the road to see my Nancy. She's no' keeping too well again and the doctor was sayin' she will maybe have to go back into the hospital.'

'Ach, that's a shame,' Shona said absently. 'Tell her I was asking for her.'

She began to move away, not feeling very cheered by her encounter with Kate. She hadn't been smiling much today and she hadn't laughed once. Also, there was trouble in her family too, everyone, it seemed, had little reason to feel happy – everybody except her. It took hold of her again as the gap between her and Kate widened and by the time she reached Laigmhor she almost felt like singing.

Ruth was in the garden, rocking baby Lorna to sleep, her look as she saw Shona full of the same hesitancy she had witnessed in Kate. What on earth was wrong with everybody? Were they perhaps jealous because she was happy and they weren't?

Ruth regarded Shona doubtfully, feeling an amazement that she could behave so normally – almost as if Ellie had never been taken from her. Fergus and Kirsteen thought so too, she had heard them talking, Fergus worried, Kirsteen trying to comfort him. 'She's either taking it well,' Fergus had said, 'or she's not taking it at all.'

Lorn had tried to speak to his sister, tried to give her the same sort of support that she had given him when

Lewis died but she had pushed his condolences impatiently aside and had gone on to discuss the forthcoming sheepdog trials.

Shona was talking to the baby, tickling her, making her chuckle.

'Are you coming in, Shona?' Ruth searched for the right things to say. 'I'm on my own at the moment and rather busy but I could make a strupak and you could talk to me while I'm washing some of Lorna's things.'

'No, you go, I'll stay and talk to the baby – I'll be along in a minute or two. It's so nice out here and I could be doing with some fresh air after being cooped up for most of the week.'

'All right.' Ruth realized that Shona was probably doing the right thing, getting out, meeting people, enjoying the air. Nevertheless there was something dreadfully wrong – why else were Fergus and Kirsteen talking, Lachlan keeping an obvious close watch on her – as if he expected something to happen. A shiver went through her. She was still trying to get used to the idea that her mother was no longer alive. Her father was feeling the same and had to check himself from setting Morag's tray, tiptoeing into the parlour to see if she needed anything – a bereavement was such a traumatic thing – yet . . . She gave Shona one last assessive look before turning away, satisfied that she was perfectly happy for the moment. She walked away across the grass and over the cobbled yard to the kitchen.

Shona waited several minutes after Ruth's departure,

making sure no one was about, either at the farm or on the road, then quite calmly she picked up the baby and walked away with her in the direction of the Muir of Rhanna. A bubble of happiness burst inside her, tumbling out to make her chuckle. How lovely it all was; the moor with its wildflowers; the dear little skylarks hovering and singing; the heat of the sun bringing out all the warm, wild, delicious smells she loved so much – the baby gazing at her with big blue eyes the same colour as the sky.

She began to croon a lullabye, one Biddy used to sing a lot, a bairn on her knee, cosy by the winter hearth; or on a chair outside, cool in the shade of summer trees. She was feeling good and very fit and her long legs carried her swiftly over the tracts of moor and along the sheep track she had so often walked with Niall – he had been happy then, now he was sad, sad because he had been the cause of that little girl dying – he deserved to feel as he was feeling, human beings punished themselves when they had guilt lying on their conscience.

The hollow at Dunuaigh drowsed peacefully in the heat. No one was here, no one would come here – not for a good while anyway. The baby was growing fretful and, little as she was, becoming quite heavy. 'Don't cry, my wee one,' she said softly. 'You'll soon be nice and cool and able to have a nap – I'll look to you, never fear. I was never guilty of neglecting my own wee Ellie – was I now?'

She found the entrance to the cave quite easily but knew she would have to make it bigger to allow her to get through with the baby. Laying the infant on the soft moss she began to pull back the undergrowth. By the time she was finished she was scratched and bleeding but it didn't matter, nothing mattered as long as Ellie was all right.

It was deliciously cool inside the cave but the baby continued to cry, her lower lip piteously curled. Shona opened her bag and began taking out baby clothes, napkins, tinned milk, sugar. It was a good thing she'd kept these things by her at Mo Dhachaidh. Everything that a baby needed was here, along with some food for herself and a few packets of tea. Spreading an oblong piece of sheeting over the dirty grey sheepskin on the stone ledge that had once served as a bed, she laid the baby on it, changed her and washed the nappy in the burn. Then she heated water on the little camp stove she'd brought, and mixing it with the dried milk poured it into the feeding bottle. The baby sucked greedily for a few minutes then her eyes grew heavy. In minutes she was asleep, one small hand across her face.

Shona made herself tea and sat back to drink it in complete contentment. She was glad that she had given the place a good clean that last time she'd been here – that lonely but happy day of exploring, finding things that had once meant so much to her. She had vowed never to come back here again but now knew that she had been meant to return. How right it seemed to bring her baby to this place – the place where it had all begun. After all, right from the start Ruth hadn't wanted her baby so it wasn't wrong to take it and make it her own – but – it was her own – what had made her think of Ruth? Ruth had no baby. She had taken away its life almost before it had started to grow in her womb. Shona shut her mind to Ruth and lay back. The world and all it meant was a million miles away – and she had Ellie back, that was all that mattered – though of course she couldn't stay here too long. *They* knew of this place, they had found her once before in this cave with a baby – one that hadn't cried or crooned like Ellie – a tiny wax doll with no life in it. Sadness washed over her but she pushed it angrily away. No time to be sad – Ellie was here, living, real. They would stay here an hour maybe and then go over to the bay at Croy where she knew of a deserted boathouse – but later they would come back – after *they* had gone. She gave a little sigh, closed her eyes and fell asleep.

Chapter Thirteen

Niall was growing anxious, wondering why Shona was taking so long to come back when she had said she would only be gone a short time. She had been so unpredictable and strange since Ellie's death, a remoteness in her that made it impossible for him to draw close to her, to communicate in the open frank way that they had shared all through their years of marriage. There was also a vagueness about her; it was there in those lovely eyes of hers, as if she wasn't taking in anything going on around her but was looking inward, retreating back over a long weary road so that when he spoke to her she had to make a great effort to travel back over the distance that separated them.

His father had asked him to keep a close watch on her, to tell him if she began to behave oddly, but there had been nothing, only that eerily calm acceptance of Ellie's death and a behaviour so normal it *wasn't* normal under the circumstances.

There had been one incident that had given him cause for concern, an incident involving old Dodie who had arrived at the door a few days after the funeral. Shona had opened the door to him and red with embarrassment he had handed her a red rose to put in Memory Corner. She had taken the flower, crushed it in her hand and had then shut the door in Dodie's face. Niall had witnessed it all from the green at the side of the house and had thought how much courage it must have taken for the old eccentric to actually go up and knock on a door. He was stumbling away, blinded by tears and Niall had gone to intercept him and to lay his hand on the stooped shoulders.

'You mustny mind Shona,' he had told Dodie kindly. 'She's no' herself just now.'

Dodie had gulped and had tried to stem the flow of tears. 'I shouldny have chapped the door,' he said brokenly, drawing his sleeve again and again across his eyes. 'I dinna do it as a rule but I missed the funeral and wasny able to put any flowers on the grave. I knew that wee Ellie loved flowers and I saw that special one growing in the Manse garden and the minister gave it to me when I told him who it was for.'

'Why didn't you come to the funeral?' Niall asked gently, knowing it was Dodie's habit to pay his respects at the graveside of his departed friends.

Dodie had turned away and gulped, 'I couldny bear to watch the cold earth swallowin' up such a young lassie. She was aye singin' and somehow I thought if I didny see her goin' to her rest I would still hear her singin' over the hills the way she used to when she was walkin' past my house on her way to visit Jack the Light.'

'Ellie will never stop singing – for any of us,' Niall

had said, his own tears threatening to choke him. He had sent Dodie on his way feeling slightly happier though he himself was utterly saddened at the idea of Shona's cruel disregard for an old man who had always placed his trust at her door.

Niall stirred in his chair, the lethargy in him making him feel that lead had settled into his veins. The house was filled with emptiness, a hollow emptiness that would never be filled – with *her* – the daughter who had filled his life with light from the moment she was born – wee Ellie, the girl child who had touched their lives with a rare happiness. She was all that he had ever needed, he had never hankered after more children the way he knew that Shona did. Now Ellie was gone and he felt utterly alone. Shona had drawn away from him and he couldn't reach her. She seemed incapable of talking to him and he felt crushed with grief. Yet, if his daytime hours were hellish enough, his night-time ones were worse still. The nightmares came then; the boat; the fire; Ellie lying still and so dreadfully burned; he could feel her torture searing through him in red hot bands, yet his father had said she hadn't felt the terrible burns – they went too deep for that.

The pain would have come if she had lived to undergo one operation after another, taking skin from the healthy tissue that was left to try and repair that which had been lost.

'Oh Christ! She's better out of it!' he wept into his hands then immediately asked himself why he was uttering such banalities. Why had it happened at all? Why? Why? He should never have left her, never listened to her – but it had been an accident. Mac explained how it had happened but somehow he couldn't take that part in – he should never have left her ... The same arguments, the same doubts, the same self-recriminations whirled round in his head till he felt exhausted. He would have to get up, go and find out what was keeping Shona, but he had to force himself out of the chair, pushing himself up on hands that still hurt, though his burns had only been superficial and were already starting to heal.

A movement on the stairs made his heart leap, and as he cocked his good ear to the source of the sound the past tragic days were wiped out and he imagined it was Ellie on the stairs – coming down – in a minute to stand in the doorway, smiling, mischief in her golden eyes as she teased him for being lazy.

'Ellie,' her name on his lips was so familiar, so dear, came out so readily. He went into the hall in a daze to see Woody bounding downwards, bushy tail waving from side to side as she scampered as fast as her legs would take her away from the boisterous attentions of Tubby who had made a good recovery and who was soon to go and live with Jack the Light, the old man who had thought the world of Ellie and who had readily offered to look after the little creature who had meant so much to her. Meanwhile Tubby was delighting in taking the rise out of the hitherto bossy and over-confident cat. Both animals shot out of the front door and the house was empty again.

'Ellie,' he whispered but it was a ghost name now, an echo which had already receded into the past. Ellie would never run, never laugh, never sleep in this house again. He had to get away, get outside, had to go and look for Shona. He was halfway down the glen when he saw the minister coming towards him. His hand was raised in greeting while he was still some distance away and when he drew closer he looked so strong, so caring that Niall wanted to reach out, to be held up by the power which emanated from him – yet he was just a man after all, as vulnerable as the next though in his calling he had to hide it. He was there to be leaned upon, not to lean.

'I was just on my way up to see you,' he greeted, 'find out if there was anything I could do.' Subtly he assessed this young McLachlan, noting the lethargy, the dull eyes heavy with suffering and he prayed that he would be able to offer some help.

Niall forced a smile. 'Maybe you can, I was wondering where Shona is. I'm just on my way down to Laigmhor to see if she's there.'

'I don't think so, I was coming out of the village earlier and saw her going off over the moors, walking very fast with a bundle in her arms.'

'A bundle?' Niall looked puzzled. 'Are you sure it wasn't a bag? She was carrying one when she left the house, said something about taking some of Ellie's things to give to Sorcha's grandchildren. There's six of them and she thought the things might fit one of them – she says it's best not to hold onto anything – that's no use to us anymore.'

'It might have been a bag – but she didn't go near the village, of that I'm certain.'

Ruth appeared on the road, frantic looking, her limp very pronounced as she came hurrying towards them. 'I've lost Lorna!' she cried before she reached them. 'She was outside in her pram – now she's gone.'

Mark James smiled at the small fair girl who had so recently lost her mother. She was too solemn for her age, she took life too seriously, and no wonder. It seemed she had had little to laugh about for most of her years. 'Has she walked away or have the fairies taken her?' he said teasingly.

Ruth was in no mood for jokes and wrung her hands together as she burst out, 'I left her with Shona out in the garden and when I went back half an hour later they had both gone – the pram was empty!'

The two men looked at each other and Niall said in disbelief, 'It canny be – she wouldn't—' He paused, it all added up, the vagueness, the remote facade of a woman who hadn't accepted that her darling child was dead. She had deluded herself into believing that it hadn't happened – in her tortured mind Ellie was still alive – she had gone back in time – back to when Ellie was a baby.

Without a word he led the way to Laigmhor. Kirsteen

had just returned from the village and quickly he told her what he thought had happened.

'Go and get Fergus,' she said imperatively. 'He'll be up on the south pasture.'

Fergus came quickly, followed by Lorn who went immediately to comfort Ruth.

Everyone was looking at each other, trying not to let their panic show. Fergus sat down heavily by the table, his jaw so tight the skin was shiny. 'It's happened again,' he said heavily. 'Twice before, Shona shut her mind to reality – when Mirabelle died and when Niall was reported dead at Dunkirk. When their son was stillborn she switched her mind off and refused to believe any of it – it's almost as if it's some sort of safety valve when reality becomes so terrible she canny face it – Oh God! My poor lassie! And to think we were believing she had taken Ellie's death so lightly! It was killing her! Christ Almighty! It was killing her.'

He was up, striding to the door, asking the minister what time it was he had seen Shona heading over the moors.

'It must have been an hour ago now – do you have any idea where she was heading?'

Fergus nodded grimly. 'Ay, indeed I do, indeed I do, Mr James.'

'I'd like to come with you,' said Mark James. 'I may be of some help.'

Fergus nodded and went outside with the men, leaving Kirsteen looking at Ruth and saying, 'I'd like to go too,

Ruth. Shona might be – difficult and might feel easier with another female.'

'Away you go,' said Ruth distractedly, 'I'll go and tell Father – I want to be with him – I don't think I could bear seeing Shona – the way she is – with my baby. It seems everyone wants her – first Mam in kirk, now . . .'

'It might be a good idea to give Lachlan a ring,' Kirsteen suggested. 'Shona will need a doctor, I don't have a doubt about that.'

Ruth was already at the phone and Kirsteen went outside to catch up with the men, telling Fergus that Ruth was ringing the doctor.

Fergus nodded and jumped into the tractor beside Lorn. 'We'd best go over by Croynachan, it's longer but the road's better. If Lachlan got the message he will no doubt take the rest of you in his car.'

They rumbled away, leaving the others to make their way to Slochmhor where Lachlan was just reversing his car onto the road.

It was a silent journey. Lachlan's mind was racing, thinking ahead to the confrontation with Shona. His heart swelled with pity for her. Poor, lonely, lost lassie, how she must be suffering – and the baby – she wouldn't give it up so easily – she would fight to keep it . . .

To stop himself from dwelling further on conjecture he forced himself to concentrate on the road ahead. The track through the moor was becoming bumpy and soon petered out to a mere thin strip of boggy peat trampled

by the sheep. Eventually he could take the car no further
and they all got out to continue on foot, catching up with
Fergus and Lorn who had decided that the noise of the
tractor might frighten Shona away. They were all running,
sharing not a word, not a thought, all too intent on reaching
the spot at Dunuaigh. It was Kirsteen who spotted Shona,
fleeing away from Dunuaigh towards the abbey ruins. They
were all exhausted and had to stop to regain wind. Lachlan's
face was perspiring, his body flung forward, hands planted
against his knees, his mouth open wide as he drew in air.
'We'll have to take a rest,' he rasped. 'She hasn't seen us
yet and we can't all get too close.'

Fergus too was drawing air in painfully, his dark face
drawn, his breathing laboured, silently cursing the weak
lung that curtailed him when the rest of his body wasn't
tired. Only the pumping anxiety in Niall's heart had kept
him going, spurred him to make a supreme effort when he
had least felt like it. Like his father he was bent forward, his
fair hair falling over his hollow face, his mouth agape. The
trauma of the last days had taken their toll of him and the
dull throbbing of blood pulsing inside his head made him
lightheaded and temporarily confused. The two younger
men were still quite fresh, Lorn only breathing heavily, the
minister showing no sign of distress. He had thrown off
his jacket, torn off his dog collar, his broad chest strained
against the thin material of his shirt. There was nothing
in the steel-like tension of his hard body which set him
apart from other men. He was the first to move again, his

long legs sprinting away before anyone was aware that he was gone. The flash of Shona's fiery hair against the sky was like a spur, beckoning him, forcing him to run faster till the distance between them had shrunk considerably. There was something about this beautiful woman that had captured him from the start. The minister in him rebelled against the notion, the man in him wouldn't allow him to ignore it. He admired her spirit, her endearing lack of sophistication; her grace; her childlike candour; her perfectly natural mannerisms – but more than any of these he was captivated by the glint of laughter in her wondrous eyes, her undoubted loveliness. How his heart had ached for her at the funeral of her daughter. She had stood as one apart, unspeaking, unmoving, like one lost, too bewildered to know what was happening, a soul adrift in an unspeakable chasm of locked-in grief. . . And now she was in desperate trouble, a runaway creature who had been driven to the despairing act of taking someone else's baby. The crying of the little one came to him, a thin frightened wail, as if it had sensed the terror, the anger, of the woman in whose arms it lay.

Shona had heard him, she half-turned and he caught a glimpse of the enraged fear in her eyes, like an animal at bay, her curtain of hair in disarray over her shoulders, her face a white blur against the yellow stones of the abbey walls.

Her name was torn from high up in his throat. 'Shona! Wait! I only want to talk to you!'

But she turned and ran, plunging into the ruins of the

chapel, the infant held close to her breast. He stumbled in after her and she was trapped, unable to go any further, ensnared by the looming east wall of the ancient ruin in which she had sought to hide. Frantically she moved her head from side to side, cursing herself for having slept longer than she meant in the cave. The faraway sound of a tractor had awakened her and she had known it was her father come to look for her, the way he had looked another time many years ago. She had welcomed his intrusion then but this time she knew it would be different, he was only here for one reason – to take her baby away. The last time it hadn't mattered, *that* baby had been dead – not like this child with the roses of life implanted into her plump little cheeks . . .

She faced the minister, a bitter resentment burning in her, mingling with a deep apprehension that fanned her smouldering anger to flames of fury. Her father hadn't come alone, he had brought a stranger with him, a man with compassion in his compelling eyes and treachery in his beseeching words. But – he wasn't a stranger, she knew him, from somewhere she knew him – she had seen him before, standing at an altar – in a church – blessing a baby. Some strange twist of fate had brought them together in a similar setting – and the baby that he had blessed was in her arms and she remembered now; he had blessed *her* baby, had held her in his arms – and now he had come to take her away. He had deceived her into believing he was a man of God – but he wasn't. If he was a good man he wouldn't be doing this to her, approaching her, his arms outstretched – reaching out to snatch her baby away.

'Don't touch me!' The scream was torn from her, plucked from her throat by another being who was inside her, warning her, goading her into uncontrollable rage. The sound of her voice rang round the chapel, echoed in the cloisters, reverberated over and over, making her want to clap her hands against her ears to shut out the dreadful noise. Ellie too was frightened by it, her tiny face was puckered, her delicate skin suffused with blood.

Over the stranger's shoulder she saw more people coming – pounding in through the arch, their white faces staring – at her – at Ellie. Her father was among them – and Niall, the man who had caused the death of that little girl and whose guilt showed in the haunted eyes and stark gauntness of his face. He had taken one child and now he had come for hers – he was moving, coming closer, his feet whispering over the moss and grasses on the earth floor of the chapel. Like the stranger, his arms were outstretched, his tortured eyes searing into her soul – the eyes of a man who pretended concern when all the time he wanted Ellie . . .

'No! Stay away! Stay away!' The dry sobbing protest burst from deep inside her head – over and over, while Ellie screamed in her arms and the woman with the sweet face cried and tried to say something which she couldn't hear for all the noise.

They were all advancing towards her and the terror

inside her swelled like a living thing till she couldn't breathe and the sky and the roofless ruin were falling in on top of her.

'No!' she screamed again. 'Don't take my baby – oh please – don't take Ellie away!' The scream tailed off to a piteous plea and Kirsteen put her hands over her face, unable to bear the tragic sight of proud, fearless Shona McKenzie, beaten, defeated; her poor face twisted in mental torture.

Shona felt her legs giving way and she sagged, spent, utterly done – but she couldn't let them take Ellie, she couldn't. In a final desperate effort she pulled her head upright, her chin tilted, her huge burning eyes showing a defiance, a last glimpse of unconquered pride. Her heart was pounding, there was a buzzing in her ears, but she wouldn't give in to them – she wouldn't.

She made a violent move backwards and twisted her ankle on a slab of stone – she was falling, falling, the faces in front of her swimming, blurring, closing in on her ... Fergus and Lorn plunged forward simultaneously, Lorn to grab the baby, Fergus to catch his daughter to his heaving chest.

Her senses swam, she heard the dull thudding of his heart in her ears. Her legs finally gave way and she sagged against him, her mouth falling open, her muscles twitching so violently she found it impossible to control her own body. Fergus gathered her to him, his lips pressed to her hair, his tears falling on the bright crown of her head.

'My lassie, my lassie,' he sobbed harshly. 'Oh God! I'm so sorry – so sorry it had to be this way.'

Her arms were torn and bloodied, the flesh of her legs ripped by thorn bushes, her dress hanging in ragged strips, exposing the soft flesh of her shapely legs. Niall tore off his shirt and wrapped it round her shoulders, his heart so overburdened with grief he found it impossible to speak – say something comforting to this demented creature who was the wife he loved more than his own life.

Part Four

Winter 1961

Chapter Fourteen

Shona wakened slowly, disorientated as she glanced round the room with its ochre carpet and soft yellow curtains. Staring up at the arched ceiling of the little alcove where sat her bed, she frowned a little, fighting down a mild sense of panic. She didn't belong here; her place was in a small white room with starched bedlinen under her and a monotonously patterned coverlet on top of her − not this fluffy patchwork quilt which caressed her body like a big soft cloud and which made a move from its delicious warmth seem like the worst possible torture.

For eternity − or for what seemed eternity − she had known only a place where the strangely oppressive silence was occasionally shattered by screams, by hopeless pleadings, sometimes from her own lips, at others from the lips of others with empty eyes and sad faces. White clinical figures had moved among those pathetic spectres, soothing, calming, often speaking in the sort of tone that might be used to still the fears of a restless child − a child . . . Her head moved on the pillow and she forced herself to concentrate on the room. It was a room filled with peace, with an almost tangible sense of happiness. Happy things must have happened here, people must have laughed a lot. The yellow curtains at the window were like sunshine – she put up her hand to trace the outline of a damp little patch on the ceiling. It was shaped like a head – the head of Jesus – how often it had comforted her to sleep as a child . . .

She sat up quickly, letting the quilt slip from her shoulders. The sharp air of late autumn swept over her making her shiver. This was *her* room – the sunshine room – which meant that she was safely home at Laigmhor in her own bed. The journey of the day before came back to her, her father and Niall looking after her, concern, kindness on their faces. Last night she had been so tired, too tired to really take any of it in, to believe that it was really happening. A great wave of relief washed over her and putting her fingers to her mouth she gazed round the room with renewed interest; the dresser with the china jug and the bowl she had washed in as a child. She could almost hear Mirabelle climbing the stairs, coming in, the pan of hot water in her hands, pouring it into the basin, cooling it with the cold water from the big flowery jug. She let her eyes rest on the fireplace with its red tiles and brass paraphernalia winking in the morning light. The fire had only been lit when she had been ill in bed and sometimes Mirabelle had sat beside it to knit or sew, rocking herself contentedly while her fingers worked busily. She wasn't ill now, but last night the fire had been lit, her father taking a shovelful of glowing embers from the kitchen fire to put into the grate of the sunshine room, quelling her protests with a few gentle words.

'Mirabelle,' she whispered, 'I've been ill – but I'm all right now – except – sometimes I'm so – lonely.'

Swinging her legs to the edge of the bed she pushed her feet into her slippers and walked slowly over to look from the window. It was a still, mellow October day, the slopes of Ben Machrie were bronzed with the dying bracken, interspersed with patches of yellow and the purple-tipped bare branches of the birch trees; the smoke from Portcull lay in a soft blue haze among the woods by Loch Tenee; a few peat gatherers were trundling towards the moors, slowly, lazily, the ponies that pulled the carts as placid as their owners. Kate McKinnon and Barra McLean were on the road below, walking close together, heads wagging busily. Kate glanced up and saw her and her arm went up, her big, radiant smile plainly discernible. Shona waved back, a trifle subdued as she wondered ... there must have been talk – so much talk about – how she had stolen Ruth's baby.

At thought of Ruth she cringed back from the window – Ruth could be down there too – worse still – she could be in the house and she couldn't face her – not yet. She didn't feel strong enough to face anyone though it was inevitable. She wondered where Niall was, Niall who had been such a regular visitor at the hospital, sitting with her, hour after hour, holding her hand, speaking to her when he might as well have talked to the wall. She had been too confused to respond to anything – anybody, she hadn't known anyone. They had all just been anonymous ghost figures moving in front of her vision, meaningless shapes who meant nothing. Later, when she knew who they were she had wanted to creep back into her lonely world again, to escape the painful memories they brought with them. And several times she had gone back, relapsed into blankness where no one could reach her. In a way she had wanted to stay in her empty drifting world forever, where there was no pain, no sorrow, just herself locked away in the private prison her mind had created. The trouble was no one would allow her to stay locked up, they were all so eager to bring her back, glimpse a flicker of the person she had been – before losing Ellie. And the torture of coming out, bit by painful bit, was the worst kind of hell of all. She had fought to get back inside herself but it had been no use. The doctors were too clever for her, they made her face reality, face the stark dreadful truth about Ellie – and when she finally came to accept that cruel bitter blow she had wanted to curl up in a ball and die too – only no one would leave her in peace to do it, they were all pulling, dragging at her senses in their efforts to win her back to health. Against her will, her body had responded, her weak flesh had cried out for sustenance, making her eat and drink, taking the vitamins the doctors told her she needed. And yet there was still so much of her locked away that couldn't be reached. Not even the look of despair in her father's dark eyes, nor the patient hope in Niall's could force her to do any more. The doctors said it would take time and patience.

Footsteps sounded along the passage and running back to bed she pulled the quilt up to her neck to wait with fast-beating heart. 'Don't let it be Ruth,' she prayed, 'I never want to face her.'

She had learned only recently that she had pleaded with her visitors not to let Ruth come near her and now she wished they hadn't listened. It would have made it easier, so much easier . . .

The door opened and Niall came in, dressed in a brown cashmere jersey that matched his eyes. His face was shiny and fresh looking – as if he had just washed – but it was so thin and his eyes held no joy – also the jaunty whistle which used to herald his approach was stilled. The grave lines of his face broke and he smiled at her, such a lovely smile – though there was a sadness in it.

'You're awake,' he greeted her, as if to see her awake was an occasion for gladness. 'Would you like me to bring up some breakfast for the pair o' us? We could have it together up here.'

But she shook her head quickly. 'No, you go ahead, I'm not very hungry yet, I've only just wakened. What time is it?'

'Nine o'clock, but you've no need to hurry. You can lie as long as you like.'

'Please don't treat me like a child.' Her tones were petulant. 'And to hell with what the doctors say! I've had enough of bed to last me a lifetime!'

He drew a deep breath and went over to the window to stare out unseeingly. The doctors had warned him it would be like this, that it would be a long time before she was the woman he had known. He wanted to hold her, to feel the warmth of her body close to his, to convince himself that all the doctors were wrong and that she had been restored to him well and whole, but he saw now it would be a long uphill process.

'I'm glad my father brought me back here.' She gazed fondly round the room. 'I don't want ever to go back to – that other house. I hate it!'

It had been Niall's idea to bring her back to Laigmhor but he said nothing of this, instead he said quietly, 'There's nothing wrong with the house, Shona, it's . . .'

Her nostrils flared. 'Oh, so it's me then? I might have known you wouldn't understand.'

'No, it isn't you, Shona, and I do understand.' He strove to remain calm. 'We – we all understand.'

'Do you?' she asked shrilly. 'Does Ruth? Do the folk around here understand why I did it – why I took a baby that wasn't mine?'

He swung round to face her. 'No one outside the family knows, except my parents and the minister – it's all right, mo ghaoil, believe me, it's all right.'

A look of perceptible relief flitted over her strained

features, she relaxed visibly and her voice was softer when she said, 'Where are you staying, Niall? At Slochmhor?'

'No, here, I've got the room next door to this. I thought it better for us to have separate rooms till you get used to things again.'

She nodded, looking at him strangely. His masculine body seemed very big in the small room and though she felt a relief at his words, something about the hard strength of him clawed relentlessly at her consciousness; an unwilling awareness of the comfort he had always given her unstintingly; the sweetness of how it had been in his arms – yet she knew she had nothing to give till she had regained her self-respect, a liking for herself again.

The doctors had told Niall to broach the subject of Ellie, bring her into the open instead of keeping her buried, but so far Shona had shown no inclination to mention her daughter's name and he knew he had to try and bring out the things that she was reluctant to face. Going over to the bed he sat down and studied her. She was like a little girl in her flowery cotton pyjamas, her hair tumbling about her shoulders in thick luxuriant waves, the expression in her blue eyes oddly trusting – the way Ellie had looked when he had lifted her high, swung her round till she was dizzy . . .

'Shona.' He put out his hand and lifting a strand of her hair let it glide through his fingers. She pressed herself back on the pillows and he withdrew his hand as if it had been burnt. 'I'm sorry,' he sighed, finding it hard to have to apologize for touching his own wife. 'I just thought you might like to talk – about things – about Ellie.'

'No.' It was a whimper of rejection. 'How can you mention her name – when you—' She halted, unable to voice the things on her mind and he stared at her, seeing accusation in her eyes, renewing a suspicion that he'd harboured for some time. She blamed him for Ellie's death, it was plain to him now and the full realization hit him like a dose of ice water.

'Shona, you canny believe that I – that I was the cause of Ellie . . . ? It was an accident. I would have died to save her but I couldn't—'

'You let it happen.' Her voice was cold, distant, reminding him of how she'd been that dreadful day when she had spoken with the remote, chilly voice of a stranger. 'You should never have gone away and left her to cope alone.'

'Ellie wasn't an infant!' He got up and began pacing the floor, agitation in every step. 'She was a bright, intelligent child with a well-developed sense of responsibility . . .'

'Unlike you,' she chipped in bitterly. She turned her head away from him. 'I don't want to talk about it – and please stop that pacing, I can't bear it. It might be better if we didn't see each other for a while. You remind me too much of things I'd rather forget. Take your things over to Slochmhor, in that way we can be near – without being too near.'

He stared at her in disbelief, his heart heavy in his

leaden chest. 'Ay, I'll do that, Shona – if it's what you really want. I'll be away in a couple of days anyway, the boat was restored ages ago but I haveny had much chance to use it. I was thinking to stay away for a month or so, see to a few things before the winter gales make travelling too risky – but I'll cut it short if you think you might need me.'

She shook her head. 'No, you do what you want, I'll be fine here with Father – I need a lot of time to myself just now – so it's as well if you go away.'

His brown eyes were shiny with hurt and he went to the door without another word. She listened to his steps receding downstairs and a sense of relief pervaded her being, mingling with an unaccountable sense of sadness for things lost, never to return.

Fergus knitted his brows and his black eyes snapped as he spoke to Kirsteen. They were in the kitchen. It was warm and quiet except for the ticking of the clocks and the smatterings of rain blowing against the window panes.

'Hell, Kirsteen,' he said heavily, 'I canny believe this. You're sure about this thing between Shona and Niall?'

She sighed, seeing in her mind's eye Phebie's troubled face when she had gone to take a strupak with her at Slochmhor. 'As sure as I'll ever be. Phebie was near to tears when she told me. In a way I was glad Niall was away – I don't think I could have faced him just then.'

Fergus banged his fist on the table. 'I was wondering

why he suddenly decided to move his things to Slochmhor. Oh God! It canny be allowed to happen again,' he said passionately, remembering with shame a long ago night when he had accused Lachlan of allowing his wife to die in childbirth. Now it seemed that the child Lachlan had delivered safely into the world had turned against his son, accusing him of causing the death of their daughter. 'That old witch Behag has a habit of saying history repeats itself,' he continued bitterly, 'and much as I hate to admit it she has a point – warped as it may be. Christ Almighty, Kirsteen! It will destroy them, eat away until there's nothing left but bitterness!'

She went to him and put her arms round him, stroking the taut lines of his jaw. 'Weesht, weesht, my darling,' she soothed, 'it won't come to that. Shona will see sense in the end. It's too early yet for her to know what she's really saying.'

'That's just it,' he said wearily, 'too early for so many things. Right now I want to run up those stairs and shake some sense into her – talk to her – try and make her see what she's doing, but one wrong word could put her right back to the beginning and none of this damned mess will ever be sorted out. Oh hell! Sometimes I wonder why any of us ever have children. You bring them up, suffer with them, suffer because of them, and just when you're deluding yourself into believing they've got their lives sorted out something like this happens. I canny take it the way I used to, I'm getting to be an old man, Kirsteen.'

She laughed and snuggled her head against his hard chest. 'Havers! You're just saying that because you want me to list all the things that make you a bull of a man both in bed and out.'

He smiled despite himself, and pulling her close, kissed her deeply. When he let her go there was a look in his eyes which she knew well. She caught her breath. 'Do you think it's wrong to feel as we do – at our age?'

'It canny be wrong to love at any age,' he answered seriously. 'I just wish Shona felt the same about Niall – I thought theirs was a marriage like ours, that could ride out the rough as well as the smooth.'

'Och, it will, Fergus, it will – just do as the doctors say and give it time.' She sounded more certain than she felt and buried her face into his shoulder so that he wouldn't see the doubts in her eyes.

Kirsteen, watching for signs of concern in Shona, was disappointed to find that there were none, and as the days passed she could keep quiet no longer. 'It will be good to see Niall back again,' she hazarded, unable to bear the unbroken lethargy on Shona's face a moment longer.

'Ay, it will indeed,' Shona said in a manner that suggested it was the sort of answer expected of her and she wasn't going to say anything to the contrary for fear of risking reprisals.

'I can't get through to her,' Kirsteen later confided in

Fergus, exasperation in her voice. 'She doesn't seem to be aware of anything – to feel anything – it's as if she's just switched off from everything that ever meant anything to her. She shows no concern for Niall – he could be lost in a storm for all she seems to care. She just sits in her room, huddled over the fire, staring into it – seeing nothing.'

Fergus's eyes blazed and his temper finally snapped. 'Oh, she's aware all right! She's just exerting every shred of that buggering McKenzie stubbornness of hers in order to keep herself divorced from us all! Goddammit! She looks at *me* as if I was some kind of rotten sore that has to be tholed. She's trying to shut herself off from life for fear it hurts her again. Well, I've had enough, I'm going up right now to speak to her!'

'No, Fergus, you know what the doctors said,' Kirsteen appealed, but he shook her arm off and stomped out of the kitchen and up to Shona's room, his face set and determined. She was at the fire, a cardigan thrown over her sagging shoulders, the hair that had been her pride unbrushed and unkempt looking, hanging about her shoulders in straggly ends. Her face was void of the sparkle that had once lit it to happiness or temper, her whole attitude was one of complete dejection.

Fergus stood looking at her, his temper worsened by the fact that she had given no indication of having heard his entry into the room.

'Right, madam,' he began harshly. 'Just how long do you intend to keep this up? You're not only depressing yourself, you're depressing everyone around you! God knows we've been patient with you but it canny go on, Shona, I won't have Kirsteen put out any longer – and look at me when I talk to you, dammit!'

At first he thought she wasn't going to acknowledge that she had even heard him, but after a few interminable seconds during which his rage boiled to exploding point, she raised her head slowly and the eyes that looked at him were dull and lifeless. 'Ay, you said something, Father?'

His nerves stretched. He couldn't believe it. She was even a better actress than he thought or else she really had missed most of the words he'd showered on her. 'You're right, I did say something,' he threw at her relentlessly. 'And since you appear to be deaf I'll say more. God knows you've been through a terrible ordeal, we all understand that. You've lost a child who was your life, but in behaving the way you're doing you're not being fair to her bonny name. You're burying her, keeping her down, you won't allow her to come out and become the precious memory she deserves to be. You've suffered, ay, but you're not the only one, we've all experienced the hell you're going through – and what about your husband? You don't seem to give a damn for him and yet in his way he's suffered more than you and for longer. You managed to lock yourself from reality, he's had to thole it from the hellish moment he saw his own flesh and blood dying in that fire. Just think about that and you might stop wallowing in self-pity and start giving some of it away for a change!'

He paused, frightened, wondering if he had gone too far but she merely turned her gaze from him and switched it back to the red hot peats glowing in the hearth. A fresh burst of rage engulfed him and he plunged on, 'That's right, pretend you haveny heard! You don't fool me and I won't allow you to go on casting your gloom over *this* house! We've had our share of grief. It's just over a year since we lost our son and by God it still hurts. That kind of pain never goes away but it has to be lived with if we are to carry on. It would be easy to go under, very easy, but for the sake of those who are left we all have to make the effort to go on. You are no exception, madam, believe me. Patience and gentleness haven't worked with you, so maybe this will.'

He was panting now, his fist clenching and unclenching at his side, his black eyes glowing red in the firelight as he glared down at her. Again she looked up, tilting her head back so that she could see his face looming above her.

'Will you please get out of my room, Father,' her voice was level, betraying nothing. 'I want only to be left in peace.'

'I will not be told what to do in my own house!' he roared, and Kirsteen, listening at the foot of the stairs, bit her lip, her knuckles on the banister clenched whitely.

'Enough, Fergus, enough,' she whispered though she knew everything he said was born of frustration and a burning desire to see his daughter happy again.

White fury bubbled in him such as he had never known

for years, bubbled, fermented, boiled upwards to almost choke him. He raised his hand as if to strike, and it was only a great force of will that stayed him. His pupils widened, his hand dropped back to his side and he all but ran from the room, knowing if he stayed a moment longer he would do something he would regret for the rest of his days.

Towards the end of November, Niall came home, refreshed, ready to believe that his wife's condition could only have improved during the time he'd been away. But when he went to see her, eagerly, his brown eyes alive with anticipation as he presented her with an enormous fluffy teddy bear with golden eyes, he received the same sort of reception as anyone else, the only difference being that with him she was more vindictive than he could ever have believed possible. It was as if she brewed small incidents in her mind till they were blown up out of all proportion to that which was real. Like Fergus, his patience had finally become exhausted and now his snapping point was reached. Against his better reason he raged at her till he was spent, but when he sat back, pale with retreating rage she merely said indifferently, 'Niall, if this is the way you're going to behave I think it would be better if you don't come back. I don't have anything that I want to say to you.'

Jumping up he went to the door, throwing back, 'I think you're right – you don't have anything to say – nothing that

I care to hear anyway. I've had it with you, Shona, all I can take and I'm damned if I need any more of it – oh God,' despite himself his voice broke, 'I wish Ellie was here – she could always be relied on for a bit of laughter when you were in one of your buggering pig-headed moods – but she isn't here, is she? That's the trouble. Maybe it's just as well – I wouldny like her to see a mother so completely wrapped up with her own feelings she's got none to spare for the poor buggers who have to live with her. Kirsteen and your father deserve medals putting up with the likes of you in their home!'

She listened to the blundering sounds made by his hasty departure. A shiver went through her. He was wrong, so wrong! He had accused her of feeling nothing for others when all the time her heart was heavy with caring. She wanted to reach out, to her father, to Niall, to let them know how much she still loved and needed them, how much she longed to talk to them. Picking up the teddy bear from the chair where he had thrown it with such joyous abandon, she cuddled it to her breast, wishing it was Niall in her arms, close to her heart. Emotions piled in on her, the first she had experienced for many months, but uppermost was a feeling of fear, fear of losing a loved one, of losing Niall. She shook her head from side to side and whimpered, 'Oh, Niall, I do love you – but I'm so – but I'm so – afraid.' With a sudden movement she threw the bear to the floor as if it had bitten her. She mustn't allow herself to become involved in that way again. It hurt, oh God! how it hurt – and she wasn't ready to take that – ever again.

Niall went immediately home to tell his parents that he was going away again and wouldn't be back for Christmas. Phebie looked pleadingly at her son, but the hurt, lost look on his face stilled her tongue.

'It might be better, Niall,' she said quietly, 'though I thought you would – at least come home for Christmas.'

Lachlan put a firm arm round his son's shoulders. 'Do as you think best, son,' he said gently. 'But remember, if you feel like coming back for the festive season we'll be waiting, you know that.'

'Ay, I know.' Niall brushed a hand over his eyes. 'I'll write and let you know how I'm getting along – but right now, I'm going to pack.'

He went out of the room leaving his parents to look at one another in bewilderment, a dull sadness in each of their hearts as they wondered what the future held for the son who was everything to them.

It was homely and cosy in Nellie MacIntosh's croft which was situated close enough to the rolling Atlantic ocean for the salt sprays of winter tides to splash into the garden where kale and cabbage somehow managed to survive and even flourish in the seaweed tossed so carelessly over the stony earth. Nellie's Croft, as it was known to all, was a favourite place of Niall's, the house in which he stayed most frequently on his sojourns to Hanaay which, with its population of a hundred and fifty, was even more insular than Rhanna. The way of life had changed little over the last hundred years, the predominant language being Gaelic and though the children learned English at school and could converse in the two languages equally well, the 'foreign' tongue was left behind when they departed back to their Gaelic-speaking homes. The ceilidhs, the Seanachaidhs, the cracks, the strupaks, were the main source of winter entertainment, enjoyed more often than not in a blackhouse where the thatch was blackened by the ever-burning peats and the raw cold of the Atlantic was kept at bay by walls several feet deep, through which no draughts, could penetrate. The Hanaay people were soft spoken and friendly, and when visitors came they left with an impression of goodwill and kindness, and almost all vowed to come back one day to an island where 'time had stood still'.

It was here, on Hanaay, that Ellie had run and played and it was on the boulder-strewn beach behind Nellie's Croft that she had found the baby otter. Now Niall walked those same lonely shores, with only the surging of the wild ocean and the cries of seabirds to keep him company, remembering Ellie, seeing her dancing in the summer spray, hearing her laughter, thinking about how the tears had sprung to her gentle eyes the day they found a dead seal, rolling and swaying in the swirling tide race. Now he had his daughter no more, she was lost, lost to him forever, never again would he know the mortal joy of her, feel touched by the happiness which had surrounded her wherever she went. And not only had he lost Ellie, it seemed he had lost his wife as well, lost her as surely as if she too had died. The cold, empty woman he had left behind on Rhanna wasn't the spirited one he had known. The light of her life had been quenched by grief and so too had the love which she had always given him so freely. He felt drained, sucked dry of all emotion, and as he walked, hour after hour, day after day, feeling neither cold nor hunger, he felt as if he too might be dead so little was there in life to look forward to.

As the days melted into weeks, with Christmas looming on the horizon, Nellie became so worried she spoke to Mac about it. She stood in the cosy kitchen, her hands folded over her rounded stomach, a frown on her plump face with its jutting jaw which made her look perpetually grim, belying her caring, kindly nature. Her salt and pepper hair was rolled into a tight sausage round her head, emphasizing the layer of fat on her neck; her skirts, worn just above the calf, revealed dimpled knees on legs which looked impossibly inadequate to support her rotund figure; her feet were splayed, stuck into big checked woolly bootees with the zips undone and the sole of one unstuck so that it slip-slapped whenever she moved. The lack of time she spent on her appearance was obvious, but Nellie had better things to do with her time and was not ashamed of the interest she took in other people's affairs nor of her eagerness to try and right the wrongs she encountered.

'The lad is growing thinner by the hour,' she told her brother grimly, 'I canny bide to watch such a decent cratur' going down like this. We will have to do something about it and no mistake.'

Mac didn't answer immediately. Seated by the glowing peat fire, his bulbous nose a bright red, his stockinged feet wiggling contentedly on the hearth, a glass of rum in his big purpled fist, he contemplated her words for quite some time. Holding the glass of spirits near the fire he enjoyed the patterns made by the changing light, his brown eyes gently panning the glass from top to bottom. With slow deliberation he removed the poker from the fire where it had been heating for the last five minutes and plunged the glowing tip into the liquid, satisfaction curling his grizzled mouth as the sizzling assaulted his willing ears and the fragrance of burnt rum filled his nostrils. With a calculated show of tentativeness he took a sip, swallowed it, his Adam's apple working in noisy appreciation.

'I quite agree wi' you there, Nell,' he nodded eventually, wiping his nose with a hairy-backed hand. 'I don't like the look o' the lad myself and that's a fact, ay, indeed I do not.'

'Well, and what are we going to do about it?' Nellie's slipper slapped the floor in agitation. 'He canny go on like this, the Lord knows. I would have him here forever if I thought it would help him but it's no', indeed it's no', and I'm blessed if I know what to do for the best.'

Mac considered his answer for a few more lip-smacking moments before saying ponderously but decisively, 'We'd best send him home where he belongs, Nell.'

Nellie sat down on a long-suffering rocking chair with labouring springs, its round wooden seat unable to contain her rolling hips which overlapped the edges in burgeoning folds.

'Send him home?' Her voice was squeaky with surprise. 'What on earth good would that do I'd like to know? Surely he came here to get away from all his bothers. The drink is going to your head, my lad, I aye said it would in the end.'

Mac ignored this. 'But he's no' escapin' all the bothers, is he? Oh no! He's brought them here wi' him and here they are just festerin' away in his mind like sores. That kind o' thing is no use to anybody. No, he'd be better goin' back and facin' his problems at their source. At least on Rhanna he has his faither and mither and if you are mindin' the way things were wi' us when we were young there is no one like a mither to ease the ails o' a sore heart.'

Nellie wiped her nose with her grubby apron. 'Ay, you're maybe right there, Mac. There's sense buried somewhere in that snowy thatch o' yours. Besides, it will be Christmas soon and everyone should be wi' their own at Christmas.' She paused and her eyes filled with tears. 'It will be sore on him, mind, Christmas trees and parties, they are all the sort o' things to mind him o' our wee Ellie. My, you know, Mac, I canny right believe myself that she's gone. I can see her now, her wee bum on this very chair I am murderin' now, thon baby otter on her knee, her bonny hair about her face whiles she laughed and talked to it.'

Mac sighed heavily, 'Ay, it's a sore life, Nell, a sore life. I loved the bairnie like one o' my own. My, we had a grand time with her over at Breac Beag – "I could fine live here, Mac," she said to me once. "I'd never have to go to school again and could just pass my time lookin' after injured seabirds and other cratur's." "And what about all those human cratur's you are wantin' to cure when you are a doctor?" I asked her. "You'll no' find many o' these hereabouts." She went all serious on me and then she threw her wee arms about me, kissed me on the tip o' my nose and called me a cunning old sea dog! Ay, she was a bairn anybody could love and that's a fact.' He sniffed and got to his feet, surreptitiously wiping his hand over his eyes, his voice less steady when he said decisively, 'We'll tell the lad tonight, Nell, it is for the best, just you wait and see.'

But that evening, seated round warmly by the fire, hearing the sea lashing and the wind moaning round the house, Niall's reaction to Mac's suggestion was half-incredulous, half-indignant. His thin face, flushed from a mixture of the fire's heat and rising agitation, looked pathetically haunted as he cried, 'For God's sake, Mac, I'm just finding my feet here, giving myself time to think! What on earth's gotten into the pair of you?'

'You are no' finding anything here, far less your feets,' Mac said firmly, though his heart was already melting at the hurt expression on Niall's face. 'As for thinkin' – you're doin' too damty much o' it and no' enough doing. You are just goin' round in circles, lad, and the longer you stay here the more fankled your mind will become.'

'Am I in the road, is that it?' Niall couldn't contain his anger. 'Or is it because I'm not paying my way well enough – if that's what's bothering you I'll give you more – everything I have if necessary.' He halted at sight of Nellie's face. She had half turned away but the crimson staining her neck gave away her embarrassment and he was immediately repentant, voicing his apologies in some confusion.

'You should know better, laddie,' she rebuked him with a nod, 'I would spend my days scrabblin' in the ground for tatties and be happy to live on tattie broth for the rest o' my days if it was going to be of any help to you but that's no' what we're meaning and fine you know it too.'

'Ach, look you, let us no' get upset now,' Mac said placatingly. 'We will have a wee tot o' rum or maybe two and talk this over like sensible chiels.'

Niall stared down at his restless hands and said in a low voice, 'It's all right, I'm a hot-headed fool, I never used to be so . . . well, you know what it is. But you're both right, it's time I was going. God knows I've done enough walking and thinking to last me a lifetime. What I need to do now is stop for a while and try to get it all into perspective – ay – that's what I must do.

The sea is calm enough at the moment so I'll be off at first light.'

Mac stared. 'But – surely you're no' goin' alone, lad? I'm all set to come wi' you. I didny become the skipper o' *The Sea Urchin* for nothing and I will no' be paid good sillar just for sittin' on my backside doin' nothing.'

But Niall seemed to have reached a decision and there was a faint sparkle in his eyes when he put his arm round Mac's shoulders. 'You stay and enjoy Christmas with Nellie and the folks here. I'm not a fool, I've learned most of what there is to know about boats and the sea – thanks to my skipper.'

'Ach, it takes a lifetime to learn even a quarter o' the ways o' the green monster.' Mac's frown pulled his bushy eyebrows into an unbroken line. He argued the point for a few minutes but Niall was adamant now, a firmness in his manner that brooked no further objections. He went to his room in order to pack a few things and go early to bed leaving Nellie and Mac wondering if they had done the right thing.

By first light next morning Captain Mac was down at the sheltered inlet of Hook Bay where *The Sea Urchin* had been anchored since their arrival. Silvery light played on the calm water which was empty but for a lone lobster boat and the skeleton of a wreck partially submerged by high tide. Mac dug his hands into his pockets and walked back to the croft where Nellie was cooking bacon and eggs on the hot plate of the range which was kept burning day and night. At Mac's entry she turned, tucking away a loose strand of hair.

'He's away then?' she nodded.

Mac sat down, rubbing his cold, mottled hands together, his big nose sniffing the air in appreciation. 'Ay, he went wi' the tide. He wasny long in hoppin' away, as if he was glad to see the back o' us, yet look at the way he was when we first suggested it.'

'He'll be better at home.' Her fire-flushed face was full of conviction. 'Sometimes a wee push is all that's needed to get a body goin' in the right direction.' She glanced at Niall's vacant chair and sighed, 'It will be funny without him for he is a darlin' boy and no mistake – and he has manners – no' like you wi' your great galumpin' starved lookin' face and your hairy hands never washed. Get into that scullery this meenit and get the dirt off yourself. You'll get no breakfast till you do!'

Mac sighed and rose grudgingly. Much as he enjoyed his visits to his sister there were times when the urge to be on the water once more was unbearable. There was a strange wild solitude to the roar of the waves and an exhilaration such as he never found on dry land. As he went to the sink to scrub his hands, his thoughts were with Niall out there on the ocean – and somehow the idea of him being alone made him – uneasy.

Chapter Fifteen

The days leading up to Christmas advanced with startling rapidity as they were wont to do when dozens of small tasks became magnified out of all proportion. The weather had been extremely mild for December but now a wild spell hit the Hebrides with vicious ferocity, bringing storms and gales which left havoc in their wake. The aftermath invariably saw folk scurrying to retrieve roof slates and bits of corrugated iron from fields and shore. Old Meggie of Nigg was unfortunate enough to waken one morning and find that half of her roof had been carried off in the night, bits of it blowing over the cliffs and landing on the shore far below. Undaunted, she immediately moved her necessities into the blackhouse which sat alongside the 'modern hoosie' and which was kept as a henhouse and storeshed combined; though, like quite a few of her generation, she always kept the living area reserved for emergencies, quite happy to remain in the cosier hoosie for as long as need be.

For Tam McKinnon the storms were a mixed blessing as he was never short of work though it was with frequent martyred sighs that he set off on his rounds of repairs, accompanied by his youngest son, Wullie, who was an excellent tradesman, despite his indolent appearance. It was Wullie who noticed that some of the slates had come off the roof of Mo Dhachaidh and Tam affected rather offended surprise as, it being dinner time, he had hoped that they could get along home without any further delay. He paused and took more thorough note of the old house, nostalgia sweeping over him at the remembrance of Biddy.

'My, my, it's lookin' awful neglected, son,' he observed, his gaze sweeping over the garden which had got off to such a triumphant start in the spring but which was now flattened by the wind and the sheep. The windows of the house were dirty and cobwebby in the limpid light of day, with the hens huddling miserably on the sills or clucking dismally among the ruins of the garden, reliant on passers-by to scatter an odd bowl of grain from the wooden barrel in the henhouse.

Tam dispatched Wullie to see to the hens and, feeling it his duty to auld Biddy, popped into Laigmhor to report on the state of the house. Laigmhor was empty but for Shona in the kitchen, half-heartedly peeling vegetables. Tam hesitated. Everyone had mourned sorely for the family who had suffered the loss of a beloved child and sympathies had been high for Shona during her illness. But as time wore on and she showed no sign of coming out of herself people were beginning to ask themselves if she ever would. Only those who had visited Laigmhor had seen her since her return from hospital and staunch as they were, they couldn't help but be offended when their approaches were met with curt response. It was with some trepidation therefore that Tam faced her for, to put it in his own words, he would 'sooner face a Uisga Caillich than a McKenzie in a black mood'.

Shona didn't turn from her task and his voice dropped like pebbles into the silence of the kitchen. He stood, shuffling his feet, wishing he hadn't been so smart, telling himself he should have sent Wullie instead. 'I'll be going then.' He sidled to the door.

'Ay, away you go, Tam.' Shona's glance fell on his muddy bootmarks on the clean floor. 'Didn't Kate ever train you to wipe your feet?' she asked sharply.

'Ay, ay, it's just – I forgot,' he said lamely, twisting his cap in his work-grimed hands, adding daringly, 'How are you keeping these days, lass? We miss you about the place. Kate was just saying she would like fine to see you more in the village.'

Shona put down the vegetable knife, wiped her hands on her apron and looked at him resentfully. 'It's well seeing you have such a carefree life, Tam McKinnon, to be saying a thing like that. Does anything other than whisky and mischief touch your life, I wonder?'

Tam's homely face crumpled with dismay. 'We all have our ails, Shona,' he chided respectfully, 'and when a man has a family to look to he has the worry o' them forbye. Now that you mention it, Kate and myself have been more than a mite worried about our Nancy. She has just come home after another operation to – well – to have another bosom taken away and the soul is a wee bitty depressed. Wullie and me have just been to see how is she. We went in wi' our faces straight and came out wi' them smilin' for you know what a joker she is and can even laugh when she is no' feelin' well.'

Shona's face had gone pale and remorse filled her heart. 'Oh, Tam, I'm sorry, I didn't know – I – I've been out of touch with things. When next you see her give her my love and tell her – I'll – I'll be along to see her soon – Nancy has always been special to me and I know how you must feel. I'm a bitch for biting your head off just now and will be grateful if you would spare the time to see to things – up yonder. Go you along and have your dinner and I'll get along and see the damage at Mo Dhachaidh for myself.'

'I'd be glad to set it to rights,' Tam interposed eagerly. 'I wouldny like auld Biddy to think we have been neglecting her house.' He reddened and left the house abruptly.

Shona took off her apron and went to retrieve her coat from the stand. A shiver went through her. Could she go back there? Back to the house where Ellie had died – back to an empty shell that held no really good memories for her? What was the point? She wasn't going to live there again . . . Even as she argued with herself she was writing her father a note, telling him where she was going. Her hands were icy as she let herself out of the house. It had been so long since she had encountered wide open spaces that panic invaded her. The wind lifted her hair, tossed it about her face. Impatiently she pushed it from her eyes and stared about her. It was a boisterous day with the clouds scudding across the sky and the tang of wind-tossed heather and peat smoke strong in her nostrils. She had once loved days like these, the excitement, the exuberance of them. It seemed so long since she had really looked at the world – breathed its life into her lungs.

She wandered along the road, her eyes roving everywhere at once. Mo Dhachaidh appeared, a lone white speck, something welcoming about the sight of it in such a secluded spot. But at closer quarters it had an air of neglect about it. A twinge of guilt wormed into her at the sight of the bedraggled feathers on the hens and involuntarily she returned a speckled round pebble to the windowsill from which it had been pushed by the hens. Ellie had collected a lot of stones like it from the seashore and Shona had jokingly told her she would grow to be an eccentric like Dodie. The interior of the house was cold; a musty odour pervaded the rooms. She compared it with the warmth, the atmosphere of Laigmhor, but knew she wasn't being fair – all it needed was people – life about it – but Ellie had been its life – the heart that kept it ticking over . . . Her glance fell on Memory Corner. Biddy's picture was as she'd left it, face down on the ledge and the remaining photos seemed to look at her mockingly, reproachfully. Her arm shot out and in one swift movement she swept the pictures and the vase with its withered flowers to the floor. The vase smashed into pieces, the photos lay scattered everywhere.

She caught a glimpse of herself in the mirror that hung on the window wall; a strange-eyed, gaunt-faced woman with lank, untidy hair looked back at her, the fire of the hair was dulled, there was a wisp of grey in the tendrils round the ears. With a little cry she snatched a pair of scissors from the drawer and hacked and hacked till her thumb and forefinger were ringed with red weals and coils of hair lay on the dirty red tiles.

'That's it,' she panted, her nostrils flaring. 'New beginnings, get rid of everything that's old, make a fresh start. Mirabelle said it was good luck to do that, good luck, good luck, good luck . . .' The words rang in her ears and she laughed derisively. 'Ellie said we would be lucky here and look how lucky she was . . .' She tossed away the scissors and threw herself onto Biddy's chair to rock herself back and forth, gazing with wide dry eyes into nothingness. Was this what it would always be like? The emptiness? The bitterness that made her snap at people like Tam McKinnon whose only crime was a happy disposition? . . . A shadow fell over her and she looked up startled to see Mark James standing beside her.

'I knocked but there was no answer.' His smile was warm but she didn't respond, her hand going up self-consciously to her head. He had visited Laigmhor several times but always there had been Kirsteen, her father, Bob . . . She wondered what had prompted him to come here, and as if in answer to her thoughts he explained that he had arrived at Laigmhor only to find it empty and her note on the table.

'It was private,' she said ungraciously, adding pointedly, 'And I came here to be alone, I don't need any sermons.'

She continued to rock, the chair creaking rhythmically on its springs. His glance fell on the strands of hair littering the floor and he grinned in his engaging way. 'I see you've been treating yourself to a hairdo. They say it always boosts a woman's morale.'

'Do they?' she said flatly. 'Are you one of them?'

'I suppose I am,' he answered evenly, choosing to ignore the heavy sarcasm in her tones.

She eyed him, struck afresh by the aura of power which emanated from him. He was wearing his dog collar but otherwise there was nothing to mark him down as a man of God. His dark hair was windblown, a wet autumn leaf was sticking to his shoe, raindrops spattered the shoulders of his heavy coat.

'Do you know more about women than you let on?' she asked dryly.

He pulled out a chair and seated himself a little way from her, his manner neither confidential nor deferential. 'Perhaps I know more than you think, Shona.'

'Really!' She laughed mirthlessly, annoyed to find that his proximity discomfited her. 'And I suppose you're going to try and impress me with how much you think you know – to comfort me in my hour of need?'

He spread his hands, fine strong hands with the nails

clean but not too clean, as if he had spent a morning in the garden and couldn't quite scrub the earth from them.

'If you want me to,' he said quietly.

She threw back her head and stared at him mockingly. 'Well, go on then, I'm waiting. I've lost a child who was my world and if you can help me to forget that then you're quite a man, Mark James.'

Slowly he raised his head, his smoky eyes met and held hers, and there was such a depth of emotion in them she found herself holding her breath. Moments stretched, laden with a strange palpable intimacy that seemed to lock them into a physical embrace. Her heart began to pound; against her will her gaze travelled to the wide, sensual line of his mouth. She struggled to compose her feelings but she was mesmerized, in her mind imagining his lips on hers, kissing her till she was beyond all resistance. It had been so long since she and Niall had held each other, so very long. For a time she wouldn't have cared if he had never made love to her again but more and more of late she hadn't been able to stop herself from thinking about him, wanting him back – but she had sent him away – rejected him – in the past week not even Phebie had heard from him and it looked as if he was staying on Hanaay over Christmas . . .

'I'm sorry – oh – I'm so very very sorry!' she burst out passionately, uncertain if she was apologizing to Niall or the man who sat so close to her. With a sudden, decisive movement he got to his feet and in two strides covered the distance to her chair. Pulling her up to him he wound his arms round her and held her close, his face against hers, the warmth of him flooding her being. She didn't struggle away, instead she laid her head on his shoulder, a beautiful kind of peace diffusing her limbs. His strength, his goodness seemed to flow into her, his silence so laden with meaning it was as if he had chosen all the right things to say. She was unprepared for the swift turn of his head. His mouth, warm and passionate came over hers in a kiss so deep, so penetrating, she was robbed of all resistance. She raised up her arms to entwine her fingers into the crisp hair at his nape, all the while exerting pressure on his head, urging him to fire, to kiss and kiss her till the raw ache of desire burned deep in her belly while her tongue met and played with his in ever deepening circles of unconcealed rapture. She drowned in ecstasy for a few brief unforgettable minutes, then he tore his lips away to lay his abrasive cheek against the smoothness of hers once more, his breath harsh and quick in his throat. Longing, strong, dangerous surged through her, her heart pulsed, her weak limbs grew weaker still. The virile heart of his body burned into her, the smell of his damp hair, his clean, rain-washed skin, was a heady concoction which she breathed and breathed into her so that she would never forget it for as long as she lived. She knew these moments in his arms were the only ones she would ever have and she savoured them while she could.

'Just once – I had to kiss you – just once!' The depth of his feelings edged his voice to roughness.

'I have lain in your arms before now,' she whispered, 'in my mind.'

'I too,' his voice was husky now, as if he spoke through tears. She became aware that he was trembling, as if some force had seized him and was without his power to control. His mouth touched her ear and she shivered, her heart twisting with so much emotion she felt like fainting. 'This is the first and last time I will ever hold you in my arms.' His words were raw, broken. He moved away and immediately she felt bereft, experiencing an echo of the bitter-sweet sadness she would know in days and years to come whenever she thought about this time – this now – with him. The fleeting interlude of intimacy was a culmination of something they had both known would happen. His lean face was etched into lines of pain, the same sort of useless longing that was in her shone naked in the blue-grey fathoms of his eyes. Her arms ached to hold his hard exciting body once more but she knew that she never would – it was over before it had begun.

He turned away to stare unseeingly from the window. 'I have committed adultery with you, as surely as if I had lain in your bed beside you.' His voice was hushed, laced with shock, and she put her fist to her mouth, exerting every shred of willpower to stop herself from running to him.

'No, no,' she breathed in protest, 'we have done nothing wrong!'

He half turned, the burning meaning in his glance quieting her. Of course she knew what he meant, why pretend it had never happened – why deny to him of all people the thing that she had sustained in her mind from the day they met? She shut her eyes . . .

'Will you always love me?' Like a bolt from the blue the words came to her, words that Niall had spoken, laden with a strange urgency – as if he had momentarily glimpsed something of what was to happen. She pressed her fist hard against her mouth but not before Mark James heard her whimpered cry of distress.

He passed a hand over his eyes. 'I didn't mean any of this to happen – I only came here to talk to you – perhaps comfort you – and somehow I've only succeeded in confusing us both.'

'No, don't say that, please don't! You came when I was in a very dangerous mood. I was hating, hating everything and everybody, the same sort of bitter resentment I've had for so long now! You came in for a bit of it when you walked through my door. I saw life and happiness in you and I wanted to rob you of it – instead you have given some of it to me. You've brought me alive again, I feel as if I can see, hear – feel for the first time since Ellie died.' She looked straight into his eyes. 'You touched me with an enchantment today that will always remain with me. I'll never get over it as long as I live. You have power, Mark James, power over women – yet – you walk alone – it's such a waste of such a bonny man!'

'Not alone, Shona, with God – and before Him with a wonderful girl who later became my wife.' He looked away and spoke almost to himself. 'Before I met her I was a wreck of a human being – I had all the vices but Margaret changed me – made me into a man. With her encouragement I followed a boyhood dream and went to college to study for the ministry and it was through her help and guidance that I succeeded in what I set out to do. I felt I had everything I ever wanted in my life – then – just over a year ago – Margaret died in a car accident – she and my daughter who was just nine years old. She was fair, gentle, full of laughter – your Ellie reminded me so much of Sharon – the same mischief, the same regard for old people and the wild creatures of the earth . . .'

He couldn't go on. Shona stared at him, reeling against the pain his confessions had brought him – it was there, in his eyes, an inward-reaching agony which he must have nursed alone for so long. She remembered the air of vulnerability that had surrounded him when first he came to the island – no wonder – oh dear God, no wonder! She bit her lip. Oh to go to him, not as a woman to a man but as one compassionate human being to another, to comfort him in his agony – but she knew she couldn't, the thing that would always be with them wouldn't allow her ever to touch him – especially when they were alone together as now.

'I – want to touch you!' she cried across the distance that separated them like a deep wide chasm.

'I know.' He smiled at her, a warm smile which spread through her like a gentle flame. 'Me too – but we have to go our separate ways now.'

'How can you bear it – to be so – alone?' she whispered.

The smile widened. 'I told you – I have my God beside me. I deserted Him when my family died and I had a complete nervous breakdown – but He didn't desert me, He was waiting for me to help me pick up the pieces of my life. Oh, there were times when I was sorely tempted to blame it all on Him but somehow I didn't think there was much sense in such useless accusations.'

'But surely – God must take some of the blame?' she faltered, trying to remember when last she had prayed.

'It's easy to blame God when we're in the black depths of mourning, a human frailty that besets us all when we are least strong.'

'But – God didn't help me!' she cried passionately.

His smile was rueful now. 'You turned away from Him – from everything. I think God can only help us by surrounding us with people who care – through them He does His work. I came here to make a new life for myself and it's working. Slowly I'm picking up the pieces but only because I've been helped in a practical way by the folk of this island. They aren't demonstrative, theirs is a staunch support and I've appreciated their lack of emotion to help me over my crisis. Barra McLean was the only one who knew what had happened to me, she was one of my parishioners in Glasgow. She helped me by not saying anything because she knew it was what I wanted, yet in a way I've hampered my own progress by surrounding myself in mystery. I'm like you, Shona, I should have allowed myself the comfort that only other people can give, but I deluded myself into believing it would only prolong the agony. It doesn't do to bury a loved one just because the light of life has gone from them. It's up to us to carry their lamp and the time has come for us both to do that.'

'I've been so selfish – and cruel to everyone.' Her heart was full to brimming and she could barely get the words out. 'I'll never be able to make it up – especially to Niall. I made him suffer more than he could already bear – by turning away from him when he so badly needed me.'

'He's a fine man, you're lucky to have him.'

'But I haven't got him,' she said miserably. 'I sent him away and because he couldn't take any more – he went.'

'He'll come back, if he loves you enough he'll be only too ready to meet you halfway.' He looked down at the litter on the floor. 'I think we should start off by clearing up this mess.'

She nodded. 'My temper got the better of me and I took it out on the first things that came to hand.' A smile lit her pale face. 'I always did blame my temper for everything.'

He studied her face. 'You're smiling, the way you used to when first I met you.'

'I'll have to learn to do more of it—' She paused. 'How strange – to be having to learn to do the kind of things I always took for granted before – before Ellie died. She was always smiling – I can see her bonny young face now – smiling.'

'You're taking the first steps, Shona, you're remembering the happy things about your daughter. As time goes by they will come to you more and more. When I think of Margaret and Sharon I think of the happy times we shared. My early pictures were all of death but now I see them healthy and rosy and full of life.'

A dry sob caught her unawares. 'I hope I'll see Ellie like that again. I try so hard to remember her skipping and laughing but it's all blotted out by memories of how ill she looked before she died.'

She gazed shakily at the strands of hair on the floor. 'Niall would be angry if he saw this. He always used to get so mad at me whenever I threatened to cut my hair.'

Mark James studied the hacked remains of her locks. 'To tell the truth I liked it myself – it was such beautiful hair – but it will grow again.' Stooping he picked up Mirabelle's picture. 'A bonny woman,' he commented softly. 'Who was she?'

She gazed at the smiling portrait in his hand. 'Who was she indeed? She was Mirabelle. She was all things to all people. She kept house for my father – she brought me up when my mother died . . .' Slowly she retrieved another picture from the floor. 'This was my mother – she's beautiful, isn't she? My father adored her. She died when I was born and he broke his heart. This handsome rogue was my brother Lewis – Lorn's twin. He was just eighteen when he died.'

One by one she went over the photos, her eyes faraway

as she talked about the people who had once enriched her life. 'This handsome man was my uncle Alick, he died rescuing my father from the Sgor Creags. People thought he was a weak sort of man but he must have been brave to do what he did. This dear lady is auld Biddy, the nurse who brought most of us into the world. She lived in this house all of her life and eventually died peacefully in her own bed. She got the MBE for long service to the community.' Shona's eyes had grown shiny. 'She used to call it a damty fine brooch and pinned it on all the bairnies who came to see her . . .' Blindly she shook her head. 'Talking about them makes me so ashamed of myself. I'm glad none of them lived to see how poorly I've behaved in time of trouble – I haven't been very brave, have I?'

'You've been human, Shona, just as they were, you mustn't blame yourself for that. We all mourn in our different ways.'

He took the pictures and began placing them on the mantelpiece, but she shook her head and cried, 'No, they belong in Memory Corner. It was Ellie's idea. She gathered them all together and every other day brought fresh flowers from the moors and fields to put in a vase beside them. Biddy goes like this – turned slightly outwards so that she can look at the view she loved. Mirabelle is facing Biddy because in life they were such good friends—' She paused and coloured, aware that he was watching her intently.

'You're alive again, Shona, don't you feel it?'

She nodded, 'Ay, it's coming back, I feel sad and happy at the same time. I want to cry but I can't – the tears won't come—' Her voice rose. 'I think there must be something wrong with me!'

'They'll come – in time they'll come – meantime, haven't you forgotten something?'

'Forgotten something?'

'Your most important and precious memory of all – Ellie wouldn't want to be left out of Memory Corner – after all, it was her idea.'

Wordlessly she left the room and went upstairs. She was gone for quite some time but when she returned she carried a picture of Ellie – Ellie laughing in a summer field, her arms full of buttercups, her golden hair glinting red in the sun, her eyes crinkled with all the joy and laughter that had been hers in her short life.

'Put it here,' Mark James directed gently. 'Facing into the room where you can see her bright young face and feel her joy when you're sad or depressed.'

A sprig of red-berried holly and a spray of bronze beech leaves had been hastily arranged in a jar and placed on the ledge. 'It was all I could find,' he explained apologetically. 'The leaves I picked from the hedge in the garden.'

Too overcome to speak she turned away and in a blinding flash Ellie came to her, long golden limbs carrying her swiftly through the fields, her brown arms outstretched as if to embrace the world, her face uplifted to the sky as if in adoration of the vast open spaces that had been hers from babyhood. 'Ellie,' she whispered in wonder, 'you're so happy.'

'Ay, Mother, happiness is like the measles – it's infectious.' An echo of Ellie's voice seemed to beat into the room, bringing with it all the frank, unquestioning hope of youth.

'I'm not – going funny in the head again – am I?' Shona voiced her fears in panic.

'You're accepting what is,' Mark James reassured her. 'And that can only be good.' He moved towards the door. 'I must go – I want to see how old Meggie is coping with living in a blackhouse.'

'Och, she'll be fine, she's a self-sufficient old soul and enjoys an excuse to get into her blackhoosie.' She thought about the day she had gone with Mark James on his visits. It had been a good day, a day of summer, of sun, of old people who faced the problems of daily living with dignity. But she had only accompanied Mark James for selfish reasons, and the same had applied when she had gone with Babbie on her rounds. Her friend had more or less implied this but she hadn't liked such home truths. She was suddenly filled with a compelling urge to right this and she said quietly, 'Let me come with you sometime, I – I feel I want to do something to help people like Meggie and Jack.'

He nodded, 'Ay, the old folk would like that. They have all been asking after you, wondering how you were.'

'Mark – I want you to know – there will always be a special place in my heart for you.'

His frank, assessive gaze swept over her and it was as if he was imprinting a picture of her in his mind that would remain forever. 'It is enough for me to know that – in some small way I have helped you to find God again. I will never forget these precious minutes spent in your company – and remember, God works in mysterious ways, Shona. Miracles do happen if you believe in them enough. You have so much of life left and plenty of time for wonderful things to happen to you. Just promise me one thing, only you and I need know of the thing that happened here today. You must never hurt your husband by telling him.'

'I won't say anything, you can be sure of that,' she said huskily.

His broad back was to her now and already he was becoming a memory. 'Think of me now and then.' His voice was low, his dark head angled slightly backwards but he didn't turn again. She listened as his footsteps went up the hall, watched as he walked past the window. His coat collar was turned up against the wind, his hair ruffling over his brow. He didn't look towards the window but walked quickly away till he was just a dark blob in the distance, a lone figure who carried God in his soul.

With his departure the house was empty again, empty and sad, as if in some way it had been badly let down. She went over to the mantelpiece and blew away the dust. 'I've let you down, Biddy,' she said to the silent room. 'I said you would never regret our coming to live in your house and I've neglected it sorely.'

She pulled herself up to her full height, a new determination on her face. Tomorrow she would come back to light fires and clean the house till it was shining. After all, this was her home, hers and Niall's – and he deserved to come back to a welcoming place, a fire to warm him, his meals ready on the table . . . Suddenly she couldn't wait to get started, could hardly bear to see the house as it was – and most of all she couldn't wait to see Niall again – to let him know that everything was going to be all right.

On the way back to Laigmhor she encountered Dodie trundling bits of corrugated iron in a wheelbarrow. She guessed that his cottage had suffered storm damage and he wasn't waiting for the laird to send someone round to repair it. She raised her hand in greeting but the familiar 'He breeah' wasn't forthcoming and though he was some way off she saw plainly the look of reproach he cast in her direction before he turned up the hill track and hurried away, his big misshapen frame thrown forward to take the weight of the barrow.

She stood dismayed, wondering what she had done to him. Never in all her years of knowing him had this happened. To lose the trust of Dodie was somehow earth-shattering. He was just an old man, smelly, eccentric, inarticulate, yet he was something more, much more than any of these. He represented everything that was steadfast and true, attributes she had rarely encountered in the more sophisticated around her. In his oneness of body and soul he portrayed the spirit of the island, in the simple faith he placed in his fellow creatures, he signified hope in everyone who knew him. To gain the trust of such a shy and humble man was something rare, accorded only to a few. She had been one of them and somehow she had hurt him badly enough for him to want to avoid meeting her.

She would have to ask Niall about it, he had been her most constant companion in the week after Ellie's death, a time of which she could recall very little, even the funeral was just a dim blur in her mind. Her footsteps quickened as she approached the cobbled yard, all at once unable to wait to see her father. It was as if a veil had been lifted from her whole outlook and she was seeing clearly again.

'I'm back, Father!' Her voice rang out. Fergus swung round from the sink where he was washing off the afternoon's grime; Kirsteen looked up from the newspaper, her newly acquired spectacles sitting selfconsciously but attractively on her neat nose; Ruth who had been to the village with Kirsteen and who had come back for a strupak, stopped in the act of bundling little Lorna into her fluffy pink sleeping suit. Ruth had been to visit many times since Shona's return from hospital but had received an even cooler reception than anyone, Shona barely acknowledging her existence after an initial brusque word of apology for what had happened.

Everyone stared at her intrusion into the kitchen and Fergus burst out, 'Shona, what in heaven's name have you done?'

She had forgotten the surprise her changed appearance

would create and for a few uncomprehending seconds she stared back at them all then her hand flew to her hair and she coloured.

'Ach, I felt like a change so I lopped it off,' she explained but still her father continued to gaze at her as if she wasn't quite real, a deep hope shining in his eyes.

'Shona,' he said and his voice was low. 'What happened?'

She looked at him steadily. 'I went to Mo Dhachaidh and had a visit from the minister.'

That was all but it was enough. Fergus nodded. 'He's a fine man.'

'Ay,' she agreed briefly then added somewhat impatiently, 'Has anyone heard from Niall at all?'

'Nary a word – but he should be home for Christmas.'

'Shona, I was wondering—' Ruth began hesitantly then rushed on. 'There's a dance at Portvoynachan next week and Lorn said he would take me if I could get someone to come over and sit with Lorna. Would you—?' She left the question unfinished, her fair skin flooding with colour at the amazed silence which hit the room. Shona's gaze strayed to the baby. At nine months she was a rosy bundle of mischief already attempting to pull herself to her feet. Her hair had darkened to a rich honey, her eyes were an intense purple-blue, a combination that was entrancing.

'You would trust me to do a thing like that?' Shona's tones were incredulous.

'Ay, Shona, I would,' Ruth said firmly, thinking about

Lorn's face when she had put the suggestion to him and her argument that it would take something drastic to bring Shona to her senses.

'If – you're sure, Ruthie,' he had said doubtfully yet with a wonder in him that this young wife of his could be so caring towards the woman who had caused her such heartache.

'It might be just the thing she needs – to be trusted once again,' she had told him and he had taken her in his arms to hold her close, his concern for his sister silencing the fears that sprang to his tongue.

Shona could only nod her acceptance before going quickly out of the kitchen, saying over her shoulder, 'I'm away upstairs to wash my hair, I'm anything but a bonny sight at the moment.'

Her footsteps died away and Fergus breathed a heartfelt sigh of relief. 'Thank God! She's herself again. Now all we need is for Niall to come home.'

'Ay, thank God!' echoed Kirsteen while Ruth lifted Lorna high in the air and laughed aloud for joy.

Chapter Sixteen

Captain Mac looked restlessly from the window to the grey sea heaving and pounding to the shore just yards from the croft. It had been a week since Niall's departure and in that time Mac had looked anxiously for the postman, hoping for a postcard assuring him all was well. But the storms had caused delays with everything, a backlog of mail had come on yesterday's steamer though nothing from Niall had arrived at the croft.

'I was thinkin' to take a walk down to the boxie and give Niall a wee talk,' he informed his sister who, enveloped in an apron made from a mailbag washed up on the beach, was at the table wielding a rolling pin with vigour.

Rubbing her nose with the back of a floury hand she nodded her approval of his suggestion. When her brother spoke of having 'a wee talk at the boxie' it was his way of saying he was going to make use of the telephone, a recent innovation on the tiny island and one regarded with suspicion by the old. Few of the houses boasted a private phone, most folks making use of the 'red boxies' scattered at vantage points on Hanaay's wild landscape.

'Ay, it would be a good idea,' said Nellie. 'Forbye

finding out about Niall it will also get you from under my feets. You've been like a hen on a hot girdle since the lad went away.'

Mac pushed his arms into a navy blue seaman's jacket and went outside, his stocky frame bent into the wind which blew over the island for 'five months of bad weather and seven months of winter'. The red boxie was perched on the edge of the windswept moors, favoured by the sheep who liked to huddle against it for shelter, or, if they could get inside, to lick the windows and demolish the telephone directories. There was a constant demand for directories on Hanaay and continuous complaints from the GPO about the carelessness of the islanders who indignantly informed them it 'wasny them who ate the damt books'.

There had been trouble all week with the lines and when Mac arrived at the box it was to see the green Morris GPO van parked alongside. The sheep had seized the chance to use the van as a scratching post while one of the more adventurous was testing the wing mirror with inquisitive lips to find out if it was edible.

'Is the damt thing no' workin' again, Tom?' Mac greeted the GPO repair man who was a native of Uist and a cousin of his. Tom the Box, a title recently bestowed on him after years of being known as College Tom on Uist, shook his head dismally and scratched a large hairy ear with his screwdriver. 'It is no' the wind this time,' he said balefully. 'The mean buggers hereabouts have been stickin' buttons into it and jammed the works.'

'Terrible, terrible just,' sympathized Mac solicitously, his big fingers jingling his change inside his pocket to prove that he was not one of the mean buggers, though on his last sojourn to the boxie he had used a carefully filed metal button and had succeeded in getting through to Uist for a lengthy conversation before the pips went. Tom the Box had become adept at freeing jammed boxes and in a few minutes his van was hurtling away over the moor road, leaving Mac free to enter the sharn-spattered interior, thankfully banging the door shut against the wind.

Gingerly he picked up the receiver and dialled the operator who, like Behag, ran the Post Office as well as manning the switchboard installed conveniently in a handy corner of the counter which meant she didn't have to leave the premises. The only drawback to this arrangement was the lack of privacy afforded callers but, as everyone knew everyone else's business anyway, no one minded and enjoyed the diversion the switchboard afforded a routine visit to the shop.

Mac had no need to give the Rhanna exchange number to Bella as she already had most of the island numbers off by heart and in a short time Behag's querulous voice came over the line. She and Bella had struck up quite a friendship via their respective switchboards and there now followed a lengthy conversation in Gaelic while Mac stood fuming inside the draughty phone box.

'Will you get off the damt wire you pair o' bleatin' yowes!' he bawled eventually. 'Some o' us have better things to do wi' our time than stand listening to recipes for cloutie dumplin's!'

Behag's mutterings assailed his reddening ears all the while she was ringing Slochmhor but Lachlan's deep voice drowned her out and Mac blew down his nose with relief. With his fingers blocking one ear, the receiver clamped to the other, he went through the usual polite salutations before getting to the point of his call which was to ask how Niall was faring.

'Niall?' Lachlan sounded puzzled. 'Niall isn't here. We thought he was with you on Hanaay.'

Mac cleared his throat, composing himself to speak calmly. 'Well, no, he left our place – well now, let me see – a week ago it was – before the start o' the storms.'

There was a silence then Lachlan, his voice frayed with growing anxiety. 'A week ago you say?'

'Ay, it would be that.'

'But – if you weren't with him – who was?'

'Ach well, he insisted on going back alone.'

'Alone!' Mac held the receiver back from his ear as Lachlan blasted the word down the line. 'Surely you didn't let him do that, Mac! He doesn't know the sea like you.'

Mac's kindly big blustering face had collapsed into lines of worry. 'I know that and I told Niall that but he wouldn't listen. He was anxious to go, in fact I got the notion he couldny get away fast enough and here was me and Nell worrying because it was us who suggested he ought to go home for Christmas in the first place.'

'How – was he while he was there?'

'Well, now that you mention it he wasny good, just sort o' loafin' about day in day out, no' doin' himself the least bit good at all, forbye he would hardly let a bite go over his throat.'

'Mac, this is serious,' Lachlan said flatly. 'A whole week and never a word from him! Something must have happened – anything could have happened – and if he got caught in the storms . . .' The words hung ominously in the air.

Mac said nothing for it seemed there was nothing he could say. He heard Phebie's voice in the background, asking Lachlan what was wrong, heard Lachlan making placating remarks. Then she obviously left the room and Lachlan was telling Mac that they mustn't waste a minute more and that he was ringing off to call the coastguard immediately.

Mac put the phone slowly down and then it was only the bleating of the sheep and the wind soughing through the chinks. Dejectedly he let the door swing behind him and seating himself on the verge lit his pipe with an unsteady hand, heedless of the biting cold which seeped into his clothing and reddened the big fingers clasped tightly round the warm bowl of the pipe.

Righ nan Dul had led a quiet life since the lighthouse at the head of Port Rum Point had been automated. His job now consisted of checking and maintenance, all of which, to a man who had hitherto carried a key position, was all rather boring and repetitive. Despite his advancing years he still maintained his position as the island's coastguard, though weeks could pass before he might be called upon. Therefore, when the coastguard station at Oban received the report of a missing Rhanna boat it was to Righ they turned and, glad of the chance for some action, he set about his arrangements briskly. The fishing boats, lying at anchor in the harbour for a week because of the weather, were dispatched to search the seaboard between Rhanna and Hanaay while he himself got his crew together and set off in the wake of the trawlers.

The weather was on their side with a light sou'westerly blowing over a quiet sea but despite the good conditions it was a well nigh hopeless task. According to reports Niall had set off from Hanaay a week ago and there had been no distress calls from him in that time. Righ knew that the fierce gales and heavy seas would have smashed a small craft like *The Sea Urchin* to matchwood in no time but there was the remote possibility she might have been able to seek safe anchorage at any one of the small islands dotting the western seas.

It was a short search and at the end of the day a fruitless one. The weather closed in early blotting out visibility and the men returned to Rhanna, their faces showing the futility of the search. A dispirited Righ wired the results to the Oban coastguard. The possibility of resuming the search next day was discussed with perhaps a light aircraft being deployed if the owner of a private plane could be found and proved willing to undertake the task. Rather wearily, Righ phoned Slochmhor with the news and when he put the phone down his heart was as heavy as his leaden limbs.

Lachlan turned from the phone and broke the news to Phebie. She gave a little cry and buried her face in her hands. Lachlan put his arms round her and held her close, his heart so full he couldn't speak but just held onto her, standing in the circle of orange light cast by the fire, from a long distance hearing the spitting of hail in the chimney breast and the windows rattling in the wind.

'Phebie, Phebie,' he said at last. 'We must be strong, we canny give up hoping, it would be the end if we did. Niall will be all right, he always could take care of himself and will likely be holed up somewhere safe and sound.'

'There comes a time, Lachy, when even people like our son can no longer take care of themselves.' Her voice was flat, lifeless. 'He went away from here a broken man, I saw despair sitting on his shoulders the likes of which I have never seen on him before – and it might be that he never intended coming home again – maybe he planned for this to happen.'

'Stop that, Phebie!' Lachlan's voice was harsh, his thin face tired and old in the shadows of the room. 'Would you take away the dignity – the compassion – of our son by even suggesting such a thing? Niall would never set out to deliberately commit suicide on that cold buggering sea or anywhere else for that matter! He's too fine and decent to lay a thing like that at the door of the people he loves and fine you know it too!'

'I'm sorry, I'm sorry, Lachy.' She sounded exhausted, her plump face haggard and grey, her voice threaded through with a terrible dread. 'I don't know what I'm saying – I – I canny think straight.'

He led her to a chair and made her sit down by the fire. 'I'm going to get us both a brandy.' His voice was softer now, his eyes compassionate as he saw the state she was in. It was in her nature to put on a brave face and no matter how many ups and downs there had been she had hitherto succeeded but now she was at breaking point and could no longer put on an act.

The brandy steadied them both. She sat with the empty glass, staring at the flickering flames in the hearth, her shoulders rounded with dejection. 'You're right, Lachy,' she sighed. 'He would never do anything like that to us deliberately.' She glanced up at her husband. He wasn't listening, his whole attitude was one of bleak listlessness and her heart went out to him. Despite personal tragedies and difficulties he still had to carry on, day after day, tending the sick, caring for others.

She went to him and sat at his feet, her head on his knee, automatically his hand came out to stroke her hair. 'It will be all right, my darling,' she whispered. 'He'll come home to us. The men will look again tomorrow.'

Reaching up she encircled her arms round his waist and

laid her head against his chest so that she could hear the
steady thump of his heart. 'I tell you this much, my lad,'
she murmured through her tears. 'No matter what happens
you and me are having a holiday as soon as Christmas is
over. I'm going to phone Doctor McLaren and ask if he'll
come and take over here for a while. He's always quite
glad of the chance to do his locum now that he's retired.
Last time I rang him he was asking when you were going
to take a break and I've decided the time has come.'

'Ay, I'd like that.' He raised her face to him and kissed
her smooth cheek. 'Thank God I've got you, Phebie, I'd
never have made it without you.'

'Nor I without you,' she said softly. They were peaceful
for a while then Phebie said almost unwillingly, 'Will Shona
have heard?'

'Ay, of course she will,' he sighed heavily. 'How she'll
stand up to it heaven alone knows. It could be the last
straw for her.'

The outside door rattled, and, as if on cue, Shona came
up the hall and into the room. She stood in the doorway,
windblown, breathless, then throwing off her coat she went
over and took them both in her embrace.

'I knew the pair of you would be moping.' She stood
back, a strength in her bearing that made them both stare.
'Niall will come back – I don't care what anybody says,
he'll come back.'

'You sound so – sure,' faltered Phebie.

'I am sure. He came back before, didn't he? And it

was worse then because we'd already been told he was dead. Then out of the blue he popped up, large as life and the only thing dead about him his ambitions to fight in the war.'

A ghost of a smile touched Lachlan's mouth. 'Ay, you're right, lass, they canny keep a good man down.'

For their benefit she smiled, trying desperately not to let them guess at the cold dread which churned ceaselessly in her belly. She had cleaned and fired Mo Dhachaidh, all it needed now was the man who would bring it alive – if – if by some miracle he was still of the earth. She daren't let her thoughts wander further. On hearing the news that he was missing her first instinct had been to run away and hide but there could be none of that now, she had to force herself to go on, to be strong when strength was the least of her resources.

'I'm away through to make us a nice strupak,' she said brightly, 'and we're going to sit here by the fire and talk about all the nice things we'll do at Christmas with Niall back and all the family under the one roof on Christmas day.'

The next day some small boys were playing on the shore at Aosdana Bay. One of them ran to the silvery tide trace and picked up a chunk of wood wedged among the rocks. 'It's a name board off a boat,' he cried, waving it high in the air.

His companions came running, one pulled away bits of sea-wrack and stared. 'It's the name of Niall McLachlan's boat. It is *The Sea Urchin*!'

The boy who had found it gaped with round eyes. 'The fishin' boats were out lookin' for him, so were the coastguard.'

'They'll no' find him now. The sea has got him.'

'Maybe we'll get a reward if we take this back and show it.'

The first boy snatched the board back. 'I found it, it's mine. If anybody's gettin' a reward it will be me.'

He ran up the beach, the piece of wood tucked firmly under his armpit. His companions ran after him, their voices carried off by the wind which sang low over the sea.

Captain Mac sat in his favourite chair by the fire, his untouched tot of rum sitting on the mantelpiece beside his unsmoked pipe. His bushy white eyebrows were drawn down so far they almost obliterated his eyes and only two brown chinks were visible. His big, mottled hands were clenched on the knees of his navy blue serge trousers, his stockinged feet, normally held in wiggling pleasure to the agreeable heat from the glowing peats, sat square and immobile on the rough stone hearth, his bulbous nose, that cheerful beacon, was as pallidly grey as the rest of his wide-pored face.

From the chair opposite an audible sigh arose and Nellie, fingers flying in keeping with her needles, wondered just how long this unnatural silence could prevail. Often she had wished for a sign of gentility in her large, blustering, noisily cheerful brother but now she saw the drawbacks of such a drastic turnabout. The croft positively held its breath, as if it too was anticipating a return to normal. Smatterings of hail battered off the boulder-hung tin roof, the wind whistled round corners but the worst had blown itself out, leaving in its wake a fresh trail of destruction and an uneasy truce.

Nellie placed another slice of peat on the fire and leaving aside her knitting, folded her hands over her stomach and patted her hair, her usual preliminaries before she plunged into conversation. But this time, as if anticipating the subject she had been about to broach, her brother sat up with a jerk and smacked his heavy hand off his knee with such force the cat was startled out of a deep slumber and glared at him out of one reproachful green eye.

'Wait you, Nell!' Mac's tones were authoritative. 'I am after mindin' something young Niall said afore he left. I thought at the time it was gey queer but never thought any more about it till now.'

'Ay,' Nellie spoke encouragingly, glad to at last air the subject of Niall's disappearance. Since the news of it, and the subsequent abortive attempts to find him, had filtered through, Mac had been so stunned he had sunk into a state of comatose disbelief and for the last twenty-four hours had

maintained such a state of near unbroken silence, Nellie had
seriously wondered if his mind had been affected. 'Do you
mind how he was when we said he ought to go home?
Angry and rebelling against the idea like a virgin wifie at
an orgy? Then how he changed his tune, said it was time
to stop for a whily and get his thoughts in order? Well,
Nell, it is my opinion he is no' dead and I think I know
where he is!'

Before she could speak he was up, downing his rum
in one gulp, shrugging into his jacket, going to the porch
to push his feet into wellington boots with scuffed collars
stained to a greeny grey. Nellie rushed out to the porch
after him, her ponderous bulk hampering not the speed
of her movements.

'And just where do you think you are going, my lad?'
She eyed her brother whose hitherto glum features were
animated, his wide mouth stretched into a most anticipatory
grin. He took his sister by the shoulders and kissed her
soundly on the tip of her big jolly nose. 'I am going to
the pub, Nell, to see will I coax some o' the lads to take
a boat out.'

'Ach! Ach!' Nellie expostulated angrily. 'The men will
no' leave their drink just to please you – besides, man, it's
a dark, bitter night out there and the tide will be out for
hours yet.'

But Mac was away, the swinging door fanning freezing
blasts of air into the house, the slap of his steps on the
crackling stalks of the frost-rimed turf, receding rapidly. A

few minutes later a laboured putt-putting came from the shed at the side of the house where Niall's motor bike was kept. The smell and the roar of it as it passed the window made Nellie screw up her face in disgust and wonder if the bodach had gone off his head altogether as what he knew about driving a motor bike could comfortably sit on the head of one of her knitting needles.

The saliva which speckled Mac's whiskers was soon frozen into spicules of ice on the four-mile journey into Port Feall. The road climbed through the moors which stretched black as peat on either side except where the white splash from the headlight fell on silver-speared banks of heather and on the rocky gorges glittering with barbs of opaque white where the burns were starting to freeze. The sky was ablaze with stars so dense in places they flared over the vast expanse like wisps of cloud. Far in the distance the horizon paled as the moon came up, splashing its light into the sea till it became a dazzling streak that stretched between the low-slung undulations of the moors and made silver basins of the numerous small inlets along the shore.

Mac's bare hands were so stiff when he reached Port Feall it was all he could do to unwind them from the handlebars. The sinews of his fingers refused to straighten and the joints cracked with the explosion of small fireworks in the dense air which seemed to compact heavily around his ears as the motor bike engine shuddered into silence.

The warmth of the tiny lounge bar embraced him

and cries of welcome came from the bar which was well supported by the fishermen who were dousing the cold of the sea from their bones in the agreeable company of local worthies and visitors alike, for quite a few exiles had arrived on the island to spend Christmas and New Year with relatives.

Captain Mac's whiskers thawed along with his muscles as his innards warmed to the appealing fire of the water of life. His tongue became garrulous as the time ticked pleasantly by, and perhaps because there was a bit of the Irish blood in him, his gift of the gab, which had earned him locally the nickname of Isaac the Tongue, soon bedazzled the listening fishermen. Niall was known and liked by them all and many a time he had stood at this very same bar entrancing them with stories of the animals who had come under his care.

'He's a good lad, a good lad,' emphasized Iain Dubh, which in Gaelic meant Black John, a huge man whose ox-like shoulders strained against the speckled wool of his fisherknit jersey, fashioned locally by Nellie herself, one of many which she sold for only a modest profit to the grateful fisherwives.

Iain Dubh was the skipper of *The Pibroch* and his towering black haired figure and fists of steel had earned him a staunch if uneasy respect from fishermen in just about every port along the western seaboard. It was to Iain Dubh therefore that the wily Mac addressed his appeal, worded in such a way that the big man couldn't resist the challenge to his ego. He'd had no sleep for twenty-four hours but fired by the whisky and the spirit of Mac's rhetoric he leapt onto a chair and, fists raking the air, black beard glistening with beer and spittle, he challenged his crew to return to the element which they had so recently abandoned with gusto.

Only the sickly and the old resisted a call from Iain Dubh and the men were unanimous in their decision to go with him to look for Niall. It was a good night to be on the sea, clear visibility and a frontal calm. They would have to wait for the tide to turn since Port Feall was a shallow harbour, meanwhile a good hour or so remained before closing time and, with shoulders hunched, the men set about their drinking in earnest, discussing among themselves which house they would go to ceilidh in afterwards.

The Pibroch, her engine throbbing steadily, her squat bow cleaving a creamy V through the translucent waves, made good time in the silent hours of night. The pale moon rode higher in the heavens, spreading her welcome beam over the endless reaches of sea, diffusing the freezing darkness so that it was possible to see for miles. The pale flicker of islands appeared ghost-like on the Sound of Barra, a satiny mother-o'-pearl ribbon under the moon. Barra itself came into view. On its narrow northern peninsula rose the bastion of Scurrival Point, an inky blotch against the ebony backdrop of the star-splintered sky. At this point Iain Dubh set *The Pibroch*'s snub snout south-westwards. He had been drinking for a solid six hours and now the whisky was curdling in his belly, its heating effects wearing off, bringing the first stabs of icy cold which pierced through his mahogany skin and shivered into his souring entrails.

Disgruntled, he stared out of red-rimmed, salt-filled eyes. The scale-encrusted hatch on the hold shimmered with iridescent hues but he had no eye for the aesthetic things in life at that ungodly hour of morning. The smell of the tarred ropes, the odours of stinking fish, engraved into the wood for all time, poured into his lungs and heaved into his belly. Roughly he bawled out an order for tea which arrived in a chipped, blue-rimmed enamel mug round which he curled his thick lips, drinking deeply of the thick, hot, sweet beverage while he allowed Captain Mac to take the wheel.

'You bloody old Irish wolfhound!' he oathed into the older man's thickly haired purpled ears. 'I'll expect a flagon o' the hard stuff after this. I don't like my Jeannie's bed to grow too cold for I've a suspicion she has other ways o' warmin' it when I'm no' there. It's a good three nights now since I straddled her backside.'

'Ach, you'll get to straddle her all you like wi' New Year comin' on and be sick o' the sight o' it by the end o' it. Breac Beag is just a few miles away now. I can see the hump o' her lyin' under the moon so just you have a wee rest and let me take the boat in.'

The rocky islets and hidden reefs which peppered the coastal waters round Breac Beag and Breac Mor were a source of danger to any shipping but Captain Mac knew every lurking spur and every sharp-fanged reef like the back of his hand. Unerringly he steered *The Pibroch* towards the haven of Valsaal Bay nestling between the half-shut claws of long ridges of pink gneiss rock where the sea foamed white. Valsaal Bay was a placid lagoon where smooth-backed rocks were coated with orange and silver lichens. Before *The Pibroch* even dropped anchor Mac's big nose was questing the wind, twitching as an oddly familiar scent filtered over the water.

'By jove, it's peat or my name is no' Isaac MacIntosh! Peat I tell you, man! Coming from an island that has no' been inhabited by man for nigh on twenty years!'

Dawn was spreading slowly across the eastern sky, swallowing the stars into its pearly grey throat. The green cap which covered the flat northern end of the island was frost rimed, the burns, which flowed from Dun Ree on the rocky southern side, were frozen, caught in the hoary breath of the bitter dawn. Further down, where the water had cleft deep gorges in the rock and carved out trenches through the machair before it spread out over the pebbles on the shore, it was still flowing though with less velocity than usual.

The men pulled the dinghy ashore and hadn't gone far when they came upon the smouldering remains of a bonfire, almost exactly at the same spot where, in the summer, Niall and Mac had piled driftwood and dead bracken to make a bonfire for a little girl who had never lived to see it.

The piping of the shore birds was almost drowned out by the seagulls' wild cries as they plummeted off the cliffs or just drifted above, mewing plaintively.

Mac scrambled over the marram dunes with such agility it was difficult to believe he had just spent a sleepless and frozen night aboard *The Pibroch*. It was easy to follow the tracks through the machair. Although there were no sheep now on the island they had left behind their marks in the numerous tracks criss-crossing the sandy ridges of the dunes. The sands here were golden, fringed by pink and yellow granite gneiss. At the shore end stood the gaunt ruins of a house surrounded by a platform of green turf, a house in the same style as the one they had so happily violated that hot summer's day not so many months ago.

Mac topped a rise and saw it, the mottled grey walls pallid against the ochre and orange splodged rocks behind it, its two tall chimneys prodding upwards to a cold, honey tinted sky. A wisp of smoke curled from one of the chimneys and Mac's heart accelerated with joy, all his sorrow, his frustration, dispersing as easily as the peat smoke drifting in a blue haze over the umber brown stain of the moor. A figure was emerging from the house which materialized into the man everyone had so valiantly sought.

'Mac!' His cry of gladness froze in the cold still air of morning. He came scrambling over the heather to throw his arms about the neck of the old man whose raucous roars of delight brought smiles to the faces of Iain Dubh and his crew.

'Niall! You young de'il, I just knew you would be here!' Captain Mac was almost inarticulate. 'By jove, just you wait till I tell Nell about this and wait till your parents and Shona clap their eyes on you! What happened? What happened, lad?'

Niall, his clothes stained, his face harrowed by lines of weariness, was nevertheless better looking than when Mac had last seen him. There was a sparkle in his brown eyes, a smile on his face, and though it was perhaps just a temporary reaction it endowed him with a life that hadn't been in him for months.

He slapped Mac on the shoulders, shook hands with Iain Dubh and his crew. 'Come up to the house and get some breakfast. You must be frozen and done in. God, it's grand to see all your buggering wonderful faces! I thought I was going to be here forever! Come on, there's a fire going. I found a load of ancient peats at the back of the house and gathered driftwood to supplement them.'

The fire was newly lit and belched more smoke than heat but in half an hour it glowed warmly in the old grate and the men, clutching mugs of steaming tea and wolfing thick corned beef sandwiches, were draped around the room on rickety furniture, some of it made out of fish boxes by the last occupant of the house.

Niall explained how he had left *The Sea Urchin* anchored

in Valsaal Bay and of how the gales had violated even that sheltered anchorage, tearing the boat from her mooring and sweeping her out to sea. Fortunately he had brought plenty of supplies and warm bedding ashore so had been in no danger of starving or freezing. 'But it was gey lonely, I can tell you,' he said seriously. 'I came here to be alone for a day or two and ended up with enough isolation to last a lifetime. It was worse at night, I couldny sleep for the wind battering the roof and there were times when I thought the sea was going to come right into the house – between that and the burns rampin' through the machair it was all hell let loose. When it calmed a bitty I lit a bonfire on the shore hoping it would be seen by a passing boat. I was up and down at it day and night to keep it piled with driftwood because I only had a few matches and struck the last one this morning to light the fire.'

Captain Mac cleared his throat and stood up. 'Are we going then, Iain Dubh? The sooner we get this mannie home the sooner you'll be back on Hanaay straddlin' Jeannie and throwin' back as much whisky as you can hold – for I tell you this, lad, I'm grateful as hell for what you and your boys did and I will no' forget it, indeed I will no'.'

The crew of *The Pibroch* unwound themselves stiffly and when the fire had been doused and the door shut on the old croft for the last time, Niall looked back and gave silent thanks for the shelter it had provided. But as *The Pibroch* sailed out of Valsaal Bay and into the open sea he didn't look back at the island again. He had gone to seek peace in its isolated loneliness and to think of the times spent there with Ellie, but that had been in the summer when the seas and skies were calm and blue and all the fairness of the world seemed trapped in the small green and silver haven that was Breac Beag. Now it was winter, summer greens had given way to cold desolate greys and he hadn't found Ellie in any of the places he'd looked. Gradually it had come to him that he didn't have to travel far to find his daughter. She was with him all the time, in his heart and mind, and on reaching that discovery he had found a contentment that embraced every corner of his bruised heart.

Yet one dark corner remained restless and afraid and as *The Pibroch* chanted steadily through the bright, cold, morning sea, he wondered what kind of reception awaited him when he at last came face to face with the wife who had shunned him and who had cast him out of her life as easily as the tide tossed its unwanted debris on the shore.

Chapter Seventeen

Shona walked swiftly over the glen road to Slochmhor huddled against the inky blackness of Ben Machrie. She knew that if she allowed her steps to slow she might lose the courage she had built up ever since hearing that Niall had arrived home on *The Pibroch*. Relief, stark and overwhelming, had flooded her being and she had stared as her father's mouth formed the most wonderful words she had heard in weeks. Yet she hadn't quite taken it all in. After tortured days of believing Niall might be dead, coupled with stark empty hours of waiting for some sort of news which might finally force her to relinquish the hopes she had so desperately harboured, the reality of her father's rich deep voice telling her the things she longed to hear, was almost too much for her to bear.

And so she had waited, waited till Niall was home, waited till Phebie and Lachlan had had their share of the sweet euphoria of seeing their cherished son alive and safe. Waited till Niall himself had had time to accustom himself to familiar things. She daren't allow herself to wonder if he was thinking of her at all, if he even wanted to see her ... if she stopped to think of things like that she would never have the courage to face him – to explain.

It was another bitterly cold night, the river was low, the burns which fed it frozen far up on the bens which were white with dustings of powdery snow. The bracken was frost rimed, millions of ice diamonds winked on the roadside grasses; the hill peaks glinted like blue steel, moving among the red clouds of sunset; the smoking chimneys of Portcull stood stark against the molten sheet of flame that was the Sound of Rhanna; the smell of frost was in the air, clean and sharp. It wasn't often that such brittle cold came to the Hebrides and it was therefore a novelty to be enjoyed as the lochans froze and children waited eagerly for the ice to grow thick enough to bear their weight.

The lights of Slochmhor were warm and welcoming, yet even so she stood for a few minutes on the doorstep, warming her frozen fingers in her mouth, going over and over in her mind the things she would say to Niall. Taking a deep breath, she gave a small peremptory knock and plunged inside, taking in swiftly the scene in the living-room, Phebie and Lachlan, peaceful by the fire, each with a glass at their elbow, a third half full sitting on the mantelpiece.

'Where is he?' Her voice came out, breathless, unsure, and Lachlan rose to put a steadying hand on her shoulder. 'He went for a walk – over by Sliach.'

She turned at once and made to rush away but Phebie's

soft words forestalled her flight. 'Will – it be all right, Shona? He's been through a lot.'

'Ay,' she said with conviction. 'It will be fine, Phebie, never fear.'

She remembered nothing of the walk through the silent woods to the reed strewn lochan of Sliach, a tiny basin, flanked on one side by the dour, barren, scree flung slopes of Ben Machrie, bordered on the other by lonely stretches of bog-riddled moor. She emerged from the edge of the trees and caught her breath. Tonight the frozen loch was a blood-red looking glass, reflecting a crimson sunset at one end, mirroring an orange-tinted moon rising up over the shoulder of the ben, at the other. The fringes of spruce round the northern shore were perfectly mimicked in the ice-locked water; the brittle cracks released by the ever-tightening ice echoed from the embracing hills, mingling with the sweet, crystal clear, bell-like notes of the wild whooper swans who came every winter to the island. They were standing at the edge of the loch, their long, graceful necks appearing to keep time to the rhythm of their own voices, the white of their feathers stained with the blood of the dying sun. It was a sight that would remain with Shona for as long as she lived. Even then she could sense the poignancy of future years when she would look back and remember the haunting beauty of Loch Sliach on that perfect winter's night. But it was Niall she would think of most, he of all her impressions, would be her most constant, her most enduring memory. He was sitting on a rock, his hands clasped round his knees, his hair a halo of fire against the black trees, the pensive attitude of his body in harmony with the splendid solitude of that wild and beautiful place.

She felt his sadness and his despair touching her like a living thing and a great sob rose up inside her. This was Niall, the boy with whom she had passed the sweet, wondrous days of childhood; the young man who had awakened her to the true meaning of unselfish love. But more than these, this was the man who was her husband, who had shared with her the years of early youth and all the tears and laughter that had gone with them. Now they were both approaching the years of their prime, years which ought to be richer, more fulfilling than any other – and she had forsaken him – rejected him at a time when their grief should have brought them closer than ever . . . The tears swelled inside her breast till she felt she would die with the pent-up agony they contained. They continued to grow in intensity till the world spun and all around was blackness and night. Her throat burned, her limbs trembled and now there was a mist before her eyes. The moon blurred and wavered, merged with its reflection in the frozen loch. A pain that was almost physical speared her heart but as the tears spilled it was dissolved away, bit by painful bit.

'Niall, oh, Niall,' she whispered into her cold fingers, 'forgive me, my darling, forgive me.'

Her leaden limbs stirred into life and as she began to run towards him, the blood coursing warmly through her veins, she felt life returning to her heart. It was as if God had touched her with His love, was breathing fire into everything that had lain dormant for so long.

She was crying, at last she was crying, the tears spilling out of her, healing her, releasing her from a prison of darkness. Her feet crackled on the frozen sedge grasses and Niall heard her long before she reached him. He stood up, momentarily hesitant, then he heard his name on her lips, a joyful sound that carried far over the loch. He held out his arms and she ran straight into them and it was as if all the long months of hurt and bewilderment had never been. Their cold lips met over and over till they were cold no more, but charged with warmth and passion – and above all, love.

'Shona, Shona,' he spoke the name tenderly. 'You've come back. I thought I'd lost you forever but you've come back – laughing the way you used to when we were young—'

'We *are* young,' she interrupted fiercely, 'I'm too young to grow old before my time.'

He laughed, the deep happy sound of it like music in her ears. 'That's my girl talking – when you come out with daft things like that I know you are yourself again.'

Their bodies merged, closer and closer, as if they were trying to fuse them together. He was hard and excitingly masculine, the rough wool of his jersey reassuringly warm against her face. His fingers whispered over the smooth contours of her face, coming to rest at the nape of her neck. In the last remnants of the sun she saw his eyes narrowing to a stern disapproval.

'Your bonny hair, what have you done with it?'

'Hacked it off! In a fit of temper. Oh, don't be angry with me, Niall. It had nothing to do with you. I was hating myself, everything about me and I took it out on myself.'

She took his hand and led him to the edge of Sliach where they sat together on a big flat stone and stared over the darkening face of the loch. The swans were still calling, the sweet musical notes like some heavenly bugle-call to the stars glittering above.

'I'll never forget this night,' she said softly, 'after all the worry of you going missing, us trying to believe the best but unable to stop thinking the worst. I knew then what you meant to me – the idea of losing you was too unbearable to even contemplate. I really would have had nothing then to live for.'

He put a finger over her lips. 'Weesht, it's over, now we must stop looking back, we must go on, Shona, but we must never stop talking about Ellie. We've buried our wee lassie for far too long.'

She squeezed his hand. 'I know that now, I want to think about her, to talk about her. Somehow I feel she's here with us, listening to the swans, seeing the beauty of the frost on the hill. I'm thinking right now of something she once said. She was singing, and when I mentioned it she was surprised – no, taken aback – as if no other state but joy existed in the world. And she told me she was happy because we were. She was like that, other people's moods affected her. When I used to get into one of my tempers with her she looked as if I had struck her but as soon as I was back to myself she would start to sing – I remember it so plainly – her wee voice singing – and those golden eyes of hers, smiling. I've infected you with my bitterness, Niall. How Ellie would have hated that, the hurt would have showed in her eyes – and she had your eyes. I look at you and I see Ellie and I think of how I blamed you for what happened when all the time it was my fault. I came back here like a child, expecting everything to be the same. I was living in a fool's paradise, selfishly, thinking only of myself and my silly dreams. I neglected you and Ellie, I should have come on that trip. If I had none of this might ever have happened!'

'Don't talk like that, Shona!' He sounded angry. 'It will eat away like a canker if you don't kill it from the start. None of us were to blame for what happened. It was an accident and would have happened no matter who was there – remember now, no looking back, promise me.'

'All right, I promise.' His hands were cold in hers and she took them between her own and began to rub briskly. 'You must be frozen, out on that island for days on your own then out here as if you hadn't had enough of solitude. Aren't your feet like blocks of ice – mine are.'

'No, I'm wearing the socks Ellie made me, they're full of holes yet they're so thick it doesn't matter – she presented them to me one night on Hanaay – a labour of love right enough. Her eyes were sparkling. She made me take off my boots and then she put the socks on for me, holding her nose in the process – she always did have your sense of humour. After that nothing would do till I tried on the red woolly hat as well. Nellie went into shrieks and Mac spilled his rum into the fire where it shooshed up in a blue light. Ellie took it all in good part, she never thought people were laughing at her, always with her. God, how we laughed that night, and afterwards, when the poor cat was rendered immobile in socks and tammy, we all laughed till the tears ran down our faces—' His voice broke and putting his face in his hands he gave vent to his emotions, his strong shoulders shaking helplessly.

'Oh, Niall, my dear, dear Niall.' She took him to her breast and stroked his hair, her own tears falling silently. 'We'll cry like this together many many times, my darling,' she said huskily. 'And it will do us nothing but good. The worst pain is when you can't cry, when all the tears are locked away bringing a bitterness that seems to eat at your very soul.'

She took his hands and pulled him gently to his feet. 'Come on, we're going home. The fires are lit and the house is nice and warm – I think we'll go early to bed, I want to lie in your arms for hours and hours.'

They saw the lights of Lorn's cottage twinkling through the trees and she was tempted to go in and share her new-found happiness, but there was an urgency in the hand that grasped hers and she said nothing more till they stopped outside Slochmhor.

'I'd better go in and get my pyjamas.' He sounded a bit sheepish.

'Tonight you won't need them,' she said firmly. 'But you'd better go and tell them – you're going home to Mo Dhachaidh.'

There was a warm, waiting feel about the old house and when they went inside they were aware of a sense of welcome, as if Biddy herself had lit the fires in anticipation of their return. Hand in hand they went upstairs, so aware of each other they couldn't find the words to convey their feelings and so they said nothing. The bed was feather-down luxury, the soft flannelette sheets, the big fluffy pillows, just asking to be used. They undressed and sank into the warm haven, firelight playing on their naked bodies, a shyness in them as they gazed at each other. Her breasts tingled with awareness as she looked at him. His body was etched against the orange glow from the grate, the soft smooth edges of it brushed with mercurial gold, his muscles rippling gracefully under his skin, his deep chest plunging to the narrow aesthetic bones of his pelvis, so taut now but which she knew could have the fluidity of a bowstring in rhythm. Then he was lying beside her, studying her face for a long long time, absorbing every contour, a flash of annoyance creasing his brow as he reached out to touch the short tendrils that were so unfamiliar to him.

'Let it grow again.' He spoke urgently and she nodded

while she traced the whorls of his ear with a gentle finger. His gaze travelled the length of her body then came back to her face and the look of love in his eyes made her catch her breath. Passionately he claimed her mouth, his tongue meeting hers, forgetting everything, all the suppressed longings of the past months surging through him in a blinding rush. His mouth grew restless, wanting more, and he tore it away to kiss her ears, her neck, before marking a pathway of fire to the enticing swell of her breasts, lingering there for ecstatic seconds before moving down to the exciting curve of her soft belly. She gave a little cry, his head between her hands as he explored further, part of her wanting to voice a protest, the other part stifling it before it was even formed in her dizzy consciousness. She had never loved him more than she did now, and she wanted to give him everything she had ever denied him, to love him with her body, her heart, her soul.

For an eternity of pleasure they played and touched till he could wait no longer. He went into her fiercely, all shreds of reason swept aside in a tide of such intense passion she turned her head on the pillow and let herself be carried with him to the final ecstasy. But as always he made her wait, tantalizing her almost beyond endurance, kissing her lips, her breasts, touching the hard swollen peaks of her nipples till she cried out as if in pain. The moon rode higher in the heavens, spilling moonbeams into the room which mingled with the firelight and bathed their fluid bodies in silver-hued flame. Far far in the distance floated the voices of the swans, silver-sweet music that blended with moonlight and the love of two people who thought they had lost one another forever.

'Shona, I love you,' Niall's voice was husky, 'I love you, mo cridhe – I love you.'

He seemed to rise up and fill the room with his masculine power. In that moment they were as one, one body, one swiftly beating heart, one soul, merging, fusing, one tidal wave of ecstasy that carried them swiftly to the ultimate, world spinning climax. And they clung together and cried, for Ellie, for each other, for all the pain that they had suffered, and as their tears mingled so too did their life forces and there seemed no end to the searing, surging flame that consumed them, sealing their new-found love, binding them together in a rare and precious world that was theirs alone.

He fell asleep with his head cradled on her breast and she had never been more at peace, more relaxed as now. Still joined to him she fell asleep and some time in the night when the fire died down and the room grew cold he pulled the fluffy quilt close around them so that they were cocooned in a nest of warmth which the bitter night couldn't penetrate.

Shona wakened first, feeling so good she thought at first she must be dreaming and that soon all the anxieties would come crowding back then she felt Niall's arms around her, holding her close, making her feel safe, cherished beyond compare. Dawn was filtering coldly over the sky which

had become overcast and even as she watched the first
smirrings of powdery snow rasped against the window
pane. She lay, too contented to move, looking at Niall.
His skin was flushed, a shadow of fair stubble lay over his
jaw, the curve of his lashes swept his cheek. She caught
her breath, loving him so much there was pain in her
heart. How he had cried last night, how many long hours
of grief must he have endured to make him break down
like that? The torture of it seared her soul and she closed
her eyes and bit her lip. She couldn't bear to think about
it and she snuggled further against him, letting his warmth
flood through her body.

He stirred and opening his eyes he smiled at her, the
sleepy smile of a man at peace with the world. 'I knew you
were watching me,' he murmured, 'I could feel your eyes
devouring me and of course I don't blame you for admiring
good looks when you see them.'

She giggled and smacked him playfully on the backside.
Lazily he enclosed her tighter into the warm circle of
his arms, a sensuousness in his stirring limbs. She lay
against him, the condensing of her breath above the quilt
changing her wakening resolve to get up and make tea.
He nuzzled her hair and whispered, 'Before you came
along last night I was doing a bit of thinking. Do you
want to hear it or would you rather lie here all day and
make love?'

'We've got all the time in the world, it might be a good
idea if we had a wee talk.'

'Well, I came to the conclusion that none of this travelling vet stuff ever really worked . . .'

'But it's got to!' she cried aghast. 'We can't leave here – not now.'

'Caillich Ruadh,' he teased. 'Will you be quiet a minute and let me finish? I meant it hasny worked me being away from home so much. At heart I'm a home-loving man and canny bear to be away from the girl who once chased me over the moors.'

She gasped, 'But – you chased me!'

'Same difference,' he returned. 'I'm trying to tell you that all I want are my slippers, my pipe and my ain fireside.'

'You don't smoke a pipe.'

'I can learn. I can learn to do a lot of things I've always wanted – such as being here with you all the time instead of gadding all over the place. I can still be a vet; there's a surprising amount of work on Rhanna to keep me going, the bairns are always on about their ailing pets and the farmers and crofters are losing their suspicions about me. We could build an extension onto the back of the house, make a surgery and waiting room. In between times we can cut our own peat and I could also do a bit of lobster fishing. *The Sea Urchin*'s a goner now anyway and somehow I canny be bothered with that kind of life anymore. What do you say, Mrs McLachlan?'

'Well, Mr McLachlan, I'd say it's the best thing my glaikit wee Niall has ever come up with,' she approved in delight.

His arms tightened instinctively round her waist and he said softly, 'I think we should make our first Christmas in this house a really special one.' He saw her face and added quickly and firmly, 'We should do everything that Ellie would have liked. It's going to be our first Christmas without our wee girl and if we just sit back and think we're going to torture ourselves. We'll do as Ellie would have done during her first festive season at Mo Dhachaidh, we'll throw a ceilidh, we'll laugh and sing and somewhere Ellie will be laughing and singing with us.'

'All right,' she conceded huskily. 'If you'll let me invite Dodie over for Christmas dinner. I've hurt him in some way and want to make it up to him – though I wish I knew what I've done for him to take it so much to heart.'

Gently Niall told her and she gave a little cry of anguish. 'Oh God! Was it just Dodie, I wonder, or have there been others?'

'As far as I know it was just Dodie—' He grinned ruefully. 'Go ahead and ask him. I'll buy a sack of onions and hang them up on the tree. He'll think they're decorations.'

'If he knows he's coming here he'll make an effort to clean himself up,' she said with conviction and throwing off the quilt she donned her dressing gown and pattered speedily downstairs to stir the slumbering fire to flame and swing the kettle on.

*   *   *

She was right. Dodie came on Christmas Day, confused, beaming, glowing brighter than a new pin. Carbolic fumes wafted from him in waves, mingling with the repugnant odour of hair oil which they suspected he had made himself.

'Tincture of skunk!' Niall decided, but set about making their guest feel entirely welcome. Dodie was touchingly grateful for everything, screeching with delight when a search through the tree rewarded him with a bulky parcel with his name on the label. He had come armed with presents for everyone, simple things, made from the treasures given up by the sea.

Tears sprung to Shona's eyes when he produced a gift for 'wee Ellie', another of his exquisitely painted stones which he placed beside her picture in Memory Corner.

He departed in the late afternoon, well pleased with his day, his pockets bulging with goodies which he was determined to share with his beloved cow before darkness set in.

Niall and Shona sat back for a brief respite before their respective families arrived for the evening, bringing with them Fiona and Grant who had come home on a surprise visit. They were a tonic, keeping everyone entranced with stories of their travels. Fiona had sailed with her husband on his Australian run earlier in the year and had remained on the Great Barrier Reef to study its marine life, along with a scientific team from one of the Australian universities. Grant had collected her on his next run and they had come back to Scotland for the festive season, much to Phebie's joy, for she missed her daughter sorely and quietly looked forward to the day when she and her husband decided to settle down on dry land.

While Ruth was ensconced in the kitchen with Shona, helping her to make tea, she confided that at last she had begun writing her book.

'Och, I'm so pleased, Ruth,' Shona said with genuine warmth. 'I just know that one day you'll be a successful novelist and unlike Rachel you don't have to move away from your own fireside to pursue your ambition. How is she, by the way?'

'She and Jon are in Vienna at the moment, having a wonderful time. He has a job there and Rachel is in seventh heaven studying and doing concerts. She writes often and is so good to Lorna, always sending her presents. She never talks about coming back to the island, even for a holiday – I suppose she's too busy,' she added rather wistfully.

'Oh, she'll come back when she's ready, she has to allow herself time to forget Lewis, though I doubt if she ever will. She truly loved him, you know; I met her once over by Burg and all she wanted was for me to talk about him . . .' She paused and went on in a rush, 'Ruth, I've never really had a chance to tell you how sorry I am for all the trouble and heartache I caused you. You must have hated me at the time.'

'Hush,' Ruth held up her hand and shook her head vehemently. 'I never hated you and we don't have to talk about it ever again – except I really do understand what made you do it. If I had been in your position I might easily have done the same. Dear little Ellie, she's gone, yet, somehow I feel she's with us enjoying Christmas in that lovely enthusiastic way she had.'

Shona's eyes were brilliant with love for the child who was gone from her life now but who still lived and breathed in the hearts of all those who had loved her most and she hugged Ruth for showing so much sympathy and understanding.

The festivities didn't stop after the revelry of the New Year. The ice on the lochans was bearing after continual nights of hard frost and everyone, young and old, took to the exhilarating pursuits of skating and curling. Nobody possessed skates but that didn't matter. A variety of weird inventions took to the ice and the bens rang with sounds of laughter and frequent shrieks. Even McKenzie of the Glen, that proud, private man, joined in the fun, leading Kirsteen over the frozen surface of Sliach, his deep laughter booming out as they slithered about with everyone else.

'McKenzie is a changed man from the old days,' commented those who were too old or too lazy to join the throng.

'Ay,' nodded old Bob. 'He has seen a lot o' sorrow this whily back but himself and Kirsteen have had the courage to stand back and count the blessings that are left to them.'

'They are people I am proud to know,' said Mac, taking a warming swig of rum from his flask. He and Nellie were staying at Mo Dhachaidh for a holiday and Mac, though disappointed to know that his days as Niall's skipper were over, was not surprised at the news, consoling himself with the thought that he could always help out with the lobster fishing. 'If ever there was two families who have earned my respect it is the McLachlans and the McKenzies.'

The rains and winds returned at the end of January and with the thaw everyone reverted back to more conventional pastimes. There was about Shona these days a serenity that brought back all her former zest for life. The extension to the house was going ahead as fast as it ever would on an island whose tradesmen only hurried when it was opening time at the hotel bar. Mo Dhachaidh had become a rendezvous for the island children and their pets and for old ladies whose cats were the solace of their old age. A back room had been hastily converted into a surgery, the hall was a temporary waiting room with the crofter's bench placed at the widest spot but even then a row of toes made navigation through the house a considerable feat of skill and patience.

Shona enjoyed the bustle around her, but looked forward to the evenings spent with Niall in the parlour when they could sit by the fire to talk or just be content to sit quietly together. Held in his arms, curled on the rug by his feet, she drew closer to him in spirit than to any other human being in the world. Each day, each night, her nightmare of the past was pushed a little further away and the sweet promise of the future came a small step nearer with each new dawn.

Part Five

Autumn 1962

Chapter Eighteen

'And was the honeymoon to your liking then, Barra?'

Kate McKinnon lowered her voice to a confidential whisper but even so the shop suddenly went quiet and all eyes were turned expectantly on the blushing countenance of Barra McLean. More than the usual number of folk were crowded into the establishment which was still referred to as Merry Mary's, though Dugald had taken over once more with Merry Mary agreeing to stay on till he could get somebody else to take her place. It was rumoured that wedding bells were in the offing for Dugald and Totie Little of Portvoynachan, a rumour strengthened by the fact that they were more and more to be seen openly together. But neither party was forthcoming on the subject so it was kept open to be discussed and pondered upon with much enjoyment.

The ferry was due in the harbour in a few minutes and though this was always an event of importance, today it was doubly so, and even as everyone talked necks were frequently stretched to watch the comings and goings outside, though this occupation known as rubbernecking was temporarily abandoned and the attention switched readily to the discomfited Barra.

She and Robbie had confounded everyone with their recent marriage and it had transpired that they had taken to each other from the start, with Ranald not even considered in the marriage stakes.

'And to think she led us to believe it was Ranald she liked,' had sniffed a peeved Kate.

'Ach, it was you who led yourself to believe it was him,' said Merry Mary with asperity, 'Barra never gave herself away one way or the other.'

But the irony of the situation had soon cheered Kate and she had set about wondering just how Behag would take to the idea of a wild city woman gaining an even stronger foothold in the family circle. But the wily Robbie had long been prepared for his sister's reaction, mollifying her by going to Lachlan to find out how to go about recommending her for a long service award. Lachlan and the laird between them had set the wheels in motion. The Lord Lieutenant of the county had been Burnbreddie's Commanding Officer and they had remained friends, Sir Gordon MacGregor coming annually to the island for the shooting and fishing. His letter of recommendation, together with one from the Postmaster General in London to the Prime Minister's Principal Private Secretary, had resulted in Behag being awarded the BEM. Her chagrin at receiving a lesser award than Biddy's had been short-lived. In her honour the laird had thrown a garden party in the grounds of Burnbreddie, during which Sir Gordon had made the award presentation. It had been a momentous occasion for her. A good number of Rhanna people had been there to see her mixing with dignitaries, newspaper reporters, and the gentry, all of whom had wanted to shake her hand and congratulate her. The sun had shone, the day had been perfect, and Behag, dressed in a printed silk dress, a splendid pheasant feather adorning her hat, her spindly legs scurrying hither and thither as she ingratiated herself with the laird's entourage, felt herself to be on a par with royalty. Her ego was further boosted when she received an invite to a garden party at Holyrood House where she had shaken hands with the Queen Mother. So taken up had she been she'd had little time to spare for her brother and he and Barra had been able to slip away to be married in a Registry Office in Oban.

Behag's hours of glory were now in the past and when she had finally emerged from her euphoric state to the full realization of what her brother had accomplished under her very nose, she had been tight-lipped with disapproval, though her BEM medal, mounted in a frame hung above the fireplace, was a constant reminder of her own importance. She had stuck her nose in the air and pretended not to notice the smirks and giggles of those who, in her own words, 'were just a bunch o' jealous nobodies'.

Robbie and his new wife had returned to take up residence in Barra's harbour cottage and everyone was keen to discover the kind of welcome Behag would extend to her newly acquired sister-in-law. But that was something to look forward to in the future, the crowd gathered in

Merry Mary's shop were more interested in matters of the moment and Kate's blunt question had given them the opening they needed. All eyes were focused on Barra and she stood nonplussed for quite some time, obviously reluctant to enlarge on the personal subject of her recent honeymoon.

'Ach, c'mon now, Barra,' coaxed Nancy persuasively, all her old vigour having returned in full after a long and anxious battle with illness. The doctors had pronounced her as good as new and Nancy had laughed and quipped, 'Ay, like a new motor wi' a few o' the luxuries missing.'

Barra looked round at all the interested faces and a dimple of mischief dented her cheek.

'Well, now that you ask, Kate,' she began then paused, making a great show of fastening a button on her coat.

'Ay, go on, Barra,' encouraged Kate, wondering if Barra was as embarrassed as she was making out.

Barra raised her head and her eyes positively sparkled though still she hesitated before opening her mouth again. 'My, thon's an awful contraption,' she finally admitted, her face made redder still with suppressed laughter. 'I have never seen the likes in all my life – no' even in my days at Art College when we had naked men posin' as models. They always covered these bits o' their bodies wi' wee clooties.'

'Ach, God!' Kate doubled up in a paroxysm of mirth. 'I must get my Tam to pose for you, Barra. I would give away a cask o' the bonny malt itself just to see him wi' a bit o' spotted silk tied round his chookles!'

'Weesht you now, Mother,' warned Nancy. 'Here is Robbie himself come to claim his bride from all you nosy vultures. My, the mannie is lookin' as red as yourself, Barra, I doubt the men have been on at him too.'

Robbie's round pleasant face was indeed a shade of violent pink, thanks to the recent teasings from Tam and his cronies. He had expected the banter and blushing furiously had finally admitted to finding the ways of women somewhat bewildering.

'They are different from the beasts I have studied all my life,' he had stated in some confusion.

'Ay, and what way is that?' asked Tam while his son, Wullie, had exploded with rude laughter and confided that his wife Mairi had always put him in mind o' a clockin' hen.

'Ach no!' protested Robbie, his face flaring to crimson. 'That isny the kind o' thing I'm meaning – it's just – well, they are different to what I expected. You see . . .' He had stopped, abashed.

'Go on now, man,' encouraged Todd. 'You are no makin' yourself clear.'

'Well, it is just – they are aye in heat whereas wi' the likes o' a cow you have to wait till it comes on.'

Tam's eyes were round and quite a few moments elapsed before he said in astonishment, 'But, surely at your age, you know that already?'

'Ay, ay, of course,' Robbie said suavely, wishing he hadn't broached the subject. 'But it is different living wi' one and findin' out that it's there all the time when you want it and no' just keekin' at you from a wee dark corner o' a hayshed.'

His astounding observation had caused an uproar during which he had made good his escape only to see by his wife's red face that she too had been subjected to merciless banter. 'The boat is comin' in,' he announced in some discomfiture, 'I saw her funnels comin' round the bay just a wee minute ago.'

In minutes the shop was empty except for Robbie and Barra who stood looking at one another for a few shy moments before Robbie crooked his arm with a flourish and invited his new wife to walk with him to the pier.

The McKenzies and the McLachlans were standing at the front of the crowd on the pier, together with Ruth and Lorn who was holding onto little Lorna, now a fair-haired toddler with rosy cheeks and huge violet eyes like her mother's. She was clapping her hands as if sensing the excitement engendered by the arrival of this particular boat. To those who most eagerly awaited it the procedure of getting the steamer alongside the pier seemed to take even more time than usual and they scanned the deck with anxious eyes, childishly vying with one another to see who would be the first to spot the long awaited arrivals.

The harbour was a bustle that day with the fishermen waiting beside their lobster boxes ready for shipment to Oban, and various parked vehicles standing by ready to collect mail and provisions.

Fergus, trying to be calm, lit his pipe with slow deliberation. Lorna standing by watching the matches blowing out one by one in the breeze.

'Light,' she nodded in a delightfully quaint fashion and importantly she teetered over to Captain Mac and pulled his sleeve. 'Light – Gwanpa.' She pointed back then took Mac by the sleeve and guided him over to where Fergus stood. 'Get light,' she said again. Mac beamed and taking out his lighter held it to Fergus's pipe which was puffing away in no time. Mac shook his head. 'The wee one is lookin' after you, McKenzie. She will never see you stuck, you can be sure o' that.'

Fergus crouched down to his granddaughter and looked into her small face. Her gaze followed the blue wisp of smoke from his pipe, her pearly teeth showed in wonder. He touched the top of her silky head. It was warm with sunshine, fragile, yet able to withstand the numerous bumps of childhood; she was barely eighteen months old, small-boned, dainty, fair skin browned by the summer sun; she was still a baby, unsteady on her legs, near enough to the breast to still need a comforting bottle to send her to sleep – yet she was so wise, this dear, tiny infant. Already she was aware that there were certain things he couldn't manage to do with just one arm and she had taken it upon her infant shoulders to protect his interests – like Ellie. The notion came unbidden to his mind and his heart twisted with renewed grief for the child who had so enriched his life. How he missed her still. Sometimes he fancied he heard her quick steps on the cobbled yard and expected her to come into the kitchen at any moment, her light child's voice greeting him or perhaps scolding him because his shoelaces were undone. She had filled all their lives with a rare and precious light and now that she was gone the world was a blacker place – yet – he looked again at Lorna and in some strange way he felt that Ellie's light would never be extinguished – not when babies like Lorna still surrounded him, in their innocent way filling voids he had thought could never be filled. She was playing with his hair, twisting the black curls round her dimpled fingers and he crushed her tiny body to his hard chest, pressing his lips to her hair, overwhelmed suddenly by the knowledge that this was Lewis's child. Everyone accepted her as Lorn's, an easy thing to do when the brothers had been so alike, but the fact remained, she was, and always would be the daughter that Lewis had never lived to see . . . he glanced up and caught Lorn watching him, Lorn of the sensitive soul and the brave heart who had taken his brother's child and called her his own.

'She's a fine babby,' Fergus said softly. 'You must be proud to be her father.'

Lorn frowned slightly. 'Ay, I am, at the beginning I used to think of her as Lewis's but now she's more mine than my own –' he relaxed and smiled, 'or rather the ones I have yet to have. She will never take second place to any that are still to be—' He drew Ruth to him and lovingly patted the swelling mound of her belly while she quickly looked round to make sure no one had seen the action. He hugged her and grinned, 'Why shouldn't I pat the bum of our baby? It makes no difference, inside or out, and come next week we ought to be having a look at the real thing.'

Fergus smiled. 'It's the baby season right enough. What do you think of your sister, eh?'

'I think she's done damned well and deserves the miracle that's happened to her.'

'Ay, it is a miracle,' Fergus conceded. 'There has been some force at work beyond our ken and, by God, it will help to make up for so much that's been taken away from us.'

The gangplank was being lowered, the passengers starting to stream down – and in their midst was the couple that everyone was waiting to see, Niall and Shona, their faces alight, Niall treading carefully, mindful of the tiny white bundle he carried. As soon as he set foot on the pier he was surrounded, cries of congratulation ringing in his ears.

Ruth rushed forward to hug Shona who was thin after the birth of her daughter, but well looking, her radiant eyes shining in her flushed face.

'She's beautiful, Shona,' said Ruth, taking a peep at the little face inside the shawl, 'I think I'll have to steal her away from you . . .' She stopped short, horrified at herself but Shona just laughed and said quietly, 'Och, Ruth, you mustny feel you always have to watch what you say. That daft part of me is dead now – and I might just take you up on your offer. Beautiful she may be but she can bawl with the best of them—' Laughingly she eyed Ruth's belly. 'Wait till you get rid of that and we can have quite a time looking after one another's bairns.'

The respective families were having trouble getting to their offspring, but finally managed to push their way through, Fergus to fold his daughter to his chest where she lay briefly, adoring the big man who was her father as she had adored him all through her life. There was so much to say, too much noise to say it in. Lachlan, tanned and healthy looking after a recent holiday, was standing behind Fergus, Kirsteen and Phebie crowding round at his back, as if they were waiting in a queue outside Merry Mary's. Shona giggled at sight of their eager faces and let out an exaggerated shriek as they descended on her. Lorn embraced her solemnly and briefly, she touched his thick, waving hair, expecting him to protest and move away but he surprised her by remaining where he was, his voice warm with sincerity when he told her, 'I'm glad for you, Shona, I feel now that you'll truly settle down to your life here on Rhanna.' The maturity of his words came as rather a shock to her and she realized that this young brother of hers was no longer the boy she took him for. Soon he would be twenty-one, yet manhood had come to him earlier, the responsibilities of marriage had seen to that. She felt a little sad at the knowledge and wondered afresh if it had been good for him to have grown up so quickly till she remembered she herself had married at eighteen and had never regretted a moment of it.

'Ay, Lorn, I will that,' she answered steadily, 'I'll be much too busy to play at houses – this wee rascal will see to that.'

Babbie's red head burst into view, her hat knocked awry. She descended breathlessly on her friend and Shona giggled as she eyed her hat. 'Babbie Büttger, you grow more like Biddy every day – even your hat is squinty the way hers used to be.'

Babbie patted her head absently, her green eyes dancing. 'Is it? Ach well, it never did fit right – it's time I had a new one.' She pulled it off and tossed it high in the air.

A gust of wind caught it and blew it into the sea and Shona choked with glee. 'What on earth did you do that for?' she asked.

'Ach, I felt like it – everyone's so happy today, the excitement of it all has gone to my head.'

'You're as daft as ever you were, too bad I won't be able to take you up on that offer you made a whily back. It would have been fun coming with you as your assistant.'

'Fibber! You wouldn't change what you have for the world and fine you know it.'

'Ach, I know, I just wondered, wouldn't you have liked—?'

'*No*,' Babbie was adamant. 'It's a bitty late now, but Anton and me are happy as we are. I'm kept too busy attending the squalling infants and often their squalling mothers without wanting the doubtful joys of having them bawling in my lugs when all I want is a good night's sleep

– anyway, it's nature's way of balancing the odds. Without folk like me there would be nobody to see the generations into the world . . .'

'Babbie! Babbie!' One of the village youngsters was tugging anxiously at her sleeve. 'Mammy has pains in her belly, she sent me to fetch you!'

Babbie threw Shona a laughing glance and followed the youngster along the harbour to a cottage which sparkled white against the tawny slopes of Sgurr Nan Ruadh. Shona gazed upwards, a quiet appreciation flooding her soul. The hills were slumbering peacefully against a blue sky daubed with lumps of cotton wool clouds; there was still a trace of summer green on the moors but the bracken was a blaze of yellow and orange amidst the purple of the heather; the tang of autumn was sharp in the air blending with the peat smoke which drifted lazily above the chimneys, billowing out to form a blue haze against the bronze of the hills. Niall handed her the baby and the incredulous wonder that had swamped her being from the moment she discovered she was pregnant, surged anew inside her breast. It was a child born of pure love, a miracle which she could hardly believe during all the long months of waiting. Now the reality of the tiny girl, with her perfect features and downy hair glinting fair in the sun's rays, was the answer to all her prayers and she felt that as long as she lived she could never ask for more out of life.

Lachlan was taking her arm, a deep joy in his brown eyes as he gazed upon the small new face of his granddaughter.

'C'mon, Shona, mo ghaoil,' he said softly. 'You've had enough excitement for one day, it's time you and the wee one came home.'

Early that evening she met Mark James down by the shore near the Manse. The sea was calm with the dying sun dappling the Sound of Rhanna to gold.

'I heard that you had come home today,' he greeted her as she came over the shingle towards him, 'but I didn't expect to see you out and about so soon.'

'I was hoping to see you,' she said frankly, 'to thank you.'

'To thank me?'

'Ay, for everything you did for me that day you came to me at Mo Dhachaidh – it was you who brought me to my senses and made me realize how much I had left to me that was good and precious.'

'And now?'

'Now I feel that I've been given another chance – that in some wonderful way Ellie has been given back to me.'

His eyes were more blue than grey just then, reflecting the pure dark blue of the October sky over the eastern hills. 'She's the miracle you needed?' His voice was low.

'Ay, you said they happened and you were right – oh how right you were – my dear, dear Mark.'

He looked long at her, saying nothing, his expression so deep she felt as if she was drowning.

'Are you – happy – happier than you were?' she asked

rather fearfully, knowing that if he was to indicate a negative reply it would be more than she could bear – yet – she had to know, to hear the answer from his own lips.

His expression was suddenly withdrawn, his eyes hooded, the dark curling lashes that had so fascinated her, drawn down like blinds shutting out the light.

'I am happy,' he said eventually, 'I've been accepted here – I love the place – the people. I think I can safely say I have found a quiet little niche into which I fit nicely.' He looked directly at her again, the full battery of his keen smoky gaze pouring into her heart. 'And I have found true friends, the McLachlans, the McKenzies, Babbie, Anton, John and Hannah Grey – and best of all I have you, my dear, dear Shona. To my dying day I will look upon you as the woman who showed me light when there was darkness, who in coming out of your own sorrow helped me to emerge from mine.'

'Oh, but—' she cried out but he had turned away, his back straight, his shoulders set resolutely.

'I'll be in kirk – this Sabbath!' she called after him. He nodded but didn't look back and she watched as he walked away, a tall dark figure with a strength in his bearing that came not from his heart but his soul.

'God bless you, Mark James,' she murmured huskily and wasn't surprised to feel a trickle of tears lying upon her cheeks. She too turned away and didn't look back as she walked home to Mo Dhachaidh – and Niall.

*   *   *

Very early the next morning she and Niall rose to keep a tryst with dawn, wrapping the baby up warmly and walking with her to the slopes of Ben Machrie where cool shadows lay over the sleeping corries. It was a pilgrimage that they had planned before their child's birth, instigated by Shona remembering something Mirabelle had told her a long time ago. She had been too young then to take in the full import of the old housekeeper's convictions but she recalled her fascination as she had listened to Mirabelle telling her, 'If ever you have a wee lassie o' your own take her up to the hills and hold her face towards the new day and then baptize her wi' the morning dew. She will live to see many a dawn breaking over the morning o' her life and you can be assured she will grow to have a nature as bright as the sunshine itself.'

Shona had forgotten these words when Ellie was born but they had come back to her suddenly and insistently during her pregnancy and she had told Niall about them. He hadn't laughed but instead had said seriously, 'If Mirabelle said it, it canny be wrong. When the bairn comes we'll do just as she told you all these years ago.'

Now they walked hand in hand to the highest spot of the windblown hill where a blinding silvery light streaked the sky behind and the air was sharp and clear as crystal. Looking down they could see for miles, the quiet smoky grey of the morning sea; the huddle of tiny white houses of Portcull; the moors stretching to the edge of the ocean. They looked at each other and smiled and as the quivering edge of the sun rose up on the distant horizon they lifted up the baby so that her face was to the morning and then they knelt on the ground and touched her smooth brow with the pearly dew from the purple heather.

'I baptize you Ellie Dawn McLachlan,' Niall's voice rang out clearly.

'And may God grant you a long and happy life,' Shona added, holding the baby's face close to her own, kissing the satin-smooth cheeks. Ellie Dawn McLachlan yawned widely then pursed her lips into a rosebud ball. Shona's laughter rang out and as it bounced against the hilltops, echoing and re-echoing, she had the strangest notion that it was Ellie's laugh which came back again and again, the joy of it ringing round all the hills and mountains that the world contained.

She glanced upwards, her heart bursting with so much happiness she knew that all things were possible, that all the life contained in heaven and earth was theirs in those moments of wondrous joy – and she didn't think it odd to see a tiny spectre moving over the face of the hills, coming towards them, arms outstretched as if to embrace the clean dawn washing over the sky, laughter pealing like a crystal bell, ringing, ringing in the crisp air, hiding in the corries, emerging again like a child playing hide and seek with parents who were getting a wee bit past it.

Niall took Shona's hand and they began to move away, feeling they were taking, not leaving, the sprite who had given them so much.

As they walked with their baby over the hillside to home, they smiled at each other again, a secretive smile, while far in the valleys behind them a wisp of cloud floated, and the singing wind, which might have belonged to the voice of a child, danced and played over the wide, wild spaces of the hills and glens of Rhanna.